the
FIFTH
POSTULATE
A SHERLOCK HOLMES STORY
L T BRADY

ACKNOWLEDGEMENTS

For Jo who has probably put as much into this as I have, if not more – I'm not sure I can ever thank you enough for kicking this into shape. And for my mum who believed in the book enough to read through the sex scenes!

And to everyone who read this and encouraged me to actually write it properly, both those of you I've met and those of you who have just helped out because you were kind enough to.

PROLOGUE

The noise of the club was loud enough that Victor could still feel the heart racing thump of it even as he stood outside, taking in a deep, pleasing breath of fresh air and let out a pleased laugh.

Revenge, he thought as he reached to take a cigarette out of his jeans' pocket, was delightfully satisfying. The stains on his fingers caught his attention and made him deepen his smile. In the artificial light of the club's entrance, the blood seemed darker than it had just minutes earlier when the stuff had come pouring out of that fucking piece of shit's neck.

It was done. He couldn't have stopped the delighted smirk even if he'd wanted to. After all these months of dealing with that irritating pair, he'd finally gotten the last word, dragged them both down to fucking nothing.

He wondered at the sight that was currently in his office. Wondered whether the drugs had taken hold; whether it was now a druggie bleeding over his floors; whether it was a corpse staining his carpet.

"You should wipe your hands," Bobby said, stepping out to stand with him and holding out a cloth. "Eyes are everywhere."

"Mm," Victor said, following the advice but with a lazy speed that made him enjoy the action even more. The white cloth was smeared pink by the time he finished and the car pulled up.

Feeling completely at ease, Victor got into it, lazing back in the seat as he was driven away and his people were left to deal with any irritating questions that the pathetic police might have.

It didn't matter, they didn't bother him. And soon everyone

who mattered would know. Know that no-one messed with the Trevor family.

Not even fucking Sherlock Holmes.

CHAPTER ONE:

The Idiot in the Bathroom

THE FIRST TIME WAS DURING one of John's okay to drink days. He'd set his plan out clearly in his head: three days a week, no more and sure as hell no less. In fact, there were times when he reckoned that Mary would have trouble keeping up with most of his mates when they were out on a bender and she'd always been the cool, scotch swigging one.

"Oi, Watson," Joe shouted from the doorway of the living room. It was a nice living room. He should tell...wait...whose house was this? They might be in Vauxhall? Who did he know who lived in Vauxhall?

"You're gonna be a doctor, right?"

Even being so drunk that he might struggle to stand, John knew what Joe was about to ask. "No," he said warily. A year and a half of his course had taught him that uni students seemed to think that anyone who spent time in a lab was instantly a fully qualified doctor who could treat all ills. Not only that, but they seemed to forget about the hypocritic...the hyprocatic...the h- that oath thing that doctors took.

God, he was so pissed.

"No," he said, shaking his head. "No. I'm gonna be a not doctor."

It didn't sound convincing, even to his ears.

"I study English," John decided, having glanced at Andy.

He was pretty sure that was what Andy was studying. They hadn't been living together long.

"Yeah," Joe said slowly, clearly not buying it. "Look, it's just a bit of sick. And I'm not the person who deals with that. At all. Clean him up and make sure he doesn't, you know, die by choking on his own puke or something."

Really?

"It's good practise," Andy called, the fucking traitor. This was absolutely the last time that John was letting himself be dragged out by that wanker.

Probably.

Lurching to his feet, John managed to glare at all of them. He even managed to stick his tongue out at Andy and flipped him the finger as he walked away. Sadly, Andy just beamed back at him before he returned his attention to saving the girl on his lap from whatever it was that was lodged in her throat.

Away from the booming music, John's head cleared a little. Enough that he took a deep breath and tried to remember that ABC thing with the breathing and oh fuck was he meant to pump in time to 'Nellie the elephant' if he had to do CPR, or was it 'Staying alive'?

Would the song choice really make that much difference?

"John?" Joe said, snapping his fingers in front of John's eyes. "Seriously, you can't pass out until you've dealt with the bastard hurling into the bog."

He damn well could. Rolling his eyes, John twisted away to start navigating the stairs.

"You know Melanie?"

What? Baffled, John turned back to Joe and tilted his head to the side. Joe stared at him and seemed to wince a little. "Who lives here," Joe said slowly as if talking to a deaf old man.

Who lives here? What did that...oh! Okay. Huh, John could have sworn it was a guy's house. Shrugging, John waited for Joe to continue.

"Well," Joe shifted uncomfortably. "Her sister does stuff. Like..." as if sensing that John wasn't in the state to infer information, Joe pinched at his nose and huffed. "Coke."

That took a moment too long to translate. "Aw," John muttered, staring at the ceiling. "Seriously?"

"Fucking relax," Joe hissed. "Just check that he doesn't need to go to a hospital. Her parents would freak out."

He and her? John closed his eyes trying to work out which one was which again. "Right," he said slowly, staring at Joe and hoping for some sort of a hint.

Hands slammed against his back and then propelled him up the stairs with more force than was probably necessary but whatever. Joe must have been drunker than he seemed because his ability to guide John was bloody awful.

Either that or he was purposefully aiming John at various walls.

The upstairs bathroom was way bigger and fancier than the one downstairs. Or at least it had been until someone had strewn towels across the tiles and had what looked like a water fight using the sink and bath.

And of course, it would probably be much classier without the cokehead sprawled over the floor, hugging the toilet bowl as if it were his last salvation. John barely managed a glimpse of it all before Joe shoved him into the room and slammed the door shut with such force that John's head rang.

Then he was left alone in a room with someone who may or may not choke on their own vomit, in a room that definitely had been used for sex and that stunk of sweat and vomit.

Great.

With a sobering sigh, John knelt down by the guy, studying him as carefully as he could under the circumstances. The guy didn't really seem to be conscious; the awkward angle of his body meant that he was contorted into a strange position that kept him upright and his head in the toilet bowl which reeked of vomit.

Wincing at the overpowering smell as he leaned close,

John put one hand over his nose and reached out the other to flush the toilet. The unconscious guy didn't so much as stir.

"Crap," John muttered as he dropped his hand to unconscious guy's throat, patting until he felt a fluttering pulse that seemed a little scattered but still strong. He studied unconscious guy, trying to work out if it was a good idea to move him into the recovery position or whether he was good as he was.

He was hardly going to choke in the position he was in. And Joe had made it damn clear that he wouldn't be cleaning up any sick. Leaving unconscious guy hanging over the toilet seemed like the best bet so far.

It did mean that John himself ended up hurling into the bath.

It was twenty minutes later when the door flung open again. By that point, John was sat with his back to the bath, head between his knees and soaking wet from where he had half drenched himself trying to clean the bath.

He was never, ever drinking with Joe again and was fully prepared to announce that to the wanker-

It wasn't Joe. The newcomer had dark, straight hair that seemed far too neat for a house-party, clothes that looked like they cost John's termly rent and a narrowed piercing gaze that reflected the slight disgust in his eyes at the sight of John and unconscious guy sitting in a room that, by that point, had to absolutely stink.

And all John could think of was that the newcomer's shirt looked silky.

Shaking the thought away, John managed to lift his hand and half-heartedly point. "Yours?" he asked aiming at unconscious guy. "Because if it is you owe me..." what did he want? "...crisps."

Yeah. He would kill for some salt and vinegar ones right now. The posh ones that cost nearly twenty pence more than the regular packets.

That or a kebab.

The newcomer's eyebrows slowly rose as if he could read John's thoroughly unimpressive thought process. "And you are?" he asked as he shut the door behind him.

"The idiot who's training to be a doctor," John replied. "And you are?"

"The one who had his drugs stolen by that idiot," came the snide reply, which was so not what John had been expecting. Taken aback, he watched as the new guy dropped down next to unconscious guy and started to rifle through his pockets, seemingly uncaring at the state unconscious guy was in.

"If it helps," John said, watching them thoughtfully. "I don't think he had a very good time of it."

New guy paused and looked over at him. Closer, John could see that his eyes were an oddly sharp hazel; the light of the bathroom almost changing them startling green-gold as they narrowed once again. The guy would have permanent expression marks in his forehead soon if he wasn't careful. Then his lips twitched, just a little, and suddenly he didn't seem quite so severe. "It helps a little," new guy said as he gave John one last glance. Then with another considering look he gave an acknowledging nod. "Sherlock Holmes," he said by way of greeting.

Sherlock Holmes? That didn't even sound real. Doubtfully, John nodded and then winced as the movement sloshed the liquid in his head around, making him feel pretty unsteady.

There was a long sigh and John opened his eyes, not entirely sure when he'd closed them. Sherlock had sat back on his heels and was watching John again. "He's also an acquaintance," Sherlock confessed. "A friend of a..." he seemed to hesitate briefly. "Never mind. How long has he been out?"

"Dunno," John said, trying to stir himself into action. "He was like that when I got here. I was gonna put him in the recovery position but," John leaned forward, staring at unconscious guy before shrugging again, "seemed good as he was."

"Hmm," Sherlock said, sounding unimpressed, though more with unconscious guy than with John. Reaching out, Sherlock flushed the toilet and pulled on unconscious guy's shoulders. For a wiry looking guy, Sherlock was pretty damned strong.

And apparently unconcerned that unconscious guy was hitting his head on the bathroom wall as he was manoeuvred around.

"Not a fan of his then?" John asked. Sherlock turned and grinned, approval glinting in his eyes before the expression vanished quickly.

"Not particularly," Sherlock replied.

"You should probably drop him a few times on the stairs," John allowed.

"What's your name?" Sherlock asked.

"Uh, John, John Watson."

"And how much have you had to drink?" Sherlock asked.

About... John held up his thumb and forefinger. "Little bit," he confessed as he tried to prove that with the space between his digits. "But you're here now so I don't have to try and be too sober now."

"You were with the party?" Sherlock asked.

Yeah. Wait. "Were?" John asked, sitting up a little straighter and then wincing as the room swam.

"They dispersed a while ago," Sherlock said, his gaze dropping down to unconscious guy. "Come with me," he decided. "I believe Sebastian might have some crisps somewhere."

It seemed like the logical thing to do.

—— · · · ——

Sitting in the taxi with unconscious guy (who wasn't quite so unconscious anymore) and Sherlock was enough to make John sober up a little as he watched London race by outside the window. In fact, it was only when they got out of the taxi and John helped Sherlock bundle almost unconscious guy into a rather fancy lift that John started to wonder where the fuck he was because he'd stopped recognising landmarks in the taxi a while ago and the building was far too fancy to be student digs.

And so was the flat itself.

"Is this yours?" John asked Sherlock. He wasn't entirely sure if he felt relieved or even more confused when Sherlock shook his head.

"I told you. Friend of a friend," Sherlock said evasively as he led unconscious guy away and down a dark hall, leaving John in the main room. Slightly unsure, John walked around the living room, approving of the huge TV and the jumbled consoles before he made his way to the window to pull back the curtain out of curiosity.

The Thames was outside and the view...well, it was of the south side of London so not as many landmarks but still, the view John had was of a wall so in comparison he couldn't really complain. Feeling a little out of his depth suddenly, John dropped the curtains and stumbled away, searching for the bathroom. There was one tucked away down the hall and he headed for the sink, splashing his face to try and regain some clarity, then reaching for mouthwash because...well... yeah. He really needed to get the foul taste of sick out of his mouth.

Sherlock was in the main room when he returned, staring at the book case as John walked back in. He turned a little, looking entirely comfortable in his surroundings as he stared at John intently. Too intently.

"Uh...What?" John asked, suddenly afraid he had something on his face.

"You've been in the army," Sherlock said. "Basic training or cadets. Something like that."

What? John looked down at himself and then at Sherlock. "Uh, yeah actually. How could you-"

"But you decided to become a doctor. Is that your aspiration? To become an army doctor?"

John stared at him a moment longer and then turned to peer around the flat suspiciously. "Am I being pranked?" he asked frankly.

"You're a virgin."

John's mouth dropped open. "I...why would you-"

Sherlock pushed himself off the wall. "Why though?" he asked himself and started to circle John. It felt like a vulture was circling. Uncomfortable with the feeling, John twisted, trying to keep Sherlock in his eye sight at all times. "You aren't unattractive," Sherlock continued thoughtfully.

Thanks, John thought, wavering as to whether the comment was genuine or sarcastic. He opened his mouth to make some comment and then flushed when all that came out was an unsure squeak that made him sound stupid.

"Want to lose it?"

"Lose what?" John asked, still trying to keep up with the circling and the conversation.

Sherlock raised an eyebrow.

"Oh," John said, nodding to himself as the meaning sunk in. Then: "Oh," he yelped. "No, no that's...uh...kind? of you, but no. Thank you."

Sherlock tilted his head as his lips pressed together in a fine line. It seemed like he was more amused than anything else though; the fine line on his forehead from earlier had vanished. "Thank you?" he queried.

Flustered, John shrugged. "I don't know how you're meant to turn that down," he sighed, staring at the ceiling and giving up trying to work out what the hell Sherlock was thinking.

"You are getting more and more interesting by the second," Sherlock said softly as he started circling properly again. "It's not the homosexual aspect that has made you say no."

It wasn't a question. "I'm not gay," John said, his mind leaping to the first answer his brain provided.

"Bisexual then," Sherlock said carelessly, as if bored by the distinction.

"Look, I don't think this is a good conversation-"

"Definitely bisexual," Sherlock said from behind John. "You're less defensive about that. So, it must be a family member then. They came out and it wasn't well received."

Vague images of his parents shouting at each other, his mum devastated and the fierce, disgusted mutterings-

"Hmm," Sherlock said as he came back into John's line of sight. "Not well received at all," he said, sounding dismissive of the topic. "What is your objection to having an orgasm with me then? I can assure you I have no interest in meeting family members so you shouldn't be concerned with any repeats of that scene."

John's mind went blank at the word orgasm. "I uh...I don't think I'm a one night stand kind of person," John decided.

"How do you know?"

"That...that's a very good point," John said and then blinked in surprise at how close Sherlock suddenly seemed. Taking a breath, John let his eyes trail up from a long neck, firm chin, the roman nose and to those green-gold eyes that were watching him intently. This close, John could almost feel Sherlock's breath on the tip of his nose.

"Why are you offering?" he asked.

The question clearly took Sherlock by surprise. "What?"

"Well...I mean you appear to be sober and I'm really not, and you obviously have experience and I don't. At all. And you look good and I'm so fucking glad I used mouthwash before I had this conversation-" Part of John winced in horror at what he had just said but he ploughed on, regardless, "-but I don't get why you're offering."

As if acknowledging the wisdom of that, Sherlock stepped back. His eyes lingered in odd places as he studied John, the line between his brows deepening as if he had some puzzle to solve. In the end the line almost smoothed out as Sherlock shook his head as he moved even further away. "You really

15

are interesting," he said to himself as he strode over to the kitchen. "Drink?"

Huh? John stared ahead then turned to follow him. "Water," he requested, feeling a little bemused by the whole thing. "So you only shag what you find interesting?"

Sherlock filled up a glass from a water filter in the fridge. "I only shag what looks to be a bit different," he corrected.

"That's possibly really insulting," John said as he reached for the glass, keeping the island style counter in-between them.

Sherlock held onto the cup as John's fingers closed around it. "You're a good kind of different," Sherlock smirked, holding John's gaze.

Determined not to be outdone, John tugged on the glass. "So you do bad kinds of different?" he asked with a cheeky smile.

Sherlock snorted and let the glass go, his gaze still not leaving John. "In all sense of the word, I suppose," he said with a considering nod. "I need data."

Huh. John swallowed his water thoughtfully. "Is that like some weird science kink?"

Sherlock's mouth twitched as he leaned forward on the counter. "You are very drunk," he decided. "Are you usually this frank when you're sober?"

John shook his head as he placed the water down. "God no," he said with a laugh. "I'm like a book. The closed kind," he said, trying to briefly demonstrate what that might look like with his hands before realising that Sherlock probably knew that. "That's why everyone tries to get me hammered."

If John didn't know better he could have sworn Sherlock looked almost disappointed. Not sure what to do, John took another sip of water and then sighed. "I don't think I want crisps," he decided.

"I imagine not," Sherlock said. Then in a tantalisingly slow manner, his hand reached across the counter. "What do you want?" he asked softly.

Unbidden, John's eyes dropped to the man's mouth. He

had good lips. Kissing lips. Bad thoughts, John thought, trying to shake them away by looking up into Sherlock's eyes which did not help matters in the slightest. He could almost see the seductive smile in those damned eyes.

"So it's because I'm interesting?" John asked carefully.

Sherlock hummed in agreement, leaning closer. The tips of his fingers reached out to touch the waistband of John's jeans, skimming a flash of skin between his belt and t-shirt.

"And if I said 'thank you but no' would that make me more or less interesting?"

Fingers walked down the front of John's jeans and Sherlock's eyes lit with amusement again as John sucked in a surprised breath. "You won't," Sherlock said with supreme confidence, his chin dipping down and his lips brushing against John's in an almost there caress that left John's lips tingling at the sensation. John flicked his gaze down, just about seeing Sherlock's hand, picturing everything that could happen...

"Thank you for the offer," he said with a grin, "but I need to go home."

Sherlock's eyed widened and his hand retracted instantly. He blinked at John a few times, baffled.

"I'm very stubborn," John announced. "And moralistic," he said with a nod, pleased at his word choice. "And I am not shagging you because it will interest you. I will shag you when you want to," John frowned, hoping that his words were making sense, "cause you haven't said that yet."

Sherlock pulled away completely, turning to the fridge to put the filter away, hiding his stance from John with the fridge door for a moment. "Where do you live?" he asked seconds later as the fridge door shut and Sherlock's expressionless face reappeared in John's line of vision.

Like he knew. "Somewhere over there," John muttered throwing out a hand carelessly.

"In the Thames?" Sherlock asked doubtfully.

"Possibly not," John allowed as he stepped away from the

counter. "Uni digs. There's this house and it's not around here. I think."

That earned him a long sigh. "One minute," Sherlock said as he stomped off into the darkened corridor where he had dumped...crap what was the unconscious guy's name again?

"Here," Sherlock said, returning with a wad of cash and lowering his phone from his ear. "Taxi is on its way."

"I'm not taking your money," John said boldly. Or the taxi, he thought privately, given that he had a fiver to his name and it was after midnight.

"Good," Sherlock said. "It isn't mine."

It was impossible not to grin at how frank Sherlock was. "You stole his money?" John asked with some disbelief. He didn't know whether to clap or cry.

"*He* stole my cocaine," Sherlock snapped.

John said nothing but let himself by tugged forward by his belt loops and dragged in a breath to argue when Sherlock shoved the cash into John's back pocket. Sherlock silenced him with a stern look, taking far too much time to slide the cash in.

"You know it's bad for you?" John asked, almost close enough to pick up some of Sherlock's natural, clean smell.

The hand in his pocket paused. "Yes," Sherlock said, as if waiting for more.

"Okay," John murmured, feeling suddenly exhausted as he turned into Sherlock's neck properly, resting his forehead in the comforting crook and ignoring that it would likely kill his own neck to stay in that exact same position.

For a moment, John could have sworn that he felt a brief press of lips to his hair but that seemed way too daft to be believed. "I'll take you down," Sherlock said.

"I can take you," John mumbled and felt the body under him chuckle as he was slowly guided to turn around and head for the door. The thoughtful hum made him scowl as they made it into the lift and John continued to lean into Sherlock, not entirely convinced he could keep himself standing up.

"'m not gonna see you again, am I?" John said as they reached the bottom.

"I wouldn't say that," came the calm reply. "You're far too interesting not to run into again."

John grinned and then groaned in annoyance as they stepped outside and into the chilled early morning air. "Cold," he complained while turning further into Sherlock.

"You're drunk enough," Sherlock said keeping him steady. "I'm sure you won't feel it soon."

Probably. "Sherlock?"

"Yes?"

"If I don't remember this it's just because I'm really wasted, not 'cause I didn't want to remember," John said with a yawn.

"You'll remember," Sherlock said confidently.

If he said so.

John had zero memory of how the hell he had managed to direct the taxi driver to the right place. Dimly he had a feeling that there may have been a half-conscious phone call to Paul and a lot of false turns which might explain why there was nothing left of the ridiculous amount of money Sherlock had stuffed in his pocket last night.

"You're alive then," Mike commented when John dragged himself out of bed and crawled onto the sofa in a pathetic, hungover heap.

"Not yet," John complained, pulling a pillow over his face in the hopes of smothering out the light or just, you know, smothering himself. "I think I tried to drink the alphabet," he grumbled to the pillow. "Pretty sure Andy tried to make me go Ale, Bacardi, Carling-"

Mike snorted. "Sadly, that was not the most stupid thing you did last night."

Huh?

John pulled the pillow down from his face and shot Mike a quizzical look.

"You left the party and followed some random guys home. How thick are you?"

"Interesting," John grinned, "I'm interesting."

It made Mike roll his eyes and bang his cup on every surface he could find on his way to the kitchen. "You're a fucking dipstick, Watson," he called over his shoulder.

John kept grinning.

CHAPTER TWO:

The Memorial of the Gloria Scott

THREE WEEKS LATER, JOHN WAS being dragged out again. He didn't usually mind it, but the pub they were going to wasn't exactly what you would call cheap but it was Connor's birthday and he liked a particularly foul type of rum that only certain bars sold so it was John's hard luck apparently. Never mind the fact that Connor was the wanker who stole his answers in lab last week.

Dickhead.

The pub was an old one, long and winding with these little nooks and crannies that made finding anyone a pain in the arse. It did however mean that they were slightly hidden from sight. Most importantly though, it meant that they were less likely to disturb the group at the opposite end of the pub who looked more like they were in the middle of some sort of wake.

Of course, it hadn't helped that Andy had loudly made a few comments about them looking miserable as fuck before he'd caught a glimpse of some old photos and gone very quiet for all of three minutes.

"Ready?" Connor called as he held his shot in one hand while the other lifted up in an arrogant wave to summon their attention. The smell of the rum was already making John's eyes water in trepidation. "One, two, three."

"God," he breathed in disgust when he finally got it down. "That's disgusting."

Paul seemed to agree as he suddenly bolted for the door to the gents.

"We should have 'nother," Connor slurred, swaying where he stood. "Now."

"When are we meeting the girls?" Mike asked, resting his hand on Connor's back to keep him upright.

"Who knows?" Andy asked with a shrug. "Takes Maggie half a day to look decent."

"That's *your* girlfriend," Mike said, a warning in his voice.

"Just 'cause you love Kirsty," Andy mocked making kissing noises.

"That's an annoying noise," John muttered, almost recovered from the shot. "And you should be nice to your girlfriend. She puts up with you."

"Yeah," Andy said with a nod. "And you know what? Part of me judges her for that."

John snorted and then shrugged when Mike glared at him. "He's got a point," John said as he stepped closer to the bar, desperately needing something to remove the taste. He managed to catch the eye of the guy working and ordered a half pint.

"How's it going with that girl?" Andy asked, leaning suspiciously close to John, which usually meant that he was after a sip of his drink. "Amy, is it?"

It was impossible not to grin. "Yeah," John said. "It's... yeah it's good." Mainly because he was, finally, having sex. Regular sex with a girl who had one of the sweetest smiles he'd ever seen.

"Who's that?" Connor asked, swaying.

"John's new bird," Andy answered with a grin. "I reckon he's a bit dippy on her."

To his horror, John could feel his cheeks start to heat and he squirmed slightly. "She's sweet," he said, not sure if he should feel embarrassed about it.

"Aw," they all chorused and John ducked his head, especially when the barman set down his drink with an amused smile, clearly having heard the last part of their conversation.

"You're all shits," John decided, paying for his beer.

Paul seemed to be taking his sweet time. He never did well with shots, and it was agreed that the others would move on while John would valiantly stay to wait for Paul to crawl back out of the toilet. Besides, Amy wasn't out tonight and John wasn't exactly sure how clubbing worked when you had a girlfriend. It was always too noisy to do anything but dance and John would be damned if he was suffering through public dancing when there wasn't the option of trying to get something out of it at the end.

That being said, sitting in a pub on your own wasn't much fun either. After staring at the crowd opposite as they drank copious amounts of rum and seemed to be having some loud debate about overflowing prisons and government strategies to cope with it, John kinda lost interest. In the end, he checked that Paul was still alive, bagged a table and started to play a silly game of tiddlywinks using peanuts and an ashtray. When he grew tired of it, he started to write down all the bones in the body that he could remember using a pen he had stolen from Argos a few days ago and a beer mat with the picture torn off the front.

Sadly, he was engrossed enough that he barely noticed he was being approached. In fact, it was only when a glass was firmly set down in front of him that John startled and glanced up at Sherlock.

"Hi," John said stupidly.

Sherlock slid in next to him. "Drink the beer, John," he ordered.

It seemed counter-productive to argue with that. John lifted the beer but, halfway to his mouth, John paused and glared at Sherlock over the rim. "There's nothing in this that shouldn't be, is there?"

"I wouldn't waste the money," Sherlock said absently, his

attention seemingly fixed on the group opposite. "Drink it and act as if you know me."

"And not like I came to your flat for a packet of crisps?" John asked, feeling a little lost.

A small smile played on Sherlock's lips. "You said you'd forget."

"And you said I wouldn't," John replied taking a sip. "So, why do I have to pretend that I know you?"

"I'm blending in," Sherlock replied, looking across the bar again.

"You're really not," John muttered to his beer. "You suck at blending in."

"Why?" Sherlock sounded offended.

"'Cause you look like that," John said, glancing at the expensive shirt that was so different to most of the people there. While it didn't cross into city boy territory, it was still enough to make him the target of anyone drunk enough and looking for an excuse. His deep brown hair was styled as well; swept back in a highly-controlled manner that John was never going to bother with.

"You may have a point," Sherlock said thoughtfully. "Come here."

"Why-"

Sherlock attacked him. Well...sort of. One minute they were just sitting there and the next Sherlock had his tongue down John's throat. And bloody hell was he a good kisser! All nipping bites and soft tongue and when John gasped it seemed to be permission to let Sherlock delve further in.

When they broke apart, John stared at him blankly.

"Now I have a reason to be here," Sherlock said, sounding monumentally pleased with himself. "Don't stare, John, you're drawing attention to us."

Utterly bewildered, John took a sip. "I...I think that," he waved his hand between the two of them, "probably drew more attention to us. And I have a girlfriend," he added, suddenly remembering that important bit of information.

"She's dull. Dump her."

John gaped, "You haven't even met her," he protested.

Sherlock didn't even look at him. "Dump her. You're already bored of her."

Bastard. John stared at the fizzy golden liquid in front of him, tracing the rim of the glass idly.

"You are aware that if one fiddles with a glass like that it is a sign they are sexually frustrated?" Sherlock asked him, hazel eyes glancing down at John's hands.

John pulled his hand away. "I am not-" he shook his head, exasperated. "What are you doing?" he asked pathetically.

"It's far too complicated to explain. I simply..." Sherlock tilted his head, as his gaze followed a woman walking by them as she returned to the wake. "In my line of work people often like to trade information for services rendered."

Frustrated, John thunked his head onto the table and covered his hair with his arms.

"Yes, that isn't at all suspect," Sherlock said sarcastically, as if his staring wasn't going to be the thing that people noticed.

Rolling his head to one side, John looked up at the man opposite. "Is it legal?"

Sherlock snorted. "What is it that you think I do with my time?" he asked, and John could see a smile tugging at his lips, even from the angle he was at. His amusement made John falter because that was a can of worms that John really didn't want to open. The options were limitless and Sherlock's amusement made it all the more likely that he wasn't exactly a squeaky clean character.

"Well, whatever it is, thank you for dragging me into it." John sat back up and reached for his beer again.

"I am merely expanding your horizons," Sherlock said as he dragged his attention back to John. "You'll find it useful when you go into the army."

John stared at him. "How did you know all of that?" he asked. "I mean, did you overhear or-"

"I observed."

"Observed?"

Sherlock sighed as if John should be intelligent enough to work it out based on that one word clue. "You don't stand in a military position but after twenty seconds you start to lean into it –which suggests some training and fondness for that training. You seem unsure of it though, as if not sure you are doing it right, so basic training, you left but you want to go back. You told me you were training to be a doctor in the bathroom. Clearly you'd never met him before or you wouldn't have had to ask me if I didn't like that annoying idiot."

"Maybe he's not that-"

"You really haven't met him. Think. No-one else wanted to deal with him when you were dragged in under the guise of being slightly more medically apt than the rest of them. The fact that you didn't know him yet still helped suggests a strong moral compass."

That sounded like a nice quality. "And the other thing?" John asked. "You know, the thing that isn't an issue any more?"

Sherlock leaned forward and John held his breath. "There," Sherlock smiled. "You don't stare at me in bewilderment anymore. You don't look quite as lost as you previously did. You were skittish, despite being attracted to me."

An amused grunt erupted from John's lips. "And you know I'm attracted to you because?"

Sherlock smirked, a pleased look crossing his face. "Because you confirmed it."

Oh. Shit, that was... John glared at him hoping to convey just how not okay that was but Sherlock was already distracted by the crowd. "Your friend should be out soon," Sherlock said with a rather distasteful look at the bathroom door. "And I must go."

"Oh," John nodded, feeling strangely disappointed.

"John." Sherlock leaned over the table and John looked up, startled. "Dump her."

"Why?" John asked, unsure how to handle Sherlock being that close.

"It keeps you interesting," Sherlock replied, and then pulled away, disappearing into the crowd.

Huh. Frowning at the crowd where he'd last seen Sherlock, John tried to wrap his mind around that.

"John?"

Dragging his eyes away, John looked up at Paul who appeared to be much happier than the last time John had seen him, holding a pint of water like his life depended on it.

"Do you mind if we sack the club off?" Paul asked rubbing the back of his neck sheepishly. "I'll buy you a pint another time if you want?"

John nodded and watched as Paul sat, the movement oddly reminding him of his conversation earlier. "Do you think I'm bored of Amy?" John asked as Paul set his glass down.

Paul shrugged. "She's your first proper girlfriend John," he said.

"Yeah...just someone said something that got me thinking about it." Now he sounded like a tit. Squirming uncomfortably, John eyed the bar to avoid Paul's gaze. squish?

"What? Did some girl hit on you?" came the amused question.

"No, a guy," John replied on automatic, and then froze, unsure what the reaction would be.

But, when he risked a glance, Paul just raised an eyebrow, "Huh...is he, and don't be emphatic, but is he more...fit to you? I mean if it were a straight competition between him and Amy. Who would win?"

John smiled at the table, "Is it gonna sound really cliché that I can tell just from meeting him twice that it would be bloody complicated? And really, really casual?"

"Do you want that?" Paul asked frankly.

It was a good question. Images of his mother frantically

flitting from guy to guy had put John off being desperate for someone to 'complete him'. No relationship was better than just any relationship. And Mary's attitude was... well, she wasn't exactly stable in her choices.

He just wanted normal. Someone to talk to, have fun with and share a life with.

"No," John said honestly.

"Then there's your answer." Paul slapped him on the back. "Though if Amy is boring you, you should probably let her down soon. Longer it drags on the worse the break-ups get."

John sighed and leaned his head back against the wall. "I'll probably never see him again anyway," he huffed.

"Uh...John?"

"What?" John asked looking down again to see Paul pointing at his shirt pocket. When he reached in there was a folded piece of paper which, when unfolded, showed a phone number, scrawled in looped writing.

John stared at it feeling torn.

"Complicated, casual? Likely to break your heart? No good will come of it?" Paul prodded.

"Yeah." John still stared at it. "But I should at least tell him that I'm not-"

Paul took the paper and dumped it in his own beer.

"But-"

"You're too nice," Paul said frankly, a slight look of apology in his eyes. "It's why you're here instead of the club. Trust me, John, I'm doing you a favour."

John stared at the floating paper and watched as it broke apart in the beer, the number blurring into nothing.

CHAPTER THREE:

The Problem with Mary

MARY WAS COMING TO VISIT.

That itself was enough to make John want to crawl back into bed and say 'sod it' to the rest of the week. He'd ended up in a screaming match with Kenny, his least favourite housemate, because (apparently) it was fine to ask John if his sister was bringing her hot lesbian girlfriend. Kenny's argument went along the lines of 'she's not your real sister' which had started yet another screaming match.

Andy had not helped by asking if the girlfriend was bi too and how well received would he be if he asked to join in.

It had ended with John yelling at Andy and giving Kenny the distraction he needed to destroy John's tea, the wanker.

Mike and Paul had been pretty good about it and John almost managed to tune Andy's comments out as it was Andy just being Andy rather than him trying to actively be a dick about it.

Then, of course, there was actually talking to Mary. The phone call where she nagged him to clean the bathroom (which wasn't going to happen because he had shared a bathroom with her on and off for three years and knew exactly how messy she was). Then there were the demands to make sure the sheets were new (which was going to happen because he had a sneaking suspicion that Kenny had managed to get his hands on those too) and her plea to make sure there was edible food in the house (which he argued meant she had to cook it), as well as the request that he meet her at the tube station (which may or may not happen, depending on how bored he was).

Normal stuff like that.

John made the usual pleas (no talking about my sister's sex life; she's still my sister and it's gross) and gave the usual warnings (don't challenge her to a drinking game, she will win). It seemed necessary to go over the usual rules about swearing (don't use anything that she says; half of it's foreign, most of it came from the military and all of it should never be repeated) and then had the usual calming talk with himself where he made a mental note not to so much as hint to his brother or his mother that he'd seen Mary otherwise the next twenty hundred phone calls would be filled with epic guilt trips.

His mum's reaction he could kind of get but he still thought Harry was a giant shit head for cutting Mary out the way he had.

Mary was, as always, a beacon for attention. Her hair was a new colour, almost pink, and John wouldn't have a clue what to say if someone asked him what her natural colour was. There was always something infectious about her, something fun and energetic that made him smile, roll his eyes and just go with it. She was fierce and brave and damned unapologetic.

Her father had been the same.

"Got laid yet?" she asked as they sat in his room. He'd mostly managed to clean it up; the washing machine had never been used so much in one week and his pile of dirty dishes had been transferred from the floor to the kitchen sink. The room itself was cramped and not helped by the fact that medical text books weren't exactly the smallest things ever written.

"Yeah," he said, flopping down on the bed next to her.

"Wow, John. Sound more enthusiastic," she mocked, shifting so that their shoulders brushed.

He stared at the ceiling and let out a sigh, "She was sweet."

Mary snorted and John closed his eyes. "Sweet

isn't enough," Mary argued. "Sweet does not make for clothes-ripping moments."

True. "There is someone, but the whole thing would be complicated."

"Sounds better," Mary said, rolling onto her side. "What's she like?"

John stared at the ceiling.

"Ah," Mary purred, rolling over onto her back again. "Well, aren't you a chip off the old block," she teased. When John said nothing, she nudged him. "He'd be proud of you, no matter what. You know that, right?"

"It's not just- I mean...Mum and Harry would make my life hell if I said I was seeing a guy. After Dad..." John shook his head. "But he's also rich, does cocaine-"

Mary started to laugh. Peeling laughs that made John grin even as he struggled to understand what it was that had tickled her so strongly. "What?" he asked, turning to face her.

"You," she said shaking her head. "Let's face it, out of the three of us you're the sensible, nice dutiful one. Harry's the wanker, I'm the..." she seemed to debate for a moment before she grinned. "The fun one," she said with a pleased grin. "Your Dad must be up there gutted that his golden boy is starting to be a bit naughty."

Gutted. Right. But Mary seemed to catch his expression and sat up with a sigh. "Not what I meant. Just, I think he would probably be surprised. And maybe feeling very protective about his golden baby boy."

John sniggered at that. "What about you?" he asked, trying to back away from the subject a little. "What happened to the fit girlfriend with legs up to her ears?"

"Women," Mary said with a dismissive shrug. "She was demanding. And she didn't have a great sense of humour. She told me she wanted jewellery so I offered to go diving for pearls and she did not appreciate it."

Oh, yuck. John rolled away and stumbled towards the

kitchen, his face going red as he desperately tried not to picture that image.

"Your flatmates don't seem demanding," Mary called after him.

"I'm not," Andy shouted from the living room. "I like diving too," he added with what had to be a cheerful grin on his face.

"I need bleach," John muttered as he covered his ears with his hands.

Despite Mary's claims that she was done with women for the rest of this month, she seemed to hone in on the pretty brunette that caught John's attention in the corner of the Walkabout Bar they ended up in.

Who also happened to be Joe's sister. Joe who played rugby with the fresher's team last year and looked like he could knock a wall down with his shoulders. That Joe.

Mary had crappy taste.

"Your dyke of a sister has taken mine home," Joe hissed at John towards the end of the night.

"What?" John said, turning around.

"I said she took-"

"No," John said, standing up properly. "Say exactly what you said."

Joe seemed to hesitate for a moment and then levelled his chin. "Your dyke of a sister," he spat.

There was no damned way he was backing down from Joe being such a complete dick. Squaring up, John fixed the bastard with a hard gaze and shook his head. "My sister will take home who she wants, when she wants and as long as she hasn't used chloroform to do it, I don't give a shit."

Joe sneered at him. "I do. My sister ain't a lesbo."

Yeah, there was no way he was backing down from that. Taking a deliberate step closer, John spread open his arms. "You wanna bet?"

It probably wasn't the best thing to say. Joe swung for him and John ducked, pushing forward to get Joe on the floor. The daft idiot stumbled back, heel catching a stool and they both went crashing to the floor where John was able to get in two good punches before one of Joe's mates came forward and caught John's head. The world seemed to tumble into a strange buzzing, high pitched sound for a moment and it was enough that Joe could shove him to the sticky floor and get a few hits in.

Where the hell his mates were, John had no idea. He curled in a little, having no chance of standing with two of them hitting him. The battery of fists and feet made him curl, trying to collect his thoughts enough through some rising panic to work out what he needed to do next. But, before he could start to think, the blows suddenly stopped. Tentatively raising his head, John caught a glimpse of Joe and his little henchman being dragged off before John himself was bodily lifted and taken in the other direction then shoved out the back exit.

"Look," the bouncer said, cracking his knuckles. "You don't come back in here. You're barred-"

Seriously? "They started it," John snarled, stumbling to a wall and spitting out blood as he tried to gather his thoughts enough to properly launch into why everyone was such a tosser.

"Your sister ain't welcome here either," the bouncer rumbled. "Got it?"

John glanced up at the guy. He was big and his arms looked twice the size of John's. Still, there was part of him that thought he could probably do some damage if needed.

The bouncer seemed to smile a little, probably recognising the expression on his face. "You'll do her no good, lad, if you get into fights for her. She won't thank you for it."

"She's my sister," John muttered. "She never thanks me."

The bouncer rolled his eyes. "Keep her out," he ordered

again as he stepped back into the bar and swung the fire exit door shut.

John glared at the closed door and kicked the wall for lack of something better to kick. It didn't help and he felt himself lurch from the momentum of it, his head unable to find a balance again. There was a sick feeling at the back of his throat which probably wasn't the best sign, and he paused to drag in ragged breath after ragged breath.

Shit. Joe had hit him in the head a few times and he'd been slammed into the floor. Plenty of opportunity for him to get a concussion or something or...yeah. John dug into his pocket to grab his phone and then frowned, patting along his pocket for keys and wallet.

Oh, be kidding!

Striding forward, John banged on the fire exit door but he was either being ignored or they couldn't hear him. Groaning in frustration, John turned towards the back alley and took a deep breath. All he had to do was work out how to get to the front of the bar, walk in and demand his things.

If they hadn't already been stolen.

It so wasn't his lucky night.

At some point, he must have taken a wrong turn because he did not find the front of the bar. And no bar would let him in to make a phone call because he didn't have any ID on him at all. Instead he kept walking, sticking close to the walls, not because he was thick enough to think that he could hide in the shadows but rather because they helped him stand up. Sort of. Ish.

He'd been walking for twenty minutes or so when his vision swayed and he curled into the wall as he waited for the dizziness to pass.

"Mate? You okay?"

John nodded against the wall and then shook his head feeling as if his brain was sloshing.

"Ignore him. Do not change the subject. We were discussing the agreement that you have with the Trevors-"

He knew that voice. John grinned against the wall, rubbing his head against it to relieve the itch and maybe the weird pressure he was feeling. "Are you still pissed off that I haven't phoned you?" he asked.

"What?" the guy talking to Sherlock said. "Mate, I don't swing that-"

Whoever the man was, he was shoved out of the way. "John?" Sherlock asked, sounding much closer now.

With his not so bruised hand, John waved uselessly behind him. "My mate dumped your number in his beer. It wasn't my fault," he said and then groaned as careful hands turned him around.

"You have had a walloping," the guy with Sherlock said, wincing at the sight of John. The guy was shorter than Sherlock and his face blurred in front of John's eyes.

That wasn't good.

"Sisters," John said as Sherlock pushed him slightly against the wall and started to root through his pockets, "are a pain. What are you doing?" he asked, trying to look down. "I think my wallet fell out during the fight."

Sherlock sighed. "Fight?" he asked, glancing at John. "Two against one is called a fight now, is it?"

"It wasn't one against ten," John said, not sure why that was relevant and then hissed when Sherlock's pats found a tender spot.

"You need to go to hospital," Sherlock murmured.

"I am a hospital," John announced. "Or something like that. A doctor," he said, pleased that the words had come out right eventually.

"You have a concussion," Sherlock said as he stepped back.

Okay. John leaned his head back against the wall which was oddly comfortable now.

"How many fingers?" Sherlock's voice asked, cutting through the comfortable, settling haze in an annoying way.

John giggled. Fingers. Heh.

"John," Sherlock voice snapped even as his fingers followed suit. John blinked, staring at the man's hand but, fuck it all, he had no idea how many fingers were raised.

"I..." he couldn't focus. "I dunno," he muttered. The wall was so comfortable that he could just go to sleep and that would be nice-

Fingers snapped right by his ear making him jump. "Do not go to sleep," Sherlock said firmly, grabbing him by the chin. "Do you understand me? Do not go to sleep."

Mm. John peeled his eyes open and stared at Sherlock, who was very close. The man's gaze was focused on John's head and he could just about feel Sherlock's hands as they carded through his hair looking for the injury. The hands encouraged him forward to rest his chin over Sherlock's shoulder, and John stared at the other guy.

"I don't know you," John said to him and then hissed when Sherlock found another tender spot.

"Probably best that you don't," the guy said. "Sherlock? I'm off. I'll catch up with you later."

Sherlock turned slightly and made an impatient, dismissive noise. John leaned forward just a tiny bit so that his nose brushed Sherlock's ear. "You smell nice."

Sherlock let out a long sigh. "You've been drinking as well," he said trying to pull John back.

So? John tried to turn his lips into Sherlock's throat and then made an annoyed noise when Sherlock leaned him back against the wall.

"You need a doctor," Sherlock muttered, looking peeved.

"I know," John said, as if that should have been obvious.

Sherlock pinched the bridge of his nose, irritated. "You have the worst timing," he complained.

"It's very white," John declared as he looked around the hospital waiting room half an hour later.

Sherlock glared at the wall opposite them. "Shocking," he said tightly.

"'m sorry about the number," John mumbled.

There was a repetitive noise. Curious, John peered at the floor and watched as Sherlock's leg jolted and jarred while his fingers tapped on one of his arms as he sat, arms folded, and the skin was going white where his nail kept catching.

"I would have phoned you," John said, staring at the nail.

"To say no," Sherlock said, not looking at him.

"Yeah," John agreed. "But I wanted to tell you that," he said shifting and then immediately regretting it as his head forced his body to over balance until he was bent over his knees.

"Why?" Sherlock asked.

"Because it was rude-"

"Not-" Sherlock's feet shifted. "Why would you have said no?"

Turning his head, John looked up at Sherlock who seemed to be properly looking at him, finally. "Same reason you can't sit still," he said pointedly.

That searching look was fixed on John. In the whiteness of the hospital, Sherlock's normally hazel eyes were almost completely cat green and narrowed almost to slits. "You realise," he said, "that even while concussed you've noticed something that none of these idiots have."

John struggled to find a good place to rest his head. "You're not usually this jerky. You're smooth."

A nurse walked by them and Sherlock watched her go, waiting until she was out of ear-shot. "Is the cocaine your only complaint?" he asked in a tone so soft that John only just about heard.

"Normal annoys you," John replied.

"Normal will annoy you too," Sherlock said woodenly. "I can tell."

"Never had it," John mumbled feeling tired again. "Want to try." He managed to crack an eye open. "I'll give you data on it if you like," he offered.

Something in Sherlock's gaze softened and he shook his head before thudding it back against the wall. He really did seem to be struggling.

"You can go," John offered. "If you need to," he added.

If Sherlock really was coming down then he needed to go and John waited for him to stand. There wasn't much more that Sherlock could really do now. And yet, when Sherlock did move it was to wrap an arm around John's shoulders and gently pull him up to sit straight. He guided John's head to his shoulder, allowing John to relax against him.

It was such a lovely relief and John closed his eyes, the brightness of the walls hurting his head. "Still smell nice," he said, his mind not quite able to get past that idea.

"You smell like lager and dried blood," Sherlock replied without venom. "You smell interesting," he said, pressing a smile to John's ear.

"I can't fall asleep," John mumbled.

"I know," Sherlock said softly. "You won't."

───────

The bed that John woke up in was unfamiliar. There was a dim memory of climbing into a taxi with Sherlock and a stern looking doctor giving him instructions that John seriously did not remember. He felt fine now though so someone must have done something right.

The room was just about big enough to fit a double bed and a side table. It didn't look as fancy as the first place Sherlock had taken John back to but then had that been Sherlock's place? Sliding up the bed and sitting against the pillows, John tried to work out whether Sherlock had ever hinted at where he lived.

He was sober.

That was weird. He'd never talked to Sherlock while sober and now he was in his bed and fuck he had no idea what Sherlock did or how old he was or whether they were still even in London.

Crawling out of the bed, John padded over to the door, still in his shirt and boxers. Dimly from behind the door, he could hear the sound of a television. When he walked out, Sherlock was perched on the edge of the sofa, looking as if he'd just been startled out of deep contemplation.

"Thanks," John said awkwardly as the silence seemed to drag on. "For, you know, last night. You didn't have to bring me back here."

"I know," Sherlock said without any hint as to what he was thinking, which so didn't help John with what the hell he should say next.

It took a moment for John to realise that Sherlock was staring at John's torso and the bruises flowering over his chest and ribs. *through the open shirt,*

"First bar fight," John said as he shifted from foot to foot. "My sister she…well…step sister. Sort of…" he trailed off, not entirely sure how interested Sherlock would be in the story, but when he stopped Sherlock looked up questioningly and gestured for him to continue. "Uh…she…she pissed off some guys so I…they called her a dyke. Wanted me to apologise for her taking some girl home."

Sherlock tilted his head to the side. "But she's only sort of your step-sister?"

John shrugged not really wanting to get into it.

"Why would you have said no?" Sherlock asked. "The real reason?" he asked, taking a step forward. On automatic, John stepped back, annoyed when his back hit the door. This wasn't happening, just because Sherlock was older and better at this sort of thing did not mean that John was going to be a complete girl about it.

So he leaned forward and kissed Sherlock.

It was just as good as he remembered it being; John was

certain he could kiss Sherlock for hours but that wasn't the point of this, he told himself sternly. Instead he pulled back, tugging at Sherlock's bottom lip with little nips and a wicked grin. For once, Sherlock looked dazed as John pulled away.

"That good?" John asked.

"I can't figure you out," Sherlock said after a moment.

"Is that good?"

Sherlock sniffed, seeming unhappy about it. It was hard not to smile at his almost childish reaction as John gathered up his things, aiming for the door. "Right, well, I'll find you I guess."

"Don't be stupid," Sherlock said with a wolfish smile. "It's my turn to find you."

CHAPTER FOUR:

Strange Dates

LECTURES COULD BE BORING, ESPECIALLY when the glamour of having them in an actual hospital on the actual Thames had worn off. The current module was being run by a guy who was so into it all that he occasionally forgot to make sure that the people he was talking to actually followed what he was saying. But, unfairly, they took a register sheet at every lecture so John could hardly get away with skipping like some people did. Especially a certain person whose name began with the letter 'A', who was studying English and dumped lectures he didn't like to chase girls because his subject didn't make him sign in.

The bruises from the week before had just started to fade away. Mary had been horrified at the state of him when he'd stumbled in. They argued: her saying that he shouldn't have bothered sticking up for hﻉr, him furious that she thought he should just keep his mouth shut. her

She ended it by giving him a hug and making him lots of hot chocolate and getting the others to promise to keep an eye out for him. Which, because his friends were all relatively lazy buggers, meant they all just let him buy the last round of drinks (the one that was usually cheapest).

He figured it would last a month, but hell, he'd take it!

Tapping his pen on his pad of paper, he sighed, feeling a little defeated. He'd already flicked through the earlier notes to see if they would help and yet, by the end, he'd simply turned over to the next blank page and stared at it hopefully, hoping something would happen and he'd become a genius. He became so lost in hopeful contemplation that he didn't notice when a long leg curled over the wooden edge behind John's row. It was only when Sherlock sat down next to him that John jumped and stared at the man next to him who was acting as if there was nothing at all unusual about the situation.

Was he dreaming or still drunk? John gaped at the lecture screen in front of him and then pinched the back of his right hand hard.

No. That hurt so he had to be awake.

"Good morning," John said, lost for anything else to say.

"Are these your previous notes?" Sherlock asked, reaching to tug the pad of paper out from under John's pen.

"Yes but..." John frowned as he watched Sherlock leaf through notes. "You're not on this course," he said carefully.

"No." Sherlock didn't seem to see any relevance in that statement. "He's very advanced."

"What? The lecturer?" John scratched under his eye. "Yeah, I don't follow half of it, so who knows."

"It's a trauma lecture."

John exhaled slowly. "Yeah, I'm not that thick," he complained. "Have you followed me here?"

"It's interesting," Sherlock said as he returned the notes and settled back the way one would to watch a film.

For a moment, John had the oddest feeling he was on the strangest date ever. Not sure what to do, John started at the PowerPoint on the screen as the lecturer sipped at his water. For some reason that seemed to help John gather his thoughts enough that he glanced back at Sherlock. "Will you be able to follow this?" John asked suspiciously.

That seemed to wound Sherlock; the man's only response was to glare at him as if mortally insulted.

"Sorry," John held up a hand to placate him. "Sorry, so

should I be concerned that you think a lecture on trauma is a fun way to spend your time?"

"It's data."

Ah, data again. John flicked the pages of his pad back to the blank page it had been open to before Sherlock had started rifling through. "Why do you need data on injuries?"

"It helps me."

This was going no-where. John slid down the chair a little, knowing from experience he was highly unlikely to find a comfortable position. "Wake me up when he's done," he muttered.

Sherlock wrenched him back up. "It will be useful to you too. Do you not want to go into the army? Do you think it will be colds you will end up treating?"

"I don't understand him," John winced as he heard himself whine. "It's not worth it. I just go-"

"To the library and stay up later than you should," Sherlock sounded disapproving. "Then why come here?"

"Register."

Sherlock was silent and John glanced over at him. "I could forge your signature," Sherlock offered quietly. "I wish to attend these anyway."

It was tempting. "Nah, my tutor will probably cotton on. It's fine."

Together, they settled back as the lecturer began and Sherlock seemed so fascinated that John almost managed to follow the first twenty minutes.

And so it began.

Sherlock didn't come to every lecture but he suddenly seemed to be around, both on campus and at St Thomas'. And, after 'borrowing' John's library card for the weekend, seemed to have acquired his own, which meant access to the collections as well as endless bitching about the layout of the library, the staff and the way that John took notes.

"What do you actually do?" John asked one evening as his eyes started to see black dots rather than words.

"Whatever I want to do," Sherlock replied easily.

Right.

The worst part was that there seemed no predictable schedule to Sherlock's sudden appearances. He would just turn up and John would stare, nod and sigh, then get on with whatever he was doing.

And Sherlock would occasionally say something weird as to why he was researching a certain topic which would cause John to try not to tear out his own hair in sheer frustration. It started off with places where John was already sat down, as if Sherlock thought he would run away otherwise, and slowly started to filter into other aspects of his day.

Though walking out of Greggs to find Sherlock falling into step with him was highly unexpected.

"Hair products?" he replied blankly as they walked.

"Yes." Sherlock seemed almost bored with the conversation as John ate his walking dinner, which pretty much consisted of a cornish pasty which, if he were honest, he was already starting to regret.

"Why?" John asked, waving his dinner around. The question seemed to be his catchphrase at the moment. God only knew why he bothered asking. It wasn't as if he ever got a proper reply.

"Because it tells me about people."

Like that.

"Ah, I get it," John said as he nodded seriously, punctuating his speech by waving his pasty again before realising he was risking having the filling fall out. A quick manoeuvre ensured that his dinner was saved. Especially as the filling was the only good bit.

"You do?" Sherlock sounded surprised.

"Yeah, you want to be a hairdresser."

Sherlock almost stopped in confusion. "No I don't."

"I can tell these things." It was hard to keep his face straight. "I can see it," he added seriously, "I mean, you'd be fantastic chatting to little old ladies about their cats and listening to all those complaints. You're an amazing people person."

"I..." Sherlock seemed thrown. "What?"

"And honestly you would look amazing wielding a pair of scissors and a hairbrush and those belt things that look like some utility belt."

"You're teasing," Sherlock breathed, sounding still a little taken aback.

"Of course I'm bloody teasing!" John grinned and turned to face Sherlock, walking backwards as he did so. It was a rare sight to see Sherlock Holmes confused and John savoured it (and was not at all distracted by how strikingly golden looking the man was against the grey day). "You as a hairdresser? Discussing what shade of yellow looks best?"

"Blond," Sherlock corrected, his lips twitching.

"Oh." John dumped the pastry shell in the bin, slightly impressed that he was managing this whole walking backwards business. "I take it all back! You are gonna be the king of hairdressers!" he said with a dramatic wave of his hand.

Sherlock's lips trembled with laughter as his eyes narrowed, scanning John in a way that meant he was trying to find something to inform him of John's behaviour. It seemed to be happening a lot lately, especially whenever he made Sherlock laugh or whenever they talked about nothing in particular and just enjoyed each other's company. It was almost as if Sherlock suspected John was hiding some friendship equation in his eyes.

"Lamp."

"What-" John narrowly missed the lamp, darting around it in what was probably an awkward dance move. "Thanks."

Sherlock just rolled his eyes, but every so often as they walked John could see a hint of a surprised smile on his face.

"You're not eating?"

"That's was not food," Sherlock said, casting a look back at the bin. "If *you* threw it away then I shudder to think what it was like."

"Hey," John complained. "I have taste. Like this is nice. Yummy," John moaned, even as inwardly he winced at how orgasm sounding the noise was. "And there's sausage rolls and cheese slices-"

"You are revolting."

"Mini pizzas and the batter you get off fish and chips."

"John, stop it."

"And kebabs-"

"You are supposed to be training to be a doctor," Sherlock snapped. "You will end up with scurvy."

"And apple donuts," John added thoughtfully, flashing Sherlock a hopeful grin.

Now that he could spot it easier, he could see when Sherlock wanted to laugh but also didn't want people to know it. "Idiot," he said fondly.

"You drink though, right?"

Sherlock looked at him with narrowed eyes. "You drink more than enough for the pair of us," he replied prissily. "Where are we?" Sherlock asked, his eyes suddenly skimming above John's head and looking around as if finally realising they had walked away from campus.

"Wow, you really were fascinated by our hairdressing conversation," John said with a smile as he reached for the gate that would probably collapse due to wood rot within the next three minutes. "Home," he said, waving at the tired, shabby house that he lived in with the other four guys. The whole area was student housing and nothing there was what anyone would call classy. "And I was talking about tea, you tit."

When he finally got the door open, and there was a technique that involved kicking it as many times as was needed and then kicking it again just to prove a point, he turned to Sherlock. "So? Do you want tea?"

As if stepping into a leper colony, Sherlock edged forward, eyes darting everywhere in curiosity, probably searching for clues. John turned back to the house, trying to see it the way that Sherlock did. All he could see though was the messy living room and the kitchen to the far end with the shabby back door that led to nowhere in particular. The stairs ran along the left and his, Kenny and Andy's rooms came off the side. John opened his mouth as Sherlock headed for the stairs where the bathroom and the other two bedrooms were.

"That's...I live with...don't get caught by my flatmates," John ended up calling as he stood in the living room on his own.

There was a noise that might be Sherlock acknowledging what John had said. Or might just be Sherlock finding something 'interesting'.

Putting the kettle on, John stared at the dirty dishes and then rooted through to find the least dirty cups to run under the tap.

What were the rules for this? What were you meant to do when someone who you had snogged twice, been propositioned by once and had been chatting to in a weird 'oh you're here we may as well talk' way for the past three weeks was in your house?

And Sherlock hadn't tried to kiss him again. In fact, he hadn't even brought up the idea of sex and John wasn't sure if he was relieved or secretly disappointed about that. John tilted his head at the kettle as he half-heartedly dried the almost clean cups, trying to work it all out.

Was he the one hitting on Sherlock now? Could you do that without knowing it?

The kettle clicked off and John started to pour the water, pulling a face as he spotted what looked like the remains of toast on a plate. Though he could hardly talk given the old sandwich on his desk.

In his bedroom.

Which Sherlock was probably-

Yelping in horror, John put the kettle down and flew through the living room and into his room where Sherlock was standing by the tiny window. John slowly reached for the plate in the hopes that the action wouldn't be seen, even as he started to surreptitiously kick his dirty washing sort of under the bed.

"If you ever wish to attract a bed mate you will need to tidy."

John wanted to sink through the floor. "Yeah, um, you couldn't like close your eyes for half an hour or so, could you?"

"You dislike one of your flatmates," Sherlock said as he continued to stare out the window, though who the hell knew what he was seeing given that it showed the alley way in between this house and the next.

"Kenny? Yeah," John shrugged, "well, beggars can't be choosers and all that."

Silence fell and, for the first time, it was awkward.

"I have tea... almost." John shifted. "And if you could possible forget what a complete mess my room is I would be forever grateful," he added, picking the plate up and hiding it behind his back.

Slowly, Sherlock turned. "You don't care that I just wandered into your room?"

That was a fair point. "Well I didn't say you couldn't," John said after a moment.

And then that look happened again, the look that said Sherlock was trying to find the hidden answer that John was somehow holding back. It was a look that John suspected he was going to get very well acquainted with.

John had expected a bit more of a reaction from his mates. He wasn't sure why exactly; they all brought friends back with them from time to time.

But it was Sherlock. Somehow it seemed as if more of a fuss should be made about that.

"Your friend," Paul said one evening. "It's him, isn't it? The 'interesting one'?"

John glared at the television. "Leave it alone," he warned. "It's not like that."

"He's a bit odd," Paul continued on regardless.

"Paul," John growled. "Leave it."

"So, what's he doing?" Mike asked as Sherlock made his way around the pub.

"Calculating." John shrugged. "I have no idea," he added when Mike opened his mouth again. "I didn't want to risk the headache by asking."

Mike seemed fascinated by Sherlock and returned to watching him with a confused eye.

Paul grinned. "Yeah...calculating," he said with a wink at John.

Startled, John turned to watch Sherlock closely, almost certain that Sherlock was indeed looking at the table edges and not at the numerous young people sat at said tables.

"God, I swear there has got to be a way," Andy declared with a longing look at Phoebe Darville as they sat watching the horse racing at the pub. "Nothing is bloody working. Fucking Turner is going to end up with her," he said with a frustrated fling of his hands.

It was Andy's latest moan in twenty minutes and John

yawned pointedly. "Oh my God," John complained, "if you complain one more time, I'm going to kill you."

"You don't understand," Andy groaned as he sprawled out across the table. "Please-"

"Buy her a whiskey and dry ginger," Sherlock said in between his rounds, which basically meant that he disappeared for about fifteen minutes and came back to stay with them until the next time he got bored. John barely bothered to keep track of Sherlock's comings and goings anymore.

"Why?" Andy asked, lifting his head pathetically.

"Buy her the drink and then ask about the race. Confess you know nothing about it but saw her watching. Say you want to learn to impress a girl."

Andy snorted. "Oh, yeah, that's a turn on."

"She'll know you mean her, you idiot," Sherlock said before turning his attention to John. "Did you print off those pictures?"

"Yes," John said, tearing his gaze away from Andy's thoughtful look.

"Where are they?"

"I don't carry pictures of that stuff with me," John said with a sigh. "They're of wounds, not porn," he added when Andy perked up eagerly. "It's at home," he finished explaining to Sherlock who nodded and then walked out the pub without another word.

"Wow," Andy said, sitting up. "He took that badly."

"He's breaking into the house," John said with a sigh as he finished his pint. "I'll go in a second and make sure he doesn't destroy the windows. Or Kenny."

Andy snorted.

And that was that. Somehow, Sherlock was in John's life. Mike was awed, Paul wary and Andy seemed to think that Sherlock was some sort of demi-god sent to help him pull girls. Whatever else he was, John had never quite had a friend like Sherlock before.

Or whatever the hell he was.

CHAPTER FIVE:

Of Lawyers and Loyalty

THERE WERE SOME DAYS THAT had Sherlock convinced he'd have been far happier if he'd been an only child.

In fact, there were a lot of 'some days'.

"You missed your hearing," Mycroft said, his arms folded. The expensive suit he wore was almost perfect, probably because he barely moved enough to give it a chance to wrinkle. Lawyers, in Sherlock's opinion, sat down far too much. And when they stood, they seemed to expect that the whole world would stop and pay attention to them.

Like right now.

"And?"

"And?" Mycroft asked, sounding on the verge of being angry. "I barely managed to keep you out of prison this time. Next time you might not be-"

God, why did he even bother? "Please," Sherlock sneered. "It's the only challenge you get. Besides, it's as much in your interest as mine. You couldn't possibly have a convicted drug addict for a brother, not in your position."

The muscle in Mycroft's jaw started to tick, which meant Sherlock had hit a nerve. "Hardly," Mycroft countered. "It would at least relieve the difficulty of having you associated with the Trevor family."

Ah, that. "Spying on me?"

"Your name is coming up in files," Mycroft said as he aimed

his gaze at the wall behind Sherlock's head. "Repeatedly. It's hardly a common name-"

"Blame our parents," Sherlock suggested, half curious as to how accurate the files were, then shrugged it away. "I wouldn't worry," he said as he reached for the remote and threw himself onto the sofa. Putting his feet on the coffee table, a habit which had annoyed Mycroft endlessly when they'd been children, he smirked and raised an eyebrow in an inviting manner.

His brother looked close to an apoplectic fit. It had always been easy to irritate him; simply look like the laziest, smuggest prick on the planet and Mycroft's left eye would start to twitch in frustration.

"You wouldn't worry?" Mycroft echoed blankly.

"You're likely to be highly disappointed if you think anyone you work with can make any kind of deductions. I'd give them a round of applause if they managed to read all the words in the file and understand-"

Mycroft let out an angry breath and turned away, his arms dropping down uselessly to his side. Clearly, he was gearing up for his return salvo.

Whatever it was, was sadly abandoned by a knock at the door. "Answer it on your way out," Sherlock suggested as he clicked the television on, bored by the encounter.

"I will not protect you next time," Mycroft snarled, leaning close in what Sherlock imagined his brother thought was an intimidating manner.

"I will weep all night with the knowledge," Sherlock replied, allowing his voice to drop to a wooden, monotone curl. He refused to watch as Mycroft collected his things, scrolling through the channels list to find something better than Bargain Hunt.

"I...uh...is this Sherlock's place?" John's voice asked after the unmistakable click of a door opening.

John.

For a moment, Sherlock froze, not at all sure how to

act with Mycroft there. The silence meant that Mycroft was probably sizing John up. Refusing to look away ,from the television, Sherlock clenched his fingers around the remote, feeling the plastic creak a little from the force.

"Is that a no?" John asked, genuinely sounding baffled. It almost made Sherlock smile because the one thing Mycroft could never quite manage to deal with was someone who had honest reactions.

Probably why he'd become a lawyer.

"And you are?" Mycroft asked, his voice lashing out with precise inflection.

"I...um...John?"

The smile faded. John sounded like a moron.

"Are you certain of that?" Mycroft asked, clearly unimpressed. "Sherlock, if you are going to spread your degenerate ways, perhaps you could pick up someone less, well..." Mycroft's pause over his vocabulary choice was deliberate, Sherlock was sure of it, "less plebeian."

It seemed enough to throw John as there wasn't the usual bantered retort from his friend. "You were leaving," Sherlock reminded Mycroft.

"But I hardly ever get introduced to your associates," Mycroft said. "Consider how much easier it will be for me to maintain my own dignity if I have other names to ensure my colleagues are distracted."

Sherlock unfolded himself from the sofa instantly, striding over. A glance at John's face showed his relief in finally being able to see Sherlock even as Mycroft's lips tilted into something akin to a triumphant smile.

Only less like a smile because it was Mycroft and the world was still rotating on its axis.

"I..." John was glancing between them. "I can go," he offered slowly.

"No," Sherlock said, reaching out to wrap a hand around John's arm to pull him closer. "And John is not an *associate*,"

Sherlock told Mycroft. "Claim that he is and I will loudly correct your colleagues."

There. He'd shown his cards to Mycroft.

"Who..." John was glancing between the two, seeming to find his footing slowly as he began to stand his ground. "Who is this?" he asked Sherlock, keeping his gaze on Mycroft.

"My heartless older brother," Sherlock announced, waving a hand in Mycroft's direction. "An endless source of pleasure and joy as I'm sure you can imagine."

John glanced at Mycroft and then at Sherlock. "Right," he said in a voice that suggested he was certain he was missing something. Sherlock kept his hand on John's arm, enjoying the connection, the feel of the practical, cheap coat under his fingers and, beneath that, the toned arm.

Mycroft's attention seemed to rest on Sherlock's fingers and then darted to Sherlock's face in question. Hating the implication, Sherlock released John's arm and stepped back slightly.

"So what do you do?" John asked, for some reason trying to salvage the situation.

"He's a lawyer," Sherlock sneered. "Specialises in international drug laws."

John snorted and grinned at Sherlock, the amusement fading when Sherlock didn't return it. "Are you serious?" he asked, quiet horror seeping into his voice as he spun back to Mycroft. "Are you...do you..." John faltered as he seemed to realise he could be getting Sherlock in trouble.

"And what do you do?" Mycroft asked smoothly. "Clearly you are not part of Sherlock's usual vagabond group."

It seemed like John couldn't decide whether to be pleased or insulted. "I...well...I'm a student."

At that, Mycroft seemed to lose all interest. A faint noise of disgust echoed through the room and Mycroft turned his full attention back to Sherlock. "Do you honestly have nothing better to do than amuse yourself with idiotic teenagers?"

"I'm twenty one," John argued, sounding put out. He may

as well have declared it to the sky for all the attention Mycroft was now giving him. Instead, Mycroft reached for the door again, which was a relief because Sherlock wasn't entirely sure he could manage another minute of lecturing from Mr Perfect himself.

But-

"He has nothing to do with the drugs," Sherlock said. "He's training to be a doctor. Try to use him against me again and-"

But Mycroft had already turned, eyebrows raised in an expression of surprise. He glanced at John again. "A doctor?" he asked. "And your thoughts on his drug habit are what?"

John was still staring at Sherlock in disbelief but suddenly seemed to realise someone was talking to him. "I...what... you know? But..." he pressed his lips together and shrugged, radiating displeasure at the topic.

"John's lectures are slightly more bearable than yours," Sherlock interjected, leaning against the back of the sofa as he folded his arms. "Possibly because he hasn't yet sold his soul to the devil in order to gain a life dedicated to discovering loopholes in legal documents."

Mycroft glanced between them and Sherlock would have given up half the cocaine in the flat to know what he was thinking. It seemed to take an age for Mycroft to nod and turn his uncomfortable, unnatural smile to John. "You said your name was John," he said, clearly pressing for more.

"John Watson," John replied, shifting a little to align more with Sherlock.

"I am Mycroft Holmes," Mycroft said, holding out his hand. "You realise that by associating with my brother you could risk your degree and future career."

Anger crashed through Sherlock. How dare he? As if Sherlock wasn't careful enough to keep John away from that side of his life. As if Sherlock wouldn't keep the drugs from touching him. As if he would allow John to be sucked into that world. As if-

The second he drew breath to argue back, Mycroft met

his gaze with a triumphant, satisfied smile as he held John's hand mid shake.

It didn't last long. John yanked his hand back as if he'd been burned and backed away, fury clear in the way his movements became sharp and staccato. "You realise you can fuck off," John snapped.

It made Mycroft's smile deepen, his gaze not leaving Sherlock's. "I realise it's been a while since you had a... friend," he said, and damn him, that pause was so deliberate that even John squirmed a little, cheeks flushing. "But do try to limit the trouble you will get him into. Even the best of us can run out of patience with you."

And, with that parting shot, he gave John a nod and left.

The only possible response was to storm over to the door and slam it shut with such force that Mycroft was bound to hear it as he walked down the stairs. Bracing his hands against it, as if his brother was going to have a sudden personality transplant and bound back up the stairs to try and get back in, Sherlock hung his head to catch his thoughts.

"Mycroft?" John asked suddenly. "And Sherlock?"

It took a moment to work out what he was asking. "Family names," Sherlock said wearily. "My father was traditional."

"Hmm," John said. "That explains a few things."

"Such as?" Sherlock asked as he straightened and turned. John had taken off his coat and was in Sherlock's former position leaning against the sofa. It was tempting to walk over, stand between his legs and fist his hand into John's windswept hair-

Friend.

Ignoring the temptation, Sherlock scratched his head and leaned back against the door, some part of him still wary that Mycroft might return for another sniping match.

John shrugged. "I have an overachieving brother too."

"He graduated two years earlier then he should have. Head hunted, revered," Sherlock said, folding his arms. "I doubt it compares."

"My brother never disagreed with our mum when it came to my dad," John said with a shrug. "My brother's as homophobic as she is."

Unfair. A small, begrudging part of Sherlock could admit that he'd chosen to avoid the same path as Mycroft. Avoid the endless comparisons, the inevitable failure to match up.

Uncomfortable, Sherlock stepped forward, not really knowing what to say. In the end, he cupped a hand around John's head and let them lean in close to each other. John allowed it, appearing calm as he exhaled a shaky breath onto Sherlock's t-shirt.

"Being the youngest sucks," John declared, trying to lighten the mood.

It would be easy to turn this into something else. To lower his chin and let his lips brush John's skin. One kiss would lead to another and another and then he could finally get this lust out of his system-

But they got on. Add sex to the equation and it would be dangerously close to dating. Dating meant demands and expectations.

Sherlock pulled back. "Why did you come over?" he asked briskly as he stepped away and flopped onto the sofa.

There was a pause as John seemed to take a little more time to change gears. "I...uh...Andy's trying to impress a girl by doing karaoke. Wanna laugh at him?"

He could spare an hour or two.

Five hours later, after being entertained by the jokes thrown at Andy, who was probably the most interesting of John's friends, Sherlock found himself summoned to Victor Trevor's side.

The Trevor's 'summoning' always irritated him. Dragged up memories of a childhood where he was told to be a certain thing, at a certain time with certain people. He despised being given instructions, despised commands.

Yet the reward was beyond compare and the jobs were... well, they were hardly the jobs that entered fully into the polite social setting that his parents had attempted to train him for.

The bar was luxurious and the drinks tab was not his problem. It was strange, going from John's friends in a dingy Wetherspoon's and ordering snake bites, sharing cheap, stale crisps around a table to sitting in a Shoreditch bar with expensive whiskey flowing as business was conducted.

They had a VIP area and the club owner was attempting to negotiate his cut of the sales that went through his club. He was good, able to bluff and improvise in order to keep up. Or at least, he would be good if Sherlock wasn't there, feet on one of the chairs as he swirled the expensive brandy around his glass and called bullshit whenever Victor glanced his way.

Growing up with Mycroft had been an education in and of itself but growing up with their father had been a trial by fire. Every inflection, every tiny move had to be taken into account when dealing with them just to work out how they were feeling and how best he could please them, once upon a time.

He'd given up by the age of ten. By the age of eleven there had been far more pleasure and power in getting the two to explode in temper.

How other people didn't see the signs, Sherlock would never know. They could put the clues together once he pointed them out, yet they never seemed to find the clues on their own nor spot the starting links that made the rest of the information click together like a child's puzzle.

For the most part, he let Victor play at being the mini KingPin he clearly desired to be. There was something almost too spoilt about him to be a real threat but, there were times when his childish attitude was often enough to give most people pause. Especially when coupled with his almost sociopathic father.

Still, if everything worked out tonight then Victor would

be in a generous mood. Since meeting Victor, Sherlock had found that his monthly spend had gone down considerably. It was doubtful they'd have sex given that Victor had been eyeing one of the girls all evening. It wasn't that much of a concern given the internal jumble Sherlock had been dealing with since the wave of longing he'd felt earlier.

It was a shame though. When they were both in the right mood the sex could be amazing. Both as high as kites, both fit and active. And Victor had expensive taste in hotel rooms, champagne and drugs.

The owner slunk away to check his accounts, a last minute glare at Sherlock which he took as a personal victory.

"He's sweating like a pig," Victor commented as he reached for a cigarette.

"He always sweats like a pig," Sherlock murmured as he swirled his glass and finished it off. "She's looking back at you," he added.

The grin was genuine and boyish. "I know," Victor said. "Her friend's been giving you the eye too. My room will fit all four of us?"

Tempting. Very tempting. "I promised Rose," Sherlock said as he placed his drink back on the table. "She needs an introduction to a mark in the next few days and this seems to be going quicker than expected."

Victor nodded. "He's all talk," he said dismissively, signalling the waitress and pointing to Sherlock's drink with a smile. "One of the first contacts my father started me with."

That wasn't surprising. There was something about the way the owner looked at Victor that made Sherlock sure he felt humiliated by the ease with which Victor could control him. "How old were you the first time you dealt with him?"

"Sixteen," Victor said with a chuckle. "Ten years he's been mine. Got himself a clever wife now, she's feeding him all sorts of ideas."

"Perhaps we should deal with her instead." Sherlock

smiled at the waitress as she brought a new drink over and removed the empty glass.

Victor chuckled at the idea and shook his head. "Jesus, let the man keep some dignity," he said as he stood. "Sure you don't want me to bring the other one over for you?"

Sherlock shook his head, amused as Victor strode off and the brunette that had been eyeing him suddenly shifted, displaying her body in what they both knew was an alluring way. The friend raised an eyebrow at him but he shook his head and lifted his glass in a toast instead. There was a flicker of disappointment but the sultry smile remained as she winked back, nodded and seemed to begin looking for someone new.

There was a note under his glass.

For a long moment, he stared at it then reached for it. Due to the dampness of the glass he almost had to peel the note away, half convinced it was probably a till receipt. But hand written in a blue pen was a small note.

Gloria Scott. 1981.

Gloria Scott? Turning the paper over a few times, Sherlock frowned in confusion. The name was familiar in some way.

The pub with John. It wasn't hard to conjure up the image of his friend sat at the table looking bored and just a little guilty as Paul threw up in the toilets.

The pub had been hosting a reunion of sorts; that had been easy enough to discover after he left John. Those who'd had family on-board some ship that had sunk, though what type of ship it had been he had no idea. The name and the date matched and yet there was something that nagged at him, as if he'd filed some information away but couldn't find where. Whoever it was that had contacted him (and declined to show) had claimed that the Trevor family had a secret and Sherlock could use that. Insurance for being involved with fickle, powerful men who had a firm hold on a large portion of the cocaine in London.

A mystery. He had loved them as a child but became

disillusioned later on when the mysteries became far too easy to solve. He could find out about this, find out who was so eager to bring the family down and-

Victor was coming over, a bag in his hand and a wicked grin.

Scrunching the wet note up into mush, Sherlock stood and nodded, convinced to join the sex party that was rapidly forming. There were far more interesting things to do, things that would likely have the added benefit of annoying his current flatmate.

CHAPTER SIX:

A Study in Sherlock Holmes

I T WAS STRANGE. SOMEHOW, SHERLOCK seemed to decide that whenever he was thrown out of a flat (which happened more than John had thought possible), he would take up residence on John's sofa. Not that John was complaining of course, but Sherlock didn't quite seem to understand the concept of asking. And, the more he came over and spent time with them, the more John was able to observe about Sherlock's sex life.

He wasn't sure which of them was more fucking insane.

———···———

They were waiting around the flat during Sherlock's fourth or fifth row with a flatmate while he was 'in-between' places. Secretly, John was starting to enjoy the moments when Sherlock would make a vague effort to avoid being homeless by being a little more helpful than usual (when he was really trying he'd give John all kinds of tips about his flatmates, friends, rivals on his course and lecturers).

And Sherlock seemed to enjoy it. He even seemed to find sitting in the living room with John's friends bearable, though he would pop in and out as it suited him depending on his level of interest in the conversation.

John felt a strange tremor of nerves when Sherlock sat on the arm of his chair for a discussion called 'What's the weirdest thing you've done in bed?'

"John?" Mike prompted.

Uh...

"Treated my partners with respect and thoughtfulness," John joked.

Andy stared at him blankly. "Yeah, you might actually win this!"

There was a chuckle and John sat back, off the hook.

Oh crap! Sherlock's was probably gonna be insane. Something along the lines of 'had an orgy with lots of coke and used half the collection of Anne Summers on a goat'.

Or something like that.

"Snowballing," Paul's friend, Rick, announced with a look that said he wasn't quite as proud of that as his voice led them to believe. Next to John, Sherlock...well, he sharpened. It was the only way he could describe it. Usually it meant that something had caught Sherlock's interest which, given the conversation they were having, was probably not the best thing in the world.

"What, like the cake-biscuit-y things?" John asked, not having a clue what the hell they were talking about.

Roughly half of the group sniggered and the other half looked relieved that John had asked. But then John's (hated) reputation as being a little naïve and a babbler did occasionally work in his favour for moments like these.

"Snowballing," Andy said and gave Rick a look that seemed half impressed and half disgusted, "is when you come in a girl's mouth and then she kisses you and you swallow."

Why?

"Oh," John said nodding slowly, "and Rick thought that was hot?"

"Fuck off!" Rick threw a cushion at him. "At least it wasn't felching. Or spidermaning."

John needed a dictionary. Or Wikipedia because maybe the Oxford dictionary wouldn't include weird sex acts that Rick liked.

They must have seen his blank look. "Felching is where you suck the come back out afterwards and spidermaning is when you get the spunk on your hand and then flick. Like spider man does."

John stared.

"Watson, what the hell do you do with your girls?"

Girls? All two of them?

"I...normal things? I don't insist we play with spunk like we're having a water fight." John shook his head. "I dunno... do they like it?"

Rick shrugged. "Dunno."

"You don't know?" Sherlock replied blankly.

Ah, yeah. That was like heresy in Sherlock's books. You should always collect all available data. It was why John just answered his questions now. It saved so much time.

"Do you?" Rick challenged.

John glanced up at Sherlock worriedly.

"This has been very informative." Sherlock stood, as if with sudden purpose. "Go back to your discussion."

"Sorry about the other night-" John said as they sat in the canteen by the lecture theatre the following day.

"Don't be, the data was extraordinary."

John stared, horrified. "What? Wait, you didn't go out and-"

Sherlock threw him a look. "No, well one but no. The attitude John, their attitude, it tells you so much about the way these boys conduct themselves, so much data. And if you know someone's attitude towards relationships and the way that they conduct themselves then..." he seemed to trail off looking a little...uncomfortable? suddenly.

John really wanted to chase up why Sherlock looked like that but, in his head, all he could do was try and work out which sex act Sherlock had decided to practise.

Embarrassingly, Sherlock must have noticed his curious

glance but he merely raised an eyebrow. "You need to have practical knowledge and their information last night was incomplete at best. For future reference felching isn't as bad as your face seems to think it would be."

Who the hell had he practiced on?

Shaking the thought away, John unwrapped the danish pastry that had been his only option at the counter, pulling the pastry out of its tight spiral. "Am I really that boring that I can't see the appeal?" he asked, avoiding looking at Sherlock.

"There's an obvious appeal when receiving."

How the hell would Sherlock receive-

Oh!

"Though giving is also an experience. It would, I believe, depend upon the partner."

Wait...sucking fluid out of someone's...really? People did that? Leaning back a little, John bounced the plastic chair, feeling the give in the material. On the other side of the canteen area that was attached to the lecture theatre he could see a few people from his course swapping notes.

That seemed far more productive than his conversation. It was kinda about anatomy though so maybe...though Christ knew what John would do if he thought they could overhear.

"That is the original intent of felching," Sherlock replied calmly taking a sip of coffee. "To be between two men."

John took a bite of his pastry, refocusing on Sherlock. "Okay, maybe I can see the appeal of that, but the rest of what they were saying...it just seems like doing it for the sake of doing it."

"You can see the appeal?" Sherlock set his cup down.

"Maybe," John added cautiously, suddenly fearful of being mocked.

Sherlock studied him for a long moment and then nodded slowly. "Good."

John winced at the icing on his fingers then licked at it.

The napkins were far too far away to bother walking over to. "Good?" he queried. Why was that good?

"It's useful," Sherlock's gaze seemed stuck on his fingers, "to know these things."

That made hardly any sense but John nodded. "Okay. I just...how does it come up? I mean seriously, if I turned to you in the middle of sex and said can I suck you off and then kiss the come back into your mouth what would you say?"

Sherlock's mouth dropped open and he tore his eyes from John's fingers to his lips.

Oh Christ!

"That's...I mean..." John felt his cheeks burning. "No, don't answer that," he cringed.

They sat in silence.

"I have a lecture," Sherlock announced. "Criminology."

"Sure." By now John was used to Sherlock's eclectic unofficial degree.

Sherlock stood, unfolding himself from the chair and pulling on his leather jacket before he paused and leaned down to John's ear.

"Don't lick your fingers like that, John. It's obscenely difficult to concentrate when you do."

Which would have been bearable except for the kiss, the slight kiss pressed into the hair just above his ear like a fond nuzzling, and then he was gone.

———————————

A week later he was drunk. And the plan was to find a way to have Sherlock tell him he actually wasn't having that much sex and that secretly he was trying to get John jealous.

Then they would snog and John would pass out and everything would be brilliant. And he'd washed his sheets last week so it wouldn't be gross.

"I just don't get it," John said as they sat in his room. "I mean, you say the body is transport and yet you have a lot of sex."

"Sex is one of the single greatest motivators of human action. I need to understand it in order to understand people. I predict that by my late twenties I'll have a comprehensive amount of data and that such proclivities won't be needed anymore."

There was only one thing John could understand from that.

"So you are having a lot of sex?"

"Define a lot," Sherlock replied idly as he took a swing from his beer and lazed back against John's pillows. "And define sex."

"I-"

"I can," Sherlock said, a smile curing his lips. "I know what activities usually fall into the category of sex, of healthy sex, of deviant, of morally ambiguous. I know what it means when people try certain activities. Their attitudes tell me more than their most secure documents ever could."

Huh. The wall was cold against his back and John glared at Sherlock, half wishing he hadn't been so chivalrous in giving up his pillows. "What about me?"

Sherlock looked a little hesitant. "Are you sure?"

John nodded. "Might help," he muttered.

Sherlock seemed thoughtful, more thoughtful than John had ever seen him.

"You care about people and want to help them. You'll suffer to ensure others aren't hurt and are a natural worrier. But you are starting to lose that. Nonetheless you will always protect first, avenge second and you will probably become a lot more competent at the second as you grow older. You are respectful but more than that you believe things need to have a purpose which is how you suffer my rudeness because you often know there is a goal at the end of it."

"I asked you about sex," John muttered after a moment, not really sure how to react.

"And I used what I know about you to tell you about your nature."

John shifted, watching as his feet dangled off the side of the bed and took another swig of the concoction that Andy had made earlier. "But that doesn't sound like me," he said eventually.

"Confidence," Sherlock said after a moment, setting his beer down on the bedside table. "Is something I should have added. You have not had ample opportunity to build your confidence in yourself."

"Is that your way of telling me to get laid?"

Sherlock laughed but didn't offer up a damned thing.

———————— ···————————

Two days later, when John walked into the pub, Sherlock was standing at the bar with a girl and looking very bored while she gestured frantically at him. While John would usually just back away (keeping his distance until she left), Sherlock had picked the Princess Louise to meet in and there was no way that John was ducking into one of the frosted glass booths with strangers just so Sherlock could continue being a dick in peace. Slowly, John skulked up, really not wanting to get involved in whatever it was Sherlock was pissing her off about.

"Ah, John, good," Sherlock said as he caught sight of him. "We can go," he added, as if she'd merely been a distraction to pass the time. And with that, Sherlock spun off to the door.

The girl was crying.

"Uh..." John looked after his friend and then damned the fact that tears always made him want to kneel on the floor and beg for forgiveness. "You okay?"

The girl shook her head miserably. "He said I was bad in bed," she sniffed and then her eyes widened in horror. "Don't tell anyone."

"John!" Sherlock called from the door in one of his most demanding tones.

Helplessly glancing between the two, John ^stepped towards to her. "He's a tosser about things like that. You're better off out of it."

Her blue eyes narrowed in on him suddenly. "I didn't want a fucking relationship with him," she snarled. "I just...I am fantastic in bed. It was the other one that was shit."

"Sherlock?"

"No, the other one."

Oh.

Oh no.

"Okay." John nodded, feeling as if he'd been dumped into the twilight zone. Not really sure how to handle it, he simply turned and left, walking towards Sherlock who by that point was so annoyed he'd decided to start the cliché act of looking at his wrist pointedly even though there wasn't a watch there.

Once outside, John paused and then huffed as he was nearly run over by the crowds. Re-engaging his brain, John followed Sherlock until he managed to catch up and they were side by side.

"You told her she was bad in bed?" John asked slowly.

"She is. The longer she deludes herself, the worse she'll get." Sherlock paused in his speech and steered John's shoulders with his hands to guide John down a side street. "Though I suppose there isn't much scope left for her skills to deteriorate further."

"Wait? So that's what you do? If they're bad in bed you just tell them and kick them out?"

Oh god, he was never, ever sleeping with this man.

"How else will they learn?" Sherlock asked and then stopped to look around. Reassessing something, he changed their direction.

"We're going to the Red Lion-"

"This is a quicker route."

John nodded and followed, trailing behind as his mind raced.

He'd been with two girls. ~~Anna~~ Amy and Bridget. ~~Anna~~ Amy had been a two month thing and Bridget had been an amazing week long marathon. In comparison, his experience with men was Sherlock. His experience overall was, he could admit, limited. He didn't think he was bad; at least he gave a damn about whether his partners got off which, from some conversations, couldn't be said about some of his mates. But then they had experience so maybe it balanced out.

Sherlock would kick him out of bed so fast that John would probably be out the door before he finished coming.

It was relatively quiet as they walked, avoiding the typical routes where flocks of students and tourists were. Slowly, John felt himself start to relax, breathing in the odd smell of multiple cuisines, the drifting noises of music from bars until, halfway there, Sherlock stopped.

"Ah," he said, turning suddenly. "Was that a bit close for comfort?"

Mortified, John turned around. Fuck this, he was going home.

"John," Sherlock called after him. "John."

Nope. Ignoring you.

It didn't take long to find his way back to a main street that he recognised rather than the winding side streets. Once he was back in the crowds, he had to slow down so he knew where to go and started to weave his way through to get to Victoria Tube station and avoid the main station. He managed to get within sight of it before Sherlock caught up with him.

"John."

Of course he'd managed to catch up. "Look, can we not-"

But they were. Sherlock had somehow managed to shepherd John into a small alcove with filthy walls that was pretty much hidden in the shadows.

"No-one would kick you out," Sherlock said carefully, his eyes dancing over John with concern; a concern that John wouldn't usually expect to see and was kinda nice for a change but he was so not in the mood.

"Great." John nodded, trying not to focus on how bloody close they were. Any second now, Sherlock would lose interest and-

"I'll show you."

What?

Suddenly aware he was pinned and not at all sure what was going on, John just stared at Sherlock blankly. His mouth opened and shut a few times because what the hell did that mean?

"She was very rigid in her approach," Sherlock murmured, closing the miniscule gap between them until John could see the flecks in his hazel eyes. "Determined to dictate what we would like."

We? Oh, right. Three of them.

Then Sherlock kissed him.

It was not like before. John felt like he was being prodded and poked by Sherlock's tongue and couldn't quite manage to engage with it. Startled, he pulled away, as far as he could in his position, and glared at Sherlock who looked amused.

"Then there was the other one." Sherlock shifted a bit. "Insipid."

This time when he leaned forward he slipped his tongue in and waggled it pathetically.

John giggled and pulled away. "That's bad."

"But manageable." Sherlock tapped at his chin. "Try to get a response."

This was possibly the weirdest thing he had ever done.

This time John tried to coax a reaction. There was some vague memory of doing this with a girl back home who had been his nervous first kiss. Carefully, he lipped and nipped until it was Sherlock that pulled away.

"See?"

"Okay-"

"Now this is you-"

John almost protested but found his mouth captured again.

This time Sherlock responded to what John did and moved with him. He didn't push as much as he had done before when they'd kissed but he kept up, occasionally surprising John.

"See?" Sherlock pulled away. "Attitude, John. Half the battle is the attitude. You keep up, you try, you have the ability to surprise and adapt," Sherlock said as he stepped back. "The rest can be taught."

Feeling really thick, John nodded.

"Now, are we going to this pub?" Sherlock asked, casting a disgusted look at the crowds.

John nodded again and started to follow him as they weaved towards a side street.

"Are you going to speak?" Sherlock asked, sounding a bit peeved as he dug his hands into his pockets.

"Soon," John said, lips still buzzing.

By the time Sherlock moved a few weeks later, John still wasn't sure what to do about his growing attraction.

"Under the bed," Sherlock called from his latest and soon to be previous living room. "It's all in boxes."

Yeah, because what was the point of really unpacking when you moved every ten to sixteen weeks? It was becoming a running theme at home. They'd be sitting watching television when someone would pipe up, "How long's it been?"

"Ten weeks."

"So we're due a stay from his lordship any day now!"

And sure enough Sherlock would flounce in soon after, announce that everyone in the world was an idiot and hole himself up on the sofa he had, at some point, decided was his.

John was a fucking demon at packing now.

Sherlock's bedroom was always fastidiously clean, despite the mess he seemed to wreck all over his flats. John had never seen any hint of anything unsavoury either. For instance, when they had moved Graham out last month (and John's skill set had been in particular demand) there had been old used condoms under the bed and dried up baby wipes and tissues galore.

The boxes under the bed were easy enough to haul onto the mattress. It was the last one that, straining, ended up collapsing in that comedy sketch show way where everything tumbled out onto John's feet.

Fucking hell.

John stared at the things on the floor, specifically at the dildo and anal beads that were currently resting happily on his scuffed-up trainers.

He was not touching them.

"Sherlock!"

A mop of dark hair peeked around the door. "Yes?"

John pointed at what was on his feet. "They're on my shoes," he said, trying to stay calm.

Sherlock snorted with laughter.

"Sherlock!"

His friend stalked in with all the grace of a cat and stood directly behind John, chin hooked on John's shoulder.

"That looks ridiculous," Sherlock commented.

"Get them off my shoes," John demanded.

"And where would you like me to move them to?" Sherlock enquired, sounding delighted at John's prudishness.

It wasn't meant as a suggestion (John knew enough variations of Sherlock's tones to know that), but the image hit him suddenly. A wonderful, slightly vague image of them using the things on John's shoes. His breath hitched and when Sherlock moved John knew he was in a world of trouble.

There had been times when John had seen Sherlock stalk someone. Usually John, sometimes someone that probably had a precious bag of coke, but this was like watching porn. Sherlock seemed to slide down John's body, those appealing eyes constantly on him, and then picked up the toys on John's shoes.

John couldn't breathe

"You've never used these before, have you?"

John shook his head jerkily.

A light went on in Sherlock's eyes. "Interesting," he murmured, as if to himself.

Then stood and packed it all away as if John wasn't standing there trying to work out what the hell was going on.

The bastard still looked highly triumphant when John announced that he really needed to go home for ten to fifteen minutes.

By late October, Sherlock introduced John and Victor when John was frantically trying to study for his exams and Sherlock was either being manically helpful by asking John a lot of questions, or terribly unhelpful by then trying to teach John what those medical illnesses implied about the way the person lived their life.

"But you're only half way there," Sherlock would complain. "You're missing things."

"I tell you what, I'll get us half way there and you finish us off," John had snapped.

Andy had snorted. "Could you two sound any more like a gay couple?"

Anyway, that hadn't been the point. The point was that Sherlock had gone off in a sulk and not bothered to contact John for two weeks (which was a blessing in all honesty) before he reappeared with Victor attached to him.

Literally attached. Like at the mouth.

Despite hearing about Sherlock's sex life and seeing various signs (the massive love bite that Sherlock had spent days complaining about sprung to mind), John had never actually seen Sherlock with his hands anywhere near someone that wasn't John.

It was by accident he supposed. Sooner or later he was

bound to run into Sherlock on a 'not John' night. In truth, Sherlock probably still thought John was studying (he was having a break for the night) and was perhaps a little less cautious than he had previously been.

Which suddenly begged the question: why had Sherlock been so careful to keep John from seeing that sort of thing.

"You looking for a threesome or something?" Victor asked, turning his head to stare at John while he stood frozen while Sherlock braced his hands against the wall and went to town on Victor's neck.

No?

No.

And no.

He was not being humiliated by this.

John dug into his pockets and pulled out the cigarettes that Sherlock had left at his. "When you have finished cleaning his neck, would you mind taking your death sticks back? Andy wants to quit and keeps annoying me for them."

Inwardly, he was torn between sobbing at the sight before him and gaping at how calm and collected he sounded.

He wanted to be that person one day; the person who barely reacted and just kept coolly quipping at stressful moments, though not in a cheesy way.

It was the best and worst moment of his life.

Sherlock froze.

Like, actually froze.

"You know this little shit?" Victor asked pulling back to look at Sherlock.

"John Watson, sofa supplier since February," John snapped. "Sherlock, seriously, I haven't got all night."

God, he was on a roll. Whatever he was doing seemed to work as, slowly, Sherlock pulled away from Victor and looked at John.

And he was high.

Great.

Then Sherlock was striding forward and grabbing John's arm, propelling them around the corner and away from the thumping club. A bottle was kicked out of their way and cigarette stumps crushed under their feet as John was pulled away from Victor.

"Don't be too long or I'll share my score with someone else again," Victor called with a sneer.

Curious, John glanced back but he couldn't see the man anymore. It seemed so strange, to see a glimpse into the other world that Sherlock lived in. Surreal almost.

And definitely a kind of trouble he shouldn't get involved in, he thought as he braced for the familiar sensation of having a wall at his back and Sherlock at his front. That was what usually happened when Sherlock dragged him somewhere.

But no, Sherlock was heading to a road and a taxi rank.

"What are you-"

"You are going home," Sherlock hissed, sounding furious. "You should be studying."

"I'm having a break-"

Sherlock spun him, the force of it had John stumbling to keep his balance and Sherlock grabbing him by his upper arms.

"Do not do this again."

"Do what?"

"Follow me," Sherlock yelled.

"I wasn't. You just happened to be there!" John yelled back, ignoring the curious glances from the smokers' corner and the people that billowed smoke up into the cold night. He caught some girl's eye and she smirked at them and fuck it, he was not backing down from Sherlock or her or anything.

Sherlock completely interrupted John's moment by dropping his grip and going for John's trouser-

-Phew, pockets.

"This," he said, pulling out John's phone, "is a marvellous invention. Use it."

"To what?" John asked, snapping his attention back. "Tell you I'm out and ask your permission?"

"Yes."

"Oh fuck off and fuck you," John snarled, wanting to turn away in disgust but kinda needing something first. "Give me my phone," he demanded.

But Sherlock wouldn't let go of it. Instead, his knuckles whitened tightly around the phone as his lips pressed together. Frustration seemed to be radiating from him as Sherlock shook the phone at John. "You are not a part of this, John-"

"A part of what?" John asked, stepping forward and feeling a flash of pleasure as Sherlock actually stepped back.

"Of this area of my life." Sherlock sounded manic now, swallowing tightly. "Do you understand? You are not part of this."

"Get over yourself. Fine, I won't put my muddy paws on your shining, perfect, party time. Happy?"

But Sherlock leaned in dangerously close. "You have got that entirely the wrong way around," he announced, his voice a threatening rumble and belying his words.

It made John pause, blinking at him. What was that supposed to mean?

Unless-

"Sherlock?" John breathed, mind racing. "I'm fine."

The phone was dropped into his hand along with twenty quid. The sudden weight made John blink down at it, watching for a moment as Sherlock's hands briefly closed over his before pulling back. "Go home, John," Sherlock said in a heavy tone as he stepped back. "Now. You shouldn't be here."

"I'm not a kid," John muttered. It was the only thing he could think to say even as his hand tingled from the way Sherlock's hand had brushed against his.

"But you are naïve," Sherlock said firmly.

Furious, John pulled away and purposefully dropped the twenty as he stalked off.

So he was attracted to the bastard. For such a clever guy, he was such a complete dick.

He was probably best out of it, right?

CHAPTER SEVEN:

One Thousand Pounds

IT WAS PROBABLY MASSIVELY PETTY, but John hadn't spoken to Sherlock since the arsehole had jostled him towards a taxi a few weeks ago and thrust money at him. Mainly because there was something embarrassing about the fact that John had gone back to check if that twenty was still fluttering in the breeze.

Being broke sucked. It wasn't as if it was completely John's fault; the house they rented was dirt cheap (emphasis on dirt) and the books he bought were second hand when possible. Granted the drinking and the takeaways and well... all the drinking didn't help, but all in all John did better than most of his mates.

The problem was that none of his mates had John's mum, his mum who had never quite forgiven his dad for finally coming out as gay and leaving her for his best friend. Certainly, she'd never forgiven John for treating Mary like his sister and would never forgive him for looking like his dead father.

Or help him out with money apparently.

Or let him go home.

Not that she phrased it like that, of course. Some daft speech about how he should stay in the house over the summer if he'd paid for it, as if he was gonna get free food and electricity handed out to him. He could phone Mary of course, but she wasn't much better off than he was. And there was Harry but his brother thrived off their mother's approval and he'd spew the same old party line.

Their mum had probably handed him a script just in case.

The sandwich shop a few roads down let him pick up a few hours a week which meant he could pay for beans and bread and sneak a few sandwiches. It was boring and monotonous and within two weeks John was chomping at the bit with the unfairness of it all.

So when Kenny suggested they go out for a night, John jumped on it.

And found himself one thousand pounds down in a poker game.

One thousand pounds.

It didn't get better the more that he said it. In fact, the more he said it the more he could feel himself start to hyperventilate. The thing was, it really hadn't been his fault and, as much as he hated to say it, it hadn't been Kenny's either.

Though Kenny's brother was a fucking arsehole.

"It's in pennies," Ralph, Kenny's brother's mate had said. "You'll be fine."

Who the hell gambled with thousands of pounds on a Sunday night?

Kenny, to be fair had shot Ralph a look within the first few minutes. John had shot him a look seconds later.

But, as it became obvious by the rising bets that Ralph was a tosser, John had been stuck.

You did not pull out of this kind of poker game.

"So. Pay up."

John looked at Kenny in horror. Kenny was slightly better at poker than John was and had only lost £200. A glance around the almost silent bar made him start to damn his own stupidity. They were completely alone in the skanky looking bar with...John frowned at the dots on the wall starting to suddenly wonder if maybe they were bullet holes.

"You bastard!" Kenny muttered to Ralph.

"Your brother stiffed me," Ralph hissed. "I told him I'd get me money one way or the other."

Kenny had just shaken his head and sighed. "Let me go to the cashpoint," he said bowing his head in defeat. "John?"

Yeah, the thing was, John could just imagine what would happen if he tried to withdraw a thousand pounds. The cash machine would probably start laughing its head off.

"I...can't," he said taking a deep breath. "You said it was pennies."

Fuck, he'd have a job at scraping ten quid together!

Ralph looked at his mate who everyone seemed to be referring to as Four Beats. The thing was that if everyone was using a nickname for a guy who looked like he was likely to pull a cigar and gun out of his pocket then John was screwed.

"It is pennies," Four Beats said with a smile, "to us."

"Yeah." John realised with dawning horror that Kenny had vanished. "I...I..." he tried to get himself under control. "Look, I honestly can't pay you. But my loan is in in September-"

"Why would I wait that long?"

"Because I can't pay," John snapped as he looked between them. "I swear, it was really stupid I know, but I thought you actually meant pennies at first! And then you wouldn't let me leave-"

Four Beats shook his head in a theatrically disappointed manner. "Johnny Boy, this is why little boys don't play at the grown-ups table."

He couldn't panic. Slowly, John started to control his breathing and relax his shoulders. Then, trying to stay calm, looked around.

Five guys sat around the room watching and Four Beats was reclined in his booth.

Breathe out. "What are you gonna do?" John asked, impressed that his voice didn't wobble.

Four Beats raised an eyebrow. "Good boy," he said approvingly, leaning forward. "Can you find the money?"

Logically. He had to think logically.

"Maybe...half of it, at a push?" If he sold everything that would keep him at uni. He shook his head. "Unless you have some suggestions?"

Four Beats smiled and beckoned him closer.

How John managed to put one foot in front of the other he would never know. Snakelike in his movement, Four Beats struck and grabbed John roughly by the chin.

"£400 now," Four Beats said, nodding in a way that pushed his face uncomfortably close to John's.

"I'll pay you the rest in September."

Oh god he was fucked if he did that. He might as well sign up to the sandwich shop for the rest of his life.

"No."

No? Confused, John looked at Four Beats. He didn't seem like the type that would be doing John a favour.

"I think you'll find that there's interest on these sorts of things."

"How much?" John asked, amazed he still had a voice left.

"How much is your loan?"

John opened his mouth. That was his whole future, every plan he had-

"What are you studying for?" Four Beats asked, his fingers digging in even more.

"A doctor," John said finding some strange amount of comfort in the phrase. "I want to be a doctor."

"And you need the money to do that."

John nodded. "Anything, I just-"

"You can find more money," Four Beats said soothingly. "But not new fingers."

There was someone behind him. Terrified, John tried to

move away but hands clamped down on his shoulders as Four Beats drew out a cigar cutter.

The metal slid over his middle finger and John couldn't move, couldn't breathe-

"Have I made my point?" Four Beats asked in an amused tone, as if John's concern for his fingers was funny. John nodded as much as he could in the harsh grip and then drew in a deep breath when he was at last released.

"I want as much as you can manage by Friday," Four Beats said with a smile. "We'll renegotiate then."

Outside, John sucked in air like he was a drowning man. Like a fucking dead man.

"I'm so sorry," Kenny said after a moment. "John, seriously I had no idea-"

John nodded, "Yeah, it's fine. Figured. I mean it'd be a fucking over-reaction to me grinding up laxatives in your sugar."

Kenny let out a strangled laugh. "Seriously?"

John nodded. "Gotta say I'm feeling less guilty about it now." He gulped in air until he felt lightheaded. "Fuck," he added, scraping a hand across his face. "Fuck, fuck, fuck."

"Look," Kenny said as he pushed off the wall and licked his lips nervously. "I've got a hundred and fifty. Then I'm screwed but I got you into this so, if you want it, it's there."

John sighed and shook his head. "It's the interest," John said, trying to remember how to stand. "That's what's gonna cripple me."

Kenny watched him with an inscrutable expression for a moment and then handed John his phone. "Start calling," he suggested with a serious frown.

God, this was humiliating.

£928

It was all he could manage.

But there was one person he hadn't tried yet.

Relatively sure Sherlock was still at the same address (though who knew with him some days), John rang the buzzer.

Only to have fucking turd face open the door.

Victor smiled and leaned against the hallway wall lazily, showing off an impressive hickey, his trousers low and unbuttoned and shirt undone in what seemed to be the picture of debauchery. "John," he drawled, tilting his head as he studied John, the smile that crossed his face very reminiscent of a cat about to purr. "Do you need a favour?"

Uncomfortable with the idea of begging for favours, John shifted on his feet, feeling like a bird ruffling his feathers. "Is he in?" John asked, determined not to seem like a complete loser in front of Victor.

Victor nodded. "I wore him out," he said, almost as if admitting a dirty secret which John didn't really want to think about.

"I just need five minutes." To beg.

"He's asleep," Victor said, not sounding at all sorry about it. "I can help you if you're really desperate-"

Frustrated, John shook his head and pushed past, determined to see Sherlock- oh great, now he was shoving his way into the flat to demand money. There was no way on earth that this wouldn't look like he was taking advantage or being demanding or-

John stopped dead at the sight of Sherlock cutting cocaine on the coffee table.

"Oh!"

Sherlock's gaze slid past John to Victor who had followed behind. "One job," he sighed, shaking his head. "That was all I asked of you."

"What can I say? He was desperate," Victor replied, sounding unapologetic as he brushed past John to sprawl onto the chair perpendicular to Sherlock. He reached out for a cigarette that was smoking in an ashtray and took a deep inhale.

The place stunk of smoke and sex and it made everything in him want to turn around, to not ask and leave them in peace to get on with it. Yet he could still feel the metal on his finger.

Sherlock's gaze paused on him and seemed to narrow, his hazel eyes searching for something as a small frown started to tug at his lips.

"Get out," Sherlock said, standing and cinching his dressing gown tightly.

John turned.

"No, not you," Sherlock snapped. "Victor, go."

Victor hadn't even looked up the first time Sherlock had said it but his head jerked up in surprise. A levelling look was thrown at John again and then at Sherlock, the cigarette hanging out of his lip before Victor inhaled and then placed the cigarette down into the ashtray, seeming to take advantage of the time it took to exhale. Whatever Victor saw was enough to make the man frown and tilt his head, like a snake eyeing up a rodent he might strike at. "I'll take my coke," he... Threatened? Warned? Teased? John wasn't exactly sure but, unsurprisingly, there was a flicker of hesitation on Sherlock's face as he looked back at the table.

What was the point? To John's horror he could almost feel tears of sheer frustration, exhaustion and terror start to fill his eyes. Four Beats would probably demand interest for days not paid and it would go on and on-

"Take this to cover your 'expenses'," Sherlock said, thrusting money at Victor as he walked past the chair and to his bedroom door, only pausing when he looked at John and then followed his gaze to the wad of money.

"How much?" Sherlock asked, seeming taken aback as he glanced between them. His gaze seemed to linger on John, scanning for clues as to how he'd gotten into this situation.

"Seventy-two," John said miserably, looking away from the disappointment he was sure he would spot on Sherlock's face.

"That's very exact," Sherlock snapped. "How much in total then?"

"I'm not asking for that." John kicked at the carpet. "I just need the extra seventy-two." There was a long silence and when he finally dared to look up, Victor was staring at Sherlock with a raised eyebrow.

"Take the fucking coke," Sherlock snapped at him.

Sherlock almost threw John into his room as he and Victor 'cleaned up' the living room. The sound of muttering voices could be heard but they weren't loud enough to pick up the tone of their conversation, let alone the words. John hovered, feeling uncomfortable, and went absolutely no-where near the unmade bed.

The noise of the door slamming shut echoed through the flat before Sherlock wandered in, somehow dressed, and shut the door behind him carefully.

"I'm sorry," John said to the floor. "I had no-where else to go to."

"Seventy pounds." Sherlock tossed the money on the bed.

John stared at it from his awkward perch against the wall. "I...Um...Seventy-two pounds," he said, trying to ignore the flush of humiliation.

"I'm sure you can find two pounds to spare," Sherlock said firmly, folding his arms. Maybe...maybe if he looked on his way back there would be some spare change-

"How much?" Sherlock snarled.

"A thousand pounds," John breathed, closing his eyes, feeling utterly stupid. There was a pause and John was bloody glad he couldn't see the expression on Sherlock's face.

"You sold your father's watch," Sherlock said eventually.

"Yeah," John looked down at his bare wrist, "well, I think he'd prefer me to have fingers so-"

"Fingers?" Sherlock's voice had turned to ice.

"Yeah." John lifted his gaze from his wrist and then slumped his shoulders at the determination radiating from Sherlock and told him everything.

"He threw you out?" Andy asked in stunned amazement and, despite the fact that Andy was miles away and tucked up at home, John could still see his outraged expression, clear as day. "The wanker!"

John shrugged. "It's his money, Andy. He doesn't have to help," he said and purposefully ignored the head-pounding, horrified feeling that wouldn't leave him alone.

Friday. Noon.

John couldn't stop flexing his fingers to check they were there. Over and over again he flexed, trying to remember the feeling just in case.

Oh god, he didn't want to do this. Every step to the door was like a step to the execution block. And, to further the aching embarrassment, he'd begged an advance. £946. It was likely the richest he would ever be. One foot in front of the other. And again. And again. Ignoring the strange look the guy at the door gave him as he walked in.

You can do this, John told himself. *You can do this.*

Walking into the main room in the day time was slightly uninspiring. What had looked opulent and expensive just looked cheap and tacky in the daylight apart from Sherlock who just looked-

Sherlock?

Stopping dead, John felt his jaw drop a little.

Sherlock sat at the table, looking as if he hadn't a care in the world while Four Beats was looking down at his own lap, lips moving as his brow furrowed with concentration.

Were they friends?

Sherlock, who had looked over at him, rolled his eyes and then scrubbed at his forehead with two fingers as if just looking at John gave him a headache. In comparison, Four Beats glanced over at him then skittered his attention back to Sherlock, before returning to his lap.

What the hell were they-

John cut the thought off before he could linger on it. Sherlock's reasons for being in the club were his own. What John needed was to get Four Beats' attention, give him the money and get it over with. With that thought, John let out a shaken breath and started to reach into his jacket pocket-

Sherlock was up in a flash, gripping his wrist and pulling him forward. Minutely, he shook his head at John.

When John looked around this time it was with a new purpose. Four Beats was basically on his own (the lackeys from the other night seeming to have scarpered) and everything was very quiet. The table looked as if it had been the stage of-

Huh. Of a poker game.

"What did you do?" John mouthed at Sherlock warily.

Sherlock smiled. "Call it poetic justice," he said as he pulled back with a last commanding look at John's pocket that clearly warned against getting the money out.

Hesitantly, John followed Sherlock to the table, just in case Four Beats was secretly assembling a knife or something. He probably shouldn't let Sherlock get stabbed for trying to help.

"Do you need a calculator?" Sherlock muttered sarcastically as he bowed over the chair and placed his palms flat on the table. "This is getting tedious."

"Don't push it," Four Beats snarled.

Sherlock looked twistedly amused and turned back to John. Then he did that 'I'm observing your pin number' look that made John want to squirm.

Sniffing, Sherlock leaned forward further and plucked up the cigar cutter. Four Beats stopped what he was doing and started to watch Sherlock instead.

Inspecting it as if it had a bloody treasure map engraved on it, Sherlock stepped back and did a few experimental cuts with it. Four Beats eyes slid to John who swallowed at the memory.

"It was a joke," Four Beats said, turning his attention back to Sherlock. "Ain't my fault if the kid didn't know that."

"Of course." Sherlock placed it on the table. "You could barely cut a cigar with that it's so blunt."

Seeming satisfied, Four Beats returned to counting his money.

Sherlock opened the cigar case left on the table and pulled one out easily. "This however," he pulled a cutter out that had a hole in the centre, just like the one Four Beats had used but the difference seemed to be that there were two blades rather than one, "cuts wonderfully."

There was a snicker-snack noise and the butt fell off in a neat, clean line. Four Beats went white.

Placing the cigar in his mouth, Sherlock pulled a lighter out of his pocket, and set the cutter down on the table as he lit up. "This is taking an extraordinary amount of time," he sighed. "Are you attempting to delay the inevitable?"

"I'm paying you!" Four Beats snarled.

"How long did he give you?" Sherlock asked, suddenly turning to John. "Before he slipped his dull little contraption onto your finger?"

John looked around. "I don't-"

"Longer than five minutes?" Sherlock asked politely, as if John's answer couldn't possibly be no.

Licking his lips nervously, John shook his head.

"Oh dear." Sherlock turned his head back to Four Beats. "Hand-"

"No." Four Beats suddenly seemed to speed up. "I'm fucking counting! He didn't have anything."

Sherlock's hand shot out and pulled Four Beats forward, making John jump. The words were too quiet to overhear but after a minute Sherlock let Four Beats' wrist go, flicking his fingers afterwards as if he may have caught a disease.

Awkwardly, John looked around, feeling weird that he was starting to feel a little, well, bored?

Sherlock kicked a chair out. "Sit," he said brightly as he smoked. "Evidently this will take a while."

There wasn't even a tiny bit of John that wanted to get that close to Four Beats again, but his legs had felt like jelly the entire walk to Shoreditch and he desperately wanted to collapse somewhere.

And god did he want to sleep.

Slipping into the chair and holding himself as if he expected Four Beats to suddenly lunge up like some Bond villain and announce they had fallen into his evil trap, John let out a long breath. As if unconcerned though, Sherlock shifted in a relaxed way appearing to be completely at home in a stale smelling club demanding money from the owner. "Here." he pushed some cards at John. "You deal."

"I- what?" John asked, barely able to keep up. In the end, he looked at Four Beats as if he would have an answer, but Four Beats seemed to be avoiding looking at either one of them.

"John, if you don't even know how to deal you really shouldn't be playing poker," Sherlock chided.

"I... I know how to deal. I don't want to-"

"Why?"

"I don't know, maybe because the last time I did, this happened," John huffed, sitting back and forgetting his earlier nerves. "Snip-snip!" he added, his fingers moving like scissors.

Next to him Four Beats winced and sped up fractionally.

"So you've learned your lesson?" Sherlock asked, blowing smoke up into the air.

"Yes!" Emphatically yes!

"No more playing poker until I teach you how to play properly?"

"Yes, no..." John glared at him. "Wouldn't it just be easier not to play poker?"

Sherlock gave Four Beats such a foul, dangerous look that John saw the man's hand shake for a moment just from the weight of it. "If you've made him boring, you won't live to see your next hustle," Sherlock sneered.

"He threatened to chop off my fingers! I'm not being boring I'm being-" John cut himself off. "Can we just talk about this later?"

"Why? We have time now," Sherlock added as he glared at the ceiling. "Honestly, how hard is it to count fifteen thousand?"

"I don't..." John's jaw dropped and he turned to stare at Four Beats. "Fifteen?" he asked in disbelief.

"And he didn't even have the excuse that he thought we were playing for pennies," Sherlock added smugly.

"Ten," Four Beats announced, putting a wad of notes onto the table.

John stared at the amount in awe. Sherlock just sighed as if he was deathly bored with the whole situation and reached for the cutter again.

"Give me a minute," Four Beats snapped.

"I've given you endless minutes," Sherlock glared at him but, after a glance at John, put the cutter down. "Though why you used the guillotine over the double guillotine is beyond me."

John glared at him. "Oh yeah, that was the distressing thing about this week. I couldn't sleep out of fear that he'd realised he threatened me with the wrong cutter. It would have been so embarrassing for him!"

Sherlock frowned. "You didn't sleep?"

"Oh God." John leaned forward and put his head in his hands. "This is surreal," he mumbled. "Do you see what I have to put up with?" he asked, turning to Four Beats because it was habit to seek out a sane person to talk to after a conversation with Sherlock.

Four Beats stared at him in disbelief while Sherlock snorted, sounding delighted.

Despite himself, John felt a manic grin starting to pull at his lips. Shaking his head, he stared at the cigar-cutter and let out an amused breath.

"Fine," he said, picking up the cards. "But no cheating."

"How will you learn to play otherwise?" Sherlock asked him, looking gleeful.

"Shut up." John started to deal.

Outside, John grinned up at Sherlock. "Thank you!" he said shaking his head. "Seriously, I thought..." John let out a breath. "I thought I was gonna be in debt with him forever the way he was threatening the interest."

"You never mentioned interest." Sherlock seemed peeved as they walked into the high street and flagged a taxi.

"It doesn't matter," John said as he slid bonelessly into the taxi. "I still have fingers," he grinned down and waggled them.

Sherlock watched his fingers dance then half stood, half leaned forward to draw the cover across, blocking the driver from view. He sat back after inspecting the speaker to ensure their conversation remained private.

"What're you doing?" John said, slightly embarrassed by how much it sounded like a squeak.

Sherlock pulled out the envelopes Four Beats had given him. "Here." He pushed the smaller envelope at John.

"You want me to hold onto it?"

"Have it."

John laughed, "Yeah, whatever!"

Sherlock's expression didn't waver and John felt something strange kick in his belly.

"You can't be serious?"

"Think of it as a finder's fee if it makes you feel better. I made ten thousand pounds today because you brought that idiot to my attention."

"There's five thousand pounds in here," John whispered, stunned, his mind barely able to process that information let alone the fact that Sherlock was trying to give him that amount.

Long fingers hesitated around his hands, a gentle touch that summoned John's attention.

"Why didn't she let you go home?" Sherlock asked, suddenly very serious.

John didn't need to ask who Sherlock was talking about. And that was the issue, wasn't it? The one question that none of his friends had asked: why had John been strapped for cash in the first place?

Unable to say anything, John stared at his shoes, his mind supplying plenty of reasons as to why his mother had been in a difficult position. The problem was, his mind also supplied a dozen counterarguments for each of those reasons. In the end, he simply shook his head and shifted uncomfortably.

Sherlock made a noncommittal noise, seeming to drop the issue, and took the envelope out of John's hands. Pulling him forward, Sherlock slipped the envelope into John's back pocket.

"A precaution then," Sherlock said softly. "Until you learn to play better."

Weakly laughing, John risked looking at him.

"Why didn't you come to me earlier?" Sherlock asked suddenly, eyes locking with his. "Why didn't you text me that night?"

Ah, that.

"Because I..." John sighed and scrubbed a hand over his

mouth. "Because...I didn't want you to think I was using you. You're always doing things for me or bailing me out and I do nothing for you. And I fucking hate seeing turd face all over you. I know that's stupid, but I still hate it and I didn't want you to think of me as some stupid kid. Or naive," he added, remembering that awful conversation a month ago.

Sherlock pulled back and seemed to study him. For a long moment John kept perfectly still, licking at his lips expectantly.

Then Sherlock moved away and sat back on his seat. "Idiot," Sherlock said fondly as he shifted to make himself comfortable.

Wait, that was it?

"You should put it somewhere safe," Sherlock said as he looked out of the window, smiling. "And not in the freezer."

Right.

"So, behind the toilet tank?" John asked hoarsely.

Sherlock's smile grew as he continued to look out the window and at the people they passed on the streets. "I was thinking the bank."

CHAPTER EIGHT:

Unconventional Advertising

NIGHT BUSES WERE FUN. WELL, they were if you ignored the people that were asleep and the ones that were trying not to throw up. John figured that he had managed it beautifully on his way back from Soho.

The door was hard to navigate though. It took a number of attempts to get the key into the lock, which meant that when it opened it was such a surprise that John stumbled through and ended up face first on the carpet. Fuck they needed to hoover, though did they have a hoover? John really wasn't sure that he'd ever seen one.

The light clicked on and John was faced with a pair of expensive shoes. They were definitely Sherlock's. John had once sat through a long and extensive conversation turned lecture about why the exact shoes that John was staring at would allow Sherlock to get away with more crimes.

That possibly should have been more disturbing than it had ended up being.

"I am wankered," John announced.

It might have been his imagination, but Sherlock's thin lips curled ever so slightly. "Yes, you are," he agreed, eyeing John up with what might have been either disgust or amusement. "Will you be staying there all night?"

Staying where? Not entirely sure what they were talking about, John decided to change the topic. "I," he said, raising his hands because that was how you made sure that people listened, "went to a gay bar. And it was gay."

The almost half smile that had been present on Sherlock's face dropped away in an instant. "What?" he asked, sounding blank, which made a nice change.

"Gay," John explained as he frowned down at his feet which were still on the doorstep. "My feet are very cold," he told Sherlock seriously, because that was a problem. Looking back up, John sighed. "If I roll over I will be sick," he said calmly.

In the light, Sherlock looked very pale. Paler. White? Which was funny because usually he looked rather tanned. Nicely tanned. Pretty skin. Lots of it because he was tall...

What had they been talking about again?

"Spinning," John informed him seriously, just in case Sherlock wanted to know.

With a rather put upon sigh, Sherlock disappeared. It was possible that Sherlock had lost interest so John was pretty relieved when Sherlock re-appeared with a mixing bowl that someone's well-meaning parents had given them for baking. The bowl was placed next to him and then Sherlock's lip curled in distaste before he wrenched John up from the floor.

Seconds later, John hurled into the purple plastic bowl.

He was miserable. If John could have reached down his throat, pulled out his stomach and squeezed out the drink then he would have. It would have been better than the slow death he faced as he hugged the toilet while Sherlock sat on the edge of the bath looking the peak of human health as he absently toyed with his phone.

"Geoff threw you out?" John asked, resting his head against the seat and half wishing they cleaned the toilet far more than they did.

"I have never lived with anyone called Geoff," Sherlock replied absently.

"Sure?" John asked, rolling his forehead against the toilet in the hopes of finding some way to cool down his aching head.

"Quite sure."

"Right." John shifted a little to peek up at Sherlock. "So why did 'whatever his name was' throw you out?"

"Too loud," Sherlock succinctly replied, and John couldn't even be bothered to ask for more details than that, not when he was in the state he was in. Groaning, he turned his head back into the toilet bowl.

"This is why you shouldn't drink cocktails, especially ones that have been bought for you," Sherlock lectured.

"They looked good," John mumbled.

The silence was telling; John could pretty much picture the unimpressed look that Sherlock was shooting him, as if John's lack of intelligence was a personal slight of some type.

"Did they have an umbrella as well as copious amounts of blue colouring?" Sherlock asked snidely.

It didn't take a genius to work out how Sherlock knew the cocktail had been blue. "Hey," John said as he pointed in vaguely.* "I'm the boss of the house and you should be nice to me." * the right direction.

"The boss of the house?"

"There was a vote," John shrugged. "I won by default. They were drunk, I rule."

And he'd won even more because Sherlock's lips were twitching in that way that suggested he was amused when he really wished he wasn't. "Finished yet?" Sherlock asked.

"Still dying."

The expression on Sherlock's face became predatory and John blinked in confusion as Sherlock's foot inched its way up his leg, towards his stomach and-

Sherlock shoved his fucking foot into John's stomach and John ended up hurling his guts up into the toilet again.

* * *

As it turned out (and unsurprisingly), Sherlock was a terrible nursemaid. After ensuring that John had thrown up every single thing he'd had past his lips for the last month, Sherlock then shoved him into his room and onto his bed while bitching about anything and everything.

"Really," Sherlock said as he bundled John into bed. "This is a complete pig-sty-"

"You're a pig-sty," John muttered into his pillow.

"You are capable of far more creative insults than that," Sherlock huffed, dragging the covers over John's shoulders.

True. Oddly pleased by the comment, John turned over and studied Sherlock, who was in the process of batting away the old socks that littered the desk.

"You," John began, pointing his finger. "You..."

"Yes?" Sherlock asked dully, appearing to give up the battle with the socks (maybe he'd smelled them), choosing to sit on the desk chair instead.

"You...are a tease," John declared, pleased to have stumbled upon the word. "That's what you are. My new friend Gay Alf-"

Sherlock winced and rubbed at his forehead as if in pain, muttering something under his breath.

"-said so," John continued, frowning at Sherlock's reaction. "And now I have to become a man slut to stop the teasing and-" he broke off as Sherlock reached over quickly and pulled down the covers to pat at John's jeans. The only problem was, he was patting at the pockets and not yanking down the zip.

"Don't take my phone," John complained. "Like phone," he added sleepily as Sherlock pulled it out. "It's clever."

The sound of beeping filled the room as Sherlock tapped away and then drew in a sharp breath. "John," he said, sounding odd, "have you read your texts?"

He'd been on the bus. "I don't want to read now." John batted an uncoordinated hand at roughly where he thought Sherlock was. The man really needed to stop talking.

"How many people did you give your number to?" Sherlock asked with what sounded like disbelief.

John shook his head, half remembering then tapped his arm.

"You bloody idiot!"

The next morning was hell. Well, the afternoon was. In the end, he crawled out of bed at three in the afternoon, half sure that men with small hammers must have inserted themselves in his brain.

Stumbling out wrapped in a duvet cover and probably resembling a sausage at best, John crashed onto the sofa opposite Andy who paused whatever it was that he was doing on his laptop, wincing at the sight of him.

"Where the hell did you get to last night?" Andy asked. "We lost you after the third pub."

John had some vague images of bright lights, blue drinks and dancing, but that hardly helped to narrow it down. "Dunno but I think I drank the place," John whimpered. "Thanks for the water by the way."

"Weren't me," Andy said, switching his attention back to the laptop. "Sherlock did it."

"He's here?" John asked, surprised.

"Outside smoking," Andy said. "Won't give me one," he sulkily added.

That was probably a good thing, John thought as he hid his face in the duvet and tried to quieten his rolling stomach. For a moment, he stared at the kitchen door and thought about getting up to find Sherlock to say thank you.

It seemed like far, far too much effort.

The bastard that called himself John's friend lazily picked up the remote and started to scroll through the channels before landing on screaming rock music that made John pull the covers over his head and try to suffocate himself to avoid the hangover.

In fact, he'd almost managed it when the covers were suddenly yanked down and Sherlock's less than amused face glowered down at him. Words seemed beyond him so John just huffed and threw a hand over his eyes in defence.

That was ruined when a strong hand gripped his and pulled it back enough that when John opened his eyes all he could see was his own arm and scrawled black numbers.

"What's that?" he mumbled blearily.

Sherlock dropped John's hand and threw himself onto the sofa next to Andy who didn't pause in his typing but still managed to flip Sherlock a foul look. In response, Sherlock lifted up a rather familiar screen and held it so Andy could see.

"Is that my phone?" John asked, suddenly feeling more alive. Glancing back at his arm he frowned at the familiar numbers that looked like...wait, was that his phone number?

Andy blinked, a smile tugging its way up his mouth before he reached out to take the phone from Sherlock. His amused gaze jumped from the phone to John and he started to snigger.

"How's he managing this?" Andy asked, putting his laptop to one side as he started to scroll through the messages. "He's hardly got the best track record when it comes to pulling."

"He's advertising well," Sherlock replied drolly with a pointed look at John's arm.

Advertising? Pulling? Half sure they were playing a joke (which, yay to Sherlock for developing his sense of humour) John sat up and then winced as the room spun. "Huh?" was all he managed.

"Hey," Andy said loudly. "This guy wants to 'show you what you're missing'. What you tell them you were missing?"

Missing?

And all of a sudden, a memory started to surface. A really dreadful one where he announced to God knew how many of Gay Alf's 'close and personal friends' that he wanted to try sucking cock to see if it was for him.

And then his arm with his number on it.

"No," John breathed in horror, collapsing back onto the sofa and lifting the covers again, as if that could block out the memory again. "Oh god, no."

"Quite," Sherlock seemed to agree, though it sounded an awful lot like the wanker was smiling.

"They've been texting?" John asked. "Seriously? I was so drunk-"

"As gathered from your love affair with the doormat," Sherlock replied, sounding way too pleased.

Shit. He'd almost managed to forget.

John yanked the covers down so quickly he could feel the static crackle through his hair. "Wait, don't read those," he demanded as Andy continued to scroll through his phone.

"Mate, you can't give me comedy gold like this and then take it away," Andy argued, sitting back as if with a good book and a cup of tea.

Great. Everyone would know now. And he was in no state to try and get the phone back. With a sigh, John staggered to his feet and clutched his duvet around him tightly. "I'm gonna go drown in the shower," he announced.

Andy nodded. "Or you could take up 'Big Dave' and his offer to have you drown in another type of fluid."

Fan-fucking-tastic.

"You have to come out again!" Gay Alf argued, chugging back a Corona. "It was hardly a fair test, you were so rat arsed that it would have been wrong to have tried anything."

John had his head buried in his arms as he sat slumped at the bar. "My mates texted everyone back," John managed to pull his head up a little, even as he whined. "I'll be chased out of town knowing them!"

"Come on," Gay Alf wheedled. "Try!"

"I need vodka," John declared after a moment. Gay Alf grinned triumphantly.

It was hot in the club; hot and sweaty and god dancing could be so much fun!

Okay, so maybe he was a little bit gay!

There was something freeing in this because girls never really flocked over and paid attention to him like this. Apparently being 'new' got him some degree of attention and John felt like liquid sex at the moment. Hands were pressed against him, deliciously clever hands and, taking a risk, John leaned back a little. The guy behind him seemed to take notice and ducked down to kiss his neck, so John rested his head on their shoulder and looked to the side to reassure himself that Gay Alf, as promised, was still at the bar.

As was Victor.

Victor?

Shit!

Yelping, John froze and the guy at his neck pulled back questioningly. With an apologetic smile, John disentangled himself from the dancing crowd and ended up half crouching to the side of the dance floor and then peeking over a table to stare at Victor.

Fuck! Ducking under the table, god only knew why, John whipped out his phone.

Am at Back Door club. Just in case you're here with turd face.

And then hugged his phone to him until he felt the vibrations that signalled a new message.

I noticed. The floor is filthy. Get up.

If there was ever a way to sink through the floor, John was sure he would have found it.

Sheepishly, John returned to Gay Alf whose eyes had followed him from the moment he'd stood up from under the table.

"You're weird, Watson," he announced as soon as John was within hearing rage. "This is why people call us queer."

"Please don't talk about it." John sat next to him, glancing towards where he'd seen Victor. There were a few new people at the bar, but turd face was no-where to be seen and neither was their mutual friend. "So, you seen Sherlock around?"

"Toilets," Gay Alf said eyeing someone up. "Oh! Don't go in there!" he added suddenly.

It was a toss-up as to whether that was because Sherlock was doing cocaine or Victor. Neither one was especially fun to think about. And, weirdly, John had never been in the position where he was aware that Sherlock was getting high somewhere where John could actually, physically stop him.

Torn, he stood still, staring at the toilets. He didn't want to see Victor and Sherlock doing anything but the thought of simply carrying on dancing while Sherlock was snorting or injecting or however the hell he took it. That didn't sit right with him.

"You like him," Gay Alf said, his voice almost too soft to be heard by the music but his expression, the sad eyes and softening quirk of his lips was enough to make John sure he'd heard right.

"We're mates," he decided, hoping to salvage his dignity.

Then he got the look that more and more people were giving him. The one that cut through his protests and made him want to squirm because he hated the idea that he was that bloody obvious.

"Yeah," John admitted, suddenly serious. "But...he...it's complicated."

Unexpectedly, Gay Alf smiled and took John's hand with a glimmer of glee in his eyes. "Let's uncomplicate it then!"

Wait. What?

With a daring grin that made something in John flutter

with expectation (and who the hell was he kidding? Interest) Alf drew John into the mass of heaving bodies. They unerringly headed straight towards a few guys who seemed to have stripped off their tops and were still streaked with sweat.

"Wait-"

Gay Alf twisted and, gripping John by his hips, backed him into one of the guys as if he were a wall.

Christ the guy was built!

"It's the oldest trick in the book," Gay Alf pressed against him and whispered in his ear. "Don't worry, it's early and no-one will push too hard."

An arm was wrapping around John's chest and a button was being undone.

"It's exactly what you were doing earlier," Gay Alf added, working from the top down. "Just with the added benefit of a potential audience!"

John could see his point, sort of. And he'd had enough of those blue drinks Alf liked that it *almost* sounded like a good idea.

Relaxing again, he grinned at Gay Alf who was a fucking fantastic dancer, able to draw people in with ease and a grin that made what he was doing look like pure fun. He'd almost forgotten why they were doing this until Gay Alf suddenly grinned and pressed against him a little firmer.

"Oh, I think he likes you too," purred Alf as he arched into John in a move that must be illegal.

But John knew that. What was the point of this again?

"You're thinking way too much," Gay Alf insisted as he nestled a knuckle under John's chin and pushed his head up to meet the mouth of the man behind him.

The kiss was filthy, almost bordering on mouth molestation in John's opinion. "Uh-" he said into the kiss. "Maybe-"

His shirt, now open, was smoothed to the side as hands ran up his chest, too many for John to count.

Not at all sure about where this was going, John tried to wriggle away to see what was going on so he could assess the situation. He had a nagging feeling he was in danger of being pulled apart in the middle of the dance floor. But the hand tilting his chin up wasn't moving and to pull away now would require more force than perhaps the situation warranted.

At the moment. If anyone started on his trousers he'd deck them.

And then the hand drew away and John gasped for air, released from the kiss. The hands (most of them) had vanished and it was back to just a nice, fun dance.

Gay Alf seemed to have disappeared...wait, no, there he was.

With Sherlock.

At first, John glared. It looked like the pair was dancing but Gay Alf was subdued and, as they moved, it was very clear that Sherlock was talking very quickly into Gay Alf's ear.

No longer fuelled by Gay Alf's scheme, the others eventually danced away and John, buttoning up his shirt, wandered back to the bar again, feeling a little confused.

What the hell was going on?

"Bit out of your depth?" Victor asked, reclining at the bar.

John shrugged and ordered a drink of water. Gasping it down, he stared out at the floor and then frowned and turned to Victor who seemed surprisingly close.

"Yes?" John asked.

The look he received was odd. Really odd. Uncomfortable and tinged with something that seemed a little stronger than dislike. And yet it was almost as if John was being weighed up like a goose at the market.

"They like you," Victor commented with a smirk. "You play wide eyed virgin boy well."

"Not a virgin," John snapped because, well, that was true.

"They like it." Victor stared thoughtfully out at the dance floor. "You're gonna be a doctor, right?"

Not entirely sure where Victor was aiming to go with this, John glanced over at him, trying to get some sort of clue. "Yeah?"

"And that business with Four Beats. A bit strapped for cash, are you?"

John stayed quiet even though his silence probably condemned him. Instead, he stared down at his drink and then took another long swallow.

"You have any idea how profitable we could be to each other?" Victor said, and the smarmy quality of his voice felt like it was curling around John like a snake. "They like you. You could be a good salesman. And supply man once you get to the good part of being a doctor."

The good part?

"How easily can you get hold of oxycodone?"

Comprehension suddenly dawned and John ground down hard on his teeth to avoid saying something really stupid because there was no fucking way he was risking his degree for Trevor. Instead, he stared out at the club that had seemed so fun and easy minutes ago and now, now he scanned the faces looking for the glazed eyes and uncoordinated movements, the jerky hands and the groups huddled in the corners.

Unfair, he thought. He was looking for it now. Half the people in here were probably as clueless as he had been. Despite the revelation, his eyes still slid to Sherlock and Alf who were still dancing. It wasn't that he'd thought Sherlock was a saint but seeing the evidence in front of him... He should be disappointed or angry but all he could think was how good Sherlock looked in the flickering club lights.

And what did that say about John?

"I could throw him into it," Victor offered, his mouth still by John's ear. "Might be able to get him to throw you a few fucks if that's how you want to take your payment."

For a second John thought he might crush the plastic cup and send water everywhere. "You make that offer often?" he asked through clenched teeth.

Victor snorted. "If he doesn't want to fuck someone then he doesn't," Victor said, pulling back a little. "You afraid he'll turn you down?"

The muscle in John's jaw started to tick and he drew in a long, deep breath; forcing himself not to react.

"Or we can leave him out of it all together," Victor offered, as if sensing that their conversation was going down the wrong path. "But if you're gonna keep coming into my places then I think we're gonna have to work something out."

My places? John frowned and downed the rest of his water. "Let me be really clear," he said, turning to Victor. "I am not selling to them or to you. I'm not putting my entire future on the line so you can get some kicks off of pain killers."

Victor's expression didn't change. "You're saying no?"

"Big time," John replied, turning to walk away. A hand on his arm stopped him and he stared at it in disbelief before trailing his gaze up Victor's arm to his face.

"Be fucking kidding," John hissed.

"Don't play with me," Victor snarled. "You ain't some uni kid that we don't touch because you have no interest in this world. You're in it. You're friends with Sherlock, Alf. You've asked for favours with Four Beats and you've come into my club. You think you're better than us, that you're above it? You're in it, you stupid shit. And when you're in it, you pick someone to do favours for."

John pulled his arm free. "I wouldn't do favours for you if your dick was gold plated and you were selling fucking pixie dust."

The furious stare made him falter a little but he refused to back down. Victor stared at him and then at the exit as if John was his minion to dismiss.

A glance behind Victor showed that Sherlock was nowhere

to be seen and Alf was watching them with a frown on his face. Catching John's eye, he just shook his head minutely as if in warning.

Seriously?

He was so done.

Throwing up his hands at Victor, John backed off and turned to storm out the club.

CHAPTER NINE:

Interlude

O NE DAY EARLIER
Sherlock stared up at the television from his position on John's sofa, ignoring the slight, nagging, craving in his blood. This sofa, the one that John seemed to favour when he had a preference, was the best mainly because it allowed him to be hidden from sight when John's flatmates came downstairs. Making them jump was often the highlight of boring days. Especially since John had gone out, again, after having just about recovered from his hangover. More than likely John was probably going to attempt to cure his aching head with another round of drinks. Possibly with Alfred Baird who Sherlock had stupidly introduced John to a few weeks ago.

He'd been introducing John to too many people.

I went to a gay club.

Sitting up, Sherlock frowned, remembering the text messages from the saccharine to the obscene. All wanting John.

John had never shown any interest in going to gay bars; it had been as if Sherlock was his one homosexual outlet. Sherlock had been perfectly content with that because John Watson was even more addictive than the cocaine that was currently starting to call to him. Sherlock had never met anyone like John, had never been more fascinated by the blush that crept up on John's cheeks when he rambled, or the infectious chuckles that made his own mouth twitch in response.

Why? Why now?

It wouldn't be possible to watch. To see John taken by the hand and pulled into that world by someone else, the world that Sherlock...What? Had wanted to show him?

Not yet.

He didn't want a relationship. He didn't want the constrictions, the ties, and expectations. Certainly, the last made his hackles rise.

Expectation.

He despised the word now. There had been a time when he had thrived on it, shattered the expectations that people had for him as if they were fragile pieces made from clumsy clay. He'd been young and foolish and desperate to be seen as something more than what he was. And now? Now he was free from his family, able to do as he wanted, whatever he wanted.

"John's asked if I want to meet up with him," Andy said as he threw himself onto the sofa opposite, tapping away at his phone in such a repetitive way that Sherlock was sure he was simply creating a message made from same letter. "At Back Door?"

Back Door. The gay club. Suddenly Sherlock's thoughts circled back to his dilemma with John. Scowling, Sherlock stood and stormed into the kitchen, rifling through John's cupboards.

As amusing as John's pulling technique had been last night, it was clear that he was ready to try a homosexual relationship. And Sherlock either stepped to the side and let him get on with it, trampling down his own personal feelings on the matter, or he ensured that John's only knowledge of such a relationship rested exclusively in Sherlock's hands.

He needed cocaine.

There were other complications too. Namely Victor Trevor's rather large ego that seemed to inflate more and more each time his father gave him another nugget of power. If nothing else, being in a monogamous relationship with John would cause a serious increase in his monthly spend.

"Want some?" Victor asked, standing by the bed, completely naked as he dug into his trouser pocket to find his stash. Stretching, Sherlock watched as Victor pulled out a plastic bag, opened it and then dipped a finger in, grinning seductively as he passed the finger into his mouth. When he leaned down, his face hovering above Sherlock's, Victor raised an eyebrow in challenge.

Knowing the game well, Sherlock craned his head up, meeting Victor's mouth and teasing open his lips in order to scoop up the cocaine dusted on Victor's teeth as if it were sherbet. Only when he was satisfied that he'd collected all that he could did Sherlock pull back and relax onto the bed as Victor moved away.

"Money's on the table," Sherlock said lazily.

"Mm." Victor jostled the bed again as he sat down. There was the unmistakable sound of a strap being threaded through his fingers. Without opening an eye, Sherlock lifted up his arm and clenched a fist to make it easier for Victor to find a vein. The pinprick, when it came, barely made Sherlock flinch.

"More?" Victor asked after depressing the plunger. His voice sounded cracked and very far away despite the fact that he was right next to Sherlock. At least he was getting a clear buzz this time rather than Victor scrimping on the quality of discount goods.

Sherlock nodded as a ringing sound started to cut through his head and ended any attempt his brain was making at solving impossible problems.

Then Victor's mouth was on him again.

Within three point seven seconds of stepping into the main room of the Back Door, the world came crashing back to Sherlock when he spotted John.

Right. Andy had said...foolish to forget. The rest of his thought process drained away as he finally absorbed what he was seeing in front of him.

In the months that he'd known John, Sherlock had never seen him like this.

His usually dirty blond hair was soaked with sweat from the heat of the club, shining a slick, dark gold against his flushed skin. The grin John flashed up at the man he was dancing with made something within Sherlock clench. John's eyes were so dark it was almost impossible to see what colour they were and his lips were glistening-

He'd been kissing someone. And, no longer hindered by nerves or being the one expected to make the first move, John moved with ease on the dance floor. There were hands roaming, hips thrusting-

Fuck.

Turning to the bar, Sherlock put his hands firmly upon it as if to ground himself and find some semblance of control.

"Crashing?" Victor asked, moving to stand behind him.

No, but he needed more. He needed to think and he could already feel that the height of his high had passed.

"Be back in a moment," Victor called into his ear, making Sherlock flinch from the way his breath tickled and seemed too close and crackling. As Victor moved away, Sherlock stared at the bar and then up at the heavens. They should have gone anywhere but here. Anywhere in the entirety of London-

His phone buzzed in his pocket and Sherlock frowned, shoving his hands into his jeans to retrieve it and read the message that was likely to be from John.

Am at Back Door club. Just in case you're here with turd face.

John.

A small, strange wave of fondness blurred with his high and left Sherlock almost unable to see for a moment. Turning, he looked, half expecting to see John still on the dance floor and then frowning when he couldn't.

Bloody idiot!

Trying not to smile at the image of John, hiding under a table (silly boy), he texted back.

I noticed. The floor is filthy. Get up.

Victor made an aggrieved noise behind him. "Come on," he coaxed, hands slipping around to Sherlock's stomach. "Got something for you."

The men's room was always a place to avoid unless you wanted to see something approaching a live sex show. Still, it was useful to have Victor with him. Even in here, the son of James Trevor managed to gain privacy, pointed glares from him and whispered rumours from the attendees always helping. Closing the stall behind them, Victor turned with triumph. "Here," Victor showed him what he had in his pocket. "You ever done this before?"

Sherlock took one look at it and felt himself hesitate. Showing that to Victor, however, would be stupid. Instead, he raised an eyebrow as if bored by what was in front of him. "No," he said, inwardly pleased when his voice didn't wobble.

"Then you should-" Victor began, looking pleased with himself.

"No." Sherlock pushed Victor back against the wall of the cubicle. Keeping an eye on him he sucked his thumb carefully then dipped it into Victor's pocket to soak up the traces there.

Then sucked his thumb again and smiled, slipping twenty in Victor's pocket.

As he left he heaved in a deep breath, suddenly feeling more unsteady than he had in a while. Ignoring the grinding bodies in the hallway, he exited into the main dance floor again and was almost sure he was finally experiencing tachycardia.

There was John, half undressed and surrounded by hungry men, dancing as if he had been specifically built to torture Sherlock. It wasn't made any better when John's head was tipped back and in the flashing light Sherlock could see the kiss. The hands. The skin. The movement.

And, like that, he knew exactly how this was all going to end. There was absolutely no choice anymore.

John's movement suddenly made him snap out of his terrified, rambling train of thought. John was tense, his hands wary and the muscles in his neck rigid against the hand Sherlock hadn't noticed earlier.

The hand that was keeping his head tilted back to the kiss.

This he could deal with. This was easy to focus on. Sliding through the bodies on the dance floor, Sherlock aimed his way to John and his friend. Sherlock had met 'Gay Alf' a handful of times; he had a lovely collection of marijuana plants growing in his shed and sold the buds for a very reasonable price. Most of the time.

It wasn't hard at all to pull Gay Alf backwards, away from John (harder not to pull him backwards and replace Gay Alf with himself) and swing him off into another part of the dance floor in a far less exuberant dance. He didn't bother to look back at John, given that he was more than capable of taking care of himself when no longer worried about offending anyone.

The boy really was an idiot at times.

"Dance with me, stay very close and do not let him see we're taking," Sherlock instructed in his ear.

"Before you start," Gay Alf started to say, "kid was gonna try it anyway."

"Was he?" Sherlock asked evenly as they swayed to the music.

"Yeah." Gay Alf shrugged. "You're lucky I know he's yours. Kid's got a good body."

Sherlock pulled him closer, tightly. "Repeat that?" he snarled dangerously.

"Which bit?"

Sherlock raised an unamused eyebrow.

"He's yours. Everyone knows it. After that business with Four Beats? The only person that doesn't bloody know it is John!"

There was little point in denying that. "What does he think about it all?"

"Says it's complicated. I swear that boy thinks you're God himself sometimes. Though he's still the only person I've ever heard bitch about you and get away with it. He sounds like your wife half the time."

Sherlock watched the bodies around them. Complicated was such an easy word for it.

"Then Alfred," Sherlock locked eyes with him, "just to make it clear: touch him again like that, make him uncomfortable like that in any way again and I will come looking for you."

"Kid can handle himself-"

"Yes. But he's also far too polite to say anything about just feeling uncomfortable. Fortunately, I have no such compunctions."

"Sherlock-"

Sherlock turned, seeing the sudden worry in Gay Alf's eyes. John was storming to the exit and Victor was staring after him with a clenched jaw.

"I reckon you got bigger fish than me."

———— • ••• • ————

Victor's mood didn't improve any when Sherlock took him downstairs and into the office underneath the club.

"You need to teach the boy some manners," Victor sneered as the door slammed shut. Turning, Victor perched on the edge of the table and regarded Sherlock in a cold manner that never meant anything good.

"What did you say to him?" Sherlock asked, leaning against the door, not entirely sure how to play this.

Silence echoed for a moment as Victor scrutinised Sherlock. "I'll need you tomorrow night. The Parker family might have had something to do with the recent sellings on our turf."

It was enough to make Sherlock pause. Victor rarely asked like this. Usually, he made it into a game, a bit of fun. This was being pointed. Slowly, Sherlock nodded.

Victor smiled and slid off the table. "And your John," he said with something akin to a snarl, "is stupidly naïve."

Pressing his lips together, Sherlock tried to cast his mind back to what the hell Victor could be referring to. John rarely lost his temper but when he did-

What had John done?

"Med students," Victor mused as he circled Sherlock. "They're profitable and a boy like that, all wide eyes? A golden boy? Get through the police no problem. Could get a good clientele as well."

It was as if he'd been turned to ice.

John dealing? Never. Even if John had a personality transplant and decided he wanted to be involved with drugs, Sherlock would never want him to be a part of the sunken world he lived in. More than that, he would never want John to be part of Victor Trevor's world and all it entailed.

Yet, somehow, John apparently was. And Sherlock could imagine how well that idea had been received. John wouldn't understand the need to be cautious, to weigh up his thoughts and actions in order to navigate his way through this game the Trevor's delighted in playing.

What had John said to Victor and how difficult would it be to fix?

A crawling shudder jerked its way through his skin.

"I mean," Victor continued, "would you fuck him?"

He couldn't quite process the connection between what Victor had said and was saying now. It seemed impossible to concentrate fully. The room wasn't quite solid and it suddenly felt as if an anchor point was very far away.

"Could be lucrative," Victor murmured into his ear and stroked Sherlock's arm. "Need a hit?"

All logical and rational thoughts seemed to skitter away from him, like insects fleeing in protection. Victor's words were becoming less clear, the meanings fuzzy and, to be safe, he shook his head briefly because they'd been talking about John and drugs and he wasn't entirely sure he could separate the two as Victor talked. Turning away slightly, Sherlock scrubbed a hand over his face, trying to contain himself. It was far too warm down in the office and he could almost feel his shirt plastering itself to his skin.

He needed either clarity or oblivion. Preferably both if such a thing was possible.

"I want the coke," Sherlock said forcibly.

"This has coke in it," Victor said, a grin evident in his voice.

It made him clench his fist in frustration and turn back to Victor. It took everything that he had to remind himself that there was nothing to be gained in annoying Victor too much; this was an easy drug flow and a cheap one too. As long as Victor was on side, life would continue as easily as it had for the past year.

"Seems like a waste," Sherlock said eventually. "You'd be expected to sell that for far more."

That seemed to do the trick as the mere hint of his father's expectations had Victor reluctantly pocket what he had been holding and instead draw something from the safe in the wall. The moment his back was turned, Sherlock clenched his hands on the desk, unable to describe the strange feeling that crashed through him.

He couldn't give this up and he couldn't watch John dance with strangers and he probably shouldn't be merging the two together. In that moment, it was like having a vision of his future, like a train crash that he couldn't stop because either way he was now fucked.

As Victor came back, Sherlock twisted himself around so that he was leaning against the desk and able to offer up his arm, already pulling up the sleeve to bare the veins to Victor and the strap that was easily wrapped around his arm.

The familiar buzz in his arm was almost a welcome as the blood flow struggled. "Are you not partaking?" Sherlock managed to ask as Victor switched on the lamp to get a clear view of Sherlock's arm.

"Don't indulge with the merchandise," Victor parroted at Sherlock, and the utter absurdity of that statement almost made Sherlock laugh. "Especially something as pricey and dangerous as this."

Pricey and dangerous? He had cocaine all the-

The sudden shock at Victor's deception was swept away in an overwhelming wave and mercifully everything stopped in way that he hadn't felt for ages, until he just didn't give a flying fuck anymore.

Colours swirled around him, forming shapes that blinked away as he chased them with his eyes. There was a room but it didn't fit into his brain and somehow John was there even though he wasn't meant to be in the room. "Do you really want me?" John asked, brushing up against him, close and yet untouchable.

"Yes," Sherlock opened his eyes and the room spun and blurred as he stared up at Victor who was pushing John down onto the table. John grinned at him, by his side, as Victor snarled down at the John on the table and then dimmed away. "Teach me," John said as he sat with a pack of cards. "I like my fingers."

Sherlock could see why.

There was a sound like meat hitting meat and the smell of blood. The pounding in his chest grew as if there was a tiny hammer trapped underneath his skin and the world swam when he swallowed.

"What have you taken?" John's voice echoed through his head, bouncing everywhere, inescapable in its demands.

"More-" Sherlock replied, struggling to follow that sentence through to its conclusion. More than he had meant to? The thought swam away before he could even remember what the start of the sentence had been.

"Fucking hell! Have you ever heard the word 'enough'? Genius my arse!"

Even though Victor was in front of him, there was suddenly Victor on the bed a few months ago, before John. "You ever tried it this way?" he asked, voice hoarse from their weekend marathon of sex, drugs and clubs.

"Yes." Sherlock had groaned, tilting his head back as the plunger shot his arse with a mixture of cocaine and water. "Not for years though," he'd admitted later as the high had faded.

"Fucking fantastic," John hissed at him. "You are such a prick!"

There was blood on the sheets again. No, there had never been blood on the sheets. What sheet?

He could smell blood though.

They'd fucked again after they'd indulged the mixture of cocaine and water, Victor still in the wooing phase of their business relationship. There was nothing in the world like orgasming while high. And Victor, for all his faults (they were legion), was actually surprisingly good in bed.

"Do you ever think?" John asked, sitting next to the bed. "I mean just engage brain and common sense before you open that mouth of yours? Or are the neurons in your brain going so quick that you don't bother to examine the solutions you come up with?" John sounded scared. "Fuck!"

They were in the room again. John's hands at his trousers.

"No." Not here, not like this. Not for John's first time.

Then he was in the school library, on the floor after hours with the girl who had introduced him to speed. Fucking into her without any real idea of what he was doing, trying what he could to start his education correctly. And then she blurred suddenly, her indistinct features becoming even harder to remember.

"You could give him anything. You're heading for an early death, Sherlock. The lifestyle you're leading will kill you and you are going to take him with you."

Mycroft.

Mycroft hadn't been in the library.

John.

The sudden wrongness of the images hit him.

I'm hallucinating.

It was utterly clear as day and yet he couldn't stop his mind from lurching and his thoughts from tumbling over and over until he became lost again.

The next time anything made sense, the world seemed too quiet and he was in bed with someone.

Victor? No. He dismissed that idea even as his mind formed the thought. No, not the right shape, size or smell.

John. It was John. Relief flooded through him and a second wave followed when he checked they were both fully clothed.

Shifting a bit, Sherlock looked down.

John was a mess. A bruise was forming by his cheekbone, round and a nasty purple from the point of impact. It looked like a hard punch had been levelled at John. Dragging his gaze across John's face, Sherlock frowned at his bloody lip, torn as if he'd been cut by a ring.

An image of Victor's hand hit Sherlock.

John had been in a fight with Victor.

And just like that everything else came flooding back in a horrific wave.

Victor had offered John a job. Victor had been sore about being turned down.

And John had to have been in a fight with Victor. There was no other explanation.

Sherlock lay staring at John's face. He was sound asleep now, curled up against Sherlock and barely moving in an exhausted slumber despite the light that was pouring in through the gap in the curtains.

Turning a little, Sherlock pressed his lips to John's hair, breathing him in as he tried to quiet his panic. His gaze slid down and lingered on John's hands, specifically at the bruised knuckles there.

He'd hit Victor back. Bloody stupid moronic idiot. Why had he-

Probably for the same reason that Sherlock's head was pounding ceaselessly and he'd suffered hallucinations all night. For the same reason that he'd clearly invited John into his bed without any memory of it.

They were in so much trouble.

CHAPTER TEN:

White Knights for White Horses

A S FAR AS JOHN WAS concerned, Victor Trevor was a complete arsehole. His places? Offering John a 'job'? Bastard.

Striding down the street, John kicked at an empty can. A deep feeling of satisfaction welled up within him as the sound rattled and echoed down the street.

"John?" someone shouted sounding slightly out of breath. "John?"

It was Gay Alf. It took a moment for John to register his voice and another to decide if he wanted to stop and listen. When Alf called for a third time, John felt himself slow down, relenting slightly at the frustrated tone that Gay Alf was using and bracing himself for whatever was to come.

"What?" he asked, folding his arms.

"You okay?"

"Yeah, I just..." John frowned down at the street as if it would have some kind of answer. "Victor offered me a job."

"Ah," Alf said, and didn't ask what the job was which probably meant that he worked for Victor, because (apparently) John was just that stupid and that thick about these things. Drawing in a frustrated breath, John shook his head. "Right," he muttered. "So what do you sell for him?"

"Weed," Alf said frankly. "And drinks when I'm not chasing after drunk idiots."

"Not an idiot," John said. "I turned him down."

"I saw. So did Sherlock."

John narrowed his eyes and glanced back the way he'd came. "So?" he asked, knowing his tone was painfully petulant.

Gay Alf glanced back at the club, looking desperately uncomfortable. "Look," Gay Alf breathed, "Victor he...you just need to tread carefully. And Sherlock definitely needs to."

"What? Why?" John asked, scraping a hand through his hair. "Are you seriously buying into this?"

Gay Alf looked away and drew in a long breath. Then, before John's eyes, he seemed to piece himself back together and into his usual friendly, easy going self. "Just try to keep tall and possessive calm next time, all right?"

Calm? John slowly returned his gaze to the club, resisting the urge to sneer and roll his eyes. "What did he do?" John asked eventually, a wave of defeat crashing over him as he thought about all the possible ways that Sherlock might have reacted to that.

"No idea," Gay Alf said with a shrug as he dug into his pockets and produced a cigarette. "Neither of 'em looked pleased though. Went down towards the office-"

And John was off, stalking his way back into the club because like fuck was Sherlock fighting his battles for him. With a nod at the bouncer and flashing the striped stamp on the back of his hand, he re-entered the club where people crashed and writhed to the pumping music.

It took a moment to readjust to the music and the lights. The throbbing crowds making it harder than it needed to be. After a few seconds, John spotted the door that said 'Staff Only' and thanked fuck he was drunk because, sober, he would have worried endlessly about what he was doing. Instead, still slightly buzzing from the alcohol, he strode through the door like he owned the place.

It led to metal stairs that spiralled down in an over dramatic fashion that wasn't helped by the deep red walls and thin strip lights above. It was impossible to stay quiet as he went but he didn't meet anyone on the stairs and, downstairs, there were only a few options to try before he stumbled across a locked door.

Damn. Steeling himself, John banged on the door. "Sherlock? You in there?"

Nothing.

Muttering some entirely foul and completely deserved comments under his breath, John rolled his eyes and knelt to study the lock. Sherlock had once tried to teach him how to pick a lock but, at the time, John had been trying to study, despite Sherlock insisting that picking locks would be useful in surgery.

Apparently, it would be a good idea to listen next time.

"Sherlock," John called again, thumping on the door. Then, using one of Sherlock's techniques, kept banging on the door, going so far as to ensure the noise was uneven and out of time to annoy the occupants further. To his surprise, it seemed to work as the door suddenly wrenched open and Victor yanked him inside, tossing John into the room as he locked the door once more.

It took John a second to regain his footing and spot Sherlock. He could barely process what he was seeing.

Sherlock looked bad. His eyes were unfocused and startlingly dark against his pale, sweating face. He sat on the floor, braced against the wall and still seemed unsteady. His nut-brown hair was sweat soaked and his entire body seemed to be struggling to cope, shuddering at intervals.

"What happened?" John asked as he took a step towards Sherlock, suddenly feeling completely out of his depth. Next to Sherlock an empty needle was on the floor and everything added up really quickly. "What did you give him?" he demanded, turning on Victor.

"Nothing he didn't want," Victor said without meeting his eyes. "Look, you're a medical student, right?"

"Seriously?" John spat. "Now? He's-"

"In need of someone with medical knowledge," Victor hissed.

"He needs more than I can give him," John decided, reaching into his pocket for his phone.

His wrist was seized in an iron grip and Victor was suddenly much closer than John had realised. "Don't be stupid," Victor hissed at John. "We don't need those questions."

"*You* don't need those questions," John corrected, trying to shake Victor off. "He needs-"

"Really? 'cause he's pumped full with cocaine. He has stuff at his place. He'll be fucked before he's even woken up. And you? Partying with a drug addict? Desperate to fuck a waste-of-space addict-"

Completely forgetting Gay Alf's words, John hit Victor before he even knew what he was doing. It was hard to tell which of them was more surprised as Victor stumbled back, releasing John's wrist to cup his nose. There was something sickeningly gratifying about the fact that blood was now seeping through Victor's fingers and dripping onto his fancy shirt.

Victor pulled his hands away and stared at the blood smeared over his fingers. His face twisted into an ugly expression and he reached for John's throat, drenched hand clawing menacingly. John tried to duck but he'd underestimated how far he was from the wall and ended up pressed against it with Victor's wet fingers digging into his neck.

"Seriously," Victor hissed at him. "How fucking stupid are you? I'm gonna-"

John didn't think it was wise to wait for him to finish. Kneeing him in the crotch, John shoved at Victor to get free and get his phone out of his pocket. The next thing he knew, a weight at his back had him sprawling across the floor as the phone was wrenched out of his hands. The feeling of cruel knees pinning him and hands scrambling roughly, biting uncaringly across his skin was oddly familiar from wrestling with his brother as a kid, but this was a hell of a lot more dangerous than that had been.

John kicked and flailed, trying to throw Victor off of him but the bastard seemed pretty good at keeping his balance and clinging on, an elbow wrapped around John's throat. From that angle, John couldn't fight back, was useless as Victor tried to wrestle John onto his back. "Hold still-" Victor gritted out, panting.

There was no fucking way that was happening. John rammed his head backwards, catching Victor's face. There was a sickening crunch and a sharp bite of pain that made John unsure as to whether he'd hurt Victor or himself. The grip on his hands eased and it was suddenly easy to scamper out from under the weight that was keeping him pinned to the floor.

A glance back showed Victor on the floor, cupping at his nose as blood almost seemed to flow out this time, cascading down with frightening intensity. The sight was enough to make John hesitate, not really sure what to do next and not entirely convinced that he hadn't made things worse.

Victor's eyes opened looking a little dazed and he stared at John over the hand that cupped his nose. With half of his face covered, it was hard to predict what he was going to do. The man stumbled to his feet, still holding his nose and took a few steps towards John.

The blow came from nowhere it was so quick. A vicious backhand that slapped John's head to the side and made him feel as if his cheek was being ripped open. The shock of it had John stumbling back, too stunned to react. He'd been in fights before, had fists thrown at him but never quite with the cold air that Victor displayed, as if he were a naughty child that Victor wanted to scare.

"Clean him up," Victor ordered, his words slightly muffled by the way he was cupping his nose. "Be a good fucking boy and do as you're told."

The thing was, John was closer to the door than Victor and Alf was outside somewhere, as was a phone...

He got about four steps before Victor caught up with him,

a hand closing around his arm, the movement almost pulling John into the path of another punch. It was easier to deal with but no less painful and the fact that Victor kept hold of John's arm meant he couldn't move as easily to absorb the blow.

It felt like something should have broken.

In the stumbling moments of disorientation and sheer hurt, Victor managed to spin him around and towards the table, shoving him down on it so that John was well and truly pinned.

"Are you fucking stupid?" Victor asked again, panting as he leaned over and dripped blood on John's shirt. "Seriously?" he added with another shove. "You're nobody," he hissed. "Nothing. And you want to start this with me?"

"He needs a hospital," John said, refusing to back down.

"No," Victor snarled. "He doesn't. He needs a nursemaid to dab his brow and mop up his sick. You are gonna stay here, do as you're told-"

"He could die."

Victor snorted, blood spraying and then winced as the pain seemed to finally kick in. His expression twisted into something ugly and his hand came down again, the back of his ring catching John's lip this time. "I don't fucking care," he hissed. "Do as you're told."

"What about his brother?" John asked suddenly, not sure why his brain was scrambling for ways to appease the dickhead.

A moment or two passed and John could practically see Victor weigh that up. The man had to be hurting, his nose was dripping blood all over John and John could feel his face starting to swell. "Yeah," Victor said suddenly as he stepped back. "You call him. He knows how to lie." With a last, threatening shove, Victor pulled away and stood up, giving John room to breathe and move again. "Good boy," he added as if John were a misbehaving puppy that had just shown promise.

So John kneed him in the crotch with a sharp smile. Victor went down like a stone and John scrambled away from him, aiming towards Sherlock this time who was still sitting at the edge of the room, sweating, dazed and not at all with it.

Spitting to the side to get rid of the taste of blood, John reached out to touch the back of his hand to Sherlock's forehead, his vision coming and going as he did so.

"How much did he-" John turned around just as the door slammed shut.

Shit.

For a few seconds, John stared at the door blankly, feeling as if the whole world had suddenly been locked away from him. The room was stained with blood from their fight and it felt like he'd been drowned in it, the taste cloying in his throat and the smell clutching to everything. The world felt metallic and too bright and suddenly unreal.

He couldn't deal with this. It wasn't...this wasn't what he'd expected, what he'd ever imagined. He couldn't-

He had to. Taking a deep breath, he turned back to Sherlock, staring at his sweaty brow and unseeing gaze. He needed to be in control and to do something that was actually going to be useful except, really, what the hell did he know about drugs apart from the fact that Sherlock took a lot of them?

He needed to see Sherlock's eyes. With some hesitation, he reached over to Sherlock and tilted his head up with bloody hands. The usually hazel irises had almost vanished, leaving behind only the faintest ring around the blown pupils.

"Sherlock?" John asked, searching his friend's face for some indication that he'd heard. He forced himself to keep breathing at an even pace even though long breaths made his face ache. He was the doctor (or at least a soon to be doctor), he should be able to do this.

He had to be able to do this.

"Sherlock?" he repeated again. "Can you hear me?"

To his surprise, Sherlock seemed to wince and blink,

momentarily focusing on John. Taking that as good as he was likely to get, John shifted to keep Sherlock's attention. "What have you taken?" he asked, trying desperately to keep his voice calm and steady.

"More," Sherlock breathed, closing his eyes as if pained.

More? What the hell was that meant to mean? Was that more cocaine than usual? Stronger drugs? Was the wanker actually asking for more?

"I don't know what you want," John mumbled as he looked around, hoping something could help him, yet the room remained belligerently still and quiet, as if he and Sherlock were in their own pocket world where life fucked up.

Pulse. He should check Sherlock's pulse. Shaking out his hands, John took a deep, steadying breath and reached for the pulse point at Sherlock's throat, fumbling a few times before he found the fast, mouse like patter that was Sherlock's heartbeat.

That might be normal for someone on cocaine. John had no idea how to gauge it, but it wasn't anywhere close to the normal rate for a sober human being. How was he meant to know how bad he was?

Mycroft. He needed to call Mycroft.

"Not for years though," Sherlock suddenly slurred as if he'd heard John's thoughts. John blinked at him and waited but Sherlock simply pulled a disapproving face, huffed and then let his head loll.

A hallucination? John pressed his hand to Sherlock's head again, feeling the oven like temperature radiating from the man. "You are such a prick," John muttered as he studied Sherlock, seeing the bulge in his front pocket from his phone. "Don't you ever just stop and think? Like...not your kind of thinking but just engaging brain and common sense? Are the neurons in your brain going so bloody quick that you don't bother to examine the solutions you come up with?" He slid closer and tried to work out how the hell he was going to get the phone out of Sherlock's pocket. "I need you to tell me what to do," he added with what sounded dangerously like a begging whine.

Sherlock remained silent.

"You never tell me anything," John grumbled as he reached for the pocket, pushing Sherlock back a little to give himself wriggle room to ease the phone out. Sherlock started to shake his head vehemently as if something crucial depended on the movement. "See how you like it," John huffed as he finally eased the damned thing free and sat back to scroll through Sherlock's contacts.

Despite how arsehole-ish Mycroft had seemed when John had met the man, there wasn't some weird code name in Sherlock's phone for him. Pressing the call button, John held the phone to his ear while keeping two fingers pressed reassuringly to Sherlock's throat to measure his pulse again.

Still too fast.

"Sherlock?" Mycroft sounded very awake for three in the morning.

"Uh, it's John? We met-"

"What is it?" Mycroft seemed to snap, which was an instant reminder that Mycroft had not dealt well with John's scrambling excuses.

"I..." John cleared his throat. "He's taken something," John said honestly. "I don't know what the hell it was but he's not responding, his pupils are blown and he's hot and hallucinating-"

"Where are you?" Mycroft asked, his tone no less demanding but different in some way. Concerned maybe?

"Back Door? The club that Sherlock goes to do...well he... it's a gay club," John said, slightly defeated. "We're in the office underneath."

"I'll be there soon," Mycroft said in a supremely calm sounding voice. "Do not let anyone in except for me."

He ended the call without any more instructions and John breathed a sigh of relief. The phone was sticky in his hands now and he pocketed it, not really wanting to deal with the smears. Catching his gaze on Sherlock's prone body, he swallowed and pressed his fingers into Sherlock's throat ensuring that the contact with his pulse was as strong as it could be.

It was strange just sitting in a room and watching Sherlock breathe. Oddly calming and utterly terrifying at the same time. In the endless silence, John became half-convinced that if he looked away, even for a second, that something would go dreadfully wrong. Time was hard to gauge; he almost ended up counting the waves of throbbing pain that danced around his head and the amount of times Sherlock blinked as if coming back to reality, only to then sink back down into whatever images his mind was conjuring up instead.

A knock at the door had John draw in a startled breath, not sure what to do. It only occurred to him as the door opened that he hadn't bothered to lock it, as caught up in Sherlock as he was, and that he was in no fit state to deal with anyone-

"John?" Mycroft asked as he entered.

"I...I didn't know if he needed an ambulance," John confessed. "I should have said-" he broke off when he saw the startled expression on Mycroft's face. "He-"

"What happened?" Mycroft asked, keeping his tone calm as he knelt down close to Sherlock.

"I don't know. I came back and-"

"No, what happened to you?" Mycroft asked. "This I have seen far too often."

"Fight," John said shortly. "Not sure if I won or not," he added, trying to joke as he watched Mycroft check Sherlock over. "Is he all right?"

"The worst has passed," Mycroft decided with a long sigh. "My brother would likely refer to this as a 'bad trip'." There was a pinched expression on his face as he drew back and returned his gaze to John. "I assume his current dealer didn't stay."

"Victor Trevor," John sighed, his lip throbbing in response to the name.

An expression flickered across Mycroft's face as his eyes narrowed, but was gone before John could decide what it was. "Does he look as bad as you do?" Mycroft asked, staying very still, as if all of his attention were focused on John.

It was a little unnerving.

"Broken nose," John said firmly. "And some bruises I'd guess."

Mycroft's gaze didn't waver and he seemed to study John. "Did the fight happen because of Sherlock?" Mycroft asked eventually.

"He wouldn't let me call an ambulance," John said, refusing to squirm. "It was..." he looked away finally. "We don't get on," he ended up saying heavily, which was stupid because why would Mycroft care about that?

"You..." Mycroft heaved a long sigh as if being in the same room with John was far too arduous to deal with. He looked down at Sherlock and then shook his head. "We need to get him home," Mycroft decided.

John nodded, not entirely sure he wanted to hear what Mycroft had been about to say.

With little pomp or ceremony, Sherlock was dumped onto his bed, eyes fluttering as he seemed to fight his way back to consciousness.

"He'll likely sleep it off now," Mycroft said with all the worldly knowledge of someone who had done this too many times. John stood, awkwardly watching, trying not to wonder exactly how many times Mycroft had done this.

"Should I tell him?" John asked slowly.

Mycroft's gaze flickered across John's face. "I don't think you could hide that from a blind man," he said with some disdain.

"That I called you," John corrected with a sigh. "He said

that you interfere." And fuck it, he was far too tired to care about how that sounded.

"He'll know," Mycroft said with a wave of his hand. "I will speak to him tomorrow anyway. He and I..." Mycroft drew in a long breath. "We need to discuss a few matters."

Great. "Couldn't you just get him arrested? I mean, you're a lawyer, right? Isn't that kind of what you do?"

Mycroft tilted his head, his expression unreadable. "I'm not entirely sure you understand the delicacy of the situation," he said eventually.

"We had a fight. He hit me, I hit him. We both look like shit. It's hardly delicate."

"And therein lies the problem," Mycroft said sharply. Startled, John frowned at him until Mycroft looked away. "You should stay with him tonight," Mycroft said firmly. "Keep an eye on him."

John nodded as he glanced back at Sherlock, surprised by how someone four years older could look so young. He ignored Mycroft as the man left the room, almost frozen in place as he stared at Sherlock.

Tonight could have gone so much worse.

"Here," Mycroft said, reappearing. "For your lip," he added as he held out something wrapped in a tea-towel. It felt like frozen peas when John took it and, wincing, he did as he was told.

"It is unwise to anger the sons of prominent drug dealers," Mycroft said quietly.

"Prominent?" John asked, pulling the peas away, the cold almost too much to cope with as he tried to talk to Mycroft. "It's hardly a respectable business."

Mycroft shot him a doubtful look but said nothing. "Stay here tonight," he said firmly. "If you need anything for Sherlock then let me know."

Seriously? "There's a Tesco's down the road-"

"Stay with him," came the stern order as Mycroft put his coat back on. "Do not leave this flat, John."

Oh. Swallowing, John looked down at Sherlock. "I thought you said-"

For a moment it seemed like Mycroft was about to say something but then he appeared to change his mind. "Better to be safe," Mycroft said in what might have been the nicest tone he'd ever used when talking to John. "Do not leave until I return tomorrow."

Right. "He's gonna hate being babysat like this," John said as he followed Mycroft out into the tiny lounge.

Mycroft made a weird, non-committal noise. "I will discuss this with you tomorrow," he said firmly as he opened the door.

The door closed softly behind him and John stared at it blankly, sure that he had missed something.

The floor was uncomfortable. John had ended up nicking a cushion from the sofa and propping it between his back and the wall to try and avoid getting that horrible numb feeling in his lower back. It really hadn't worked that well but at least it had kept him awake long enough to keep an eye on Sherlock.

It was about quarter to six when Sherlock finally stirred.

Worried, John crawled forward, not entirely sure if it was a positive sign or not. Switching on the bed side lamp, John peered down at Sherlock, hoping to get a better idea, and breathed in a sigh of relief when Sherlock frowned and recoiled slightly at the sudden brightness. His face was regaining some colour and his hair was stuck in awkward angles from the sweat that had bathed his body but he no longer looked ill.

Thank god.

Reaching out, mostly to reassure himself, John pressed two fingers to the pulse on Sherlock's throat, able to find it with unerring accuracy this time. The beat under his fingers was calmer, steadier and far more normal than it had been.

Sherlock's hands came up, awkwardly grabbing for the fingers that John was pressing against him. "Mycroft," Sherlock mumbled, apparently refusing to open his eyes. "You called Mycroft."

"Yeah," John said slowly. "Well..." he cleared his throat when the words threatened to stall. "Didn't think you'd appreciate being left on the floor of Back Door all night. Not the most comfortable place to be."

A hazel eye cracked open and stared at John before glancing at the cushion in the corner. "You're managing," Sherlock murmured, his face scrunched up and eyes drooping shut.

"I'm young," John replied softly, trying to make him smile a little. It was impossible not to stroke his hand through Sherlock's hair in an attempt to soothe him. "Go back to sleep," he instructed.

But Sherlock was shaking his head and frowning as if something important had occurred to him. Both eyes cracked open this time and his gaze fixed firmly on John. "What?" he managed to croak as he reached out with his hand as if to touch John's jaw, but his hands were far too uncoordinated to manage. "What happened?" he asked, sounding a lot more with it suddenly.

"Fight," John said simply. "Ask me about it tomorrow."

"Mm," Sherlock said, hands dropping to the mattress. He inhaled loudly and then lifted the covers. "Here," he ordered as he created a space for John.

"I'll be fine on the floor-"

"Get in," Sherlock said in what could only be described as a stroppy tone. "You're exhausted."

It probably wasn't the wisest plan. Probably wasn't anywhere close to being a wise plan, but John lay down in the area that Sherlock had indicated and felt a relieved shiver go through his muscles as he lay flat and warm once the covers were dropped. Sherlock shifted closer to him, spooning into his side and laying a propriety arm over John's stomach.

It was nice and endlessly reassuring to feel Sherlock's

breath against his neck. There was something about feeling the continuous warmth on his neck that matched the rise and fall of Sherlock's chest as it pressed against John's side that made him feel warmer than the duvet ever could. Turning a little, John placed a kiss to his forehead and breathed Sherlock in before he turned off the light.

Everything felt safe and cosy. It was that perfect morning sensation that made him want to bury back to sleep and ensure he stayed in the exact same position because he would never again be this comfortable. It was made all the better by the skin under John's lips. Feeling relaxed, he smiled and then froze when pain lanced through his entire lower jaw.

"You should have put more ice on it," Sherlock said, his voice sounding oddly flat.

Probably. John had no interest in dealing with it and moved closer to Sherlock's warmth. "Mm," he said after a moment. "You okay?"

There was a very long silence. "Did you hit him?" Sherlock asked in that same strange tone.

"Broke his nose," John yawned. "I think. Bled a lot," he added, half sure he could fall back to sleep again and desperate to try for it. He wriggled further into the bed and let out a contented noise.

It took a while to realise that Sherlock was lying stiffly in the bed, his breathing tight and tense. Stirring, John lifted his head to stare at Sherlock in confusion. "Are you mad at me?" he asked, baffled.

Sherlock's jaw was clicking as he stared up at the ceiling. "You broke Victor Trevor's nose," he said in a clipped, tight tone, as if it were taking Sherlock an inordinate amount of control not to hit John.

What?

John sat up and then immediately regretted it as his stomach churned and his vision blurred briefly. "You were hallucinating in the corner," John said to the wall, narrowing in on a slightly stained piece of wallpaper. It wasn't exactly the fanciest place that Sherlock had lived in. "And he wanted me to just watch you. What if you'd overdosed?"

"I do not overdose," Sherlock replied. "I'm not as stupid as other people."

That sounded like...John turned to stare at Sherlock whose eyes skipped away from his and instead lingered over John's face. "Are you seriously having a go at me for standing up for you?"

Sherlock rolled his eyes. "I do not need to be defended," he said, sitting up with fluid movements that seemed unfair given the state he was in last night.

It was so ridiculous that John felt himself huff out a laugh, though whether from shock or disbelief he had no idea. God knew that expecting Sherlock to acknowledge someone else had done something useful was probably as close to impossible as you were likely to get, but usually he made some sort of backhanded compliment.

"Yeah," John said as he eased himself out of the bed. "Won't do that again."

There was a long, heavy silence from behind him as John moved towards the door, and that pissed him off even more. The clear disapproval, as if he'd been wrong or stupid to try and look after Sherlock last night, rankled him until the idea of walking out seemed like backing away from a fight. Pausing with the door half open, John slammed it shut again and whirled back to Sherlock.

"What do you want from me?" John asked, staring angrily at Sherlock who was eyeing him up with obvious trepidation.

"Evidence that there's a brain in there somewhere," Sherlock sneered as he turned to sit on the edge of the bed and reached for his phone. It was almost as if he was bored by having John there.

Great.

"Fuck this," John hissed. "I'm done."

He wrenched open the door and strode out into the living room, aiming straight for the exit.

"John," Sherlock called from his room. Not sure why he turned, John glanced back to see Sherlock leaning against the door frame, phone in his hand and an odd expression on his face. It seemed to take an age for Sherlock to decide what he wanted to say. "You shouldn't have hit him."

Bloody hell. "You didn't hit him. You didn't ask me to. I'm sure I haven't ruined you and your boyfriend's special time-"

Sherlock's free hand practically clawed through his hair. "You are so unbelievably stupid," he sneered, as if pained by the very idea of John.

"Fine. I'm stupid. So why the hell did you follow me home or bother to be my friend? If I'm that much of an irritation-"

Sherlock leaned his head against the door frame and muttered something at the wood. "You," he said loudly and then drifted off with a shake of his head.

"What?" John demanded as he strode forward. There seemed to be no answers forthcoming. "I...what?" the very word seemed to stick to his tongue because Sherlock Holmes defied reason and logic, despite spouting it off everywhere he went. "What did you even take last night?" John asked, just to have something concrete to ask.

It seemed to confuse Sherlock enough that he actually answered. "Speedball," he said, sounding almost surprised himself. "It was speedball," he repeated, looking away as if something about that didn't sit right with him.

As soon as the idiot deigned to look back over, John made movements with his hands that must have reminded Sherlock that, unlike him, John wasn't exactly an expert.

"Heroin and cocaine," Sherlock said, pushing off the door frame and turning back to his room.

What?

"How is that a-" John cut himself off, furious. "You call me thick?"

"I called you stupid," Sherlock corrected as he wandered

back to his room to pull on a hoodie. John hovered, not too sure whether to follow him in or storm out. The indecision kept him rooted in place. Baffled, John closed his eyes as he tried to work out where the hell to go with that.

"Is that a normal thing to take?" John asked, opening his eyes slowly as Sherlock rubbed at the back of his neck and adjusted the hoodie slightly.

Sherlock shook his head, a flicker of frustration crossing his face. Seeing Sherlock look anything less than annoyingly confident was strange and massively wrong. "Why did you take it then?"

For the first time since they had met, Sherlock actually shrugged.

Shrugged.

"What does that mean?" John asked, trying to work it out. "Did he make you-"

"You are not this much of an idiot usually," Sherlock complained, turning away and attempting to make the bed in way that even John thought showed shit effort.

"Are you still high?" John asked as he watched Sherlock actually clean for once.

"You were dancing," Sherlock snapped suddenly, throwing the pillow onto the bed with sudden violence.

"And that drove you to drugs?" John asked in disbelief. "I'm not that bad at- Wait." He thought it through for a moment. Sherlock's weird kisses when they'd met and his offers of sex had faded away until John had thought...but his reaction to John at Back Door suggested something entirely different.

It was probably a left-over concussion that made John step closer and risk, well...talk about the thing that they'd both avoided for months. "So, you were jealous?"

There was a sharp noise as Sherlock clicked his tongue behind his teeth. "Do not get ideas," he said tightly. "I have no interest in a relationship."

"I don't want a relationship with you," John snarled back on automatic, even as his brain stuttered over the idea and found it far too appealing giving how bloody insane the man was. "Would you fucking well turn around so I can have a proper conversation with you?"

Sherlock stared up at the ceiling in exasperation and then turned. His eyes jumped straight to John's cheek and then his eyes. He winced at the sight and shook his head. He dug his phone out of his pocket and glanced at it again.

"You said you'd stay until Mycroft arrived," Sherlock said, stepping around John like he was a piece of furniture.

God, he was far too tired for this. John trailed out into the lounge and collapsed on the sofa as he tried to work out what the hell he was meant to do with that information. Closing his eyes, he doubled over and groaned into his hands.

A bag of peas wrapped in a bath towel was pushed in front of him. "Use this," Sherlock said, sitting down next to him. "You have no idea how terrible you look."

John sighed as he pressed the ice-cold parcel to his face. "I think I do."

Sherlock was quiet again which seemed so unnatural for him. "So," John said, turning a little so he could face him. "I hit someone that I shouldn't have and you took something monumentally stupid. Call it even?"

He expected a flicker of a smile but Sherlock's lips didn't so much as twitch. Instead, he sat back into the sofa cushion with his elbow on the arm of the chair and rubbed his index finger over his lips in thought.

"Is this going to cause you trouble?" John asked, not quite able to voice the secret hope that if it caused trouble for Sherlock's drug supply it wouldn't really be the worst thing in the world. But Sherlock shook his head slowly, his eyes studying John's hands.

"And," John felt his voice falter, slightly fearful of the consequences of what he was about to say, "you were jealous?"

Sherlock's hand dropped from his face back down to the arm of the sofa. "I told you," he said firmly. "I don't want-"

"I'm so sick of everything being so serious," John

complained. "Let's...I..." God he probably sounded like such a moron. "We can have sex and be friends."

Sherlock's head tilted sharply, like a bird narrowing in on prey but he said nothing.

"Just something to think about," John muttered as he squirmed, a little uncomfortable.

"John-"

And, as sod's law would have it, Mycroft chose that exact moment to walk through the door.

CHAPTER ELEVEN:

Getting Lucky

I T HAD SEEMED LIKE THE wisest plan was to flee while the Holmes brothers discussed Sherlock's moronic decision to take Speedball, like that was what normal people talked about. John still couldn't get his head around it, even after spending the entire day in his room, pissing away the day and pressing anything cold to his face in the hopes it would keep down the swelling. It was only late into the evening that he admitted defeat and (once he heard the door go and the room outside go quiet) snuck out to get some food, only to run straight into Andy.

"What the hell happened to your face?" Andy asked around the piece of toast that was hanging from his mouth.

"Fight," John replied shortly as he strode into the kitchen.

"No shit," Andy said with a large gulp as he swallowed down his toast. "With who?"

John pressed his lips together as he opened the cupboard, wincing as the aches and pains made themselves known. "Doesn't matter," he said eventually, trying to avoid Andy's gaze which was hard given that the git had followed him into the kitchen.

"Hmm," Andy said, lifting himself up to sit on the only free space of the counter that wasn't covered by dirty plates, cups and cans. "Let me guess. Was it Sherlock or Victor?"

Great. "Victor," John said as he leaned back against the counter opposite Andy and started eating a pop tart.

"Did you get him back?" Andy asked.

John nodded, not feeling quite as triumphant about it as he had hoped he would.

"Why'd you do it?"

"He-" John hesitated briefly. "Have you heard of speedball?" he asked quietly.

Andy nodded and then winced. "Sherlock took it?"

"Yeah," John said. "He was out of it. Victor kept giving me orders and I wanted to take him to the hospital. We...I dunno. Sherlock wasn't exactly pleased about it this morning," he added as he finished the pop tart and rubbed the crumbs from his hands.

"I bet," Andy said with a pointed look.

"Andy-"

"I know. You don't-" Andy frowned, looking a little stuck before he shrugged the idea away. "Fuck I'm way too hungover," he murmured. "But John, Sherlock...he does care about you."

"Yeah, maybe." Crap, he was waffling again. "He said he didn't like watching me dance so..." John steeled himself, though it was hardly as if Andy could judge. "I asked him if...I asked him if he wanted to just shag and still be friends."

"While you looked like that?" Andy asked doubtfully, a grin starting to creep across his face. "How the fuck did you two manage?"

"We didn't," John said. "His brother turned up so I never heard his answer." He caught sight of Andy's disbelieving look. "The drugs are a big issue between them. It's never a good idea to stay with them while they discuss it."

"Bet ya," Andy said after taking a minute to absorb that idea, "fifty quid that Sherlock is here tomorrow to take you up on that."

Yeah, John wasn't quite so sure. "You didn't see him this morning. He was supremely pissed off."

"With you? Nah," Andy said, jumping off the counter.

"Fifty quid then? Think about it – either you get fifty quid or sex," he said with a grin.

True. John nodded and shook Andy's hand. "Come on," he said. "May as well see if I can beat your arse at Call of Duty as well."

"You wish," Andy laughed.

The next evening, John tried to demand the money from Andy. It was only when the following morning rolled around that Andy, looking more confused than disappointed, gave John the money.

John left it a week before he found himself pissed off enough that he decided to hell with it, he may as well have it out with Sherlock. Either they argued and that would be that or...or...

Well, he wasn't really sure what would happen but somehow it seemed as any alternative would be worse than them fighting.

His face was healed enough now that he didn't get suspicious looks from people at the bus stop anymore. It was as if the minute a guy in his late teens or early twenties turned up with clear evidence of recently being in a fight people decided that they needed to move their shopping bags away from him. Like he'd been trying to steal from Asda's or something.

There was part of John that kind of suspected Sherlock wouldn't be living in the same place as he had been last time but it seemed worth a try anyway. The lift was broken so John hauled himself up eight floors and into the hall.

A man was coming out of Sherlock's flat and for the life of him, John couldn't think of a reason why the man would have any business with Sherlock. He was older, bearded and his long coat had a few patches where the material had worn away. As he got closer, he could see that some of the stains had been bleached out, leaving lighter patches in the almost dirty tan coloured fabric.

John felt his heart sink as he glanced at what had been Sherlock's door then back at the man again.

"Is-" John started, stepping into the man's path with an apologetic look. "Does Sherlock Holmes still live here?"

A suspicious look was cast towards him. "Why?"

Why? That almost sounded like the man was covering for Sherlock rather than claiming not to know him. "I'm his friend," John said because damn it, until Sherlock said otherwise, that was the story John was gonna stick to.

The suspicious look simply switched to a doubtful one and the man scoffed. "Ring the bell and find out," he suggested before turning and walking away.

Right.

Refusing to let his nerves overtake him, John braced himself and knocked on the door.

The door was yanked open. "What could you possibly have forgotten?" Sherlock's voice faded away as he stared at John before shifting his gaze to the hall behind. Seconds passed before Sherlock gave a nod to what John assumed was probably the man waiting at the end of the hall.

"Did I pass?" John asked sarcastically.

That seemed to regain Sherlock's attention. "Why are you here?" he asked blankly. It was enough to make John pause for a moment, feeling unbelievably unsure about the situation. Refusing to be cowed, John tilted his chin and looked pointedly at the lounge over Sherlock's shoulder, not really wanting to talk to Sherlock with a witness.

In the end, an irritated sigh was all he got in response as Sherlock stepped to one side and allowed him entrance. There were boxes; half of Sherlock's things were in them and the rest were strewn around the floor in piles. It was probably the most organised John had seen Sherlock when it came to moving.

It hardly helped that Sherlock sat on the sofa, oddly

reminiscent of a king on a throne as he swept a hand at John, as if commanding him to start talking.

"You're a dick," John said simply.

A frown burrowed its way in-between Sherlock's eyebrows. "And you felt the need to come all this way to tell me that?" he asked, sounding a little less confident.

"I haven't heard from you in a week," John said, folding his arms. "And-"

"I haven't heard from you either," Sherlock defended.

"Are we still friends?" John asked, staring down at Sherlock and feeling perverse relief that Sherlock looked slightly panicked at the question.

"Why wouldn't we be?" Sherlock asked, sitting up properly.

"Last week you-" John broke off and tried again. "Clearly what happened with Victor-"

Sherlock waved a hand dismissively. "I overreacted," he said. "It's been dealt with." He cleared his throat and shifted, his pose still as arrogant as before but his expression faltering a little and ruining the effect. "Anything else?"

He was being weird. "Okay then," John said slowly. "So why are you still pissed off with me?"

"John, whatever histrionic idiocy you have concocted-"

"Don't," John said simply. "Don't do that. Is this 'cause I brought up having sex then?"

Sherlock froze, as if one wrong move would set off some kind of bomb. "I...that was...no," he said awkwardly.

"That was no?" John asked doubtfully. "Is that your answer?"

Sherlock's hazel eyes narrowed at him. "That was your answer," came the snappish reply.

"Because you said that I was interesting and that you wanted to try different things. It was hardly-" John drew in a frustrated breath. "You've still never said that you want to have sex with me."

Sherlock stared at him and John could practically hear

the insults he was being called in Sherlock's head. And his damned lack of answer made the whole thing a million times more awkward.

And he was trying so hard not to think about what Victor had implied last week.

"Doesn't matter," John said, trying not to let it show on his face how surprised he was when his voice remained strong and even. "We can just...we're good friends, right? And now that it's off the table, we'll be better, right?"

God only knew who he was trying to convince. Sherlock leaned back, a surprised look on his face as he slowly nodded. "That would probably be the most sensible option."

Okay, wow. John sucked in a long breath and sat on the coffee table. "Okay," he said, staring down at his hands. "Okay so-"

He barely managed to look up when he was suddenly aware of Sherlock in his space, lips close to his and hands bracketing his body.

Huh? Glancing down at Sherlock's hands, John swallowed deeply, hating that he could almost hear the nervous gulp. "You literally just said-"

"That it wouldn't be sensible," Sherlock said, leaning even closer and nuzzling at John's chin with his nose. "But," he breathed as his mouth slowly ghosted across John's jaw and drifted gently up to his ear. "I want you," he finished with certainty.

John turned his face, finding Sherlock's mouth with his own which earned him a pleased noise from the man. Kissing Sherlock was...John hummed in pleasure at the feeling. Sherlock's hands slid from the table, up John's back to pull him forward onto Sherlock's lap. The warmth and contact like this was different to what they had previously. This was more desperate, more full on.

John slid his hands down Sherlock's front, his neck craning as he tried to keep their lips together, even as his hands scrabbled at Sherlock's stomach to find the hem of his t-shirt, intending to lift it as far as he could but-

"I'm not taking the job," John warned, detaching his lips with effort. "If this is what this is."

Sherlock rolled his eyes and leaned in for another kiss before he seemed to process John's words. Leaning back, he frowned up at John. "Job?"

"Victor," John said, shifting on Sherlock's lap. "He said that if I dealt with him that he'd..." John pulled a face, all too aware that he had absolutely no idea how to phrase it.

"Of course you won't deal for him," Sherlock said, tracing his teeth over John's collarbone. "How stupid do you think I am?" he asked as his hands climbed John's back, lifting his shirt as they went.

John grinned and leaned to the side, letting them both sink down into the sofa which was a mistake because suddenly they were a bundle of arms and legs and pointy knees, sharp elbows and sensitive bits. Laughing, John found himself on his back and staring up at Sherlock as his shirt was yanked off and thrown off to the side. Pulling Sherlock back down, John hummed with content into his mouth, working to finally get Sherlock's t-shirt off.

"Why would you dealing affect this?" Sherlock asked suddenly, sitting up and away from John's hands.

"Huh?" Like John could follow Sherlock's thoughts at this moment.

With visible irritation, Sherlock glared down at him. "Why would us doing this make you refuse a job? Unless-" Sherlock tilted his head to the side and then swore viciously. "I wouldn't have sex with you to get you to deal drugs," he said, sounding hurt.

"I know," John said, trying to work out if it would be a good idea to tug down Sherlock's jeans. Slowly, his brain started to come back online. "But...did you? Do that? Have sex with people for his deals?"

Sherlock stared down at him and then leaned in. "I had

sex with who I wanted to have sex with," he said clearly. "If it killed two birds with one stone then all the better."

"Who you found interesting?" John asked quietly.

Sherlock smirked. "Yes," he breathed, wriggling down ever so slightly to get at John's neck. "You are interesting," he said as his teeth dragged across John's skin. "And different," he added. His lips returned to John's suddenly, kissing him with frantic nips and touches that left John breathless. "Now stay still," he ordered, ducking back down to John's chest, hands going for John's jeans. He glanced up at John with wry amusement. "You don't need to look quite so nervous," he said pressing a kiss to John's hip. "You have had a blow job before."

Eleven of them.

"Yeah," he mumbled as he hid his face with his arm, sure that it was heating up in embarrassment.

Sherlock gripped him by the hips and straightened him out a little. "Leg," he ordered, taking no notice of John's mortification apparently. Confused by the frank, brisk order, John dropped his elbow off of his face to stare down at Sherlock questioningly.

God that was a good image.

John first moved one leg as directed until it was over Sherlock's shoulder, then the other one. He found himself licking his lips as Sherlock slid his hands under John's arse and up to his hips to hold John, very much in control of everything he did with his hips.

Then Sherlock lowered his mouth.

John let out a strangled cry. He'd forgotten how bloody amazing this felt; lips and tongue and warm, wet heat. He tried to keep himself utterly still, as A~~nn~~a Amy had once requested, and twisted his head against the cushion, trying to keep quiet.

Then Sherlock's wonderful mouth disappeared and he suddenly leaned up, John's legs still on his shoulders.

John had no idea he could be that bendy.

"I told you she was insipid," Sherlock muttered, frowning.

"Huh?"

"Stop tensing, stop holding back and do not bite your lip," Sherlock ordered before he slunk back down and resumed his previous actions.

Experimentally, John let his hips snap forward a little when Sherlock did a particularly wicked thing with his mouth and was rewarded with a praising stroke of his hips and a pleased noise.

It was impossible not to watch. Awed at the sight, John hesitantly lowered a hand to Sherlock's head and gently, careful to exert no pressure, started to stroke his soft nut-brown hair.

Sherlock's tongue became torturously mind blowing and suddenly John panicked because there was no way he could hold off too much longer and it seemed terrifyingly quick to blow his load but Sherlock wasn't slowing down.

He should probably tell Sherlock.

"Close," he whispered, dropping his hand from Sherlock's hair to let him pull away easily.

Sherlock's tongue just kept going.

Shit!

And then John was caught in a strangely wonderful cycle of almost going over and holding himself back to give Sherlock time to pull away. John tried to wriggle his hips back but Sherlock's grip turned to iron.

Fuck, fuck- fuck!

Mentally apologising, John turned his head to the side and, not wanting to bite at his already sore lip, shoved a knuckle into his mouth instead just before he tumbled over.

It was amazing! Endless waves that made his toes curl and fingers ache. Sherlock wrung every ounce of pleasure from him, every wave was followed by a smaller one until John collapsed. He winced as he straightened out his slightly gnawed knuckle.

A careful hand pulled his knuckle down to examine it and John watched Sherlock frown at them.

"Sorry," John squirmed. "I...that was fantastic!"

"Travesty," Sherlock muttered under his breath.

Horrified, John froze.

"No," Sherlock wriggled back up to him. "Not you. Your education in this. This would not have happened had you said yes to me the first time," he added, almost petulantly.

Unsure, John watched him, trying to catch some glimmer of an explanation from the man above. "So it wasn't dreadful?"

"You would be the judge of that given that it was I who was performing," Sherlock replied, looking amused.

"Do you-"

"Want you to help me pack?" Sherlock asked as he sat up. "Yes. See, we trade."

John huffed a laugh into the sofa and stretched, enjoying how relaxed he suddenly felt. "In a bit," he bargained.

A box was shoved onto his bare stomach making him groan at the weight. "Try to be a bit quicker," Sherlock suggested as he strode off back to his room.

Okay then. "I'll do you later then, yeah?"

"Pack," Sherlock's voice echoed from the bedroom.

Jesus, in a bit.

Andy shot John an amused look when he walked back in. "Want my fifty back," he said, practically preening from the sofa.

"You said within twenty-four hours," John argued as he skulked back towards his room. "And how did you know?"

Paul, who was staring at the TV turned around and tapped his neck with a pointed look. Baffled, John strode into his room and pulled open the wardrobe to stare in the mirror at the love bite nibbled into his neck.

Fucking Sherlock.

"Great," John said, walking back out.

"Marking his territory," Andy said with a grin. "He wants the whole world to know you're his boyfriend," he mocked in a baby voice that made John cringe.

"Fuck buddy," John corrected. "We're not together."

Andy and Paul exchanged a long look. "Who decided that?" Paul asked cautiously.

"Seemed best," John said dismissively. "What?" he asked when they both stared at him in disbelief.

"Nothing," Paul said quickly, looking back at the TV. Seconds later, he glared at Andy who hadn't stopped looking at John.

"Uh..." Andy nodded and then turned back to the program like his life depended on it. "Good for you?" he said, sounding uncertain. "Two," he added, as if hedging his bets.

Their reaction was weird. "Drop it," John ordered as he sank into the sofa and kicked at Andy for some foot space.

"Dropped," Andy agreed. "Completely dropped."

Still slightly suspicious, John settled into his seat and stared at the screen, trying not to smile.

CHAPTER TWELVE:

Andy's four Simple Rules to Success

"So," ANDY ASKED AS HE bounced himself down next to John. "How goes the dumb arse idea?"

"You wanna give me more to work with?" John asked as he looked up at Andy over the medical book he was studying. It was his own private triumph that the book was getting stuffed full of post-it notes and pencil notes in the margins. Almost like he was a real medical student.

"You and Sherlock," Andy explained as he shuffled into the other corner of the sofa. "Fucking," he added helpfully as he tried to tap a rhythm onto the cover of John's book with a sock covered toe.

"Fine," John replied shortly. "How are you and Cindy?"

Andy tilted his head in question, mouthing the name thoughtfully.

"Three weeks ago," John replied drily.

"Big boobs?" Andy asked.

"Red head," John said as he looked back down at his text book.

"Oh..." Andy said, as if that were a revelation. "Yeah, she was..." Andy nodded, "not one of my best friends who I started shagging so not anywhere near the same. Don't change the subject," he said, punctuating each of his last few words with a tap of his toe onto the book. "Is it weird?"

Weird? "No," John said, feeling a familiar, weary resignation fall over him. "Just...finding out a bit more," he said slowly.

154

"Like?"

John tilted his head. "Are you turning into a teenage girl? This is like gossiping," he said with distaste.

"Yeah, well. You're gay now. Get used to it," Andy said without care.

John rolled his eyes and sunk down the arm of the sofa. "Bi," he groaned, trying to block out Andy's face with his book. "Or just...fuck off, why do you care?"

"Because I want a gay best friend who can help me pull fit girls," Andy said frankly. "You're like Mecca, John. A mate, not competition-"

"Bi," John reiterated and then resisted the urge to throttle Andy when the man just waved him off.

"Anyway," Andy said pointedly. "Back to you and Sherlock."

"He-" John sighed and put the book to one side, peering up at Andy who was still grinning down at him. "I dunno. He hasn't read any books that we did at school, barely watches TV or films. Basically, unless it's a horror or a crime themed, he doesn't want to know. Has to have a mystery. Watched true crime shows for three hours the other night. The TV did one of those countdown things about criminals, all the way from James Armitage to Steven Wright and we had to watch because it was 'useful'. You should have heard the rant he gave when he caught me watching the Lion King the other day." John hissed as that piece of information left his lips, but Andy seemed content to let it slide. For now.

"Fratricide didn't count then?" Andy asked instead.

"I mentioned that but I got this stupid rant about how lions aren't people as if I was a moron," John muttered. "Got the entire plot of 39 Steps though. And a never-ending comparison between it and the film and book. And Hitchcock. Never talk to him about that. It never ends."

Andy grinned. "Could have told you that," he said. "It was on late one night. I called it crap. We didn't speak for a while."

Reluctantly enjoying the discussion, John shimmied up a little from his slouch. "Okay, so we bumped into Jack

Robinson, you know, the guy on Paul's course who switched to do philosophy? I thought Sherlock would know all about that stuff but he listened for one whole minute and then stood up and walked away shaking his head. Pretty sure he thinks it's a waste of time. That and politics."

"That's probably Mycroft's fault," Andy said.

"He knows law though," John argued.

"That's probably the drugs fault," Andy said in the same tone, making John feel a bit like a traitor when his lips twitched.

"Knows a lot about them too," John said with a sigh. "It's a pain in the arse." He tried to ignore the sinking feeling that came hand in hand with any thoughts about the drugs.

"What else?" Andy asked, tapping at his arm. "Come on. Impress me with your knowledge."

John shifted, a little uncomfortable before he focused fully on Andy. "You want something," he decided.

The eye roll that he was given confirmed it and Andy shifted forward seriously, rubbing his hands together thoughtfully. "The guys and I had a chat."

"And?" John asked, sitting up straight and steeling himself even as a flicker of anger rushed through him. He couldn't quite decide whether to hold on to it or not.

"You and Sherlock. Doing this. You know it's stupid, right? I mean even before this there were some serious sparks."

"Sparks?" John asked, feeling his voice flatten with how unimpressed he was.

"We just...okay so you say that you don't want to be more than fuck buddies?"

"We aren't more than-"

"So, maybe you should have some rules to ensure that you don't...that no-one gets hurt."

That...wasn't as bad as it could have been, John decided. Relaxing a little, he stared at Andy's sincere brown eyes and then gave up. "What rules?" he asked, rubbing a hand over his forehead.

"So," Andy started with a worrying amount of enthusiasm, "no dates. Or dinners."

"We eat out all the time," John muttered.

Andy sniggered at that. "Okay well, no paying for each other's dinners or having intimate meals, just the two of you."

He could do that.

Sherlock had him against the wall, kissing him frantically despite the fact it was freezing out and John's back felt like an ice-cube.

Shivering, John pulled away, "Wanna swap positions?"

"The wall's cold," Sherlock said with a smirk.

"I'm aware of that," John muttered pointedly. It made Sherlock's smirk turn into a grin but he stepped back and made an impatient 'get on with it' gesture. Taking him up on it, John stepped forward towards Sherlock's lips again. "Why haven't we been doing this all week again?" he asked in-between kisses.

"You," Sherlock nipped at his now healed lip, "were injured."

John's stomach rumbled loudly in answer.

"Come on." Sherlock pulled back from him.

They wound their way through the streets and John, vaguely bemused at Sherlock's route home, let himself be dragged along.

Until it became obvious they were going to a restaurant and Andy's list rang in John's ears, loud and clear.

"I have cold pizza at home," John said as he stopped suddenly.

Sherlock stopped to turn and look at him, seemingly baffled. "What relevance does that have to this?" he asked. "It's a Spanish restaurant."

"Yeah...uh...I haven't got enough money on me so I'll find a cash point."

"It's fine. I can pay."

Shit. "Okay...should I see if anyone else fancies Spanish food?" John started to pat his pockets looking for his phone.

Sherlock was looking at him as if he'd gone mad. "Why?"

Somehow, John didn't think the whole rule thing would go down well. "Why don't we just um...go there," John said brightly as he pointed.

Sherlock turned slowly in the direction of the McDonald's and stared. John felt a strange flicker of relief, despite the fact that Sherlock was staring at the place as if he'd never seen anything like it before in his life. There was no way that anyone could call that a date. The posh git probably hadn't ever been in one.

"No." Sherlock's voice was very firm, as if John had just suggested they play with syphilis. "I am not paying for that."

"I'll pay."

"You said you had no money," Sherlock said as he whirled on John. The whole thing was not going to plan at all. With a huff, John folded his arms, deeply uncomfortable.

"I said I didn't have enough money for that place," John tried to explain, determinedly not looking at Sherlock, even though that would probably piss the man off even more.

Sherlock's jaw twitched. "Go have your cold pizza, I have things to do," he snapped suddenly.

Helplessly, John watched him turn to storm off. Without any conscious effort on his part, the words bubbled out of his mouth. "It's in the rules," he called, and then inwardly winced when Sherlock stopped, seeming to pause for thought before he turned around.

"Rules?" Sherlock queried.

"For this situation," John said delicately. "To avoid complications. No dates."

Sherlock actually seemed to be seriously considering that, which was weird. "And how does Andy define no dates?"

John wasn't even gonna bother asking how he knew that.

"I dunno. Not eating with just each other or paying for each other. Whatever it is that people do on dates."

Sherlock looked away, his head tilting as if he were batting the idea around in his mind.

"Right," he said, turning to stride up the street. Not entirely sure what it was Sherlock found to be 'right' about the situation, John stayed where he was and watched Sherlock walk away.

"John," Sherlock called, still not turning around.

Was that a summons? Slowly, John walked after him, not quite fast enough to catch up and lose the admittedly rather nice sight of Sherlock's arse underneath his leather jacket.

"Must you?" Sherlock asked as he turned down another street. "Or are there rules about my arse too?"

"Pretty sure you'd dictate those," John called, feeling suddenly more at ease. Jogging a little to catch up, John fell into step beside Sherlock. "So where are we going?"

"To find company," Sherlock said, reaching out to pull at John's arm and steer him around a sharp corner.

"Company?" John asked. "Is this company people that you know or are we just finding some random strangers?"

The smallest smile crossed Sherlock's face and he slowed down a little. "I'm not having dinner with random strangers," he said. "It's not far."

"So these are your friends?" John asked, enjoying the easy pace they had set. Across from them a main road buzzed and lit up the street with the lights from a theatre.

"We share interests," Sherlock allowed. "Here," he said, turning them abruptly down a road and towards a rather fancy looking hotel.

"You can't pay for me," John muttered as they walked up the steps. "How much is-"

Sherlock steered him away from the menu that was nailed to the wall and through the doors. "We have company," he said, as if that somehow erased John's argument or as if Sherlock had decided that this was going to be the day where he proved *that he actually had been taught manners by whoever the hell it was that had raised him and Mycroft.*

There was a group of people that Sherlock steered John towards. Two who looked like they were in his parents' generation and two who seemed to be roughly the same age as Sherlock.

"Sherlock," a woman from the group called out with a smile. "How lovely to see you again, darling." She stood to greet Sherlock who responded with impeccable manners rather than the disinterest that he usually showed. "Sherlock, you know my father, Stuart."

There was an odd smirk on Sherlock's face. "Stuart," he said, shaking the man's hand. "How is the banking business?"

Banking?

Sherlock knew someone in banking and was pleasant to their face? John blinked in disbelief.

"And this is?" the woman asked.

"Ah," Sherlock said, turning to John. He glanced at the two other men and then looked back at John. "This is my uh... friend," he said with such an awkward look that John was almost taken aback by it. "John."

"Lara," the woman said, introducing herself. "And this is Clark and his son Julian. Would you care to join us?"

"We couldn't impose." Sherlock looked around again as if uncomfortable. "We...um..."

"Stay," Julian urged with a smile. "Please. Lara and her father have been so generous. It would be lovely to meet more of her friends."

Sherlock looked down at him and smiled- wait. Had Sherlock just smiled shyly?

Sherlock could smile shyly?

Not too sure what else to do, John stepped back as a waiter pushed another table next to the one the four were sitting at and brought over some chairs. Somehow, Sherlock ended up next to Julian and John was between Sherlock and Stuart.

This was so not what he'd had in mind.

Thankfully, the food made up for it. Sherlock ordered for him in an off-handed manner while he and Lara talked with Julian. Not long after, a plate of steak and chips appeared and John couldn't have given a crap about how awkward the dinner was because the food was probably the best he'd had in months.

Then a hand crept along John's leg.

It made John pause, not because he wondered who it was but because so far Sherlock had been acting like a completely different person for half the night. Turning a little to catch a glimpse of Sherlock's face, John raised an eyebrow at him in question.

And then blinked at the amount of empty glasses that were being collected. Across from him Julian's father seemed to see the same thing and frowned in disapproval.

"Spanish would have been better," Sherlock murmured, his voice just for John's ears alone.

"You seem to be doing okay," John replied quietly.

Sherlock's head turned, facing John more square on and his expression dropped for a moment as he rolled his eyes. Then he winked and sat back again, swirling his drink around his glass even as his hand climbed higher up John's thigh.

"That business proposal you offered my father last week," Sherlock said suddenly to Stuart, "has he been in touch with you?"

Father? Sherlock's father was dead. John was pretty sure about that. Mostly sure-

"I believe he wasn't sure about it the last time I discussed it with him," Stuart said thoughtfully.

Somehow, someway, an apologetic look crossed Sherlock's face. "He did say he wasn't going to go for it."

Stuart looked as if he'd expected the news but was disappointed anyway.

"Cigarette?" Sherlock said, leaning back to look at Lara and

Julian. Julian started to nod but seemed to catch his father's eye and slumped in disappointment before he shook his head. Lara nodded eagerly and slipped out of her seat. "Order me a coffee, please father?"

Sherlock nodded at that. "An espresso."

"Of course," Stuart said with an indulgent smile as the pair walked away. Julian watched them longingly and his eyes drifted down Sherlock's back.

John glanced at Clark to see an ugly expression cross his face for a moment. Great.

"I'll see if I can find that damned waiter," Stuart decided as he checked his wallet. Clark glanced at the movement then smiled as if pleased by something.

"Don't you dare try paying the bill," Clark said in a tone that even John could tell was false.

Stuart laughed it off and shook his head as he headed for the desk.

And then there were three. John opened his mouth but the expression on Clark's face made him close it again, dissuaded from making small talk.

"I might just..." he trailed off and pointed vaguely over his shoulder in the direction that Sherlock had gone in.

"I would," Clark said coldly.

Right.

Standing, John slid out from the table and threaded his way awkwardly through the restaurant and out to the front of the hotel where there was no-one to be seen. Pausing on the step in confusion and letting his breath fog in front of his face, John looked left and right as he did his coat up tightly against the chilly night air.

A hand pulled him back and he could feel Sherlock laughing behind him. "Magnificent," he whispered into John's ear and then steered him down a side road.

Lara and Stuart were waiting in a taxi but Lara's hair had changed and was now red and curly while Stuart had loosened his tie and had a softer, more amused look on his face. "Police?" Stuart asked.

Sherlock shook his head. "Related to one though," he said, leaning briefly into the taxi. "Not a wise choice," he added with an almost rebuking tone.

There was a noise from the restaurant they'd come from and Sherlock looked up, meerkat like, and seemed to stare thoughtfully before he pushed John into the taxi. "They were quicker than expected," Sherlock said as he followed John into the taxi.

Lara laughed. "The great Sherlock Holmes miscalculated."

Sherlock scowled as he tapped the button that allowed them to talk to the driver. "Vauxhall," he demanded and Lara groaned.

"South of the river?" she asked in some disgust.

"If I help you with your marks then you should drop me off where I ask," Sherlock replied in a snooty manner. "And John," he added with a pleased smile.

"Who paid?" John asked curiously, tilting his head.

They all smiled.

"They were a poor choice," Sherlock mused. "You're better at picking marks, usually," he added with a slightly arrogant sneer. "Still, it was an interesting place to eat," he said as he locked gazes with John.

"Oh." Oh. Had they just...John glanced through the back window of the taxi and then sighed. Well, no-one had paid for anyone else he supposed. That hadn't broken Andy's rules.

"And," Andy said, leaning back as if he were enjoying himself. "Condoms."

Huh? John slammed the medical book down pointedly and glared at Andy. "I'm a doctor," he said. "I know this bit."

"Yeah," Andy said. "But you know jack shit about heat of the moment and having gay sex."

Which, John had to admit, was a fair statement. "So I should buy some," he said quietly.

Packets of condoms were thrown at his face and John sighed as they landed with a smack in his lap. Then there was another thud as a bottle of, oh god, lube was added to the pile.

"I don't even know what to say to that," John said as he stared thoughtfully at the pile in his lap.

"Say that I'm a generous bastard," Andy said, shifting on the sofa to get comfortable. "I've gotta go back to campus to get some more now. Do you have any idea how long that's gonna be?"

***

October 10th

There were certain things that Sherlock liked to watch. Certain things that John hated.

Like horror films.

It was the only reason why Sherlock was over the day after Andy's birthday when they were all nursing hangovers and half-heartedly sharing a takeaway.

Obeying his own rules for not being in a relationship, John hadn't sat near Sherlock. Instead, he sat on the beanbag that the house had somehow acquired (probably through Paul who became part magpie when he was drunk).

They were on the third horror film of the day and John was already starting to feel bored. If it had been interspersed with an action film or two...or three then perhaps he would have been more aware and interested, but as it was he was half dozing and only staying put because he was too tired to even think about moving.

"Human centipede," suggested Andy who, by some awful quirk of fate, was closest to the television.

John glanced at Sherlock who was the only person not hungover but seemed almost as bad as they did, which probably meant he was coming off of something else entirely. What was worrying was that Sherlock stiffened and then settled back as if about to be deeply amused by what was about to happen.

It didn't take long to work out why. Paul yelped and turned away, covering his entire face with his arm while Mike tried to wrestle his way past Andy to the television. All the while Andy cackled with laughter and Sherlock watched, a smile tugging his lips as he watched the drama.

"You're a wanker," John hissed at him, trying desperately not to look at the television. When he risked a glance in the direction of the yelling from the sofa as Mike and Andy rolled around for the remote, he caught sight of Sherlock staring at him.

"What?"

A look slipped over Sherlock's face. A cheeky, lustful look that made John blink in disbelief. "Are you serious?" John asked, glancing at his friends to check that none of them were paying attention.

The look continued and Sherlock's gaze turned thoughtful as he flicked his gaze at John's door.

Hey, it was way better than what they were currently doing. With a smile, John stood and stumbled his way to his room well aware that Sherlock was following behind him.

They were hardly fooling anyone, John thought as they stumbled into his room and pushed the door closed behind them. "You have disgusting taste," John mumbled into Sherlock's mouth and then coughed when Sherlock laughed into his mouth.

"You are insulting yourself," Sherlock replied, nosing his way down John's neck and nipping a path to John's collarbone.

"Whatever," John said, pulling Sherlock back to the bed. The next thing he knew, they were lying down, pulling at each other's clothes, peeling off t-shirts and jeans until there was an expanse of skin to explore and-

Track marks.

It wasn't the first time he had seen them but it was the

first time John had the opportunity to explore the marks that littered Sherlock's arms. In what he knew to be a cowardly move, John avoided them, focusing instead on Sherlock's chest and then moving his way down. Allowing himself to get lost in the sensation, John nuzzled at the tented fabric of Sherlock's underwear and, after looking up for permission, pulled them down.

Curious, John studied the dick in front of him, slightly awed at the fact that he was allowed to look and feel. When he leant forward Sherlock moved like a bullet, clenching a hand around John's chin.

Not at all sure if this wasn't some weird sex thing, John stared at him and waited.

Shaking his head, Sherlock pushed John back by his chin. "Condom you idiot," he hissed.

"We're not having sex," John said, confused, even as he glanced at the drawer where he had shoved the condoms that Andy had given him.

Sherlock's eyes widened as if horrified by John's stupidity.

"Oh," John wriggled and Sherlock let go of his chin. "I know that!" he hissed. "But you didn't use one on me so I figured-"

"John, you are neither particularly promiscuous nor well acquainted with needles. You're fine and statistically, transmitting via me giving you oral is-"

"Right." John said quickly, cutting him off because so not sexy. "Yeah, of course." He frowned as Sherlock sat up and moved over to the drawer, apparently having seen John's glance. "Thanks," he said, silently berating himself for being such a moron.

Sherlock shook his head and turned around, tossing John the condom. "Thank me in other ways," he suggested as he returned to the bed.

Right. John grinned. That he could do.

"Any other words of wisdom?" John asked as Andy stared mournfully at the condoms.

"Just two more," Andy replied. "No gifts."

"Gifts?" John asked doubtfully. "Shit," he said sarcastically as he snapped his fingers. "I was gonna go and buy him flowers."

"Christmas is coming up and his birthday," Andy argued. "It falls under the same category as buying dinner for each other. No sweets, no 'ooh that reminds me of you' objects. Nothing. Nada."

───────

Though it wasn't unusual to see Sherlock leaning against a wall and texting half of London whenever they met up, it was a little weird now because it had become so massively clear that it was the crooked half that Sherlock knew. Still, there was something strangely comforting about it.

"More restaurants to scam?" John asked as he stood in front of Sherlock.

Hazel eyes flicked up to John and then back to the screen. "Not restaurants," he said, tucking his phone away. "I need to get a present."

"Okay," John said as they started to walk. "Did you accidently kill someone?"

"I never do anything accidently," Sherlock dismissed, catching John's elbow so that they could cross the road, an almost shark like smile on his face for a flash of a second.

"If you do everything on purpose then you are no-where near as smart as you pretend to be," John said, amused.

Sherlock's eyebrows raised in his patented 'I'm not amused but can't think of a comeback right now' look. "I need you to buy a present for someone interested in maritime prisoners. Relatively recent history."

John snorted and then heaved a long sigh when Sherlock's expression remained serious. "Maritime?" he asked in some horror. "What like with the sails and cords and port?"

Apparently, John's knowledge of anything to do with the ocean was so shit that it made Sherlock stop and glare at him. "Maritime history. That's all. Imagine it was some army related nonsense."

"Since fucking when do you need someone to pass a general knowledge test when buying a present? Just go on eBay."

"EBay does not have what I need," Sherlock snapped.

John threw up his hands. "Fine," he said shortly.

Sherlock twisted on his heel and continued down the alley. It was painfully uncomfortable as they walked together in silence.

"Here," Sherlock said suddenly, gesturing at an old shop front that looked like it was gonna stink of piss.

Great.

Inside wasn't quite as bad as John had suspected. It smelled of damp boxes and the faintest whiff of old cider. The shop was like an old junk shop, random chairs and stacked tables with strangely shaped glass bottles. The counter was at the back of the shop, as if you had to prove your worth by making it through the endless heaps of crap. John wasn't entirely sure how the hell the owner never had anything nicked from the front.

"Uh...Hi?" John said, slowly slinking over. "I'm uh...I was wondering...do you have anything about maritime history?"

The old man behind the counter stared at him and then stood with an almighty huff, as if exhausted by the very idea.

Sighing, he turned to look at Sherlock but found himself alone in the shop. Turning back, he swallowed and then smiled hopefully at the grouchy bastard in front of him.

"Anything in particular?"

"Uh...prisoners?" John asked, knowing that it seriously sounded as if he wasn't too sure. "I...it's for my...uh..." he glanced at the old man and then dismissed the idea of calling Sherlock his boyfriend because fuck would that be a disaster waiting to happen. "Mate," he said, not too sure if Sherlock was still able to hear.

The man eyed him and then pulled down a huge, heavy book. "I have a number of things in stock."

What the hell was he meant to buy?

"I..." John looked over his shoulder hopefully. "If you were into this, then what would you want?"

His eyes rolled in annoyance. "Do you not know anything more specific?"

"No," John said, hunching his shoulders because even he knew he looked like a complete idiot at the moment. The only mercy seemed to be that Sherlock hadn't followed him into the shop. "Can I just...he really likes the recent stuff. Can I have a look?"

Strangely, the man seemed to take some pity on John and nodded, turning away and heading into the back of the shop. Apparently saying 'recent stuff' had helped to narrow it down because he came out with two or three boxes.

The next ten minutes were spent rifling carefully through what was put in front of him. There were a few interesting things, John had to admit, including the old experiments from the late seventies and early eighties to put prisoners on a boat. The man pulled one or two things out as John looked and put them to the side. "Not for you," was all he would say.

The other stuff was prisoner of war based during various conflicts. The old American and British records were all separated neatly and John poured over them with some interest. The man seemed to soften a little.

Having no idea what it was that Sherlock was looking for, John traced a scrapbook that held the World War II newspaper clippings with some longing. Nothing in the pile screamed Sherlock Holmes and he was starting to feel a little lost.

Digging into his pocket for his phone to text the daft git, John frowned when suddenly there seemed to be nothing in there. A frantic clutch had him close his hands around some paper but-

"You seem to like this one," the man said, tapping at the scrap book. "I can make you a good deal."

John hadn't even thought about payment.

Wait.

Pulling his hand out slowly, he stared at the notes that Sherlock had clearly replaced his phone with. The man seriously needed to stop pickpocketing him.

It was as good a guess as any.

"Yeah," John said, smiling. "How much were you thinking?"

When he left the shop, with what was probably a good deal, Sherlock was waiting down the street, a satisfied and smug look on his face.

"What did you do?" John asked, stopping across from him and folding his arms so that the carrier bag slapped against his front in an undignified way.

Sherlock shook his head, the picture of innocence. "Nothing," he said.

He was holding himself awkwardly.

Striding forward, John went for Sherlock's zip only to have his hands caught. "Not here," he said with a hiss. "I'm relatively certain that the CCTV doesn't work here but-"

"You did something to that shop," John hissed. "He was a decent bloke-"

"He's a black-market dealer who uses the shop as a front. Why do you think he took some of the stuff out of the boxes?"

Wait, what? "How did you know that?" John asked, tilting his head.

"Even I can't steal black market items from a shop without being inside of it," Sherlock whispered into his ear.

John felt his jaw drop.

"Keep that though," Sherlock said, his fingers brushing against the bag in John's arms. "I liked seeing you that interested."

When John glanced up at him, there was something soft and uncertain in Sherlock's eyes. "You liked watching me babble about military history?" he asked doubtfully.

Instead of replying, Sherlock leaned forward and kissed

him softly. Given that they were in public, it was an unusually gentle and sweet kiss for them and it made John's toes curl in easy pleasure.

"Keep it," Sherlock whispered again.

It didn't even occur to John until much later that he'd sort of accepted a present.

"And the last one?" John asked, trying not to roll his eyes.

Andy shifted and eased forward, his entire stance changing as he became more serious. The unusualness of it made John freeze, suddenly wary.

"Don't you dare fall in love with him," Andy said in what was probably the most concerned tone he had ever used. "Firstly, it's a cliché and secondly, you can't go into this thinking things will change."

It was on the tip of John's tongue to point out that this wasn't some chick flick and that he wasn't a moron but...but that was the thing, wasn't it? Because John wasn't entirely sure that he wasn't half way there already.

"I know," John said seriously.

Andy nodded and then sat back and shifted as if suddenly uncomfortable with their conversation becoming an actual serious discussion.

"You all right?" John asked, feeling a little amused at how ill Andy was starting to look.

"Feel dirty." Andy sighed. "I need to go and get shagged," he decided, standing up quickly and reaching for his coat.

John nodded and raised his thumbs in the air with a sarcastic grin to show just how great that sentiment was as Andy went to wash away any trace of being momentarily serious.

"I'm still not entirely sure why we're doing this," John said

as they walked through the market. "You never used to do this many cons, unless you just used to be better at hiding them."

How was this now his life? They were talking about con jobs like it was normal. John was still half convinced he'd have the police show up at his door one night, despite the fact that his biggest fault was that Sherlock just seemed to use him as a genuinely innocent front in order to cause a distraction.

"I owe people favours," was all that Sherlock would say, his mouth puckering up into a frown.

"More than usual?"

The frown deepened and John rolled his eyes, leaving it alone. All things at the moment seemed to point towards Sherlock having gotten himself into some trouble with the drugs and John didn't think it would help to bang that message home over and over again.

"So what was it?"

Sherlock glanced at him and then shook his head. "It was stocks and markets. Everything is electronic these days. It's an easy enough formula to replicate."

"You sound almost annoyed about that," John said, bemused.

"It...it depends on the team. Some enjoy the elegance of it and some-" Sherlock's mouth firmed into a thin white line again.

"They don't sound like your usual crowd," John said softly, relieved as they managed to finally get free of Spitalfields.

"They're not," Sherlock said, but he offered nothing more than that. "They would not be my preferred group of people to work with but they do have a specific set of skills."

"So you're learning from them?"

"We traded," Sherlock said, not quite meeting John's eyes.

"I still don't get why you need me for the clean-up?"

"She may recognise me. We were in the same room briefly. Momentarily introduced. I need a fresh face."

Not entirely sure how he felt about that, John nodded and simply fell into step with Sherlock as they made their way down the streets of east London, occasionally glancing up at the different kinds of flats above. It wasn't a place John went to often; too trendy to be cheap and a little daunting during the day, but it was fascinating to see the massive mix of languages, cultures and dress. John even saw Sherlock flash a fond look at the sign for Whitechapel.

"Were you ever a fan of the Ripper stories?"

Sherlock's face brightened with a smile for the first time that day. "I had case files on it as a child," he said, a mix of nostalgia and embarrassment tinging his voice. "Pointless in the end. There's no way to confirm even the strongest theory."

The smile soon fell off his face as they entered another street. This time he looked, well, if John had to put a name to it, he'd say Sherlock was nervous.

They approached a pretty nice looking building and Sherlock tapped on the intercom, drawing John's attention to it as he pressed and the buzzer started to ring.

"Mrs Chowdrey?" Sherlock asked as the muffled connector echoed out from the speakers. "We're from-" He frowned the way he did just before he was about to manufacture a massive lie when the buzzer simply clicked them in.

Sherlock almost looked ill.

"Here," he said, turning to John. For a moment, John thought he was about to say something but instead Sherlock drew out an envelope from the inside pocket of his jacket. He said nothing as John took it and peered inside, just about able to see the money inside.

"How is this a con job?" John hissed.

"Shut up," Sherlock snapped as he shoved John through the door. "Just get her to believe it and accept it. I don't care how."

Fuck.

Armed with the floor and flat number, John started to climb the stairs, his heart racing. He wasn't entirely sure what he expected when he knocked at the door, but an exhausted woman with red-rimmed eyes, strawberry blond hair and a baby in her arms wasn't quite it.

"Uh...Mrs Chowdrey?"

She nodded, bouncing the dark-haired baby on her hip. "What are you here to take?" she asked.

Huh?

"I assume you're from the bailiffs or the loan shark or-" she shook her head.

"I uh..." he glanced at her hair again. "I'm from the Red-Headed League."

She blinked at him and then lifted her eyes to his decidedly not red hair. "Oh, my brother runs it. I have to help out sometimes as punishment for calling him carrot top and ginger ball-" John trailed off and winced. "Sorry, massively out of practise with this."

She closed her eyes and then leaned to one side of the hallway. "I'm not able to give anything to charity. In case you didn't pick up on it, I'm broke. Bankrupt with a sick husband and no family-"

John held up a hand. "We...uh...Okay so I haven't had to explain this before. Bear with me," he said, flashing a smile. "So we were founded by some red-heads who felt a little hard done by and collected together some money." He winced as she started to glare at him. "In order," he said hurriedly, "to give it to other red-heads in need. A bit like a..." he moved his hands in a way that he hoped would help. "Self-helping charity. Anyway, your name came up so...here," he said, handing her the envelope.

She blinked at him a few times and then took the envelope, awkwardly bouncing the baby. Her jaw dropped when she saw it and she gaped at it, then at him.

"The Red-Headed League?" she asked with disbelief. "You seriously expect me to believe that I'm getting enough money to pay off half my debts because I'm ginger? What do I have to do in return?" she demanded, tears suddenly brimming in her eyes.

Shit. That wasn't what was meant to happen. That... he glanced at the baby and then at the boxes behind her and the gaps in the walls where pictures had clearly hung.

Something clicked. Sherlock's unhappy frowns that week, his complaints about the people he was with. "Or," John said, taking a monumental risk. "A friend of a friend felt that you'd had an unfair week for your circumstance."

Her eyes narrowed and there was a strange wobble in his heart as he glanced at the phone lying on the table by her.

Then she nodded and slipped the envelope into her back pocket. "The Red-Headed League," she muttered. "Well, you weren't involved in that farce last week."

Unwilling to give her anything, John just shrugged. "Have a good day," he said with a nod and turned away.

It seemed weird to wait for a thank you when she'd obviously lost more than he was giving back.

Downstairs, Sherlock was leaning against the wall, smoking and staring at nothing. "She told you?" he asked in a monotone voice.

"You gave her back more than you earned," John said, walking over to lean against the wall next to him.

"The con," Sherlock said, still not looking at anything. "When she tried to pull out before the money had been exchanged... they blackmailed her. She has a sick husband and a new baby, was trying to find a quick fix so she could have a break and..." Sherlock shook his head.

"Why would you work with those people?"

This time Sherlock did look at him. "Because there was something more important at stake," he said, giving John a strange look. "I told you, I needed their skill set for something."

"And I'm not allowed to know what," John said with a disappointed sigh. "You didn't have to do that though," he added, glancing up at the flat.

Sherlock said nothing as he finished off his cigarette.

"I'll take advantage of anyone's stupidity," Sherlock muttered as he flicked the butt to the floor and ground his shoe on it. "I'll use anyone's secrets against them but not against people who are desperate, who made one stupid mistake."

175

"And hers was?"

"She kissed one of the team," Sherlock said with a shrug. "It was on camera and it looked like more than it was. After seven months of struggling alone while her husband was ill-" he rolled his eyes. "If that's the most terrible thing you've done then it makes you a better person than most."

"Hey," John whispered, cupping Sherlock's face. "Doing this makes you a better person than most."

There was a doubtful look on Sherlock's face but he leaned forward all the same until their foreheads touched and they shared breath. It wasn't even a kiss yet it felt like one of the most intimate things they'd done.

"I thought you'd-" Sherlock seemed to be struggling a little with the words. "It shouldn't have happened in the first place."

Probably not. John simply turned a little to brush a kiss to Sherlock's cheek, overwhelmed sometimes by how much he...

John prodded at Sherlock until the man rested his head against John's neck. John stared at the flat above and then closed his eyes and held onto the idiot he was falling in love with.

CHAPTER THIRTEEN:

Cocaine and Canapés

O
KAY, ADMITTING THAT HE WAS in love with Sherlock was the first step. Admitting that Sherlock was bat-shit crazy was the next one. Admitting that anyone who loved the bat-shit craziness needed to go and have a beer seemed to be the next order of business. And that was exactly what John was doing when Sherlock slammed through the front door and stormed into the living room where John was watching a Christmas film.

Andy had stomped off, complaining that it was way too early given it was only the eleventh of December.

"Why aren't you dressed?" Sherlock demanded.

John looked down at his t-shirt and jeans then up at Sherlock. "You're usually smarter than this."

"Get in the shower," came the hissed demand followed by a patented Sherlock Holmes derisive glare that meant if John didn't do what he was told Sherlock would throw him in the shower.

Unfortunately, it seemed the more you saw that look, the less threatening it became. "Get lost," John suggested, turning up the television to a level that almost made him wince but was guaranteed to drown out Sherlock's voice.

"John! I'm studying," Andy yelled from his room. "And this time I kind of need to pass. Get in the shower. Now!"

"I hate the lot of you," John muttered, getting up.

When he emerged and wandered into his room, Sherlock was standing with a bag John hadn't seen before. Without so much as a pause for thought, Sherlock yanked at John's towel then shut the door, which was hardly the order that John would have chosen.

"What the hell is going on?" John demanded as Sherlock plugged in a hair dryer and shoved it at him.

"We'll be late." Sherlock turned the dryer on and John jumped at the sudden blast of hot air. "Aim it at your head," Sherlock suggested snidely.

Yeah. John stared at him for a moment and then pointedly turned off the dryer. For a moment, he stared down at the damned thing and took a deep breath while trying to ignore the fact that he was completely naked. Steeling himself, he looked up at Sherlock and glared. "I can dress myself!" he hissed.

"Evidently you can't," came the snippy reply as Sherlock reached out for the hairdryer and tossed it on the bed.

"What the hell are you going on about?"

"There's a-" Sherlock winced and actually looked uncomfortable; a genuine kind of uncomfortable rather than the faked expression that John had seen from Sherlock during some dodgier moments. "A gathering with food," Sherlock finished staring at the ceiling.

"You know the rules-"

"This is allowed," Sherlock muttered as he then made John step into a pair of trousers. Trousers John didn't own because they looked like they cost more than his entire education.

"By our rules or by the actual laws of the land because I am not being used to con someone-"

"It's more important that you're dressed," Sherlock declared, deciding to ignore his questions which was never a good sign. "Hands," Sherlock demanded and then started to manoeuvre John into a white shirt. A white shirt that felt like it was made of fifty pound notes.

"Sherlock-"

"Stop protesting, you're wasting time."

"Fucking hell this is a suit!" John moaned as he saw the jacket and felt the sudden urge to sit wearily on the side of his bed. The only positive side was that the comment seemed to distress Sherlock, as if this was the first time he was faced with John's lack of class, before he added the jacket to the ensemble John was currently being forced to wear. As Sherlock backed away to study John thoughtfully, John stared longingly at the door, trying to decide if it was worth going along with this plan, whatever it was.

"Take the jacket off," Sherlock ordered suddenly as he rummaged around in the bag.

"Wh- why?"

"John!"

Defeated, John stripped the jacket off and then shook his head emphatically when he saw Sherlock draw out what looked like a waistcoat and a bow tie.

"No," he said firmly.

"Believe me, where we're going you'll want them." Sherlock picked up the hairdryer and handed it back to John with a look that was as close as he got to pleading.

He was such a sucker for that look. With an annoyed noise (one that he damn well hoped Sherlock knew was an annoyed noise) John took the hairdryer and ran it over his hair a few times until satisfied. Sherlock seemed to be waiting with some form of gel on his fingers that he combed through John's hair and styled to his own taste.

"This had better not be some weird bedroom kink of yours," John sighed as he watched Sherlock's eyes narrow, catlike in concentration.

"No kink of mine involves you being fully dressed," Sherlock replied absently and then cocked his head. "Two of them," he corrected after a moment. "But there are far more that are higher on the list."

"Are you conning anyone?" John asked, trying not to smile.

"No," Sherlock said, stepping away and nodding at John's

appearance. "Given the last time, it seems wise to avoid involving you."

Good. "I need my oyster card," John muttered as he scanned his room.

"Here," Sherlock said, holding the card between his fingers, because of course he'd spotted it. "For the journey back. For the way there..." he tilted his head allowing John to take the card and tuck his wallet and keys into his coat pocket. "I believe we are right on time."

Right on time? "Where are we going?" John asked as they walked out of his room and to the front door. Tossing his coat on, John winced as he stepped out into the cold air and the slight smattering of rain that felt like little ice bullets.

Sherlock guided him to the taxi and settled in with a neat little shuffle leaving John to bound gracelessly into the taxi.

"And who is paying for this dinner?" John asked as he pulled the door shut and the taxi pulled away from the pavement.

Sherlock shrugged. "I am not," he said as he stared moodily out of the window. "Someone with too much money. It's..." his mouth twisted into an ugly expression. "A waste of time," he seemed to decide. "No-one there will be of any interest. Nosy, boring sycophants."

"Why am I going?" John asked as he tried to ignore the sinking feeling that made him want to beg the taxi driver to turn back.

Sherlock clicked his tongue against the roof of his mouth. "I asked for a favour and now have to...it's blackmail," he said, sounding oddly defeated. "I ask for advice and then have to spend my whole evening listening to the opinions of others on topics I do not wish to hear about."

"Yeah," John said, watching him carefully. "That didn't really answer my question."

An almost smile broke the sour frown. "You'll make it bearable," Sherlock admitted, turning his head to look at John. "As only a friend can."

There wasn't really any way that John could say no to

that. Even when the taxi pulled up to an old stone building, the type that were two a penny in London but still had the façade that screamed John was not the kind of person that would be allowed through the doors.

The doorman on the door seemed to add to that.

"I fucking hate you," John breathed as they stepped out of the taxi. Strangely, that only seemed to make Sherlock breathe easier as he nodded to the porter.

Inside the opulently decorated hallway (which must have been polished within an inch of its life), Sherlock strode up to a silently waiting man standing by a large book. The man nodded at him and smiled politely. Uncertain, John looked around and really wished he hadn't. Even the ceiling had ornate regency plater and pictures on it. Everything seemed so quiet and elegant and John had eaten a day-old pizza with ketchup three hours ago.

"Can we take your coats?" someone asked, appearing as if from nowhere. Refusing to jump, John nodded and shrugged off his coat before realising that all of his stuff was in the pocket and needed to be transferred over. The waiter or butler or whatever he was showed no signs of annoyance but rather waited patiently for John to fumble through his things.

Sherlock, when John looked, was dressed up as well. His chestnut brown hair contrasted sharply with the whiteness of his shirt. The whole thing complemented his skin making him look almost golden in the light. Sherlock's strong nose (that almost didn't work with his face) seemed to fit in a hallway riddled with pictures of people with the same classical, almost roman features. And the suit...ah, well. It was a work of art, John decided, as he let his gaze roam appreciatively. Strange because he had never really given a crap about Sherlock's clothes before now; they both wore the normal jeans and t-shirts and hoodies unless they were out.

John was starting to see why Gay Alf was so adamant that they should dress up once in a while because Sherlock was... yeah, they should do suits more often. In private though because when they were out John couldn't do a damn thing about how delicious his...his...

Not having a name for what they were was so fucking annoying.

"What?" Sherlock asked, seeming slightly exasperated.

"Just seeing one benefit of this," John grinned.

Sherlock let his eyes travel down John wantonly. "I imagined you would see my way of thinking," he said as he stepped close and kissed John thoroughly.

"Are we allowed to do that here?" John asked as they broke away.

"Somehow, I doubt that's a concern," Mycroft said from behind John.

Sherlock, prat that he was, just dipped his head down to John again, a smile on his lips that he tried to kiss into John.

"Tosser," John murmured against his lips, even as he grinned in response, which earned him an approving wink.

"Mycroft, how pleasant to see you," Sherlock said as he smiled with such insincerity that John almost cringed. "Blackmail any other relatives?"

"Is that a conversation that you really wish to have?" Mycroft asked calmly and with what seemed to be genuine curiosity. Interestingly enough, it made Sherlock falter and look away, uncharacteristically off balance.

"Let's not loiter." Mycroft turned away before John could really study his expression. "Mother is waiting."

Mother?

John stared up at Sherlock in horror. "Tell me this isn't your family," he hissed.

"Believe me if I was adopted I would have found evidence years ago and taken action," Sherlock said very loudly. "A more boring group of people you would be hard pressed to find. They have no interest in-"

"No," John said firmly, all too aware of how long Sherlock's disparaging lists of complaints could be. "I meant tell me this isn't me meeting your family."

"You dislike me lying to you," Sherlock replied airily.

"I hate you," John hissed at him. "I am going to kill you painfully and slowly."

"In that case, try to do it before we have dinner." Sherlock placed his hand on John's back as they moved into the large room filled with elegant looking people holding long gleaming glasses of bubbling drinks or smaller, more florid glasses half full with deep amber liquid.

There wasn't a beer in sight.

"Sherlock!" A tall, graceful woman with hair in an intricate bun-thing that must have taken a shitload of patience walked over. "Look at you."

"Mother," Sherlock said tightly. "You look...well."

"Yes, and you look as if you're not high," she replied in such a sweet tone that it took John a moment or two to register what she'd just said. Stunned, he looked at Mycroft who appeared to be a little bored with the proceedings. "And this must be the new one," Mrs Holmes said with an edge to her voice.

"Friend," John corrected automatically.

"Really? Is that what we're calling it these days?" Sherlock's mother studied him as if he were a new rodent in the garden.

"Mother," Mycroft interrupted swiftly. "This is John Watson," he said as if there were weight or some importance to John's name.

Stranger still, it seemed that to Mrs Holmes there was. She blinked at him, as if the rodent had just stood up and started spouting Shakespeare. "Oh! Well...I'm Violet Holmes," she smiled at him then looked back at her youngest son with a scathing glare. "You might have told me," she scolded.

"I might have," Sherlock said, "had the conversation about my attendance been anything other than a monologue from you."

"Don't start," she said softly. "John," she smiled, her face suddenly lighting up. "Mycroft has been telling me all about you. So you want to be a doctor in the army? How exciting," she said as she linked her arm through his. "Tell me all about your studies."

"I..." John looked at Sherlock for help but Sherlock was already heading towards the bar with Mycroft trailing after him. "Should we-"

"No leave them to it," Violet said, sounding a little strained. "I must confess, John, I have no idea why Sherlock brought you here."

Unsure of how to take that John looked at her quizzically.

"But, whatever his reasons," Violet continued with a reassuring smile, "I am glad to finally meet you."

John was almost sure he felt the same way.

To John's horror, he was seated between Mycroft and Sherlock who had been speaking in hushed tones and some form of glare communication all night.

"Do I even want to know what you are planning?" John asked as Violet sat down opposite them. He'd been right before, Sherlock's father was dead but apparently was now being used as some bizarre code word for Sherlock's growing fan base in the criminal world.

"I don't have a plan," Sherlock huffed. "If I did, we'd be gone. This is the best I could do. We'll get it over with; she'll stop nagging at me to meet you. End of." And, as if to prove that, Sherlock reached for his glass and knocked back the drink.

John pinched the bridge of his nose to keep himself calm, unable to remember the last time he had seen Sherlock drink so heavily. Though it was hardly as if Sherlock was going to go and snort something in the bathroom of an event that Mrs Holmes apparently hosted for charity every Christmas.

"Sir? Wine?"

John looked up at the waiter and tried to picture the look he would receive if he just asked for a Carling.

"Sure," he nodded.

"Red or white sir?"

"Red."

"The Merlot? Pinot Noir? Shiraz? We have a lovely Syrah."

What the fuck?

Slowly, John looked at Mycroft who was sipping at something that looked like red wine.

"Uh..." he looked back at Sherlock.

"Shiraz," Violet interjected to his relief. "I tried some earlier John, you really must experience it. It's," she seemed to rethink whatever it was she had been about to say, "lovely and fruity."

The waiter nodded and retrieved a bottle from the tray.

"Thank you," John mouthed at Violet who just smiled at him from where she was seated opposite.

"Sir?" the waiter asked Sherlock, his voice lowered as if in trepidation due to the black cloud practically storming above Sherlock's head now.

"A triple of your most expensive whiskey," Sherlock replied without emotion.

Mycroft glared at the ceiling.

The sulking didn't end there and while John would usually kick at him under the table until he talked, he had a feeling that might be frowned on here.

Just a little bit.

When the army of waiters put down their food, almost as one, John stared at the plate feeling just a little bit lost.

"What the hell is this?" he hissed at Sherlock.

"Foie gras," Sherlock said as he stabbed at it.

John looked down and then at the silverware next to his plate. Hand hovering, he tried to see what other people were using to eat their starter.

"It's like pâté, right?" John asked, staring at the stuff that had been sculpted into an elegant half-moon shape and feeling a flutter of amusement when Mycroft actually squirmed at the question.

Sherlock plucked a knife from John's pile and pushed it at him. "Use this," he instructed.

Trying to copy what everyone else was doing, John took his first bite.

It was horrendous. Actually disgusting. It took effort to swallow it down and not spit it back onto the plate. Next to him, Sherlock snorted, a hint of a smile tugging at his face finally.

"It's gross," John whispered to him. "Oh god, is it gonna look bad if I don't eat it?"

The smile was threatening as Sherlock turned a little to him. "Not to your taste?" he enquired politely.

Miserable, John tried again and this time shuddered, the taste making his eyes water.

Then, mercifully, a knife came from Mycroft's direction and he took half of the pile from John's plate. "There," he said as if nothing had happened. "You're doing very well."

Pleadingly, John looked at Sherlock.

"No," Sherlock took another neat bite.

"Please," John wheedled. "You brought me here!"

Clicking his teeth in annoyance, Sherlock stabbed what was left of the foul stuff and transferred it to his own plate. "You owe me," he murmured into John's ear.

───────────

The next course had a shrimp. Complete with feelers and eyes and John wasn't entirely sure that the damn thing wasn't staring at him. He hovered his fork around it, lost as to what to do.

Sherlock was cracking away, using the plate provided in a manner that said he'd probably learned to do this properly before he could walk.

"Sherlock-"

Sherlock switched their plates quickly and then set to work again.

"Is this punishment for McDonald's?"

When the main course finally arrived, it looked sort of normal.

John studied it carefully, peering over the beef and poking at the potatoes. There had to be something weird with it, right? And the fact that it wasn't something obvious probably meant that it was even more dangerous.

"You have had roast beef before," Sherlock hissed.

"Yeah, slices. Not a chunk!"

"Stop playing with your food," Sherlock said moodily.

"How wonderfully ironic," Violet muttered into her wine. "I never thought I'd see the day, darling."

All of Sherlock's growing good humour vanished and he glared at his food. Feeling uncomfortable, John figured he may as well give the food a go. Besides, he'd eaten Andy's concoctions before, surely that had to have given him a strong constitution? He loaded up his fork and had a bite.

"Bloody hell!" he blinked, the meat almost melting in his mouth. "This is amazing!"

"It was cooked by a Michelin star chef, there is no need to be stunned," Mycroft muttered.

"Yeah, but he cooked the other stuff as well. This is...I don't think I've ever had anything this good in my mouth." He glanced at Sherlock. "No offense."

There was a slight hitch in the conversation before Sherlock suddenly burst out laughing as John went red. Mycroft just reached for more wine as if pained but Violet looked almost enchanted at the sight of Sherlock laughing.

At least he was good for something, John thought, pretty sure that he was now as red as the wine he was trying to hide behind.

By the time the waiters cleared away the plates, John was pleasantly buzzed on Shiraz and almost relaxed. Enough so that he merely rolled his eyes when Sherlock stood to stride after Mycroft who had left the table once he had finished his main meal.

"So are there any repeatable stories you can tell me about my son?" Violet asked with a hopeful smile.

"Probably not," John grinned. "Though he did come to my third dissection."

"To support you?" Violet asked, looking a bit taken with the idea.

"No, the lab assistant was ill so he pretended to be the cover and did a passable effort of assisting in pancreatic surgery."

Violet stared at him and then her smile suddenly grew. "My Sherlock? Surgery?"

"Well, you know. On a cadaver. But yeah," John said, feeling the smile become infectious. It was probably stupid, given what a moron he'd been to ignore Andy's advice, but he could pretend for one night that he was allowed to find things about Sherlock sweet.

Violet started to giggle, "And he got away with it?"

John nodded, taking the last sip of his wine. "Yeah, that was more impressive given half the students knew he was fibbing through his teeth. They thought it was brilliant. He's a bit of a legend at uni now."

Delighted, Violet looked over at Sherlock as he sat down. "A legend?"

"What are you talking about?" Sherlock asked warily as he sat, his fingers briefly finding John's.

"Your dissection lesson," Violet smiled, "evidently you're quite the hit."

Looking a little confused by her reaction, Sherlock looked at John. It seemed as if Sherlock had no idea how to respond to that. "I'm not sure that's-" he started to protest, as if by some miracle he had gained some semblance of false modesty.

"Please. Every time we get a new lecturer I'm hounded by people wanting insight from you. You wouldn't believe how much easier it is to please a course tutor when you know their pet peeves!"

"You don't mind the deductions?" Violet asked.

"No, they're bloody...I mean...uh...brilliant! Just brilliant," John replied honestly.

Violet smiled and Sherlock looked utterly bewildered at the pair of them. He leaned back as the waiters approached with food and Mycroft joined them, his lips pinched together in tight disapproval as he avoided both John and Sherlock's gazes.

What the hell was going on between the two of them? Baffled, John looked between them and then leaned back when another plate was placed in front of him. It was some posh tart with what looked like cream but probably wasn't.

An awkward silence fell over their group as they dug into their food and Violet chatted to the man next to her in a cheerful tone. Even so, every few seconds her eyes would dart between her sons and John kind of wondered how much of an influence she had been on them.

The idea of putting up with all three Holmeses seemed like a monumental task if they shared the same ability to deduce at a glance.

Not a worry you have to put up with, John reminded himself as he stabbed into the tart with a little more force than was necessary.

Right.

The silence lasted as the dessert was cleared away and all the way through the eons of time before coffee was served. It was only when the man next to Violet stood to dance with his wife that Violet swung a disapproving look at both Mycroft and Sherlock before she focused on John like he was the second coming or something.

"So, what about your parents, John?" she asked. "What are they like?"

John shrugged. "They're...fine."

"Why is it that young people seem so reluctant to discuss their families?" Violet sounded disappointed.

"I can't imagine," Sherlock stirred his coffee endlessly after dumping enough sugar in it to make his teeth rot.

"Really?" her voice had turned frosty. "Tell me dear, what was so terrible about your upbringing?"

She and Sherlock locked gazes for a moment, causing Mycroft to sigh.

"Watch your temper, Mother," Sherlock tapped his spoon on the side of his cup, the noise particularly grating. "We wouldn't want a scene now would we," he said, emphasising the word scene as if it was offensive.

John snorted, "Right, your mother's lovely. I can't imagine her chucking a saucepan at your head."

Sherlock snapped his attention instantly to John and Mycroft paused mid-sip.

"It's an expression." John shifted. "So, bathroom?" Then fled the table.

Shit.

Shit!

Bloody red wine.

John leaned over the sink and stared at himself in the mirror.

"Idiot," he hissed.

The door opened and Sherlock walked in, closing it behind him.

Watching him in the mirror John sighed, "So, anyone buy the 'it's an expression' excuse?"

"A saucepan?"

"She missed!" John said quickly. "It's not quite as bad as

it sounds," he said, sighing when he heard what that excuse sounded like out loud. "She was a bit drunk at the time," John admitted. "We...there was a disagreement about Mary and Dad and..." John shrugged, not really remembering how the hell it had started, only the look of surprise on his mother's face after she had done it.

It was probably pathetic that he'd taken some comfort in that.

Sherlock's stare was fathomless.

"She apologised afterwards. When she was sober," John added, not entirely sure why he was still bothering.

Sherlock stood behind him, locking eyes with John in the mirror. He pressed a kiss to the back of John's head and wrapped his arms around him. Welcoming the silent comfort, John covered Sherlock's arms with his own.

"And your brother?" Sherlock asked quietly.

John shrugged. Harry had remained silent both during and after. Always did. "Families," he said, looking hard at the tap in front of him. "Who'd have 'em?"

Thankfully, Sherlock seemed to take the hint and nodded, his nose brushing the side of John's neck. The comfort was welcome, as was the quiet and lack of questions and advice, which was admittedly weird for Sherlock.

What wasn't weird was the way that Sherlock's hands started to move towards the buttons on John's trousers.

"Sherlock-" John breathed in warning as clever hands started to pull the fabric open. "I-"

"Watch," Sherlock instructed as his hand found its way in and John gasped, struggling to keep his eyes on Sherlock.

"Not me," Sherlock scolded softly. "You. Watch you."

"I'm not that interesting!" John teased, arching into the delectably talented hand, his own fumbling behind him to slip into Sherlock's trousers, grinning as he watched the man's eyes flutter a little.

"Yes, you are," Sherlock said, and it was the certainty in his voice that made John falter.

"Watch us." Sherlock started to stroke faster.

John nodded and bit back a strangled groan as he started to move his hand again.

Thank god he'd washed his hands after.

"It was lovely to meet you." Violet smiled warmly at him as she shook his hand.

"Thank you for having me!" John struggled to find the words. "It's uh...been amazing."

Her grip on his hand tightened as she looked at him, as if searching for words. "I believe I should be thanking you," she said, sounding very serious.

"For eating?" John tried to joke.

"For the first dinner party in five years where I have had my son sober."

"Nah, he was drinking-" Oh. John looked over at Sherlock who was talking with someone vaguely important looking. "I don't think I had much to do with it."

"I have never seen him look so happy," Violet insisted. "And I can tell you, John, that is completely down to you and your relationship with him."

"Oh...no...we aren't together," John swallowed. "We're friends. He doesn't want anything more."

Violet raised an eyebrow. "Then my son," she said carefully, "is a complete idiot."

"Yeah," John said with a wry smile as he glanced at Sherlock again.

If only Sherlock agreed with her.

CHAPTER FOURTEEN:

I Won't be Home for Christmas

I T WAS STRANGE, BUT SINCE having dinner with Sherlock and his family, John had barely seen the man. There were reluctant replies to a few of his messages, and most of them were to avoid meeting up.

"I did tell you," Andy said as they ate Chinese in front of the X Factor one Saturday night. "Did I not tell you?"

"Tell him what?" Mike asked from where he was sat with his girlfriend, Kirsty. He was on the floor with his head by her knees as she curled up on the sofa and looked strangely comfortable in the position.

"Not to fall for his fuck buddy," Andy said as he picked out a mushroom and put it on the lid where it joined the rest of the cast-offs from his meal.

"Shouldn't have started it in the first place," Paul said, glaring sullenly at the television. It seemed wise to ignore him given that Paul had been dumped and was still in a sulk about it two weeks later.

"Did I ask for this conversation?" John asked as he hovered his finger over the volume control on the remote.

"No," Andy replied honestly. "But unfortunately the contestants this year are more boring than your sex life so bad luck there. Has he texted?"

John glared at him.

"You're just friends with benefits," Kenny said because,

apparently, he was going to try to be a present and worthwhile member of their household that night. "Just...go out, get laid."

"He's in love," Andy said with a fake kissing noise. "And like the worst gay guy I know-"

"Bi," John corrected, already bored of that. "I had girlfriends; I like girls."

"Yeah but they don't like you. Stick with your strengths," Andy suggested and then laughed as Mike threw a balled-up sock at him. "I'm being cruel to be kind," Andy protested as he caught Mike's gaze, the pair of them grinning like idiots. Mike shook his head and muttered something about Andy being a tit under his breath.

John stared at the television screen for a few minutes, turning the idea around in his head. Tapping his thumb on his phone, John fired off a quick message to Gay Alf.

The reply came back shockingly quick and John smiled down at it before he stood.

"Fuck me, are you actually doing it?" Kenny asked with disbelief.

"Yup," John said, drawing in a deep breath. "See you all after Christmas, I guess."

"New Years," Andy said, staring at the television. He seemed to be worrying his lip between his teeth, though god knew John had to be reading that one wrong because Andy being concerned seemed so unlikely. "We'll do something. Or could catch you when you get back in," he said in an awkward tone.

"Because I'm gonna be shit at pulling guys too?"

It suddenly got very awkward and Andy winced while looking to Mike for help. Mike, however, was staring determinedly at the TV as if it was his life's work not to get involved with their arguments. When it appeared that there would be no reply, John turned and stormed out of the house, striding down the street to the tube station.

Fuck 'em.

Alf met him outside the tube station and took him somewhere different this time, which was strange because Alf was doing one of the barmen at Back Door and hadn't paid for a single drink when he'd taken John out last time. When John questioned it, Alf just shrugged and then pulled a rather muscular man over and shoved John at him.

It was a relief, not having to worry or think about Sherlock. He could dance and kiss and kind of ignore that niggling voice at the back of his head that reared back in horror at what he was doing.

He and Sherlock weren't dating. They weren't a couple and Sherlock didn't want him that way. Why the hell should he feel guilty about this?

The thing was, despite enjoying the freedom, the alcohol soon loosened his mouth enough that he started to talk whenever someone was willing to listen. Shouting in the ear of the person next to him, trying to be heard over the thumping beat that drowned out most noises, John could barely hear what he was saying himself.

He barely processed what he was saying.

At kick out time, John stumbled out of the club with his arm around some guy that he'd pulled all by his lonesome and, dammit, he was drunk enough to feel smug about it.

The taxi ride home was a complete blur and there was a guy next to him that apparently lived close to John and was gonna help him home which seemed nice. Half asleep and half trying not to throw up, John mumbled his thanks.

It took him ages to get the front door open. Giggling with the guy as he struggled to get the key in the lock while the guy murmured all sorts of ridiculous innuendoes in his ear. In the end, they both tumbled through the door and how the hell no-one woke up, John would never know.

"Tea," John gleefully whispered, delighted by the idea. "I can give you tea."

The guy laughed and John waved at him to make him be quiet, as if he were a ~~composer~~ conductor in some weird orchestra. The kettle seemed to make far too much noise too, so John tried to shush that as well.

The guy laughed, bringing his arms around John and nuzzling into his neck.

"Tickles," John mumbled, trying to hunch his shoulder.

Hands slid down his side and John frowned, trying to work out if this was what he was meant to do. He was pretty sure that they had been dancing and almost completely certain that this was the guy that he'd left with but who the hell knew anymore?

"Uh..." John said, not entirely sure.

"You said you wanted to make your ex jealous."

Kind of. At least they had been talking then. John hummed and turned into the guy, accepting the kiss that was perhaps way more wet than he was used to.

"Not an ex," John muttered against the guy's lips.

"Fuck buddy," the guy corrected, as if he couldn't give a shit about the difference. "I can be your fuck buddy too."

Right. Well, that seemed kind of reasonable. John let the guy continue the kiss as his mind tried to work out the rest.

God, he was so drunk that he could barely think. There didn't seem to be any good reason not to do this except for the fact that he wasn't entirely sure that he wanted to. The guy seemed to take the kiss as a sign to continue, his hands undoing the buttons on John's shirt and pushing it open and to the sides before starting in on John's jeans.

Sherlock, waiting, arms around John, poised to lift up his shirt.

"I offered once."

Then the guy was kissing him again, pulling him forward, hands now sliding down his hips to his arse. "You have no idea how much I want this," the guy whispered against his lips. "You're fucking fit," he added as he pushed John backwards and somehow, the back of his legs were bumping against the sofa.

"I-" John's words were swallowed up by the next kiss and the world tilted. It was comfortable being on the sofa and all he kinda wanted to do was sleep.

"I have never seen him look so happy. And I can tell you, John, that is completely down to you and your relationship with him."

Laughing as Sherlock smirked and travelled down his body.

"Are you clean?" the guy asked, pausing as he started on his own jeans.

John blinked at him, confused.

"Condom you idiot," Sherlock's voiced hissed at him.

Still uncomfortable, John watched the guy as he stripped his shirt off and moved to lean down.

Sherlock at the poker game.

Sherlock introducing John to his mother

Sherlock jealous.

Sherlock with less track marks than usual, without love bites that John hadn't made.

Sherlock cupping his head as they slept and pressing a kiss to his forehead.

OH!

John scrambled away from the guy and stood panting down at the dazed looking man who he didn't remember asking back or asking for help or...or anything.

"What the hell are you doing?" John demanded, scraping at his mouth. "I'm fucking drunk!"

The guy looked as if he were about to move towards John. "You're upset-" he said in a coaxing tone.

"Yes," John hissed, suddenly conscious of the fact that his flatmates were still around and god almighty this was like the stupidest thing he'd ever done. "Of course I am! Jesus, Sherlock's a total wanker at times but he's never done this!"

"Don't be dramatic," the guy snapped. "I was trying to

comfort you." Looking a little upset by the idea, the guy reached for his shirt. "Tosser," he sneered as he stood up and fastened his jeans.

"Yeah," John sneered. "I'm the tosser-"

"You wanted it," the guy insisted. "You let me come back with you."

John stared at him in disbelief. "Fucking get out before I hit you," he ordered, fiddling with his own jeans.

The guy seemed to take it at face value because he skulked off without another word...well, unless muttering under his breath counted.

John stood in the middle of the suddenly quiet lounge, staring at nothing and completely unsure as to how he should react to that.

Pathetically, John hid from his flatmates. It would be impossible to even put a number on the amount of times that Sherlock had told him he was incapable of lying convincingly and John couldn't bear the idea of letting them see how stupid he'd been. Knowing all of them, they'd probably take it as further proof that he'd fallen in love when they'd told him not to.

He texted Gay Alf to let him know that he'd gotten home safe and prayed that the guy knew as little about John as John had known about him, otherwise the gossip addict that was Gay Alf would know by lunch time.

By the time the door went for a final time, when finally the friendless wonder that was Kenny left to go home, John breathed a sigh of relief and crawled into the shower. And if he took an hour in there then at least there was no-one to bitch about it.

Letting out a determined breath, John stared down at the

bag with the clumsily wrapped presents and wondered at his sanity for the fifth time.

Who the hell knew why he had done it. Stupid really, to get a tie for Mycroft to say thank you for eating that fucking foul starter and perhaps a bit overly hopeful to buy Violet a nice bottle of Shiraz (according to Gay Alf) as a thank you for the wine incident. And the fake certificate that he and Mike had jokingly made Sherlock for passing the dissection module which loads of his course-mates had signed as the 'course leaders'.

That said, it seemed a bit stupid to not give them after the time and money. Besides, it would probably be a maid who'd open the door (at least, Sherlock's family looked as if they might have maids). Or he could ring the bell and run. Yeah. That wouldn't look at all bad. Knowing his luck, they'd probably think he was a bloody terrorist and call the bomb squad. Still, he might get Christmas dinner out of a prison sentence so it wouldn't be a complete loss.

Either way he couldn't help lurking at the family house Sherlock had once pointed out to John.

Crap, what if he got the wrong house? The Holmes' didn't seem exactly neighbour friendly.

Why the fuck was he getting so worked up over this? Sherlock hadn't texted him for almost a week, he probably wouldn't give this so much as a second thought. It was as if Sherlock had picked up on John's feelings and had backed off a gazillion miles to ensure that his feelings on the matter were pretty damned clear. Whatever Sherlock felt for John, and he wasn't dumb enough to think Sherlock felt nothing, it wasn't enough for Sherlock to want a relationship.

In the end, he took his chances with the bomb squad and ran after ringing the door bell, feeling like a complete pillock.

------•••------

After he'd successfully avoided getting arrested or receiving the pitying, baffled stares that were usually levelled at the insane, John collapsed on the sofa with some old Christmas films and settled in for Christmas Eve.

He'd probably need to get used to this. Since his mother had found out about Sherlock, or at least the gay thing, she'd refused to speak to him. Harry had been quiet too, awkwardly quiet which meant he didn't know how to handle it and no way in hell was John going to ~~him to~~ beg for scraps of family comfort from that wet sod.

Banned from the house for Christmas.

It was sad that he wasn't even that surprised. And sad that it had been his step sister who had texted while on her Christmas holiday with a guy she had met at some rave.

Telling her seemed pointless. What was she gonna do now except for feel bad for him?

Jesus, it was lucky that he didn't have any company tonight. His pity party was in danger of annoying himself.

Which was why he jumped up from his lazy sprawl over the sofa when the door slammed open just after eleven.

"What the-"

"Why are you here?" Sherlock demanded, storming in. "What did she do?"

"I live here, piss off."

Sherlock, bastard that he was, switched the light on and walked over to pick up a bottle while John winced away from the brightness that was like a bloody axe chopping in blinding pulses behind his eyes.

"You've been drinking."

"No shit," John hissed, trying to adjust to the light and keep track of the bastard.

"You-" Sherlock's hand shot out to tilt John's chin up roughly as he stepped forward.

Oh.

Oh. The hickey. Great.

The hand holding his chin spasmed in fury.

"I didn't break any rules," John announced, pulling

away. "I'm 'benefitting' from the arrangement. Not that it still exists, but-"

Sherlock grabbed him and yanked him up then almost bodily hauled him into the bathroom.

"What is your fucking- No," John hissed as Sherlock started to strip off his shirt. "No, I am so fucking pissed off with people trying to strip me."

That look, that murderous look crossed Sherlock's face again as he ignored John and continued until John was clad only in his boxers. Then he hauled John into the bath and Jesus, sometimes John forgot that the man so freakishly strong.

"Really?" John asked as Sherlock reached for the shower head and turned on the spray. Too tired to really care and process it all, John watched as Sherlock tested the water temperature on his own arm before placing the shower head back in the holder and aiming it at John.

For some reason, even though he knew it was coming, it still startled John enough that he yelped when the water hit him. In typical heartless fashion Sherlock yanked the curtain back, hiding John and his complaints from view.

"Stay in there until I get back," Sherlock snarled.

Fuck him.

Though the shower actually felt pretty good as the water started to heat up. Warm and refreshing and actually kind of perfect.

Fine, but he wasn't doing it because he'd been told to do it. He was doing it because he wanted to.

An indiscriminate amount of time later Sherlock yanked back the curtain and turned off the shower.

John rested upon the wall with his head buried in his folded arms. It was oddly comfortable as the cold had long since seeped from the tiles.

"Why are you here?" John asked, not moving.

A towel was wrapped around his shoulders. "I asked first."

"Apparently two gays in the family is two too many." John turned, just about edging into being bitterly amused by the whole topic. "It must be her. First my dad and then me. It's like a pattern or a curse on her or something."

Sherlock didn't say a word but guided John out of the bath and into his room.

"So why are you here?" John asked dully as Sherlock moved about.

"Why do you think?"

"Dunno. Didn't get visited by three ghosts tonight, did you?" John asked snidely.

There was a long sigh from Sherlock. "Get dressed," he suggested. "Trying to talk to you like this is more trouble than it's worth."

When he came out, John was feeling much more sober and much more...well, humiliated by the whole thing. It wasn't exactly a good thing to have the person that you kind of... sort of...well...loved, come over when you were a quivering, useless wreck.

Pathetic wasn't exactly sexy or impressive.

"You didn't have to come here," John said awkwardly as he walked back into the lounge. "That wasn't why I gave you the presents."

"I'm aware of that," Sherlock replied, sounding distracted by the topic.

"So why are you here then?" John asked, taking a seat in the armchair. "We haven't talked in ages."

Those hazel eyes fixed on him and then Sherlock sighed. "Your mother...she told you not to go home?" he said eventually, his voice tight as he perched upon the arm of the sofa opposite.

"Yeah," John said with a nod as he dropped his hands to the arm of his chair. "Her finding out about us...it went down very well," he added with a sarcastic lilt to his voice.

"How did she find out?"

"I told Harry. The others were talking about it while I was on the phone," John said, with a shrug. "He asked; I didn't lie."

"You should have," Sherlock said, standing up.

Well, wasn't that great. "So, mystery solved," John said leaning his head back. "Off you pop then."

"Don't patronise me," Sherlock snapped, looking irritated.

Really? John looked away. "Then leave," he suggested icily.

Sherlock said nothing, his lips pinched tight as he fixed a long, deep stare on John.

Sighing, John stood up and wandered over to the kitchen, if for no other reason than to get some space and distance from Sherlock while he worked out what the hell he wanted to say.

Something touched his neck and John flinched back, startled. Turning, he glared at Sherlock, "Would you make some bloody noise when you-"

"How drunk were you?" Sherlock breathed tightly.

Shaking his head, John turned away and pulled out a glass of water and then rolled his eyes when Sherlock snatched it up and took a deep gulp. "You're such a fucking drama queen," John ground out as he turned to get another glass. "You make everything into such a big deal-"

Glass shattered against the wall.

Stunned, John turned back to Sherlock who was staring at the broken shards of the tumbler with irritation.

"What the fuck was that?" John yelled.

"It's fine," Sherlock mocked. "It's fine?" He took a step forward. "It's fine that your mother is an abusive parent, it's fine that you have no money or support, it's fine that someone takes advantage, it's fine, it's all fucking fine!" he ended up screaming at John. "It is not fine!"

"What do you want me to do? Cry and whinge about it?" John yelled back. "It is as it fucking is. My mother's hopeless and I manage. And don't start on about people taking advantage, you have no idea what happened-"

"Enlighten me then," Sherlock challenged.

"You can't do this!" John shoved past him. "You can't. I can cope with this thing we have as long as you don't do this!"

"Do what?"

"This! Acting jealous, acting as if you want me to meet your family and treating me like- I can't do that! Do you have any idea how fucking cruel you're being?"

"Treat you like what?" Sherlock followed him back into the living room. "John?"

"Just get-"

"John!" Sherlock yelled, grabbing him. "How do I treat you?"

"Like I fucking matter to you!"

Sherlock looked as if he'd been hit by a brick wall. Hot embarrassment welled up and John made a dash for his room only to have long hands grab him and try to pull him close.

No.

Struggling to get away proved easier said than done and they ended up toppling over onto the sofa. The feeling of someone else on top of him wrenched at memories that were far too raw and John started wriggling desperately to get free.

"John," Sherlock sounded as if he were talking to a wild animal. "John, calm down-"

Shaking his head, John tried to squirm but, at some point, Sherlock had managed to wrap his arms around him, pinning his elbows to his waist with one arm and cupping his forehead with the other to keep his head steady.

He wasn't getting free.

Exhausted, John slumped, biting at his lip to keep what

was either a scream of pure frustration or a sob of pure sorrow at bay.

"Why didn't you say?" Sherlock asked quietly as John's breathing evened out.

"Because I told you I could do it and I can. But it's hard when you make it so easy to forget."

Sherlock nodded slowly against his hair as traitorous hot tears burned in John's eyes.

Wait.

"Why the fuck are you nodding?" John breathed, voice wobbling.

Sherlock was silent then shifted his grip on John. John didn't bother to look at him until he felt Sherlock shift a little and a hand appeared. And, in that hand, was a present.

"That's against the rules, "John said, feeling exhausted all of a sudden.

"I know."

Snorting at Sherlock (though why the hell he had thought Sherlock would stick to the rules he would never know) John sighed and took the present.

"You do know this is exactly what I was talking about?" he said without inflection as he started to unwrap the paper.

"Just open the damned present," Sherlock said, sounding oddly unsure.

It was a box.

Unimpressed, John looked at Sherlock.

"Open it, you moron," Sherlock muttered, looking more like his usual self.

Rolling his eyes, John opened the box.

Inside was his father's watch.

Stunned, John dropped the wrapping paper and pulled the watch out, turning it over to check the inscription.

So you'll never have to ask again!

A joke between his parents; his father had used the "What's the time?" opener to pick up girls when he'd been younger and it had been how they'd met. The story had been told so many times when he'd been younger, before his father had left, before he had announced he was gay and John's mother had been distraught by the news.

Back when they'd all been happy.

"I can't believe you found it," John breathed, remembering how upset he'd been when he'd discovered the pawn broker had sold it on almost instantly. "How the hell did you find it?" he whispered, unable to stop fiddling with the watch.

"We can't keep on like this, John," Sherlock said quietly, ignoring his question.

Don't say that, don't. But even as he thought it, John nodded as he stared at the watch.

"I've changed my mind."

"What?" John blinked at him because that didn't sound like how Sherlock would start the break up conversation.

"It seems," Sherlock licked his lips and seemed to gather strength, "that being in a relationship with you would be far less distracting than not being in one."

Detangling that, John stared at him, "You want to be with me because it's less distracting?" John asked, gearing up steam.

"John-"

"No. You fucking stay on the sofa. Or go home. Either way I'm going to bed," he announced and then paused, "or break into one of the other rooms as you did bring me the watch."

"And if I told you I loved you?"

John stared at the door.

Oh Christ, he must have drunk enough to start auditory hallucinations. That was surely more likely than Sherlock Holmes, Sherlock bloody Holmes, announcing he loved someone.

"I...what was-"

"Do not make me say it again." Sherlock was staring at

the skirting board as if he could burn a hole through it. "It's a process."

"A process?"

Sherlock nodded grimly. "And against my will and judgement," he added, sounding slightly put out by the whole thing.

John gaped at him. "And how long-"

"You were interested by an artefact and it made even a miserable arsehole of a man become pleasant. And it made me-" Sherlock broke off as he glared down at the floor. "I don't want a relationship but I love you and it seems impossible to do anything else." Sherlock seemed to be over enunciating his words as if to take his frustration out on the bloody English language. "Not having you in my life is unacceptable, having you as a friend is a lie, and having this arrangement is," his eyes flicked to John's neck again, "painful," he admitted. "I dislike the lack of viable options."

"Why don't you want a relationship?" John asked slowly.

Sherlock's gaze dipped to the corner of the sofa, as if he could see into the past. A small frown was creasing his forehead.

"Sherlock-"

It seemed to work. Sherlock swallowed and seemed to steel himself before he answered. "Because you'll ask me to stop."

There really didn't need to be any clarification on that.

"Probably," John agreed hesitantly.

"But it appears neither one of us can walk away either," Sherlock decided as he sat with a sigh.

John shook his head in agreement.

They sat in silence.

"I do love you," John said suddenly. "I realised I hadn't said it. And I do."

Sherlock reached for him and pressed their foreheads together. "It won't be enough," he warned.

"Maybe, maybe not. But…I don't think that I can't not give it a go," John breathed, their lips almost touching.

In answer, Sherlock simply tipped his lips to John's, closing the gap to kiss him gently. Contentment, sharp and unexpected, bubbled up within him as they exchanged small, sweet nips and kisses, taking in each other's breaths. It was weirdly perfect until John broke it with a slight giggle.

"What?" Sherlock asked, pulling away with a frown.

"I was just thinking," John smiled and stroked at Sherlock's hair, "it must be love if you ignored the double negative."

Sherlock snorted, an answering smile forming on his face. "God help me," he sighed as he drew John close again.

***

Going to bed was nerve-wracking. Never before had John been so aware of where Sherlock was and what he was doing.

Lying next to each other, Sherlock stroked a hand gently up his arm in repetitive strokes.

"So we're together?" John asked.

Sherlock smiled against his skin. "Yes, John."

Hmm. "What time do you want the alarm set for?" John asked as he tried to bury himself into Sherlock.

"Go to sleep, John."

"Then tell me quickly!"

"Whenever you want to get up."

"When do you need to be home?"

"Mother is expecting us at one."

"Right." John dropped the clock, letting it crash back onto the bedside table. "Us?" he squeaked.

"Mmm, if you wouldn't mind telling her we are together that would be wonderful. The woman has nagged me about it every spare moment."

"I don't want to put her out-"

"It's hardly as if there aren't enough dinner plates. She has a small army of them."

"Whoa, how many rooms do you have-"

"John. Go to sleep."

John grinned impishly. "Boyfriends talk in bed," he said petulantly, rolling the word on his tongue to get the feel for it.

"Partners do not," Sherlock grumbled.

Partners.

"Like cowboys," John said sleepily.

"As you wish."

CHAPTER FIFTEEN:

Family Portraits

H ANDS PRESSED HIM INTO A *corner, pulling and scratching at him-*

John startled awake and lay staring at the wall as he tried to even out his breathing, not really sure why he had startled awake. It took a while to realise he was alone in bed.

Crawling out of the covers, John sleepily padded into the lounge, frowning at the sight of Sherlock, who was standing in the kitchen, his mouth twisted as he peered into the fridge. "You have no food," Sherlock announced as he shut it. "At least nothing without fur and the ability to respire."

"I consider that a personal triumph," John grinned. "Do you have any food at yours?"

Sherlock looked suddenly skittish. "My mother may have some."

"You got chucked out of a flat again, didn't you?" John grinned. "I knew it! It's like a Pavlovian response now; you get chucked out and then boom," he said, clicking his fingers, "you feel an odd need to come here and beg the use of my bed."

"Clearly," Sherlock muttered sarcastically, apparently unbothered by the fact that all the cupboards were open from his search, because evidently the great Sherlock Holmes couldn't be bothered to close them.

John was within touching distance now and there was an odd shyness creeping up on him because he was actually dating Sherlock. Finally and properly, which was kind of amazing and weird rolled up in one confusing ball.

"Hi," John grinned, patting Sherlock's arm.

A fond smile grew. "Idiot." Sherlock ducked for a quick kiss. "I'm thirsty and your water is disgustingly filthy."

"No, you just haven't built up any tolerance to it," John said, clapping him in mock sympathy on the shoulder as he pulled away. Seeing the resigned look on Sherlock's face, John rolled his eyes. "One of the others might have hidden a bottle of pop in their room."

Sherlock was off like a flash.

Ten minutes later, the raid was complete and they ended up with a bottle of Fanta and a tube of Pringles.

"You honestly need to learn how to cook," Sherlock huffed, his eyes narrowed and fixed on John as he happily demolished the crisps. "It's a wonder you haven't suffered from scurvy."

"I drink orange juice," John argued, oddly enjoying this.

"So your specialism won't be nutrition then."

John shook his head. "Couldn't imagine anything more boring," he said, then hesitated. "What about you?"

Sherlock reached for a crisp. "You mean a job I assume?"

"No," John said, shifting. "I mean...there's the gambling and the cons and...the drugs-"

"Not a dealer," Sherlock said absently, as if it were a typical thing to have to correct.

"Okay," John allowed. "But how did you even start doing all of that? I don't suppose that your mum or dad had any contacts."

Sherlock snorted at that and leaned against the front of the sofa, his knee drawn up with his elbow resting on it. "University," he confessed. "I was... bored," he said heavily. "Everything was boring and slow. I could have passed the course in my sleep. Mycroft was excelling and he was the favourite. I don't do well playing second fiddle to anyone."

"Noticed that." John watched him closely. "So what happened?"

"Mycroft started going into law so I started to break the law." The statement was said as if that was perfectly normal and John lifted his hand to hide the small smile that was threatening. "It was interesting," Sherlock continued, though his eyebrow lifted a little at John, obviously catching the attempt at subterfuge. "Playing with people's reactions, watching them as they committed a crime and tried to justify it. Or didn't as the case may be. There are no expectations. No-one looks at you and expects to see you excel at conning others or tricking them out of money. It's...there are no rules." Sherlock looked at his hand as if he might one day hold the answers. "I like that."

"Your mum knows," John said softly.

"Yes, she cut off my trust fund," Sherlock sneered, seeming a little bitter. "Apparently, my 'frivolous lifestyle' will not be funded by my ancestors, though I imagine they would approve."

"So you make it up in other ways. Do I know them all? I mean do you..." John racked his brains for an example. "...strip?" John asked jokingly.

"Once. Tedious."

John's mouth dropped open and Sherlock snorted in amusement.

"Git," John tossed a crisp at him. "You could do so much more though, you know that right?"

"Such as?" Sherlock asked. "Live and work and be a good citizen and die at a respectable age? It sounds so...ordinary. Like something a million and one people across the world could do. I want...I want to do something that only I could possibly do. I just need to find it."

"You will," John said softly. "If anyone could it would be you."

There was a warmth in Sherlock's eyes as he watched John, the light turning them an almost gentle golden brown. "You want to ask about the drugs though," he said quietly.

John shrugged. "Is there any point?"

"Probably not," Sherlock admitted. "But I don't deal, John. I never have. I've helped Victor."

"I remember," John said tightly. "As long as you wanted to, right?"

For a moment, Sherlock looked confused and then he shook his head. "Not dealing, I meant with people. Other dealers. My skills set, the deductions. It's been useful more than once. Especially when police interference had been expected."

Police? "You haven't got anyone hurt-"

"Please," Sherlock said dismissively. "Victor isn't brave enough to hurt a police officer and his family isn't stupid. There is nothing to be gained by being on the end of police vendettas. As for the meetings, usually they're with people who are protected by their own gang."

Gangs?

"Sounds more than it is," Sherlock said. "Think of me as a lie detector. It helps deals go smoothly."

That conjured up strange images. "Victor's family are in this deep then?"

"Mm," Sherlock said as he put the lid on the Pringles. "They certainly have their secrets," he added in what sounded almost like a triumphant tone. It was so unexpected that John blinked at Sherlock in confusion before the man waved a dismissive hand. "They simply had an unusual climb to power," Sherlock said. "One that means they are not as strong as they would like to believe."

"And how do you know that?"

Sherlock took a swig of drink, his eyes shadowed before he shook his head. "No matter," he said.

"Sherlock-"

"I don't wish to tell you."

Oh. Well, at least it wasn't a lie, John supposed as he tried to absorb that. But there was something else, another question that was forming, even though it didn't really matter what Sherlock's answer was.

"Would you ever want me to-" John started to ask.

"No," Sherlock said forcefully. "Never."

That was a relief. "How come?" John asked, twisting the cap onto the bottle.

"I'm not sure," Sherlock frowned at that. "You have a lot more invested in keeping yourself clean. You're going to enter a profession where you cannot possibly hope to get away with using."

Nodding at that, John dragged the duvet around himself. No-one could argue with that.

———————————

The house was just as big looking as it had seemed last night. Pausing, John stared up at it, neatly nestled between the others on the street and very white against the grey sky.

Sherlock seemed to sense that he'd come to a halt and stopped himself to turn, looking at John curiously.

John flashed a nervous smile. "It's really, really posh, isn't it?" he said, looking at the house again, hardly able to believe that it was just one home. It should be a museum or flats or...well, something.

Turning back to the house, Sherlock seemed to study it, as if trying to see it from John's point of view. "Imposing," he declared after a moment. "The inside is not much better."

John scratched at his cheek and looked longingly down the road, thinking of the closed shops they'd passed by. "There aren't like stag heads or anything are there?"

Sherlock seemed to be off on another planet. "No, far too unfashionable nowadays."

That didn't help. At all. John stared at Sherlock in disbelief as the man walked up to the door and pulled his keys out of his pocket, looking perfectly at home on the street with its wonderfully white exterior and grand doorstep.

It didn't get much better inside. Suddenly feeling self-conscious, John hunched in on himself as he studied the interior. It was light and airy; the walls painted a cream that made John sure that simply brushing up against it would create a stain. The tables were a dark wood with glass tops and John walked forward slowly, trying to be careful as he peered at bowls that looked so expensive he was sure someone was about to tell him off just for breathing on them.

"What are you doing?" Sherlock asked, watching him with a confused expression.

John shook his head. "Looking," he whispered.

"Why are you whispering?" Sherlock asked, not bothering to match John's volume.

"It feels quiet in here," John answered, still keeping his voice low and, damn, looking like a moron.

Smirking and sliding his fingers to link with John's, Sherlock tugged him into the main hallway, beyond the stairs and into a room behind a deep, dark wooden door.

"Here," he announced, pushing John forward into what seemed to be a reading room. "You can stop nagging me now."

John stared down at Violet Holmes, who was sitting in what looked like a comfortable chair next to a large book case with a warm lamp to compensate for the dreary day. She still looked very elegant in what he supposed she considered informal wear. She stared up at him just as blankly then, with a long sigh, bookmarked the page she was reading and put the book to one side.

"Should I assume he is why you stormed out of here last night in such a temper?" Violet asked silkily, raising a very familiar eyebrow at her son.

"Of course. How else did he deliver the presents?"

Oh god, the presents. John felt his entire face heat up in horror. "Sorry about that," he muttered, resisting the urge to kick at the carpet like a naughty child.

Violet looked at him steadily, emotions flickering across her face too quick to read. Finally, she switched her gaze to Sherlock.

"Would you like a drink, John?" she asked, standing up.

John glanced over at Sherlock, hoping for some lead on what kind of drink he was being offered but Sherlock was staring at his mother with wary, narrowed eyes. "Tea?"

Violet smiled. "Take a seat, or feel free to look around. Sherlock?"

There was a fleeting squeeze to his wrist and then Sherlock followed his mother out of the room.

"Okay," John said to himself as he looked around the now silent room. It was a cosy living room he supposed, with plush chairs, a roaring fire and pictures that wouldn't look out of place at a gallery. Bored after half a minute, John wandered over to an old looking bookcase that was carved from dark gleaming wood and held old tomes.

What would it be like to grow up here? John could remember the few times he'd visited his grandmother before she'd died. He'd hated it – the constant berating for being messy or for knocking things askew. It had always been a relief when his dad had grabbed him and Harry and tossed them outside with him for a game of hide and seek in the garden.

How Harry forgot what a good man their father had been, John had no idea.

Next to the book case, on a little side table, was a card. John stared down at it, knowing what it was and feeling reluctant to pry.

It was a funeral card. Curious, John picked it up. From the dates and the name Siger Holmes (which seriously? Siger?), John could guess that it was Sherlock's father. Apparently, he'd died two years earlier.

The sound of the door closing gently made John look over at Violet who stood quietly by the door.

"Sorry," John said, putting the card down. "Just curious. Wasn't sure when Sherlock had..." ah, that sounded like he was snooping. "My father died six years ago," he said, wincing at the voice in his head that snarled it was five years, ten and a half months ago.

No-one ever wanted to hear the precise time.

"I see," Violet murmured, standing the card up on the mantelpiece properly. "It's a dreadful age to lose a parent, when you're a teenager-"

"I don't suppose there's ever a 'good' age," John said sadly. "It was terrible timing," he added trying to lighten the mood with a pained smile, "but then he always had shocking time keeping skills!"

Violet smiled, a hint of the woman from the dinner weeks ago finally reappearing. "I'm at a bit of a loss here, John," she confessed as she tilted her head to the side in a way that was rather reminiscent of Sherlock when he was thinking. "Neither of my sons have ever brought anyone home before."

"Much less at Christmas, right?" John took a deep breath. "I'm sorry, he told me you were expecting me."

"Well, I suppose he did shout something about it over his shoulder when he launched himself through the front door like a spitting cat," Violet sighed. "It was all a little...abrupt."

John had a distinct feeling abrupt was frowned on in this house.

"He's making the tea," Violet murmured and then glanced at John as if just remembering that he was there. "I suppose we had best check on him before the process becomes some grand drama."

John was suddenly hit with the image of a much younger Sherlock, tongue between his teeth as he concentrated on his latest research with his usual focus and grinned at the thought as he followed her.

Violet was already marching into the kitchen where the makings of a Christmas dinner wafted in the air and the cooker...stove maybe? (either way, it was huge) was filled with shining pots and meat was roasting in the oven. And, next to the impressive thing, was Sherlock. In his hands was a letter that Sherlock was peering down at and studying with interest as he ignored the kettle.

Violet yanked it out of Sherlock's hands, apparently far too used to seeing sights like this. "Do not read your brother's mail," she ordered, "and the counter is not for sitting on."

Looking unrepentant, Sherlock slid off and wandered to John. "Would you like a tour?" he asked mockingly. "Evidently I have been forgetting my manners."

Violet slammed a cup down on the counter, hard.

Great.

John made a show of looking around. "You don't have any ghosts, do you?" he asked thoughtfully.

Sherlock looked unimpressed. "Ghosts?"

John nodded. "Mm. Or secret passages? I'm always up for a good old secret passage."

"There's the back stairs for servants," Sherlock said after a moment's thought.

"Servants?" John asked, freezing in horror.

"Oh yes, did you not see the huge army of them when we came in?"

"No." John backed away, slightly panicked. "Oh, Christ almighty," he muttered to himself.

"Stop being cruel to the poor boy," Violet scolded gently.

"*That*," Sherlock whispered, learning forward, "was for McDonald's."

―――――――●∙∙●―――――――

"Where's Mycroft?" John asked as Sherlock paraded him around Mycroft's bedroom.

"Working."

John grinned, tickled by the idea of anyone working on Christmas and then stared as Sherlock's face remained impassive, as if missing the joke. "Wait...Seriously?" he asked.

"He'll be back for dinner." Sherlock toyed with the drawer that was locked. All of them were locked.

"It's Christmas day," John protested, feeling a momentary twinge of sympathy for Sherlock's brother.

"Mycroft doesn't do holidays." Sherlock took out what looked like a thin strip of metal and started on the lock. "The word simply isn't in his vocabulary. I did ask Mother once if he was born in that suit but she insists I'm being dramatic."

"Are you trying to break into his drawers?"

"Yes."

"Okay." John rocked back on his feet. "Am I your lookout?"

Sherlock turned to him thoughtfully. "No. I think he'd be more confused if he didn't catch me."

John nodded as if that argument had made perfectly logical sense which, probably in the Holmes world, it did.

"Come here," Sherlock summoned.

John walked over, part of him tisking in disapproval that he should make sure this 'coming when summoned' did not become a standard part of their relationship. "Yes?" he asked when he was stood close to where Sherlock was kneeling.

"Sit."

Shrugging, John sat.

"Now," Sherlock seemed to bend and twist until he was sitting behind John and scooted them both close to the drawer as he placed the lock pick in John's hand, "put it in."

Grinning, John obeyed.

"You need to feel what's there through the rod. Tell me how you think the lock is keeping the drawer fastened."

It was hard to work out what the metal was bumping across, his brain unable to translate the shape of the hole. "I'm not sure," John confessed.

"You want to be a surgeon-"

"You tell me what part of the body is as hard as metal. And which part of the body has air pockets for me to wiggle a scalpel around in."

Sherlock huffed against his neck, arms coming around

John. "Try," he suggested, "and surely you can think of part of the body which has a hole you need to manoeuvre a rod in."

Pausing, John tried not to snigger. "You need to have serious words with your doctor if you reckon that's what we do to our patients," he teased.

One of Sherlock's hands was creeping down. "Focus on the lock, John," he ordered, even as his wandering hand slid under John's jumper.

"I can't concentrate with you doing that!"

"You might be in danger when you next do this. You might be desperate. It's best to recreate the stress you'll be under when teaching you." Sherlock's hand was now pulling at the buttons on his jeans. "You need to work out what you need to do, John. Move the pick in a pattern, vertical or horizontal – you choose. Tell me what you need to do."

"I need to push it round...I think!"

Sherlock hummed in approval. "Will it work if you just use what's in your hand?"

John pulled the pick out and studied it. "I think I need another one."

Sherlock nodded against his neck. "Here," he said as he dug in his pocket and placed three others on the floor. "Pick."

John hovered his hand over the choices as Sherlock dipped his hand into John's boxers, warm hands wrapping around his cock. "Warm," Sherlock murmured, "getting warmer, warmer."

John selected one and got a few rewarding strokes. "In it goes," Sherlock breathed.

"Tease," John hissed as he shifted to get a better angle on both Sherlock's hand and the lock. "Now what?"

Sherlock paused and put John back into his jeans, zipping him up with far less care than John liked. Just as his clever fingers finished, he turned his head. "Mycroft," he welcomed sarcastically. "How's the office?"

"You have your own carpet to defile, Sherlock."

"Yours is far cleaner. It's always more fun to dirty the clean things up."

"I noticed."

Sherlock went rigid, anger in every pore of his body as he and Mycroft stared at each other. Sensing an epic staring competition was about to begin, John wriggled free and stood, eyes darting between the brothers.

"I've missed something, haven't I?" John asked, lurking uncomfortably by the desk he had just been trying to break into.

"You could always clean your own carpet," Mycroft said, still staring at Sherlock as if John hadn't spoken.

Sherlock snorted, finally looking away as he pushed up to standing. "Why bother?" he snarled, already walking to the door. "It will never be as pristine as yours," he added bitterly as he left the room.

Mycroft let out a long sigh.

"Uh," John stared down at the lock picks still on the floor and the two still in his hands. "Apparently you're used to finding this..." he waved the lock picks in the air to make it clear what he was talking about.

"But not you," Mycroft seemed to be pondering something then looked in the direction Sherlock had just gone. "You and he-" Mycroft stared as if he could see his brother through the walls. "I presume he did not bring you here just to masturbate over my carpet."

"Please never say that word again," John begged as he stared at said carpet.

"John?"

"We...we're trying it." John shrugged. "A bit. A lot." Wincing at his words, John scrambled to explain. "We...we're together."

Mycroft snapped his gaze to John. "Really?"

"Yeah?"

Mycroft stared at him a moment longer and then nodded. "John?"

"Yeah?"

"Would it be terribly inconvenient for you if you left so I could get changed?"

"Oh!" John nodded and then shook his head. "Yeah, no...I mean. I'll go. I'll just..." He ducked to pick up the lock picks. "And I'll...see you at dinner!"

He could have sworn he almost saw Mycroft smile as he ran out of the room.

The dining room was decorated with the same elegance and clean lines of the other rooms. Rather than crackers and bright decorations there were huge sprays of flowers and green leaves in large glass vases with gleaming crystal glasses filled with intricately shaped napkins. The table was large enough to fit eight people and had high backed, dark chairs that were almost throne like in their appearance.

John watched as Sherlock stood by one of the chairs, fingers tracing the grains of the wood with a far-away expression on his face. Smiling sadly at the sight, John turned away and wandered back to the kitchen.

"Do you need a hand?" he asked. "I can carry things."

Violet shook her head. "You're a guest."

John shrugged. "I'm also mad enough to date Sherlock. I think you can let that rule slip for once."

Violet flew around, looking stunned. "Dating? But I thought you said-"

"Turns out he's not such an idiot after all," John said with a wink. "Well," he considered the idea for a moment, thinking back to the conversation that had taken place when he and Sherlock had agreed to change their relationship.

"Oh," Violet seemed to be trying to absorb that fact. "Oh my, I should have used the better silverware," she muttered to herself.

"Mrs Holmes?" John said hesitantly, "Please don't take

this the wrong way but I'd really rather pretend that you didn't have better silverware. Mainly because I'm convinced I'll somehow break the ones already out there and they look fancy enough."

She stepped towards him. "You're a very sweet boy," she said with a smile. "And I believe I said you were to call me Violet."

John nodded. "Thank you."

She let out a breath. "Right then. You can tell Sherlock to make himself useful and get the wine and tell Mycroft to not spend twenty minutes changing, he can carve."

John nodded. "And I can do what?"

"Deal with Sherlock's temper tantrum when he discovers he can't carve," Violet suggested with a very familiar, wicked look in her eyes.

John nodded. "So I'm supervising the drink making."

Violet nodded, laughing.

Sherlock and Mycroft both looked a little confused at their orders, but obeyed nonetheless; though Sherlock seemed to have a few choice words for John when they wandered down into the cellar.

"You have a cellar?"

"Why are you down here?"

"Helping?"

Sherlock glanced upwards and muttered something under his breath. "Look for a pinot noir," he snapped.

"Okay." John wandered over to what looked like white wine.

There was an irritated noise and a hand grabbed his elbow and shuffled him about, aiming him at the reds and pushing him forward.

"I thought it was white!"

Dinner went as well as could be expected and was surprisingly easy. Better than it had been a few weeks ago. Mycroft made a few comments about John's taste in food so Sherlock made a few select comments about Mycroft's dress sense. Violet seemed to bear it all with a strange smile before she turned to John.

"Would you like to see some baby pictures?" she offered, and John was reminded, once again, that Sherlock had inherited that devious nature from somewhere.

"Love to," he said when the Holmes brothers stared in horror.

Served them right.

John grinned down at the scrawny kid with silky golden hair and a fiercely stubborn expression which seemed to glare suspiciously at the people beyond the frame.

"You *were* cute!" he announced to Sherlock as he sat on his boyfriend's bed. "You must have had everyone wrapped around your little finger!"

"No." The answer was frank. "I believe my father considered me to be far too wild and unpredictable."

That couldn't have gone down well, especially as Sherlock would have found that to be something to be pleased about. Sherlock's face was half illuminated by the street lights as he watched the people below, eyes narrowed and fixed on the world beyond the glass.

"Play a game?"

"Like?" Sherlock sounded rather dismissive of the idea.

"See if you can coach me to deduce your childhood from the pictures?"

Sherlock's head turned to him. Then, nodding, he walked over and settled himself so that he was sitting by John's head as he opened up the album again and flicked through.

"Here," he said, turning the page. "This was taken when

I turned eighteen. There's a painting of it somewhere in the house too."

John shifted his elbows so he could peer down. "But wouldn't the photographer have put you all in position?"

"You tell me," Sherlock replied, combing a hand through John's hair. "Start with me, you know my expressions. Tell me what you see."

Eighteen-year-old Sherlock glared out of the photo, every part of him stiff and rebellious. But there was a slightly unfocused look about the younger version of Sherlock, his jaw set as if someone had annoyed him but he wasn't sure how to proceed.

"You...you were angry. You'd had a fight?"

"Your evidence?"

"Your fist is clenched. Wait, no..." John looked at it closely and noticed the way it wasn't quite clenched. There was a faint blur around it, as if the hand had been in constant motion. "You were using back then?" John asked, looking back at Sherlock.

A thumb brushed his neck. "Yes."

John chewed at his lip.

"Stop worrying about how I'll react," Sherlock breathed by his ear. "Just look at it. Properly look at me and tell me what you can deduce."

How? How was he meant to look and see what was starting to bloom in his mind? That Sherlock was standing slightly outside of the group, separating himself it seemed. "Mycroft was tense," John added, glancing at the rest of the family, frozen in their portrait.

"What?" Sherlock sounded startled. "No, he wasn't."

But John nodded his head. "Look, he's holding onto the chair and his knuckles are practically white. Not sure I've ever seen him look that annoyed," he added, trying to ignore the fact that he hadn't met Mycroft often enough to really be able to make that judgement.

Still, Sherlock pulled the picture forward, dissecting it with his eyes. Even after a minute he didn't seem to have anything to contradict John's observation.

Sitting up, John pressed a kiss to his ear. "Were they very strict?"

Sherlock nodded, seeming to refuse to drag his eyes from the photograph. "Everything had a schedule, a time and a place. It was...is endlessly dull."

Wrapping his arms around Sherlock, John placed his chin on a bony shoulder and tucked a leg under his bum so he was at an easier height to look over Sherlock's shoulder. "Yeah?" he asked.

"To dress for dinner when people have already seen you all day, to make endless small talk about idiotic topics; it's useless. Petty and useless and they made their lives around it. And then they expected me to do the same." Sherlock suddenly shut the album and John could practically feel the restless energy burning within him.

"Do you know what I was thinking? The other day when I was drunk and pretty much making up shite poetry about you to Gay Alf?"

Sherlock tilted his head, his chest moving in amusement. "Poetry?"

"Ignore that part. Anyway, I was sort of thinking you're like this storm."

Under him Sherlock tensed, as if unsure how to take that.

John guessed perhaps that had been a bit vague.

"Promise not to mock?" he argued, suddenly shifting his grip to pick up Sherlock's little finger with his own. "Pinky swear?"

"How old are you?"

John wagged their fingers. "Too late," he grinned. "Anyway, I was talking about storms."

"Go on then," Sherlock sighed, "babble away."

Nipping at his neck, John smiled. "Well see it's like when

you have a hot day, and everything is nice and happy but it's plodding along and no-one feels like doing anything at all. They just laze about and everything is blurred and hot.

"Then the storm comes along. It's wild and messy and everything is chaotic and sped up. It's amazing, like waking up suddenly. It's a bit dangerous and haphazard but it's like you can breathe again." John took in the smell of Sherlock, smiling. "It cuts through the endless days and it stands out, it's an event.

"It's indescribable and amazing and there are these flashes of pure brilliance. It's temperamental and I'll probably never manage to keep up with it but that's part of the fun." John squeezed Sherlock then pulled away. "And it's way more fun to have sex in the rain than on a muggy day," he added with a grin.

Sherlock remained silent, fingers tracing the album's letters, but he looked calmer, less tense.

Nodding at the sight, John slipped his trainers on, kissed Sherlock's forehead, hunted for his coat then moved to slip out the door quietly.

"John?"

"Yeah?" he asked, tapping his fingers against the door handle.

"Thank you for the present."

John nodded and left.

CHAPTER SIXTEEN:

From a Distance

Victor Trevor – 28th December

The sounds of yet another party echoed through the room, despite the firmly shut door. It didn't exactly bother him; he'd grown up with the sounds for years and fuck those places where it was quiet and calm, but there was a flicker of unease bubbling away inside of him. Had been ever since-

Victor cut off the thought as he glanced in the mirror again. The swelling had gone down and it no longer looked as if he'd dipped part of his face in eyeshadow, but he could see the bump that hadn't been there before and the slightly crooked nature to his nose now. Running a thumb down the bridge made the fault feel worse that it probably was.

It wasn't the cosmetics of it (though that did burn a little). No, it was the way he wasn't allowed to go out and prove to the world that he wasn't weak just because some jumped up little shit had dared to punch him in the nose.

There were looks now. Speculative looks that made Victor bristle and snap back. The whispers that maybe, just maybe, the Trevor family was getting weak. The horror and awe that had been around since his father had snapped his fingers and Beade's body had been found by the docks (symbolic, his father had said with a grim smile) was fading and fading fast.

Fucking Sherlock Holmes and John Watson.

They were together, Victor knew that. Together as in boyfriends holding hands and skipping through flowery fields and all the crap that came with it. He'd heard a few of the staff at his club talking about it in quiet whispers last night. Nervous glances were being thrown at him after he'd lost his temper last month and-

Well. The waiter that had ended up hospitalised from that hadn't really been a looker anyway. Fuck knew what he'd been doing working in Victor's club. He did have standards after all.

Speaking of.

Noise crashed over him as he opened the door and made his way along the hall. His father's club was bigger, brighter and older than his, filled with beautiful people: powerful and well connected. No-one stopped him as he walked into the private office. He smirked, feeling almost like a prince in his palace again, reassured once more after his conversation with his father. After all, this was their world and Sherlock Holmes' desperate scrabble for information was pathetic against their power and influence. His father had pointed that out, cold smile lighting up his face as he'd sat back during the last one of Victor's rants.

"He's an addict," his father had said with a shrug. "Some cause trouble, some cause concerns but at the end of the day, boy, they buy what we sell and they do as we want, whether they know it or not. The minute he slips, we'll deal with it. Until then," his father had taken a sip of whiskey that was probably more expensive than the house that fucking John Watson rented, "let them have their little illusion of power. It won't last long."

And it wouldn't, Victor thought as he watched some shop owner get beaten upon the plastic covered floor of his father's private office. It never did.

Andy Davidson – 2nd January

God, Christmas had fucking sucked arse. Though watching his great-aunt get his cousin hammered and then watching his aunt glare for as long as she could keep it up while his uncle decided that twister was the ultimate game for his seventeen-year-old drunken son had been pretty funny.

And everyone in the world knew that no-one, dead or alive, could top his nan's roast potatoes. Though admittedly, someone probably should have worked up the guts to tell her that the cream in the profiteroles was off.

Still, it could be worse. He could be John. Paul had mentioned that John had been at the house until Christmas Eve and had showed no signs of going home. Poor guy. Probably could do with a pint, and Andy had some left-over beef in his bag that his mum had given him. He could share.

"John?" he called, kicking the door open in what he felt was an appropriately dramatic entrance. "You-"

Oh for fuck's sake!

John stared at him from between Sherlock's knees, Sherlock's cock in his mouth in what was clearly a sixty-nine position.

"So," Andy dumped his bag on the floor, deliberately leaving the front door wide open (serve them right for looking in, the tossers). "Good Christmas?"

John opened his mouth and Sherlock's condom covered cock sprung free as he gaped at Andy then gasped and smacked at Sherlock's thigh as the git clearly continued. "Stop, you arse," John hissed.

"It's all right." Andy looked at his watch. "I reckon it will take me ten minutes to unpack. You can be finished by then, right?"

John looked like he'd happily spend the next thirty years of his life working solidly to invent a time machine. "Sure," he said tightly and then squirmed.

"Sherlock," Andy called as he turned to go upstairs. "Always a pleasure!"

"Andy!" John hissed. "Close the fucking door."

Oh, that.

Prude.

His great moment of unpacking (which had included dumping his suitcase in the corner of the room and tipping it over), had revealed that he was missing a tube of Pringles he'd hidden from his greedy flatmates and that his condoms and lube were no longer in his bedside drawer.

"You owe me a pack of condoms," Andy announced as he walked down the stairs and back into the lounge.

John, clothed and mouth empty, seemed to be avoiding looking at him straight on. "We didn't steal your condoms. I'll give you back the Pringles. Made a hell of a Christmas breakfast," he added with a cheeky grin.

"You fucking better," Andy agreed. It was the rule. If John wanted to pretend it was funny, then it was funny. "So I suppose your fuck buddy is the one I should talk to about the condoms."

"Andy-"

Sherlock tossed the box at him as he walked back out, looking unconcerned. "Useless anyway," he muttered.

"How are these useless?"

"Oh God, let's not discuss this!" John pleaded, burying his face in his hands.

"Easily breakable." Sherlock opened the most used drawer in the entire kitchen and pulled out the takeaway menus.

"So? You pull out and pop down to the free clinic for the morning after pill." Andy turned to John. "P.S. You can't get pregnant." He turned back to Sherlock. "Or you. Not sure which way round you're happiest with."

John made a squeak of sheer horror; it was brilliant how easy it was to embarrass him. Sherlock, on the other hand, seemed unfazed, damn it. Andy was so losing that bet about getting him to finally show some embarrassment. It was like the guy had absolutely no threshold. "Clearly living with two doctors hasn't raised your health awareness," Sherlock muttered.

"If you count them two as doctors. Personally, I call them being anal and likes anal."

A sofa cushion came flying at his head. "Fuck off!" John sounded as if he was torn between laughing and begging.

"So, what we having to eat? I need compensation for seeing your cocks. It's rules!" Andy announced.

"Then I believe John should get reparations for seeing your naked arse eight times in the past year."

Curious, Andy turned to John and tilted his head questioningly. "Really?"

John flushed. "You don't close your door when you're 'eager to close the deal'. Ever. We all walk by with a hand covering one side of our face."

"Pervert," Andy muttered. "So you two cleared everything up then?"

John nodded. "Indian?"

"Yeah." Andy stared at Sherlock. "Sure." He turned to John. "You go pick it up. My eyes are still wounded."

"He has legs," John complained, and then his gaze slid to Sherlock. "Oh fuck it, why even bother pretending that's gonna happen," he huffed as he went to his room to get his shoes. "What do you two bastards want?"

"Look," Andy said as he heard the gate squeak. "You need to make up your mind about what you're doing with John because-"

"You encouraged him to go out," Sherlock said, folding his arms as he leaned against the kitchen counter.

"Yeah," Andy said, still not entirely sure that had been his finest moment. Especially since John had been incommunicado the following day, but he figured they could talk about that later. "Look if you're jealous then that's your tough shit. John did nothing wrong. You ain't together-"

Sherlock looked put out. "I refuse to explain my relationship with John to you of all people."

Fair enough. Andy shrugged. "All I'm saying, and I speak

for all of us here, is that if John has a chance to have a proper boyfriend then he should go for it. You're nice..." Andy broke off as if struggling for the right word. "Interesting enough," he settled on and was almost amused at the flicker of pride in Sherlock's eyes. "But we all know-"

"We are dating," Sherlock sighed. "And, in the future, sending someone out when they are feeling...like that, it rarely ends well if they go out alone."

That was a fucking huge amount of information to take in at once. Confused, Andy screwed up his face.

"You and John? Properly?"

"Yes." Sherlock looked as if he'd rather be on the rack than submit to this.

"How long?"

"Nine days. Would you like the hours and minutes as well?"

"Who the fuck does that?" Jesus, Sherlock could be fucking weird at times.

Andy passed out on the sofa, his belly full from the takeaway and head fuzzy from the beer. John and Sherlock must have left him to it.

When he woke, it was to laughter and a significantly brighter room so fuck only knew what time in the morning it was.

Hell, who was he kidding? It was probably afternoon.

"Stop it!" John hissed through his giggles. "You'll fall and break your bloody neck!"

"But it looks interesting."

There was the sound of someone scrabbling up to stand on the counter and then the sound of a long exhale. "That does not look interesting, it looks like toxic death!"

"How is that not interesting?" Sherlock asked with what sounded like utter bafflement.

"Because it's gonna eat up my deposit!"

"John don't be an idiot, that went years ago, Andy's 'hide the used condom' idiocy saw to that."

Oh, yeah, that had been brilliant. There was a sudden yelp and then an almighty crash. The sound of plates smashing had him sitting up instantly, slightly concerned that something had gone wrong.

John and Sherlock had both somehow tumbled and ended up half wedged in the sink.

John started to cackle.

"We may have pulled the counter away from the wall," Sherlock announced, twisting to stare at the edge.

John cackled even more. "God, I'm gonna be utterly broke when I leave here," he said mournfully.

"I could always teach you how to play poker," Sherlock offered suddenly.

John grinned.

And then Andy saw it. Saw Sherlock's eyes suddenly warm and the almost sweet smile that tugged at his lips. So he buried back down into the sofa and let himself drift off to sleep, lulled by the quiet sniggers.

Pair of morons.

———————————————

"Oi."

Sherlock paused at the door and turned to Andy with a very sceptical expression on his face, as if he doubted the following conversation would be of any use to him.

"You and John-"

"Must we go through this again? It's dreadfully dull watching you think."

"So help me if he ever comes home with a needle in his arm I will fucking rip you up to kingdom come."

He expected a clever comeback and one he probably didn't fully understand.

He didn't expect the nod of agreement.

"Good," Sherlock said tightly then walked out.

Andy let out a breath.

Fuck he was still hungry. He paused and thought about it before hunting down the takeaway boxes from the other night.

Mycroft Holmes - 7th January

It wasn't particularly as if Mycroft Holmes had anything against John Watson. Indeed, spending Christmas with him had been relatively pleasant, especially considering that Sherlock was in the room and barred from any class one substances.

No, there wasn't anything he could claim to dislike about John's inherent personality except a slight frustration against those who had a natural charisma and seemed to get ahead in life. It was what John had done rather than who he was.

Namely, John Watson, idiot extraordinaire, had gotten into a fight with Victor Trevor and broken the man's nose. Really, Sherlock should have had far more sense and explained things clearly to John, but his brother had always enjoyed indulging in drama.

Had, apparently being the operative word these days.

"You have nothing else?" Sherlock demanded, shifting in the chair where he was slumped into the leather.

"Nothing I can give you," Mycroft replied. "I am not your personal google machine."

It was concerning that even now, when Sherlock was determined to show no weakness, his brother's lips firmed in worry as he drew in a deep breath. His eyes were tired and his movements a little more staccato than usual.

"How long did you think you could continue to blackmail Mr Trevor for?"

Sherlock's eyes snapped to his, wary and angry. "You knew," he said, his tone aiming for nonchalance and falling painfully short.

Mycroft didn't even bother to dignify that with an answer. "Why not just let the boy have the beating for breaking Trevor junior's nose and be done with it?" he asked, a sudden wave of tiredness threatening.

"He was defending me-"

"Then you should have taken the beating," Mycroft suggested. "But blackmailing him? You know what rats do when cornered. More than that, Sherlock, you know how dangerous this man is without being provoked."

His brother looked close to sulking. "If you cannot give me any new information then we are done," Sherlock snapped after a moment, drawing up as if to stand and walk away.

"You are sinking," Mycroft warned. "You are better than this, Sherlock."

"I am trying to protect-"

"Then that is your problem," Mycroft replied, sitting forward and catching Sherlock's eye firmly. "When I prosecute men like Mr Trevor, I lay a case out like an exact science and-"

"I hardly think it will help me to play you in this situation," Sherlock started to complain.

"It will hardly help you if you treat this like a game," Mycroft snapped. "You are tinging this situation with romanticism which produces the same effect as working a love story into the fifth postulate of Euclid. Believe me, Sherlock, you will fail."

For a moment, Sherlock drew back as if burned, his fingers falling from their tight clench around the arm of the chair, and sliding uselessly down. It was almost as if Mycroft was witnessing the first moment of awareness, of seeing how deep the pit was that Sherlock had dug for himself.

But this was Sherlock, it hardly lasted long. Any momentary awareness of mortality faded quickly and was replaced by snaps of temper in its wake.

"I have more on Jim Trevor than your people have amassed in the twenty years he has been building up his cartel," Sherlock sneered as he stood. "If you are lacking in information then it just shows how pathetic your knowledge is. Do not judge me by your standards."

His brother took one last disgusted look at Mycroft's desk and then stepped away, his long legs striding for the door.

"Does he know?" Mycroft asked. "The danger he is in currently? That there is retribution hanging over his head, held up only by the grace of your ability to manipulate the Trevor family?"

Sherlock paused at the door.

"Are you that desperate to play the hero for once?" Mycroft mused, opening his drawer to flick through his diary for his next appointment. "That, Sherlock, is possibly the most pathetic twist in this tale."

The door of his office slamming shut was all the answer that he needed.

Alfred Baird – 13th January

Where the hell had John got to? He'd been around a few minutes ago, looking around with those big wide eyes that were so not his thing.

Maybe a little bit.

Man, he was tense. And there was a guy in the corner, all tall and thick necked and dumb looking.

Smoke first. Shag later.

Outside was fucking freezing, he needed to move to LA or Las Vegas or something.

Walking a bit of a distance so the bouncers wouldn't smell his spliff (and, knowing most of them, ask for a drag) Alf wandered down one of the side roads before he pulled out his lighter.

There was a moan which was fantastic because that meant action which meant some entertainment on a cold winter's night. With what he imagined was probably a shit eating grin on his face, Alf put away the lighter, stepped into the shadows and turned the corner.

Holy Christ on a bike!

John Watson and Sherlock Holmes. He couldn't see what the hell they were doing, it was hidden by their coats, but there was an unmistakable elbow rhythm that made him grin.

Good for them, though they were mental bastards to be doing it in this weather.

There was a strangled gasp from John and his hand clenched the base of Sherlock's neck as he buried his head in the taller man's shoulder. Sherlock's arm was braced against the wall with his fingers curled.

John was doing the work then? Good lad.

It appeared they had finished, John let out a shuddering breath and mouthed at Sherlock's neck as his elbow stopped frantically pumping. Then he pulled back a little, holding up a drenched hand in the half-light cast by the street lamp.

Sherlock stepped back and dug into his pockets, pulling out a pack of what looked like baby wipes.

Alf blinked and then restrained the urge to chuckle.

"Here," Sherlock said, holding them out to John.

"You're not gonna ask me to lick my fingers?" John asked cheekily.

Yeah? That would work!

But Sherlock was stonily silent and John ended up sighing. "Are you ever gonna get checked out?"

What would be the point? Sherlock Holmes wasn't known for his patience - intravenous was his preferred method and you never could be too careful when using needles.

John wiped his hands, looking unhappy. "Are we ever gonna fuck?" he asked sounding frustrated. "I'm not a fucking blushing bride."

They weren't fucking? And God only knew why Sherlock, weirdo that he could be, took the soiled wipes and put them back in his pocket.

"Not in an alleyway," Sherlock said frankly. "And not here – why were you in this area?"

"Huh?" Alf could almost picture the confusion on John's face. "Why here? They were handing out flyers for free entry and a free vodka shot so..." the way John trailed off probably meant that he'd shrugged away the rest of the sentence.

Sometimes Alf did worry about the dipstick. He seemed so completely unaware of how pissed off Victor Trevor was about his wonky nose. Secretly, it was fucking hilarious, but Alf wasn't daft enough to mention it out loud.

Bad enough what happened to Frank at Back Door when he'd commented on Victor's face the following day.

"Besides," John carried on. "I'm not asking for fucking flowers and a water bed or something, stop making it into such a big deal."

Water bed? Those were such a ball ache. John really was an inexperienced plank if he thought those were ever a good idea for sex.

"Because you are more than just a quick shag against some filthy wall!" Sherlock kicked at an empty bottle fiercely. "You deserve more than that. And I-" he cut himself off, turning so Alf could see part of his face and the expression on it.

That expression that did not belong on Sherlock Homes' face and, for the first time, Alf started to feel a tiny bit uncomfortable, as if he were watching something he shouldn't be.

John dug his hands into his pockets and said something quietly. Whatever it was softened Sherlock in a way that rarely happened and Alf watched as Sherlock dipped his head, nudging John's lips up with his own. Whatever he said to John was far too soft to hear, and then he leaned forward the rest of the way and kissed him.

Alf was hardly a stranger to kissing. He'd got that kissing disease back in his late teens and no-one had been surprised. Filthy kisses, funny kisses, friendly kisses, sweet kisses, wet kisses, angry kisses and happy kisses.

But this was careful. Dreadfully careful and intimate.

Oh shit, he shouldn't be watching this.

He stepped back around the corner and risked losing half his spliff to the bouncers.

CHAPTER SEVENTEEN:

Night Physics

University Year 3: 23rd January

"John? Would you mind staying behind after?"

That wasn't good! Never in his life had John been asked to stay behind for anything...well, nothing that had been good. Throwing a pleading glance at Mike, John leaned in as they finished putting everything away. "Does Doctor Harrison look mad?"

Mike looked at him then peered over John's shoulder in an obvious way. "Uh...he looks like he's trying not to laugh."

"You have absolutely no subtlety," John complained with a glare.

Looking unfazed and unconcerned at that, Mike shrugged. "Oh well, can't have it all!"

There were a few students that wanted to see Harrison after the session. He was a popular man on their course; he'd worked on ships, in prisons, and even in a war zone. If John could have anyone's career it would have been Harrison's.

Unfortunately, there were loads of others on their course unit that felt the same way, so John flicked through his phone while he waited. In the end, he started looking through a couple of recent pictures on Facebook which then led to spending more time than he liked looking back at old photos.

Sherlock looked pretty young in some of them. And then

there was turd face in the background of more than John would like to admit.

There were days when John was so glad he'd broken Victor's nose.

A hitched breath made John look up into Doctor Harrison's face. "You wanted to see me?"

Doctor Harrison stared at John's phone. "I...yes," he said, seeming to give himself a shake. "Yes. You seem to be doing well. Is that..." he pointed at the phone. "Your friends?"

Huh? John looked down and then smiled. "My boyfriend and...Victor," John said, not really wanting to give a relationship link between Sherlock and Victor.

"A friend of his?" Doctor Harrison asked.

John shrugged and put the phone to one side. "Am I in trouble or-"

"No," Doctor Harrison said, giving the phone one last glance and then refocusing on John. "I've been impressed by your work this term."

John smiled, pleased with the compliment. "I'm enjoying the unit," he said honestly. "I think I'd like the idea of being a surgeon, like you were abroad. I kind of want to go into the army, be a PQ officer."

"That's unusual," Doctor Harrison said, seeming to settle into the conversation as he pulled up a stool to sit opposite John. "But you're doing well enough that I can't see any problems on the medical end. How much do you know about the army?"

"My stepfather," sort of step-father, "was an officer and I used to be in the CCF and did some basic training. I loved it. I wasn't always good at it but," John shrugged, "I haven't changed my mind."

There was an approving smile from Doctor Harrison. "There's a large degree of leadership needed," Doctor Harrison said, "and I think we may be able to help each other."

Really? John scrunched up his nose, baffled at how he could possibly help.

"There are two students that have missed a few classes. A family death and..." Doctor Harrison seemed to consider his words carefully. "And a sensitive issue. They need to be caught up and it would certainly look impressive on your application form."

"Leave no man behind and all that?" John asked, grinning. "I... thank you, but why me?"

"You are one of the few who I think could cope with the extra work load at this point in the year. That said John, should it affect your studies you must come and tell me and under no circumstances are you to chase them up. If they don't turn up to a time you designate then you need to let me know."

John nodded, unable to keep the smile from his face but for the life of him, he couldn't work out why it was that Doctor Harrison gave his phone a last, lingering glance.

"I'm a genius!" John announced as he let himself into Sherlock's room. It was a sign of how good they were that John had a key to Sherlock's new flat and could let himself in when he felt like it. "Not your sort of genius but still!"

Sherlock was typing and only lifted his eyes from the screen. "I see. Their reward for your hard work is to make you work harder?"

John nodded excitedly and grinned as Sherlock's brows drew together in confusion, clearly torn as to whether he should be amused or continue to be derogative.

John shut the door and dumped his bag on the floor. "You know," he said, walking over to the bed Sherlock lay sprawled on, "I'm like a teacher now!" He crawled up the bed and straddled Sherlock's legs. "Wanna be teacher's pet?"

Sherlock actually winced. "We need to improve your seduction technique."

Undeterred, John peered over the back of the laptop and read the article about...cow tipping? Unsure if he was reading that correctly, John threw an accusing look at Sherlock. "You changed what you were looking at," he sighed dramatically. "Well, if you think I need to improve, I suppose I'll just go and stand outside the building propositioning people until I see what works."

"Keep a chart," Sherlock suggested, the screen changing again to an email about some shipping documents that looked almost familiar. "I'd be fascinated to see the results."

Amused, John reached out and fished a pen and paper from the side table. "Okay," he said, tipping the screen forward so he could use the back to rest the paper upon. "Let's see. I could just randomly undo people's jeans and see what happens?"

"If you're determined to get arrested there are far more interesting things you could do."

"Like cow tipping?" John asked.

Sherlock flashed a smile as he continued to type. "Try to be a little more imaginative."

"For being arrested or trying to seduce someone?"

Sherlock childishly stuck his tongue out at John as he typed, fingers flying over the keyboard.

Bored, John wriggled off Sherlock's legs and sat on the bed, staring at his bag. He should really get started on his notes but he couldn't be arsed. So instead he lay on his stomach, head by Sherlock's bare feet. They were oddly cute for a man for whom nothing at first glance could be called cute. Unlike the rest of him that was tanned, Sherlock's feet were a lighter shade of gold, fine boned and arched.

John pressed a kiss to his skin. Sherlock's toes curled reflexively and John grinned, stroking a finger over a vein he could see travelling under that fine, smooth skin. It was different enough that John got caught up with it and didn't realise that the typing had stopped.

"Sorry." John turned to look over his shoulder. "Am I distracting you?"

Sherlock pulled a stubborn face. "No," he replied and snapped back to the screen.

Suddenly feeling impish, John twisted a little, trailing his finger along the vein to Sherlock's ankle and nudging the cuffs of his trousers up with his nose as he used his tongue to follow his fingers.

The typing didn't slow. If anything, it sped up.

Making a small noise of complaint when the trousers prevented him from going much higher, John reluctantly continued his path above the fabric, pressing kisses and feather light touches up Sherlock's leg.

"How much more have you got to write?"

"Two more minutes," Sherlock's voice had dropped and John hid his triumphant smirk in Sherlock's leg.

Any further up would lead to a problem – namely the laptop and Sherlock's hands. Pausing to consider the situation, John thought about the options.

And then decided to slide a hand up to wander between Sherlock's legs.

The tapping paused.

"Finished yet?" John enquired.

"Checking before I continue," Sherlock corrected as his breathing sped up a little. Enjoying himself, John bit his lip on a cheeky grin and watched his hand disappear further and further until Sherlock suddenly snapped his legs shut, trapping John's hand before it could go any further.

"Hey!"

"One minute," Sherlock assured him, his thighs solid against John's hand which conjured way too many dirty images in his head. With one hand gone, John slid his only remaining one down to his own jeans' buttons.

When he looked back up the typing had slowed but was still a steady drumbeat as Sherlock, not at all focused on the screen, tilted his head to watch.

"One more minute?" John teased.

"Three if you keep distracting me," Sherlock said pointedly.

"Then let me strip off and in a minute that will be one less thing to worry about."

With a nod, Sherlock released his hand and John sat up on his knees, pulling his jumper and t-shirt over his head in one smooth move.

Sherlock was looking over his laptop screen but snapped his gaze down again when he saw John had spotted him. John wriggled out of the rest of his clothes but Sherlock never once looked up again.

It was amazing that the man could have such iron control in some things and absolutely none in others.

No sooner had John sat back on the bed when Sherlock practically tossed the laptop to the floor with a crash that made John lean forward in concern, only to be attacked by teeth, tongue, hands and acres of Sherlock Holmes at his best.

"So, do you still want me to practice my seduction technique outside?"

Sherlock huffed a laugh against his lips. "Maybe just to refine it."

John changed tactics and tried to wrestle Sherlock down onto the bed, ending up on top of the man and laughing down at him. "I'll bet you made at least one mistake on that email," John teased.

"You can check if you like."

Nah, John had far more important things to do, like stripping the smug idiot underneath him.

When Sherlock was a writhing mess (and John was the smug one) he reached out only to realise that they were at the wrong end of the bed for ease of access to the condom drawer.

"Here."

John gaped down at him. "Do you produce them or something?"

"You were prepared," Sherlock nodded at his jeans.

"Thief," John accused without heat, slinking forward again and holding his hand out for the condom. But Sherlock seemed to be looking at it thoughtfully.

"Unless we don't need one?" John said, hating how hopeful he sounded.

"Of course we need one." Sherlock's thoughts seemed to have strayed, and then he lowered his hands, John assumed to roll the rubber over his cock. Surprised, John just shrugged and leaned down to kiss him, unable to remember the last time Sherlock had done that himself-

Mid kiss, John yelped in surprise as the condom slid on him instead. Stunned, he glanced down, watching Sherlock's long fingers roll the damned thing down.

"I haven't-" what the hell did Sherlock think he'd done? "I swear I've never-"

"Of course you haven't," Sherlock's replied as he rifled through his trousers.

John blinked. "I'm so trying not to be offended or a git but why do I need one then?"

Sherlock pressed something into his hands.

Lube.

Stunned and a tiny bit awed (or was that terrified) John looked up. "But I thought-"

Sherlock brushed a strand of hair out of John's eyes. "You have had sex before John," he reminded him firmly.

"But-" how the hell was he meant to explain that he had kind of wanted Sherlock to take control, at least until John felt more confident or at least knew what to do. What if... Christ the amount of 'what ifs' running through his head at the moment was insane.

Sherlock leaned up and kissed him. Bracing his arms on either side of his head, John followed Sherlock back down so his partner wasn't craning his neck. And the things was, whether or not it was Sherlock's intention (and knowing

Sherlock, John doubted that it was), John had a chance to look after him for once, to take the lead and give something back.

It was a strange epiphany.

It wasn't scary to prepare Sherlock – they'd done that sort of thing enough times and John was confident enough with that to know what Sherlock liked, what made him grip at John's shoulder and breathe shakily into John's ear.

Grabbing a pillow with his toes and manoeuvring it up in a manner that probably wasn't as smooth as he'd liked to believe, he slid it under Sherlock's hips, angling him up and pressing a kiss to his hip bone as John withdrew his fingers.

Awkwardly positioning himself, he aimed forward carefully until he was seated just inside the opening ring of muscle before bracing his elbows on either side of Sherlock's head. Running a hand through hair that was turning a sleek brown from sweat, he kissed Sherlock slowly. Then, taking a steadying breath, he pushed forward millimetre by millimetre.

Under him Sherlock shifted, locking his leg around John's waist and tipping himself up for a better angle. It took a fucking epic amount of control to not just thrust in manically and instead keep the carefully controlled, slow push.

"John-" Sherlock hissed against his lips. "Move."

"Please," John whispered, brushing lips against Sherlock's cheek. "Let me do this my way."

Sherlock restrained the urge to sigh with pleasure as gentle lips trailed across his shoulders. John's hand, linked with his, was pressed into the bed by his head as the other gripped his hip, smoothing a careful thumb over the skin there.

The pace was decadently slow in a way he'd never experienced before, as if orgasm would be an afterthought. There was a heady temptation to control the long, wonderful thrusts with his legs, to pull John in at a far greater speed, but he had promised, and this was new, uncharted territory. Terrifying in its intensity.

248

John's lips never stopped moving, whispered words that Sherlock could barely make out but that were said in a gentle, reverent tone that made his body hum with pleasure. Gentle kisses that made his heart flutter and careful brushes of lips and tongue that made him arch and gasp.

"Sorry," John whispered. "I get a bit overly affectionate." He let go of Sherlock's hand and ducked his eyes.

Sighing in frustration, Sherlock grabbed at his hand, linking them again "If I disliked it, I would tell you," he muttered, searching John's lips out.

"Promise?"

Sherlock nodded, shifting a little and enjoying the gentle sparks John was eliciting from his body. It hadn't taken John long to find his prostate and, while not exactly perfect, he was showing signs of improvement.

Nothing slow had ever been this good before. Slow was ordinary, dull, pointless, brain rotting and boring but this? It was like being able to stop everything and experience the world completely as it was at that single moment.

And John? John Watson like this was utterly devastating. Sweat was turning his hair darker and his face was flushed from the incredible restraint he was showing. John's usually light eyes were darkening with desire until their colour was like shot silk, impossible to gauge. John's bitten lip was all Sherlock's own work and the faintest flush on his throat and chest from Sherlock's minor stubble created something primitive within Sherlock. John was his.

But it was the stunned, awed look that John would occasionally give him that was intoxicating. The slightly terrified, slightly protective look as if Sherlock was something he considered precious.

John was a bloody idiot if he thought that, but something in Sherlock still warmed to the idea, misconceived and idealistic as it was.

"Stay with me," John whispered into his ear. "Please," he added, stroking Sherlock's temple.

"I am," Sherlock licked a strip up John's jaw line, fascinated by the way bones and blood and flesh made up this wonderful man. "Thinking about you," he added. "Just you."

There was a slight shiver that ran through John's body, relief or arousal Sherlock couldn't tell and a small part of him hated that John had thought he was elsewhere. John's hand slid down until it was wrapped around Sherlock's cock.

"John-"

Not yet. He wasn't ready for this to end yet. John shot him an apologetic look. "This is really hard!" he confessed looking strained.

Feeling a wave of emotion, Sherlock brushed a thumb over John's mouth. "How long?" he asked watching as John nipped at the tip of his thumb.

John let out a shaking laugh, "Er, how long have we been doing this? You arched earlier and I thought I was about to burst a blood vessel!"

Smiling, Sherlock thrust into John's hand, frowning when John removed it. "You're close," he hummed, creeping his own hand down.

John breathed heavily. "You aren't," he said frankly. "I don't want to rush you."

Any other time Sherlock would have snapped that he was being foolish, but there was something telling him not to, telling him to go as carefully with John as John was with him. "Go slow then," he said, pressing a kiss to the shaking arm braced on the mattress.

John nodded and dipped his other hand again, creating gentle strokes that made the earlier sparks of pleasure suddenly crackle and jolt. A sudden, wonderfully aimed stroke, both inside and out, made Sherlock hiss with sheer pleasure and clench, which in turn made John swear. "Fucking hell," he almost cried, sounding wrecked as he bit at his lip and looked down. When John glanced back up his eyes were bright. "That was really good," he breathed. "You're killing me."

No, it was completely the other way around.

He could feel it, creeping up, tingling from the base of his spine. Such a strange feeling to have the pleasure build like this – Sherlock was used to orgasms that were like a hit of cocaine – instant and blinding or instant and disappointing. Never this strange spiral of being aware and tugged under a wave at the same time.

John sucked in a surprised breath, his face close to Sherlock's and shaking.

"Need you," John said in a wrecked whisper, just before his orgasm finally crested. Endless waves of pleasure hit him and he was dimly aware of John making his own sounds.

It was only afterwards that he remembered to feel irritated with himself. He'd missed John, missed seeing his face. Was continuing to miss it as John collapsed onto him, burying his head in Sherlock's shoulder. His breath was coming in fierce pants, as if he'd run a marathon. That had been far better than expected. In truth, Sherlock had been prepared to guide John along and soothe his nerves. Where the sudden confident, considerate and patient lover had sprung from, Sherlock hadn't a clue.

But he wasn't complaining.

John was truly magnificent when he believed in himself. Perhaps he should slip a twenty into the pocket of the doctor that had made John bounce into the room as if he'd won something wonderful.

"Think I died," John complained, muffled by Sherlock's collarbone. "Best way to go though."

Not wanting to reply to that, Sherlock stroked his free hand down John's bare back.

Groaning in complaint, John pushed himself up and carefully pulled out. There was hardly any pain, just a pleasant ache that felt more like muscle burn after a good exercise. John shifted out of bed to head for the bathroom, yanking on Sherlock's dressing gown. "Back in a sec," he called, wobbling out and shutting the door.

Alone, Sherlock sat up, feeling strangely bereft.

He could make people scream in pleasure, make them cry and beg, writhe and grab with desperate hands. He could deduce what people wanted in seconds, knew every kink that was out there and had tried most. There were things he could do to John that John had never dreamed of, things that would make John's toes curl and his voice hoarse. But what John had just done...Sherlock had no idea how to even begin replicating that. How to make sex and fucking into something slow and heady, patient and loving.

There was a phrase, skittering at the edge of his mind that he couldn't even bring himself to think of because of the sheer sentimental drivel associated with it but, god help him, it seemed to fit.

They had just made lo..

No.

John wandered back in, mouth curled in amusement. "Your flat-mate's trying to drown himself in beer," he announced. "We may have been a tiny bit too loud for," he frowned at the clock, "half past four in the afternoon."

The people who cared about that had clearly never experienced John Watson.

"I'm shattered," John complained, sliding into the bed still wearing Sherlock's dressing gown as he reached for the laptop. "If I fall asleep you may have to rescue this. It's taken enough hits recently as it is," he added, curling up around the machine.

Drawing up his knees and placing his chin upon them, Sherlock studied John closely. He was still so young; the boyish charm and easy grin were strongly apparent. His skin unmarred and smooth. Last year it had been an exercise in self-control when summer had come and John had stripped off his shirt to welcome a golden tan while playing football or rugby. Deliciously tempting honey gold skin had distracted Sherlock more than once. His hair was tussled from Sherlock's hands and just the length Sherlock preferred.

He had to be kept safe.

Sherlock refocused on the laptop, certain that he'd closed all the tabs. It was only when John made an annoyed sound that Sherlock raised an enquiring eyebrow, feeling his heart flutter a little. Despite not looking over, John answered the unspoken question.

"Not one mistake!" John looked dreadfully disappointed. "How do you manage that?"

Ah, the email. It was unlikely that John would manage to make the leap from the email to what Sherlock had been working on.

"You're reading my message?" Sherlock asked, watching him.

"You left it open," John tutted, smiling. And, from the ease in his shoulders, John didn't suspect a thing.

Sherlock reached out to peel the dressing gown off of John to pull it around himself. John cracked a yawn and leaned further into the pillow, smiling as Sherlock pulled the covers over him to replace the warmth of the dressing gown.

In the bathroom, Sherlock braced against the sink, staring at his reflection. Turning, he knelt and slid the bath panel open to stare at the tiny packets of cocaine.

Sitting with his back against the toilet, he thought.

CHAPTER EIGHTEEN:

Public Services

I T HAD BEEN A LONG shift and, to top it off, there had been a grisly murder which Sergeant Sidney Bradstreet had picked up within the last half hour.

The man had been called William Jameson and he was twenty years old, beaten to death, the poor kid.

A crowd had formed (bloody vultures) and, in a filthy mood, Sidney stormed to scare them off. The problem was, once he had finished, one hadn't moved. Not entirely sure if the man wasn't perhaps just shell shocked at having seen a dead body, Sidney tried to push his foul mood away and swallow back the immediate scathing retort that begged to be used.

"Are you all right," he asked, his tone a little too short still.

"Yes." The man nodded, and closer up he looked younger than Sidney had expected, more like a student. Rich, Sidney would guess from the expensive leather jacket, but still just a kid. "But I live over there." He pointed.

Really? All attempts at making an effort to be an upstanding officer faded away in an instant as did any building sympathy. "Go around," Sidney suggested with some frustration.

"No." The guy rolled his eyes. "I am not adding an extra twenty minutes to my journey time." And with that he ducked under the tape.

When Sidney had been in his twenties he wouldn't have dared pull a stunt like that but...but then he had seen all kinds of stuff in London that he would never have dreamed of pulling when he'd been younger. So he just, well...floundered, stunned for a moment as he looked over at the Inspector helplessly. Thankfully the Inspector seemed to have heard the conversation and was even more shattered than Sidney was. She just shook her head and gave Sidney a pointed look.

Which translated to: keep an eye on him and just let it go.

The guy stopped halfway across the road and paused to stare down at the body. Watching him, Sidney had a sudden moment of guilt. Members of the public shouldn't have to see that sort of thing. But, when he walked forward to take the man's elbow and gently lead him away, the man tilted his head sharply to one side. Then turned around, looking up at the flats above.

"I assume you're about to arrest the occupier of the flat up there? Fourth along and third up."

Humouring him, Sidney nodded. "Sure. You need to get moving."

Hazel eyes narrowed and flicked to all the key components before refocusing on Sidney. "The murder weapon was a wooden bar from a window box. All but three of the flats above have one. The window box from directly above is rotten, first window in on the top level was painted before its removal, which leaves the one I just pointed out to you."

Sidney frowned at him and then stared down at the body, wondering if he was just that tired that he'd missed what was apparently an obvious clue or whether the man in front of him was just the local nutter. "And you know it was a window box because?"

With an exasperated sigh the man strode forward and Sidney barely managed to yank him back before he touched the body and ruined the evidence for court.

Seemingly insulted at the touch, the man yanked his arm out of Sidney's grip and studied him for a moment.

"Oh," he said, sounding disappointed. "Can't you...did you really miss all of that?" he asked as if in disbelief.

"I..." baffled, Sidney glanced at DC Declan who was making his way over. With a helpless shrug, he pointed at the guy without a clue of what the hell to do with him.

"You all right there?" Declan asked.

The guy turned, his face catching Declan's torch and illuminating tanned skin, one of those hooked noses that seemed to be favoured by the old rich families and eyes that weren't quite focused and would look more familiar in a crack den.

Great.

"He's high."

<hr>

The phone wouldn't stop ringing. Refusing to move, John unwound an arm from the sheet he was sort of using and patted around for his phone.

"Mm?" he asked as he put the phone to his ear.

"Is this Mr John Watson?"

"Sure," John agreed, almost certain he could get back to sleep now that the ringing had stopped.

"Do you know a Sherlock Holmes?"

Ah yes, his git of a boyfriend who had texted... huh, when had he texted? John opened his eyes to check the clock, twenty minutes ago? Jesus, he could sleep quickly. John groaned into the phone. "If I say no can I go back to sleep?" he asked, pretty sure that in that time Sherlock couldn't possibly have come to any harm.

Though it was Sherlock.

There was a pause. "He's been thrown in the cells to cool off."

"Okay," John said, still half asleep.

"I need you to pick him up."

Pick him up? If that bloody git had been fibbing with those texts about being home safe, John was going to kill him. "Fine, what club are you?" John huffed.

"Club?" The voice on the other end of the phone sounded genuinely confused. "Mr Watson, this is the police."

Fuck's sake!

Sherlock Holmes. Strange name, but it fit, somehow.

Sidney wasn't exactly sure what he'd been expecting after the phone call to John Watson (probably another addict), but the sleepy-eyed kid that turned up looking as if he'd just rolled out of bed was not it.

"You called him? Why did you call him?" Sherlock Holmes said, sounding a little on edge.

"He was in your call history the most." Sidney shrugged as he pulled out the paper work and attached them to the clipboard. "For your fine, Mr Holmes." He glanced back at John Watson, feeling a momentary stirring of guilt rise within him.

What was this kid doing with a drug addict calling him? He didn't appear to be showing any signs of addiction. Slightly aware that he was spacing out, Sidney focused on the pair again and specifically at Sherlock who simply stared down at the papers as if repulsed. Then he turned imperiously to the kid, who was clearly trying to use the top of the reception desk as a pillow and said, "You do it."

John Watson just flipped him the finger and buried his head in the crook of his elbow. "G'way," he mumbled. "I hate you."

Rolling his eyes, Sherlock Holmes just picked up the pen and clipboard and for a moment Sidney relaxed.

Until the nutter tried to slide the clipboard under the kid's arm and put the pen in his hand. The kid stirred, glared and stood up straighter, flipping through the pages with a sigh.

"Let's see. Name: Dickhead, first name: Massive!" Sidney watched as the kid started to write on the page.

A look revealed that John Watson was actually writing down Holmes, Sherlock, which was fine.

"Occupation: Idiot," John added calmly. "Address: Long suffering boyfriend's sofa."

"Partner," Sherlock corrected, sounding as if he'd done this many times before.

They were together? Sidney studied the pair, not quite sure if he'd have put them together. He kept his eyes fixed upon the kid.

"Fill out the form yourself then," John threatened. "Next of kin: Mycroft Holmes, in big, big letters to show how much you love him."

"You." Sherlock was peering around the wall at the detainees waiting in reception, his eyes darting over them.

"And Violet Holmes," John continued. "Long suffering angelic family."

Sherlock glared heavenward for a moment and then returned to his staring.

"Ooh," John said, twisting around and smiling at Sidney. "This is a good one. Reason for fine and amount of fine." He looked over at Sherlock. "Go on then, light of my life; what did we do today?"

"You really shouldn't have woken him." Sherlock glared over John's head at Sidney. "He's beyond irritable in the morning."

"Drug use," Sidney said and inwardly sighed when John didn't look at all surprised. "But no possession though."

John nodded and started to write, this time in silence. Sherlock's face screwed up a little and he glared at the people around the corner.

"You use?" Sidney asked quietly, reaching out for the numbers for anonymous groups, but John shook his head.

"Christ no," the kid said. "I'm training to be a doctor. That would be my career up in flames."

Sidney looked over at Sherlock and John followed his gaze.

"Don't get me started," John said with a sigh. "And those will not work with him, believe me," he said, catching sight of the cards.

"There are groups for families and friends affected by drug use," Sidney offered. "If you need it."

"He doesn't," Sherlock snapped.

John ignored the pair of them. "Here," he said, handing the paper over to Sherlock. "I would sign it for you but then we'd both be thrown downstairs for fraud."

"Don't be so dramatic," Sherlock muttered, taking the pen. "I wouldn't be thrown downstairs."

John shrugged and leaned back on the desk. "Do they have beds?" he asked grumpily, "'cause that's a bloody tempting idea right about now."

"You put down Mother and Mycroft," Sherlock snarled.

"'Cause they're your next of kin!" John looked at Sidney beseechingly. "Tell him to get on with it, take me home and make me tea."

"Mr Holmes." Sidney tried to nudge him along. "Your signature."

But Sherlock was focused on the form. "You are aware you don't actually need this chicken scratch scrawl to be a doctor?"

"Okay," John said, sounding for all the world like someone who would say anything just to get some sleep.

"Occupation?" Sherlock slammed the form down. "Unemployed?" he snarled disbelievingly.

John looked at him wide eyed, then glanced at Sidney. "What else was I meant to put?" he asked, sitting up.

Sidney leaned back and reached for his cuffs with a sigh. "Is he a dealer?" he asked John.

"No!" The pair of them spared him a second's glance; Sherlock sounded as if the idea was beneath him and John sounded horrified.

This was not worth it. Sidney released his hold on the

cuffs, acknowledging that it would never go further than an arrest and would eat into what was already a very long shift.

Looking thunderous, Sherlock signed the papers and then peeled out the money from his wallet, tossing it on top.

"That's a lot of cash," Sidney muttered, giving John a pointed look.

John nodded, seeming to completely miss the point that it took quite some illegal activity to come up with that kind of cash.

"Out of curiosity," Sidney said as he ran the money through the till. "That stuff you were saying about the window box and the murder. You were just full of it right?"

"This is our police force," Sherlock muttered to John with a wave of his hand. "Comforting, isn't it?"

John eyed him up and then looked at Sidney. "What do you mean?"

"He claimed he solved a murder within two minutes of being on the scene."

John seemed thoughtful. "Window box?"

Sherlock tapped his fingers on the counter. "Blunt force trauma, but cuts and scrapes so it had to be an uneven surface, sharp in places. There were small splinters around the body and deep holes which would indicate the object was old wood and still had nails in it. There were flower beds in the flats above; all of them had one and those that didn't could be explained away apart from one. If the killer wasn't in the flat then there will at least be evidence there. It seems more likely that the murderer is the occupier though, only someone living there would have known how easy it was to pull the wooden board off. Otherwise it would have been a foolish attempt to even reach for the board."

Sherlock sounded as if it was the most boring thing imaginable and John's mouth had dropped open slightly.

"Come." Sherlock turned on his heel. "John!"

With an apologetic shrug, John followed.

Still stunned, Sidney sat for a moment before he dialled down to the DS still down in the morgue.

"That body, the wounds...are there any splinters or indications of it being pierced by a nail?"

"Uh...I'll check..." there was a pause. "Yeah. Bloody filthy as well, Sid."

Holy mother of Christ.

John ran down the steps, sure he had lost Sherlock until a hand reached out and grabbed him, pulling him into the shadows to snog him senseless.

"I can't believe you did that," John gasped when Sherlock finally pulled away. "It's unbelievable."

"Yes well," Sherlock shifted uncomfortably, "in hindsight it wasn't the best idea to walk through a police squad while high."

"I-" John shook his head. "I wasn't talking about that, you berk!" he said, swatting at Sherlock. "I was talking about you solving a murder investigation like that."

"It was simple," Sherlock complained.

John laughed and wrapped his arms around Sherlock's neck. "Brilliant," he argued. "Did you see the Sergeant's face?"

That earned him a smile. "Yes." Sherlock looked rather smug. "He did look rather impressed, didn't he?"

John grinned and then walloped him over the head. "Do not text me until you are in the flat and your front door is shut!"

CHAPTER NINETEEN:

Love and Death

3rd February

Sherlock had gone bloody insane. Or was really angry. Or bored. Hell, it could even be all three; it wasn't as if Sherlock ever did things in halves.

It took the ninth pointless argument for John to snap.

"God, if it annoys you so much go home," John muttered, watching Sherlock tear his room apart looking for who the hell knew what.

"I just need to think," Sherlock snapped. "I can't think."

Every time they had a fight recently this came up. Sherlock's assertion that he couldn't think properly, that he was unable to process what he saw, that the world was crawling and buzzing all over him. It made no sense and John had tried everything: sex, massages, talking, walking, cooking, sacrificing his friends to Sherlock's deductive skills, laughing about his cooking, everything. The thing was, nothing seemed to be working. It would always end with Sherlock stomping off home and reappearing after three or four days, only for the mad cycle to begin again.

Maybe this was what relationships were like when the honeymoon period wore off. If so, it was a fucking miracle anyone made it to ten years, let alone fifty.

So a new tactic had been developed: ignoring him.

John dropped his gaze to his text book and kept reading,

trying not to wince as his belongings went flying around the room. Wanker.

"John? Did you hear me? I don't know where your passport is."

"Top drawer, left. At the back," John replied in a dull tone.

"I didn't know where it was," Sherlock said, sounding affronted.

"Now you do." There was no way he was being dragged into this.

"That is not the point," Sherlock snarled, actually snarled as if he were a dangerous, wild creature suddenly summoned into John's room. "You told me."

God, he was getting a headache, and he wasn't even sure why. "Next time I won't then," John answered, reading the same sentence for what felt like the fiftieth time.

"You are deliberately missing the point," Sherlock muttered as he leaned against the wall, his face looking pale and almost feverish.

"To this pointless argument? I wonder why?" The information wasn't going in. At this rate, John would have to throw Sherlock out. Again. Though hopefully, Sherlock would leave on his own accord. The idiot was already seething and knocked something off the top of the drawers. Probably a glass from the sound.

John kept reading. "I'll happily listen properly if you tell me what the real problem is."

Silence.

Okay then. John drew in a long breath and then let it out when Sherlock slammed out of the room, hating that he felt a flicker of relief that he was finally alone.

10th February

Valentine's Day was fast approaching.

It was not a particularly favourite time of the year. In fact,

Sherlock would go as far as to say that it was a loathsome time of the year that should be abandoned post-haste and forgotten about as quickly as those blasted card shops that had been constructed just to irritate people into bothering about certain days of the year.

But it was the done thing to treat your 'special someone' (another abysmal phrase) to a good day and John should be treated to a good day, or at least not made to feel as if Sherlock didn't care.

The things he did for love.

There were limits though. No flowers (John would think he had gone mad and the damn things would probably shrivel up and rot within five seconds of crossing John's threshold) and no chocolate (John wasn't a huge fan of chocolate). There were to be no cuddly toys or jewellery exchanging hands, which left a lot of the usual Valentine's Day gifts unacceptable.

What did one get when they were in a committed, monogamous, homosexual relationship? There should be a website, or a guide or something to help. Usually Sherlock would go to John for such problems but, sadly, that was not really an option.

The card shop was a trial. Beyond idiotic. Rows and rows of mundane, dull poetry and empty messages. Silly animals gazing adoringly at each other (exactly what was it about the day that made people entertain the idea that animals and romance were somehow linked?) and cartoon characters that looked as if a five-year-old had been sitting down with some frazzled moron for half an hour (not that it would be surprising to discover that idea was close to the truth).

It was made worse by the fact that he had managed five days this time. Five long, long days shadowing John just so he had something else to focus on because, at the moment, trying to work out how to find evidence to link the Trevor family to their sordid past was proving to be beyond him. He couldn't think, couldn't see the links. And that was the very last thing Sherlock wanted.

11th February

"So dare I ask what you two are doing for Valentine's Day?" Mike asked hesitantly. "Or is it gonna disturb us all to hear your plans."

"Nothing," John replied firmly from where he was sitting with Sherlock's feet on his lap while munching on a bag of Ready Salted Crisps that were all that had been left in the cupboard. When there was a long silence, John looked up and saw Mike glancing between the two of them looking suddenly wary. Curious, John looked around and then at Sherlock who seemed to be startled by the revelation.

"Please, it's hardly your kind of thing," John said, squeezing one of Sherlock's feet. "Candlelit dinners and long moonlit walks?"

"I was unaware those activities were set in stone." Sherlock was frowning now.

John shrugged. "I'm not a big fan of it," he said. "I thought you'd be fine with not doing anything."

Mike cleared his throat awkwardly. "Uh..." he looked away, seeming frustrated.

"Did you want the sofa?" John asked, then restrained the urge to sigh when Sherlock pushed his feet firmly into John's lap as if to prevent him from ever moving again. "Don't be such a child," John muttered. "You've been nagging me for an hour to go and see the new exhibit at the science museum."

Sherlock nodded and took his feet off John's lap, swinging himself to sit up. "Fine. Shoes, quickly," he announced, darting into John's room.

It was like having a small puppy at times.

"I...I was kinda hoping for some advice," Mike said awkwardly. "About what to do with Kirsty on Valentine's Day."

John shrugged. "Sorry mate, no idea."

"You've never taken a girl out on Valentine's Day?" Mike asked, disbelieving.

Once.

"No," John said firmly, ignoring that line of thought. "I told you, it's not my thing. Now, if you'll excuse me, I get to take Sherlock to his version of a sweet shop for however long it takes for security to throw us out."

Sherlock appeared again, dropping John's shoes and coat onto the sofa. "Quickly," he barked.

John smiled grimly up at Mike then laughed as Sherlock huffed a sigh and decided to try and put John's shoes on as if it were John who was acting like a small child.

<hr />

12th February

Clearly, John had some strange issue with the day. But every couple Sherlock saw were doing something for Valentine's Day and, as far as he could tell, it was a win-win to follow the crowd. Either John secretly did want to engage in the activity but was afraid of being mocked for it or there was a genuine reason for his uncharacteristic hate of the day, which Sherlock would discover by getting John to participate in the ritual.

However, there were some difficulties, such as what to buy.

"Make it special," Paul told Andy as they sat watching TV while John was out picking up the Chinese.

"I am not scattering roses on the bed, last time I did that I got a fucking thorn bush in my arse!"

Hyperbole. Sherlock remained silent, trying to focus on the rhythm of his fingers as he tapped against the sofa arm. He kept losing count.

"Not like that, you berk! I meant make it personal. Like her favourite sweet or perfume. Something that shows you actually pay attention," Paul argued.

Personal. Interesting and feasible.

"But I have a feeling that means paying attention," Andy said slowly. "Fucking hell, Paul; this is me we're talking about."

What would John want that was personal?

Sherlock lost the rhythm again as a sudden shudder ran through him, dancing away his vision for a few seconds. God he wanted cocaine.

Clenching his hands into fists he glared at the television, trying to ignore what his body was telling him.

John liked drumsticks; the sweet, chewy things on a stick and would bemoan that they no longer used sherbet in the middle. He liked old medical books with intricate drawings and would flick though them with fascination, sneezing at the dusty pages. John liked food and John probably needed to eat out because there was only so much salt the human body could take from frozen pizzas before it started to complain.

Then activities. John liked the cinema. Sherlock was not that patient. But Sherlock could manage a film on the laptop. Maybe. An old one that he could make fun of and John could defend between giggles.

That surely covered chocolate, personal present, dinner, activity, even if he had needed a tiny sprinkling of what was left from under the bath.

14th February

When John opened his eyes, Sherlock was staring at him, fully dressed and waiting like a kid on Christmas morning.

"What did you do?" John asked warily, freezing under the bed covers.

"Would you like tea?"

Really nervous now, John slowly started to sit up. "Oh God, have you finally killed someone?" he asked.

Sherlock glared. "Why would I kill someone and ask you if you wanted tea?"

Because it was Sherlock? "Okay," John said slowly, looking around the room for a clue as to what was going on.

"Tea would be great," he said, still half expecting that it had been a trick or that he'd missed something.

Sherlock nodded and disappeared.

Sighing, John yanked some clothes on, figuring *that* if this was Sherlock's way of announcing he was about to become a fugitive John had at least better be dressed first.

"You're meant to stay in bed," Sherlock complained as he walked in with a steaming cup. "How can I bring you tea in bed if you're not actually in the bed?"

John had to repeat the sentence back to himself to ensure he'd heard correctly. Utterly bewildered now, he sat on the bed and pulled the cover back over himself. Sherlock rolled his eyes and passed him the cup. "I suppose that will do," he sulked.

Not sure what he was meant to do, John just drank his tea, relatively sure he wouldn't get scolded for that.

John stared down at the milky liquid, impressed at how good it actually tasted. "Is this my tea?" he asked suddenly.

"I bought you tea bags," Sherlock said, watching him closely.

Huh. Well at least that sort of made up for the gallons of tea Sherlock had drunk over the past year for free. "It's good." John studied it as if the brand would suddenly appear in the cup.

"It's Darjeeling tea."

That sounded fancy. "Is it a new thing?"

Sherlock closed his eyes and sighed. "Yes, John. Brand new," he said in a voice that suggested John was being an idiot.

Who cared? He had good tea. "Thank you." John grinned. "It's amazing."

Sherlock seemed pleased with himself and nodded even as John's phone went off with an alert.

What time tonight?

John sighed at the text from his brother, thumbing over the buttons thoughtfully.

"Here." John stared at the bunch of nettles that was presented to him. Raising his eyes slowly, he stared up at Sherlock.

"Why?" he asked slowly.

"Have you ever studied them?"

"No," John said frankly. "No, they never came up, strangely enough, in GCSE science."

"If you become a GP people might come in after being stung by them." Sherlock laid the nettles on the table. "You should have an in depth understanding to prevent the morons from returning."

John watched him set out some kitchen stuff and what looked like equipment stolen from uni onto the battered old coffee table then looked down at his text.

Anything was better than focusing on tonight.

"I'll get dressed then," John said.

"Your tea," Sherlock argued.

Right. This was so weird.

"Drumstick?" Sherlock asked.

"Hmm?" The nettles were actually kind of fascinating and Sherlock had brought some Dock-leaves with him as well to explain how the reactions worked.

A brown paper bag was rattled at him impatiently and John obeyed the silent command, digging his hand in and coming out with a wrapped sweet on a stick.

Sucking thoughtfully, John watched as Sherlock explained the next process, barely focusing on the words but on the man instead. The sharp, analytical gaze as he calmly, patiently (who would have thought that word applied to Sherlock?) and methodically worked his way through what he was doing. It was a side John didn't get to see all that often. A wave

269

of fondness wormed through him as he watched Sherlock, sitting cross legged on the floor as he leaned onto the chipped coffee table, intent on his experiment.

John pulled the stick out of his mouth in surprise when he tasted sherbet.

"Where did you find this?" he asked, delighted.

"Old sweet shop in an arcade," Sherlock replied, sounding distracted.

John popped the sweet back in his mouth happily and then smiled. Perhaps the last two weeks had just been a blip.

Reaching out, he pressed a kiss to Sherlock's lips, exchanging some of the sherbet which made Sherlock make a strange noise that almost sounded like a protest mixed with laughter.

14th February

John was oblivious.

It was oddly endearing and, for a moment, Sherlock almost found himself wishing they could do this more often.

It wouldn't be healthy for John though, given that he'd already scoffed four drumsticks. Though watching him lovingly suck at the last one had been an experience Sherlock wouldn't mind repeating.

One day, one day he would have John's tongue on him like that, unhampered by latex. For now, it was enough to reach over, pull John forward and kiss him, exploring the sweet strawberry sugared taste from the sweet and to lick at the remains of the sherbet, now that he was used to the sensation. For a moment, he found himself imagining it was cocaine then cut that idea off sharply. Never. Not with John.

Pulling John further forward, his partner ended up straddling him where Sherlock sat. It was an interesting angle to watch from as John fumbled with his buttons. Sherlock tugged John's t-shirt up, over his head and ran eager hands down his back, enjoying the feel of warm, smooth skin under his fingertips.

"Bedroom," John gasped. "I'm so not having a repeat of Andy."

Chuckling into John's mouth at the memory, Sherlock nodded and let John go. John was grinning down at him, holding out his hand and glancing up out of habit.

Then John's eyes found something that made the smile falter. From his position on the floor, Sherlock turned to see what he was looking at.

The clock.

"Sorry," John dropped his hand and went to retrieve his t-shirt. "Tomorrow, yeah?"

What? That wasn't right!

"We have dinner," he said dully, and god how he hated himself for that.

"Huh? No, we don't. Why would we have dinner?" John looked blank as he yanked his t-shirt back over his head.

John really was stupid at times. Sherlock took what he hoped was a deep, calming breath and looked at John pointedly.

It took a minute.

"Wait." John looked around as if able to see for the first time. "You, this…" He closed his eyes. "I told you," he muttered, "I told you I didn't want to do Valentine's Day."

"Evidently it is Valentine's Evening you object to."

John's face went blank for a moment then he turned and stormed into his room.

Interesting. Sherlock did up the buttons on his shirt. This was definitely not a confidence thing.

John appeared again; coat on, shoes on and jamming his wallet into his jeans pocket, where, just before it snapped closed, Sherlock could see a train ticket. It was slightly raised in the sleeve indicating John had just checked it was there.

John was going somewhere, pre-planned, booked and paid for on Valentine's Day evening without telling Sherlock.

Furious, Sherlock grabbed at John's arm, trying to deduce where he was going, why he was going, who he was meeting. But fear of what might be happening was keeping him from being able to pick apart what he was seeing.

"Who are you meeting?" he demanded, still trying to infer the evidence he needed.

"I told you not to do this," John hissed. "I asked you not to and you ignored me so don't you dare act as if I've been the arsehole here."

John was deliberately trying to anger him, which was irritating and worrying and infuriating.

"You are not leaving until you tell me why you are going," Sherlock demanded, feeling his control of his temper start to quake.

It was entirely the wrong thing to say.

"I do not need your fucking permission!" John shouted, eyes alight with anger. "I am not your pet or your toy, you go off for days on end without asking me for permission even though I know exactly *where* you are going and *what* you're doing to yourself so don't you dare start acting like the petty jealous boyfriend-"

"You know where I am going. I don't know where you are going!" Sherlock yelled back. "This is not the same-"

"How about I assure you I'm not going to shove some dirty fucking needle in my arm or deal with people who want nothing more than to fuck me over in every possible way," John snarled, suddenly vicious. "That's more than I ever get!"

Sherlock let go. Stunned, he watched John storm for the door and slam out of it.

How...what had just happened? He stood, unable to process it and damnit he knew why he was struggling, why he couldn't work out what he had missed. Something had set his partner off because John wasn't the type to pick fights.

If he was then he and Sherlock would do nothing else with their time.

What was he meant to do? He couldn't think without it, he couldn't have John with it. He couldn't protect John without it, yet he couldn't keep John happy with it.

Two days. He'd managed two days this time and even with that gap he couldn't work out what had happened, couldn't see why John had suddenly exploded.

He was missing something, he knew he was. He'd missed signs and indicators that he usually would have picked up on in seconds if he weren't dealing with the cravings.

It made him ache.

One more. Once more to figure this out.

It was blindingly simple once he thought about it. In fact, it was so obvious that Sherlock spent most of the train ride inwardly berating himself for being so idiotic and selfish. If he couldn't work out that John was upset because his father had died six years ago on Valentine's Day then what hope did he have in using the blackmail material from the Gloria Scott to combat Victor's threats.

John hadn't talked about the place where his father had lived with his partner. There had been a few mentions of a local pub and a strange story about cows and sheep that Sherlock hadn't really paid attention to.

Still, inexcusable.

Getting off at Dorking, Sherlock walked, not really sure where he was intending to go to find John. A graveyard perhaps? Folding his arms, he trudged off in a likely direction, trying to ignore the wind that whipped around him.

It was embarrassingly dark by the time he remembered that John came from a family who, from the sounds of it, thought of a pub as a 'home away from home'. From that point on it was simple and within twenty minutes he managed to track John down.

John was sitting on his own, staring at a half-finished pint of beer. He was in a booth, which suggested that at some point he'd had company. His brother possibly, but he was long gone now. That was annoying; Sherlock had wanted to meet the pathetic man who hid behind his mother for every facet of life.

Unsure, because John looked so miserable, Sherlock walked up to the booth and waited. As if sensing a gaze upon him, John tore his eyes from the pint and stared at Sherlock without blinking.

"You're not meant to be here," John said, his voice weary and wavering with what might be sorrow. Probably was.

"Took me a while," Sherlock replied, trying not to let his own annoyance with himself show.

John said nothing for a moment and then sighed, picking up the pint and downing it. "We'll go then," he said without any inflection.

"Have you eaten?"

"No." Yet John was standing up as if they were going to go somewhere. It was only once he was on his feet that Sherlock realised just how much John had drunk. The man could hardly stand, his hand reaching out to grip the edge of the table. Stunned, Sherlock reached for him, placing a steadying hand onto John's back.

"You have not been drinking beer," Sherlock commented, not really knowing what else to say.

"Harry's," John mumbled as he leaned into Sherlock. "We had shots."

Really?

"Toasted Dad with his favourite rum," John said, sighing as he leaned into Sherlock, his breath ghosting over the pulse point in Sherlock's throat. "That bit was good."

"He died," Sherlock said, letting his hand stroke up John's back in what he hoped was a soothing manner. "On Valentine's Day."

"Mm," John agreed. "We talked about me and you. Was fitting. Harry doesn't approve by the way."

Shocking. But John had been upset by it, had drowned his sorrows in alcohol and if Sherlock had found him sooner-

It was pointless to debate that. Instead, Sherlock pressed a kiss to John's head and tugged at him, trying to lead John to the door. "We should go home," he said quietly.

John made an affirmative noise but swayed heavily causing Sherlock to have a sudden vision of him on the train with John, trying to keep him alert and awake and not vomiting on other passengers.

Guiding him back to a chair, Sherlock leaned down to John's ear. "Stay here, just for a moment," he said, running a hand through John's hair.

"So not walking," John said as he tipped back as if struggling to balance against the wall.

True. Satisfied that even John couldn't cause trouble where he was, Sherlock strode over to the bar.

"Your friend isn't having any more," the woman behind the bar said, eyeing him up suspiciously.

"Is there a room nearby?" Sherlock asked. "He won't manage the train."

The suspicious gaze vanished and she nodded. "We got a few upstairs," she said. "Sixty quid."

It was a ridiculous amount for where they were but, given the state John was in, the easiest solution. Nodding, and handing over his debit card, Sherlock returned to where his inebriated partner slumped and crouched down in front of him.

"We're getting a room here," he said as John opened his eyes, blinking at Sherlock in a way that suggested the room was spinning around him. "We just need to go upstairs."

The doubtful look John levelled at Sherlock would have made him laugh at any other time. "'m sorry," John said as he slowly sat up. "Shitty Valentine's Day."

Ah. "I wouldn't worry," Sherlock said as he lifted John's arm around his shoulders to support the idiot. "It allows for easy improvement next year."

The snort sounded more like his John. "True. Given myself scope."

"Indeed," Sherlock replied as they weaved towards the doors where the woman from behind the bar was standing. "There are better things to do than drink the bar dry."

"You would know," John replied, and that was enough to make Sherlock grind his teeth together in frustration. Every time they had a fight, John would bring that up. It was getting repetitive and horribly predictable.

They walked up the stairs in silence, the process taking far longer than normal with John's abysmal balance. By the time they got to the room, the woman (Meg, Sherlock could now see from the name badge that she'd hastily pinned on at some point) was looking impatient as she held open the door, a key in hand.

"You need to be out by ten or you'll have to pay for the next night too," she haughtily informed Sherlock as she waved the key at him.

Snatching it from her, Sherlock sent her a scornful look. "Your hospitality is astounding," he muttered sarcastically.

Apparently, she didn't feel it was worth a parting shot and simply walked away, muttering under her breath.

When Sherlock flipped on the light switch, a plain double room lit up. There was a neat wardrobe and dressing table complete with tea and coffee paraphernalia. A door which Sherlock assumed led to an en-suite, a bed and a chair.

The latter seemed to be the best option for now. After lowering John into it, Sherlock closed the door, switched on the bedside lamps and then switched off the main one. And then there was nothing to do but talk.

"Do you want to talk about it?" he asked carefully as he knelt down in front of John to undo the laces of his shoes.

"Nope," John said, popping the 'p' with satisfaction.

"Where was Mary?"

There was a long hum. "She stayed away," John said eventually. "Wanted me and Harry to bond."

Ah.

"You and Mycroft," John said suddenly. "You don't speak much."

"We have little reason to," Sherlock replied as he started on the other shoe. "He's a lawyer and I interact with criminals. It hardly makes for easy conversation."

"Where you close? When you were younger?"

Sherlock paused in what he was doing and looked up. John was slumped in the chair, his elbow resting on the arm as he gazed down at Sherlock thoughtfully.

"No," Sherlock said as he sat back on his heels. "He was always much older than I was. Always perfect and doing the right thing. The proper thing. We have very little in common."

"Does it bother you?"

Not particularly. Sherlock shook his head. "We are different."

"Both clever though."

"Our applications of it are very different," Sherlock said as he continued untying the shoe. "You cannot imagine that my parents were pleased that I ended my university career early and..." he hesitated, unwilling to bring up the topic.

"I was Dad's favourite."

Sherlock glanced up, surprised at the fact John was acknowledging it. Tossing the shoe to one side, he made what he hoped was an encouraging noise.

"My mum, she adores Harry. Thinks he could shit rainbows all day long and solves world peace with every word. My dad...I dunno. Maybe he liked getting a look in with me." John shrugged. "I lived with him, did I ever tell you that? Picked when he got settled and," John drew in a ragged breath. "We did alternate weekends."

Sherlock didn't dare breathe a word.

"I went on my first date," John said with a sad smile. "Dad came to pick me up and-" he tapped his hand on the arm of the chair and stared at it. "Funny how life can fall apart so quickly," he said, frowning down at nothing.

If he were honest, Sherlock didn't have a clue what to do next, but he stood and tugged John up with him. "Do you need a shower?" he asked.

"No. Not gonna throw up," John said, wobbling a little. "Just. Need to sleep."

Nodding at that, Sherlock started to pull John's shirt over his head. When his partner's head reappeared through the hole in the fabric, John was gazing at him thoughtfully.

"This is weird," John decided. "You. Doing this."

"I've looked after you when you're drunk," Sherlock snapped. It was hardly worth pointing out that he'd had to deal with John drunk far more times than John had needed to deal with Sherlock when he was high.

"Happy drunk," John corrected. "Not miserable bastard drunk. You're better than I thought you'd be."

"What were you expecting?"

"Like I'm answering that when I'm drunk." John snorted as he collapsed onto the bedcovers. "Hotels always have puffy duvets," he decided.

Avoiding that was probably a wise idea. "Your step-father," Sherlock said as he pulled back the covers, intending to roll John onto the other side of the bed. "Your father's partner. Did he let you stay with him?"

"Couldn't. Weren't married, weren't anything legally. Mum had me back the next day. Kept sneaking back though. Drove her up the wall," John said, almost sounding proud of it. "Went into basic training just to have a way of seeing him."

"He died," Sherlock said, trying to piece it all together.

"Signed back up," John confirmed. "Needed to. Dad's wages had..." he sighed as Sherlock rolled him over. When John was face up again he shifted, curling around himself to study Sherlock as he knelt on the bed. "We should get married," he decided.

"You're drunk."

John didn't look all that surprised by the rejection. "I said we should," he defended. "It was just that they, they couldn't. Mum...sometimes I wish it had been her."

And, in typical John Watson fashion, he looked guilty the moment he said it. As if to hide from his words, John rolled over and buried his face in the pillow.

"I would have liked to have met him," Sherlock said quietly as he reached out a hand to John's hair. "And your step-father."

"He'd have liked you," John mumbled into the pillow. "Would have thought you were a brilliant mad nutter."

He sounded like John. "He'd have approved?" Sherlock asked, not even sure why he bothered. Approval was hardly necessary, especially from a dead man, but it seemed like it would appeal to John.

"No," John said, rolling over after a moment's thought.

Sherlock frowned and looked away, hardly needing the reasons why spelled out to him.

"I approve of you," John decided, yawning and batting at Sherlock with what was probably meant to be a pat of the cheek. "In lots of ways."

It was getting pointless now. Sherlock moved away and wriggled off the bed as John made an unhappy noise of protest.

"It was good," John said to nothing, shifting into the pillow again. "This morning."

It was hatefully pathetic how easily John could thaw out his bad mood. "Go to sleep, John," Sherlock instructed.

It was about half an hour later when John's phone rang. Sherlock had spent most of the time sitting on the chair, his feet drawn up and dug into the bed to share the warmth of the covers as he scrolled through his emails.

At first he ignored it, trying to use the last remnants of the cocaine to keep his focus on the case, to keep his thoughts fluid and easy.

But it could be that brother or even the mother...

Reaching forward, Sherlock plucked the phone off of the covers and stared at Mary's name.

"He's drunk," Sherlock said as he answered the call. "Your plan failed."

"Dramatic," she said, sounding far too mellow. "You always sound so dramatic."

God, not another one. "You're high," he accused. "Marijuana?"

"You got it." She sounded wonderfully unapologetic. "Is John awake?"

"He and Harry seem to have fallen out," Sherlock said, glancing at John's sleeping face. There was absolutely no indication that he would stir.

There was a long sigh. "Knew it was a long shot," she said frankly. "History repeating itself."

"You mean my relationship with John," Sherlock asked, trying for equal candour.

"Yes. Too many wounds."

He had a strange urge to curl up around John, even as he lay dead to the world and stinking of alcohol. Realistically, a homophobic brother and mother who saw John's father as the reason for their broken family were never going to be a healthy presence in John's life.

"John'll make an effort to-" Sherlock started.

"Why? She never helps him financially, never invites him home. Christ, she's not even listed as his next of kin, I am. What eighteen-year-old knows anything about that sort of stuff let alone changes it?" she asked, sounding far less mellow. "Did he tell you that his bitch of a mother dragged him home the next day? He was curled up with us on the sofa, crying and she-" Mary laughed bitterly. "She fucking accused my dad of trying something with him."

Unsurprising. Probably an accusation made from jealousy and grief than a desire to hurt but the result was always going to be the same.

"You should visit," Sherlock said quietly.

"Give him a few weeks to get his head sorted," Mary argued. "He'll just snap back if I try at the moment. I'll be in London in a month."

"Until then?"

"Are you asking for help?" she asked, sounding amused. "John said that you'd probably carve out your eyes before-"

"John is dramatic in the extreme," Sherlock argued. "I always seek expert advice."

In the pause that followed, Sherlock could just imagine the raised eyebrows.

"Then quickly exceed their words of wisdom," Sherlock added, almost peeved that she'd managed to infer that much from her conversations with John. Sure enough, laughter cackled down the phone and he glared at John.

"He'll be out of sorts," Mary said as her laughter faded. "Don't push him, let him sulk."

God, how tedious. "For how long?"

"A week? Try and use sex?"

"Is that your usual method?"

"Don't be gross," she said calmly. "My method is to sweet talk some cute girls into snogging him. You wanna bet I'm better at that than you?"

Not really. Sherlock stood and paced around to John's side of the bed. "Did you know his mother threw a saucepan at his head?"

There was a long silence this time.

"You let him keep too much to himself," Sherlock decided. "Aim for three weeks instead." With that parting remark, he ended the call.

The next morning was hellish. Morning crashes were hard enough without a sulking, hungover John Watson throwing up in the en-suite. The train ride back was painfully quiet and John seemed surprised that Sherlock continued to follow him onto the bus back to his.

"You don't need to be here," John said in a short tone as he opened his bedroom door. "If you have things-"

"You told me about your father and Harry," Sherlock said, leaning against the door frame.

"I know."

Ah. "I wasn't entirely sure how drunk you were."

John nodded and then sighed, running a hand through his hair. "Thank you," he said suddenly. "For coming after me, even though..." he frowned. "I should have just told you."

"Why didn't you?"

"Because I knew it was stupid," John said, sitting on his bed. "I still thought that maybe Harry might...he might..." John's eyes flickered brightly in the light as he looked away and shook his head.

"I would have said it was stupid," Sherlock admitted. It seemed to make John smile briefly as he looked back at Sherlock. But the smile faded as John's eyes scanned him and a disappointed sigh fell from his lips.

"You're crashing," John said softly.

"Don't start," Sherlock snapped. "You were drunk out of your mind last night. I...this...it helped me find you."

"I'm tired," John said, talking over him. "Just-" John made a small sharp gesture with his hand as Sherlock pushed himself off the door, half determined to leave before John told him to go. "Come here," John asked in a smaller voice.

Oh.

Sherlock walked over and sat down as John stood, drawing back the covers as if to copy what Sherlock had done with him last night. "I thought you'd argue more," Sherlock said as he lay down.

"I'm too hungover to argue," John admitted. "And you're right. It'd be hypocritical and a wankerish thing to do so we should just sleep."

It sounded heavenly. Sherlock let his eyes close as the bed dipped and John lay next to him, pressing close. Within moments John was asleep, apparently exhausted from the previous day. Too exhausted to argue about the drug use...

He wasn't usually though, Sherlock thought as he breathed in deeply and tried to ignore the panic that was starting to stir at the back of his mind.

One day, very soon, John was going to ask him to stop. And, if yesterday had proved anything, it was that he couldn't. Not yet.

Not if he wanted John to stay safe.

CHAPTER TWENTY:

The Cleverest Cocaine Addict in all the Land.

THINGS HAD BEEN WEIRD SINCE they'd gone to Dorking. Well, since John had gone and Sherlock had followed him there. For one, Sherlock was quieter. Not that it was unusual (Sherlock could hold radio silence for days if he chose to), but it was more of a pensive, introspective silence that made John thoughtful by default.

Which, although it was sort of handy for his unit tests, wasn't exactly...well...them.

And then there had been Mary who had turned up out of the blue even though she'd been in Italy the last time John had spoken to her. She and Sherlock seemed to have held some powwow over the phone and for neither love nor money could John get anything out of the pair.

It kinda sucked that they stuck together. John had the distinct impression that had he tried anything like that with Mycroft the man would have snorted on his way out the door, back to his fancy glass law firm that Sherlock periodically bitched about.

Whatever it was, something had changed and John couldn't quite put his finger on it. It didn't help that his memory of Valentine's evening was shot to hell and it really didn't help that he had the distinct feeling he had missed something in the lead up to it.

Fuck, you needed to be Sherlock Holmes to work out what was going on in Sherlock's brain.

Still, uni was going better.

"Have you started thinking about your placement?" Doctor Harrison asked John as he handed him back his research paper.

John gaped at the mark. "Seriously?" he asked with a grin. "This is...this is bloody good!"

Doctor Harrison sighed. "John?" he said and smiled when John looked at him enquiringly, "It's a wonderful mark that you have worked hard to get. I was asking about your placement."

That was ages away, sort of.

"Um, no." John shook his head. "Next year seems ages away."

"Well it isn't," Doctor Harrison said firmly. "You need to start looking and applying. You could have your pick of placement hospitals."

John couldn't stop grinning. "Wow," he breathed. "Thank you."

"Perhaps a little outside of London."

What?

"Why?" John asked, putting the paper down on the table.

"There have been some concerns within the faculty...we've been hearing rumours about your other half. So far it hasn't affected your work but working at a hospital, full time, is very different to being in university." Doctor Harrison sighed. "We are not dictating to you John, it is your life and your decision, but perhaps a little bit of physical distance would help you in the long run while you are training."

"Rumours?" John asked carefully. "What rumours?"

"That he is difficult. Demanding." Doctor Harrison met John's eyes. "Addicted and involved with...people it'd be best not to involve yourself with."

John careened between fury and gratefulness, standing still as he tried to decide which emotion was stronger.

285

Sherlock might act like a dick at times (or often), but this was his boyfriend that Doctor Harrison was talking about. His brilliant, wonderful boyfriend who, while obnoxious as hell, would never knowingly do something to screw John's career up.

"You have developed over the past year beyond expectation. Whether that is his influence or not, clearly something had helped you along. But you are still young and you are placing yourself in a very difficult situation. All I am saying is that you can make it a little easier on yourself."

"Yeah." John nodded and then turned to walk away before he told the man to go fuck himself.

"What are you looking at?" Sherlock asked as he wandered into John's room. His sudden, unexpected appearance made John frown, as did the jug of custard he was carrying.

"How long have you been here?" he asked dumbly.

"Two hours," Sherlock replied. "You closed the search, why-"

"Hospitals," John said absently. "Why do you have a jug of custard?"

"Why are you looking at hospitals?"

"Placements," John replied. "Doctor 'I like to shove my nose in other people's business' told me I should start looking."

Sherlock suddenly looked pleased. "I know at least three Doctors that can be blackmailed," he offered.

John laughed. "Only three?"

"It's been a slow year."

Sherlock put the jug down. "Ah, no!" John said looking up again, "If you put it there it will stay there, get green and then you'll start nagging at me to clean my room."

Sherlock nodded and pointedly left the jug where it was.

Shaking his head, John shifted over in case Sherlock wanted to sit. "Out of curiosity," he said, "how would you feel about-" he broke off suddenly, unsure if he should even bother asking.

But not finishing a sentence with Sherlock was like blood to a shark. "What?" Sherlock tilted his head, eyes scanning. "Why on earth would you leave London?" he asked, sounding taken aback.

"Just something Dr Harrison said," John replied, trying to keep his tone light.

"You should stay in London. The hospitals here tend to attract the best Doctors therefore it would be idiotic to move. Besides you would have to get a flat-share and it could prove to be distracting if you didn't get on with them."

"You mean if you didn't get on with them when you came to visit."

"Mm," Sherlock replied without any commitment. "It's a foolish notion to have someone leave London. I simply do not understand why any of your lecturers would suggest-"

John stared at the screen resolutely.

"I wouldn't," Sherlock said after a moment. "I never have. Your university career comes first. Your aspirations-"

"I know," John said, watching him. It was so strange how someone so anti his own education could be so fiercely protective of John's. "It'll be hard. I was gonna go into the army for it but..." John hesitated and considered.

Leaving Sherlock behind seemed impossible now.

"You'd do well," Sherlock said quietly as he turned and suddenly picked up the jar of custard. "But you'd do well wherever you go. Pick...pick as if I wasn't part of the equation."

"But you are," John said, slightly baffled by the custard again. "Seriously, why do you have that?"

But Sherlock just smiled in a strange way and then leaned forward to John, hazel eyes scanning him. Just as John opened his mouth to ask what the hell it was, Sherlock swept forward and kissed him, quickly deepening the kiss into something that made John groan into his mouth.

"Put the custard down," John murmured against Sherlock's lips and grinned as he felt a chuckle vibrate through Sherlock's body. As he moved, John wrapped his legs around Sherlock's waist and gasped at the friction building between them.

It was getting comfortingly familiar now to move against Sherlock, to reach out and know that a touch to his neck or drawing his teeth across Sherlock's collarbone would gain him a hiss and a broken moan. ~~That~~ He could fumble at Sherlock's t-shirt and jeans with ease and pull them from him without needing to stop and look anymore. They moved with the ease of familiarity, stretching out across the bed without risk of falling off again and bringing half the household up to their room in a panic.

How people said that they got bored of a monogamous partner, John had no idea. It was delicious to twist until he could feel Sherlock mouthing against the back of his neck as his hands tormented John, eliciting groans and causing him to arch in their spooning position. One hand had two fingers buried in John while the other brushed over his cock and balls in soft, teasing strokes that made John thrust and whimper.

"More." John fisted into the pillow, clamping his muscles down and around Sherlock's fingers. "Please, more."

Behind him, he could feel Sherlock rest his forehead on the nape of John's neck, clearly in a position to watch his fingers scissoring in and out of John.

Then Sherlock moved away slightly, keeping his fingers moving inside John with careful strokes while the other hand patted around for something, reaching for a bag that he had dumped under John's bed months ago.

John loved that bag. He wriggled, desperate and eager, and trying not to smile as he bit his lip. Sherlock rolled back, pulling his fingers out and something blunt was pressed against John.

John twisted to look and Sherlock accommodated it, pressed a kiss to his shoulder.

"Watch," he whispered as he pushed the toy slowly in.

It hurt a little; not in a bad way or a sharp way, just a dull ache that was so unfamiliar his brain immediately decided it had to be pain. John shifted on the bed as Sherlock pressed kisses down his back and lifted one of John's legs higher to accommodate the toy.

"Okay?" Sherlock asked against his skin.

John nodded, sweat forming on his brow from the heat of the night and their activities. "Just feels really solid!" he gasped as the rest of the plug suddenly went in and fitted where it was meant to. "Christ." He turned into the pillow again.

Sherlock rolled him onto his back and crawled up his body, kissing his way to John's lips. "More?" he asked politely.

Eyes wide, John nodded and sighed with relief as Sherlock wrapped lube wet fingers around him. The other hand was waved in front of John's face where it seemed like some kind of a remote was in it.

Sherlock settled back a little, watching John hungrily as he twisted the gadget around his fingers.

"Game?" he asked as he twisted his other hand in a particularly delicious way.

"Now?" John panted. "Sure?"

"If you shut your eyes or look away from me, this goes off."

"What goes-"

The plug suddenly started to vibrate wonderfully and John arched, twisting and breaking eye contact-

Immediately the thing went dead and John nearly screamed in frustration.

"What about you?" he panted, knowing there was no way he could help Sherlock in this game.

"You know where the bag is should you wish to have your revenge afterwards."

John grinned. "God, I love you," he said, opening his eyes and nearly babbled with pleasure when Sherlock flicked the button.

When you were friends with Andy, getting post in the morning was often used as a reason to celebrate. Getting high marks and then having sex? That was a reason to get pissed to hell.

It was the absinthe challenge that did it. Andy had made them stand there, at the bar, looking like tits as they held the burning liquid in their throats. After came the desperate urge to drink anything just to quench the fire in his throat.

"You," Andy said, half hanging onto John's shoulders, which was a bad idea as they both rocked precariously. "You should go home and fuck something."

"He has a name," John muttered, trying not to laugh at what he imagined Sherlock's face would look like if he heard the conversation. "Think he's out. Clubs."

"Clubs?" Andy asked, perking up and gesturing to someone behind John. "I like clubs."

No. John shook his head. "Not one I can go to. There are like rules and things. And he might be conning lots of people. I can never keep up."

"Mm," Andy said, swaying into the bar. "I laugh in the face of rules."

It made him snigger. "So you think I should go find him?"

"Find him, fuck him, buy him drink," Andy agreed. "Spread the love. In all ways," he added in a conspiratorial tone.

It sounded like a plan. The only problem was actually physically leaving the relative safety of Andy's presence. Stumbling forwards, John managed (somehow) to make it to the door and out into the fresh air.

It was colder than he'd expected and the sudden wall of outside-ness made him pause, reaching for the wall as he waited for the world to stop spinning. By the time it did, he felt slightly more alive and the edge of the pavement looked like it could be fun to balance on.

It took longer walking like that. It was great fun though; everyone he met was so happy and friendly, but that was possibly because he was failing miserably to stay in a straight line while humming 'I'm a little teapot' which had been stuck in his head since Andy started screeching it at the top of his lungs earlier.

Words were fun.

"Gay Alf!" he cried happily as he spotted his friend smoking by the wall by the Back Door night club. "I'm balancing really well."

Gay Alf glanced up from his phone and blinked at him owlishly before glancing back at the club. An odd look crossed his face as he hesitated.

"You are wankered!" Gay Alf said slowly. "What you doing here?"

"Sherlock," John said, wobbling and trying to catch his balance. "Well, I'm gonna be doing him," he said cheerfully. The world seemed very quiet but there was music thumping underground from beyond the steps and it sounded fast and fun. "I want to dance," he announced.

Gay Alf sighed. "I think you should come dancing tomorrow," he said soothingly, an almost reluctant smile tugging at his face as he pulled out his phone. "You go home now and sleep this off."

John shook his head and stumbled when the world spun. "Oh my god, the world moved. That's 'cause I... I got high marks on my course!"

Gay Alf nodded, thumb moving over his screen to activate a call. "Yeah, that's the reason. Not the fact that you drunk enough to start a small ocean."

John looked around confused. "'s not wet."

"Hey, you close to the club? Got something of yours that looks like he's dunked himself in a tequila bottle." Gay Alf said into the phone.

"Blugh," John said, screwing up his nose. "It was disgusting," he added, feeling the need to warn Gay Alf.

"Yeah." Gay Alf took a drag as he listened to his phone. "Okay." He hung up the call. "So, how was your night?"

John nodded. "Andy bought me a drink," he whispered. "And then ten more."

"No kidding." Gay Alf blew out chuckling puffs of smoke. "Come on. Let's kinda get you sobered up."

Sobered up? "Andy wants me to get Sherlock to come back with me," John mumbled. "I don't think I've seen him properly drunk."

Alf didn't say anything but came close, aiming John towards the street opposite. "He'd be a fucking moron to do both," Alf said after a moment. "How are you this drunk anyway? It's nine o'clock."

Nine? "Why are you here then?" John asked as they stumbled across the road.

"Opening up," Alf said dismissively. "And you shouldn't be around here," he added seriously. "Hasn't tall and irritating told you this?"

"He has strange ideas," John replied. "And he's secretive. Like a ninja. Secret ninja," he decided. "It's annoying. I think I should be cleverer."

"You're training to be a doctor, how much smarter do you wanna be?"

"Pft," John said. "Huh, funny noise. Pfft!" He laughed at it as Alf steered them into a café that was almost empty.

"Ken," Alf called and grinned at the Asian man who glanced up from the counter. "You got a coffee lying around?"

"Is that Alf speak for can I have a coffee without paying for it?" Ken asked, raising an eyebrow.

"Depends if you can do it," Alf replied with a disarming smile.

"You're good at shagging people," John decided.

A rumble of laughter went through Alf as Ken threw them both an exasperated look. "Not everyone that talks to Alf is turned gay," Ken muttered, reaching for the coffee machine. "So he's drunk."

"Please, be a real favour if you could?"

"Sit him in the corner," Ken instructed. "I swear to god, Alf-"

"Yeah, I know. But they're always for a good cause."

Sherlock walked into the café during John's second coffee, a strange look on his face as he paused. He looked flustered. Oddly flustered, and his hair looked like he'd ran his hands through it a few times. John was the expert on Sherlock's hair when it'd been clenched over and over again. But he didn't look like he'd been out. There wasn't a jacket in sight and the long sleeved blue jumper was all he wore against the March weather. It contrasted rather well with his bloody lip and reddened cheek.

"You," John said, circling his finger in what he assumed was roughly the right direction. "You I want to shag."

Alf snorted and then pulled an apologetic face towards the till.

"Because you are a man," John continued slowly, punctuating every word with his finger as he concentrated on standing upright.

"Glowing recommendation there, Sherlock," Alf laughed as he tugged John back down. "You can't stand," he defended when John turned to glare at him.

"Where have you been?" Sherlock demanded, ignoring Alf. His cheeks were flushed and he looked almost manic.

"Here!" John answered brightly. "With coffee."

"Before that?"

"There," John pointed towards the door where Sherlock had just stepped through.

"John!"

John shrugged. "Between here and there?" he offered hopefully. "I think I went a very strange route," he said as Sherlock stood in front of him. He blinked up, remembering vaguely that he'd already decided that this was a bad angle for Sherlock's slightly hooked nose.

It was better when Sherlock knelt down by him, his hands shaking slightly as he reached for John's sides.

Sherlock shook his head fiercely, gripping John firmly by the neck. "Andy said...we couldn't find you," he breathed, sounding small.

"I came here."

"And it took you two hours."

"Nooo," John looked at Gay Alf who nodded slowly. "Really? Fuck that was a bad route!"

Sherlock's shoulders shook and he nodded minutely against John's lap, almost bent over his legs now. Baffled by the behaviour, John turned in his grasp. "Gay Alf," he stage whispered, "I think he needs cocaine. You go find some."

"How the hell did you manage to walk here in this state?" Sherlock muttered under his breath.

"I balanced," John said, spilling his trade secret.

How they got back to Sherlock's, John had no idea. He half slept on Sherlock and half spent too long throwing up on the side of the road somewhere. All he did know was that he woke up in Sherlock's room about four hours later, feeling on his way back to normal again as someone stroked his hair.

"I'm gonna kill Andy," John muttered, not daring to move an inch.

Sherlock stroked the side of John's neck with the back of his fingers. "Taken care of," he replied.

"Literally?"

"Not quite."

"Oh my god." John pushed into the pillow. "I don't even remember anything after the second pub. Other than Andy screeching at me to down things."

The hand on his neck stopped stroking. "No?"

John risked turning over and stared at Sherlock's bloody lip. "Oh. How the hell did you get that?"

"You'd disappeared by the time I arrived." Sherlock's hands were tracing his cheek now. "No-one knew where you'd gone."

"My phone-"

"You left it in the bar." Sherlock swallowed as he nodded to where it was on the side table. "There had been a fight down the street, both parties taken to hospital in critical condition-" he looked away shaking his head. "I thought-"

"Shit," John breathed turning to him. "I'm so sorry."

Sherlock just shook his head.

"Did you punch Andy?"

"Yes. But only because he dragged me away from the plebeian paramedic who wouldn't release the names of the injured parties."

John stroked a hand through Sherlock's hair, trying to calm him down. "Uh...where was I then?"

Sherlock shook his head. "Walking to Back Door in the most convoluted route known to man, singing nursery rhymes apparently."

John winced. "Smooth eh?"

Sherlock remained silent as John dragged himself to a sitting position, burying his head in his hands. "I threw up, right?"

"Yes. Often. You'll need water."

John peered back at him. "You weren't at the club then," he said, studying Sherlock. "You were at home?"

"Unlike you, I do not spend most of my time in bars and clubs."

Woah. Blinking at him in disbelief, John twisted slightly. "No, you spend your time in drug and gambling dens."

Like the warning sign it was, Sherlock's chin tilted and his eyes narrowed. Silence lay between them, thick and heavy. Almost unbearable in its weight.

He wasn't taking it back. There was no way he was taking it back.

"I'm having a shower," John mumbled after a few minutes, shifting off the bed as Sherlock stayed where he was.

The lack of reply felt strangely like a scream.

———————————

Feeling a little more refreshed, but almost as if the world was part of a half dream, John hesitated outside of the bedroom door. Despite their almost not quite fight, he hadn't heard the door go and it was rare that Sherlock would leave while John was in his flat.

Hell, it was weird that Sherlock would leave without feeling as if he had made his clever ideas heard.

The thought was enough to make John square his shoulders as he walked in, almost spoiling for the brewing fight. Sherlock was sitting on the bed, eyes narrowed at him.

Suddenly, going for a shower seemed like a thick idea; he really did not want to be mostly naked while having this fight. And, annoyingly, Sherlock seemed to have decided not to say a word and let John hang himself with his own words.

Fine then.

Determined not to be the first one to break, John reached for his underwear and jeans, yanking them on in quick, sharp movements that he hoped clearly communicated how fucking pissed off he was. Sherlock's gaze was almost stabbing into his back as John towel dried his hair, aware it was probably sticking up all over the place.

"Where did you leave Andy?" John asked, half just so that he could say something.

Silence.

Fuck him then.

The shirt he'd worn earlier was nowhere to be seen and, thinking about it, probably wasn't exactly in the cleanest state if his vague memory of the journey home was anything to go by.

God, he was going to have to ask to borrow a shirt. Just

the idea made his cheeks burn with humiliation, so he stared at the wall as he built up the courage to ask.

"Top drawer on the right," Sherlock said, his voice sounding flat.

The instruction grated and John couldn't even really put his finger on why that was the case. He needed the shirt, he hadn't had to ask but it was the assumption, like he knew John so well and was so clever.

The cleverest cocaine addict in all the land.

The burning anger was enough to fuel his courage and turn around, arms folded as he leaned against the chest of drawers and matched Sherlock stare for stare.

"Is this where you tell me we don't need to have a conversation because you, genius extraordinaire, know exactly what I'll say and do and how it will end."

Hazel eyes bored into John. "We both know how this will end."

That was...Hurt, John swallowed and looked away, opening the drawer and-

"You know what," he said, slamming the drawer shut. "Let's have it anyway. Let's finally fucking talk about how you want the drugs more than me."

"You're twisting that-"

"How?" John snarled. "How am I twisting that? You said that you didn't want this because I'd ask you to stop. And even now, even..." he pressed his lips together to stop himself from saying something that would make him far too vulnerable. "You won't."

"I told you when we started that I wouldn't change."

And there it was. Sherlock's defence and the thing that John could never win against. "Then you should never have claimed to be in love with me."

He didn't really want to see Sherlock's reaction to that. Instead, he pulled the drawer open and yanked on the first

long sleeved t-shirt that he could find, wanting nothing more than to leave quickly and finish getting blind drunk.

The bed creaked as Sherlock stood and John sucked in a long breath, trying to steel himself for this. Pulling the t-shirt over his head helped, made him feel less vulnerable and as if his temper might melt away if Sherlock came close.

"You can accuse me of many things, John," Sherlock snarled. "But not that. You have no comprehension of what I have been doing-"

"I don't fucking want to know," John snapped as he shut the drawer and turned, barely able to hold onto his temper. "I don't want to know about you shooting up in alleys and clubs and thinking that you're earning brownie points because I don't have to watch-"

"I need it," Sherlock hissed at him. "I need it to fix your bloody mistakes."

"My mistakes?" John breathed. "My what? Am I forcing you to do drugs?"

Sherlock's lips thinned into a tight line. "Some patience would be appreciated," he said eventually. "Until the situation has changed."

Patience? Seriously? Had he just said-

"Be fucking kidding me," John yelled, shoving at him. "You want me to what? Wait?"

Sherlock hesitated, almost as if he couldn't decide what he wanted. "I...there is something I have to finish first."

There was something he had to finish?

Stepping forward, John stared at Sherlock whose eyes narrowed again, clearly sensing danger. "When exactly will that be? Should I book it in the calendar?"

"John-" Sherlock started, frustration seeping from his voice as he glanced heavenwards. "You don't-"

"I have to wait for you to finish? A con? A poker match? Finish being interested? What? What am I waiting for? What is more important than us?"

"You drink," Sherlock snapped back. "You get drunk more nights than not-"

"Because I am not sitting at home and waiting to be told this is the night where you took more than you could handle!" John yelled. "I am not wringing my hands in fear for someone who thinks that speeding up the world is better than sharing it with me."

"That isn't..." Sherlock scrubbed his hands over his face. "This isn't..." he shook his head and looked around, almost as if he was stuck on repeat or lost-

No, not almost as if he was lost. It was because he was fucking crashing.

"Be kidding me," John murmured, backing away. "You were high, weren't you? When they couldn't find me? When you got into a fight? You were fucking-"

"And you were drunk."

"God," John groaned. "I cannot keep-" he pulled back and stared at Sherlock in disbelief. "Tell you what, I'll stop when you stop. There, how's that for a fucking good deal."

It was like firing a shot. Sherlock froze and John could practically see the frantic thought process as Sherlock paled a little.

It hurt. He'd never asked because...God, because he was terrified that this would be the reaction. That, despite how much Sherlock claimed to love him and hate the drinking, his boyfriend would say no. And he was going to, John could see it in his eyes.

The world blurred as traitorous tears burned and John turned away, refusing to let Sherlock see.

"John," Sherlock whispered. "Don't."

But John shook his head, scrubbing at his eyes as he started to search for his keys and wallet and any fucking other thing because there was no way he was ever coming back.

He'd managed to get his keys shoved deep into his pocket when Sherlock's hand clamped around his wrist.

"You are the one thing in this world that I love," Sherlock hissed sounding desperate. "I-"

"No I'm not!" John yelled. Infuriated, he reached onto the bed and rummaged for the trousers Sherlock had been wearing earlier, knowing his particular brand of paranoia all too well. He pulled out a tiny bag from the back pocket. "This," he said holding it up to Sherlock. "This is the one thing you love. This and that," he said, flicking a finger at Sherlock's forehead. "I don't even come close."

"You are so thick!" Sherlock sneered. "It's because I love you that I do them-"

John laughed in sheer, stunned amazement at his gall. "How-?"

"I have told you!" Sherlock shouted. "I need to be able to think to keep you safe-"

John turned away. "I am not listening to this again. Whatever bloody soap opera you have playing in your head is fucking stupid."

"You punched Victor Trevor and broke his nose," Sherlock yelled suddenly. "Do you have any idea what the repercussions of that are? You walked into his club, refused a job and broke his nose."

What? John paused and turned to him, eyebrows furrowed in confusion. "And? If he was going to press charges-"

The laugh that erupted from Sherlock was bitter and twisted. "He won't involve the police. He isn't interested in their brand of justice."

It unnerved him, he could admit that. Made him hesitate, hand on the door knob as he eyed Sherlock up.

"You stood up to a man that cannot be seen to be weak. You, a nobody university student, humiliated him. You have no idea how fine a line you and I have been walking, how much I have done."

John's fingers closed on air as he stopped dead, unable to drag his eyes away as Sherlock came close, his eyes wild in his pale face and hands jolting.

He was a mess.

"You actually believe it," John breathed. "This fantasy that you have."

"It is not..." Sherlock pressed his lips together. "I have balanced so many gangs keeping you safe, so many people..." he staggered forward. "And now...I can't stop. I can't be useless for months on end. Not until it's finished. You just have to give me more time," he said, reaching out for John. "Just a few more weeks. Maybe a month or two."

It was...seeing him like this, it wasn't right. His head swam and John almost felt like vomiting again, disgusted by the sight. "Sherlock-"

The man actually dropped to his knees. "Just...a little more time," he said, and his eyes flicked to John's left hand which still held the drugs.

God.

John stared at the bag of white powder, his jaw clenching as he brought it close to his chest and looked down at Sherlock. At the bloodshot eyes, at the new marks on his arm from where his sleeves had ridden up, and at the spasms in his hands.

Then looked up to his face and the pleading expression, the slight edge that showed Sherlock thought he had made a convincing enough argument and was about to relax.

John leaned forward. "You sound like a junkie," he hissed.

The words hit Sherlock like a slap John would never deliver and Sherlock swayed backwards looking stunned. Taking the chance, John straightened up as Sherlock remained kneeling.

"And you can tell all these people that you reckon lurk in the shadows, all these excuses, that you've just done their job for them." John yanked the door open. "And you probably did it better than they ever would."

He slammed the door behind him.

CHAPTER TWENTY-ONE:

The Deficiency of Probity

THE MUSIC WAS THUMPING IN the pub, almost too loud to have a proper conversation. Thankfully, it so wasn't what he was interested in.

"Four shots," John said, leaning on the bar as the guy behind looked up.

"Of?"

"I don't give a shit," John muttered. "Whatever's on offer."

The barman looked hesitant and then shrugged, turning to a bottle of Jägermeister. Resting his elbows on the bar, John buried his hands in his hair and stared at the soaked mats on the sticky, damp wood.

"Generous of you," Andy said from his left. "I thought-"

"They're not for you," John said as the shots were placed in front of him. Handing over twenty quid, John stood back up properly.

"You're meant to be with Sherlock," Andy said.

John downed the shots. One after the other without a pause, needing the burn of alcohol to help him focus and forget the fucking wanker he'd just walked out on.

"John?" Andy said, sounding serious suddenly. "What happened?"

Turning, John studied the bruise that was forming on Andy's jaw. "Pretty sure we just broke up," John said, turning so that his back leaned against the bar. He was probably getting all kinds of stains on Sherlock's shirt.

302

Andy blinked. "No," he said, sounding as if John was being mental. "You guys? Don't be stupid. It was just a fight."

"Told him I'd give up drinking as he hates it so much," John said, lifting his gaze to the lights above. "If he'd give up the drugs." He didn't want to see the pity in Andy's eyes. "He didn't even consider it."

And wasn't it telling that even Andy, king of banter, couldn't seem to think of a damn thing to say.

"He ain't gonna change overnight," Andy offered.

"He ain't gonna change," John spat as he pushed off the bar and aimed to walk over to Mike. A hand on his arm stopped him and John stared at it, frustrated. "What?"

Andy glanced back at the bar and then at John as if he was going to say something. He looked as if he were struggling and then shook his head, letting John go.

Good.

One more month. One more fucking month. Why couldn't John wait that long?

Sherlock stood, surveying the disaster that was now his flat. It was hardly surprising that wrecking the place hadn't helped improve the situation but it had helped. For a split second, it had helped.

There was something that would help for longer though.

Under the floorboard by the bed was everything that he kept from John's sight so that it wouldn't cause...well, this situation. Why John couldn't see the effort that he made or how hard he tried, Sherlock had no idea. Too stupid, too thick, tooutterly oblivious and naïve to the world.

With shaking hands, he lifted the loose floorboard and set it to one side. Underneath were needles and equipment. He stared at it all, suddenly aware of a relief that flooded through him. A Pavlovian response to the sight.

He needed it. Wanted it. And John had never even tried to give up the alcohol for him. Never.

He tried to ignore John's voice, the offer he had made before walking out of the flat.

A loud buzzing noise pulled his attention away and he blinked down in confusion as his phone lit up with a text message from Andy.

? Johns here & drinking like it's going out of fashion.

Drinking? He was drinking?

All compunctions vanished. If John could be that pig headed then so could he.

None of the bastards that called themselves his friends were being particularly sympathetic. Well... Paul had always had his doubts about Sherlock but he seemed no more against it than usual. So John sat at the corner of the pub, probably exuding his foul mood if the way everyone avoided him was anything to go on.

Was he really that wrong? Sherlock was an addict; everyone thought he needed to get clean. Everyone except for the man himself.

"You punched Victor Trevor and broke his nose. Do you have any idea what the repercussions of that are? You walked into his club, refused a job and broke his nose."

It kept circling around and around until John felt dizzy, his four shots and the beer he was currently nursing not really helping matters. Because, what if Sherlock had a point? What if Victor was trying to get to John in some way?

He'd have done it ages ago, an unsure voice muttered at the back of his mind. Surely?

Unless...Sherlock had been withdrawn that morning, had vanished for days on end around that time. Had he been...

What? Protecting John like he was some fucking useless damsel in a fairy tale?

It was annoying that John couldn't quite dismiss the idea. Sherlock was insane half the time, yes, but he was rarely needlessly paranoid. And he was clever, really clever.

In which case...maybe he couldn't go through withdrawal. Maybe there was an actual real reason and John was being the arsehole.

Unable to circle around the idea anymore, John pulled out his phone. Feeling like he was somehow admitting defeat, even as he scrolled through to find Sherlock in his contact list, John called.

The call was ended after one ring.

Fucking fucker!

Ignoring his drink, John stood and headed towards Andy who was dancing with some girl that John was pretty sure Andy had already shagged (which would make a change) and pulled Andy's phone out of his back pocket.

"Don't call him," Andy said, turning around with a weary look on his face. "You're drunk. Drunk phone calls are never-"

John held up a hand, managing to ignore the rest in the thumping beat of the dance music. Weaving back out, he headed for the door and stepped outside into fresh air and relative quiet.

This time, the phone rang for longer before it was answered. Sherlock really was such a wanker and why the hell John had thought this would work when Sherlock would probably end the call as soon as he heard John's voice-

"Sherlock Holmes' phone."

It was a woman's voice. For a moment, all John could do was gape at the empty road and look around as if some explanation would appear in front of him.

"Is he there?" John asked, trying to keep his voice level.

"He can't come to the phone right now. Can I take a message?"

John was damn sure he could hear Sherlock in the background, and even more sure it sounded like the background noise of some fancy bar. "Who are you?" John asked, striding a little away from the pub door.

"Someone that he wants to talk to," came the smart arse response.

"You know what?" John suddenly snarled. "It doesn't fucking matter. Tell him to go to hell." Only the fact that it was Andy's phone kept John from throwing it into the street as he ended the call with a vicious jab of his thumb. It was no-where near as satisfying.

"Hey," Mike said, suddenly appearing out the door. "You okay? Did you get hold of him?"

"Got hold of the woman who's been given the great honour of his phone," John snapped. "He is such a- He won't change, will he? He'll just keep pissing everything away on drugs and-"

"John," Mike said, sounding deeply uncomfortable. "I've never been the biggest fan of him and I know that there isn't a universe in the world where it's good that he takes drugs but.... that's a big change to expect overnight. And you're drunk, he's high. Just leave it alone until you're both in a sober frame of mind."

"He thinks that me drinking is as bad as his drug habit," John spat.

Mike still looked hesitant, even looked away at that.

"Oh, piss off," John hissed, shoving Andy's phone at Mike. "Piss right off with that one. You drink, Andy's as bad as they get-"

"You drink to get drunk," Mike argued. "We drink while having fun."

He was not having this lecture, not from someone who had tried to justify Sherlock's drug use and reaction tonight.

"Why are you all on his side?" John yelled.

"You need to go home," Mike argued.

John backed away, raising his hands and admitting defeat. "I'm done," he said, backing away. "Go screw yourselves-"

"John," Mike called after him. "Where're you going-"

"Somewhere to have fun while I drink," John snarled. "Don't come. You'll ruin the mood."

He felt a flicker of guilt at the way Mike's face dropped. Seeing the awkward way his friend stood, as if baffled as to what to do next, made John almost hesitate. But a bigger part of him felt even more annoyed. Everyone was painting him as the fucking villain tonight. If they were that determined to have him play that part then fine.

He'd perform it gladly.

"He sounded pleased," Dahlia said as she handed Sherlock's phone back to him.

"He was drunk," Sherlock dismissed as he tucked it into his pocket and turned back to his companion.

"And yet still so much more polite than Trevor," Dahlia mused as she walked off. Sherlock restrained the urge to roll his eyes at her, refocusing his attention on Hudson who had been waiting silently, suspicion deep in his eyes.

"We shouldn't meet in public," Hudson hissed seconds later. "Our whole ruse depends on Armitage thinking that Evans was your original source-"

"You are drawing attention to yourself," Sherlock said as he reached for his drink. "And you'd have to be a moron not to seek me out. He sent you the note; he knows that you are fearful. And half of London now knows I have something on him-"

"Not enough," Hudson said, hunching over the bar. He looked as old and careworn as he had the first time he'd come pounding on Sherlock's door. He hung his head down close to the rather immaculate, polished surface of the bar. "Even now, we don't have enough."

"We merely need to link Armitage and Trevor together-"

"How?" came the desperate response.

The man was useless. Sherlock swallowed, already feeling the height of his buzz fading away. "I have held up my end," he said after a moment. "I have found all of his records, ensured that they cannot be doctored or altered. I have found all the data on his current activities, found evidence. The sole reason we cannot move forward is because you have failed to find a way to prove that James Armitage, legendary murderer, criminal and forger is Jim Trevor, dealer and current bane of our combined existences."

"I told you-"

"Your word will not hold up in a court of law. You will not hold up in a court of law," Sherlock hissed. "You won't even hold up three streets away from a police station, so let's not pretend that-"

"It's his handwriting," Hudson snarled. "In the note, it was his handwriting-"

"Handwriting analysis will only take us so far," Sherlock said, sitting up. "I have one of the most pedantic and annoying lawyers in the country waiting for our evidence and even he will need more than 'I say so' and 'their handwriting sort of looks the same'." He closed his eyes, trying to keep John from entering his thoughts and distracting him. "What about his body? Any identifying marks?"

Hudson flashed him a baffled look. "How the hell would I know any of that?" he asked. "He weren't screwing anyone there. Only people that would know are the women he's banged. And the doctor. But he's dead and there weren't a single woman on that ship."

Irritating. Sherlock let out a frustrated noise and leaned back down, trying to find some sort of- damn it, some sort of answer. One single answer that would give him the evidence that he needed to go to John and fix this. All of this.

One single answer and he couldn't think.

"The other side's going all right though," Hudson added

as an afterthought. "Just dunno how long it will take for someone to notice the money-"

"Not an issue," Sherlock replied with a smirk. "The trail we've left will work in our favour. Believe me. As long as we can back it up with that link."

The smug feeling faded almost as quickly as it had arrived.

He needed more. That was the problem. Without the cocaine, his mind was so slow and dull-witted. More this time, perhaps that would help him work it out.

James Armitage was Jim Trevor. It was likely that James Armitage had deliberately been caught and imprisoned because he had a plan to escape and be declared dead by the very people he wanted to hide from. James Armitage was, without hesitation or doubt, someone who could be convicted.

Jim Trevor was not. There were far too many police and politicians and stupid pathetic people under his control, under his influence.

One single piece of evidence to prove that one man was the other. One irrefutable piece of evidence that couldn't be buried or hidden or need time to be proven beyond doubt. That couldn't be muddled by subjective views or clever lawyers.

One single piece of evidence.

It was a familiar path to walk, very fucking familiar given that he had walked it only seven hours ago. This time though, the club was clearly active; thumping music could be heard a street away and floods of people could be seen at the entrance.

There were a few faces that he recognised from last autumn (had it been that long since he'd properly been at Back Door?) Jesus, the last time he'd properly been in the club had been the night he'd decked Victor Trevor and broken his nose.

There was a flicker at the back of his mind that going in was a stupid idea. Paranoid? He dismissed the thought process as he strode down the stairs after paying way too much to get in. Sherlock was rubbing off on him. All those childish games and lies-

Which might not be lies, a vicious voice whispered.

"You come to my place?" Victor's voice hissed at him-

-were getting to him. Simple as.

Downstairs was a mess of bodies and bright lights all moving in time to the music that barely allowed John a chance to even think. The bar wasn't packed but it wasn't empty either, and John edged closer, trying to spot a familiar face.

"Is Alf on tonight?" he asked the first barman that caught his eye.

"I'm better, sweetheart," came the purred response.

John fixed him a stony glare, which probably wasn't the best way to get what he wanted, but screw it. He wasn't exactly in the mood. The guy moved away, hopefully to get Alf and John threw a warning glare at anyone that looked like they might come over.

This probably hadn't been the best place to come to, but Alf worked where he did so...yeah.

Maybe this had been a really stupid idea.

Finally, Alf appeared, hurrying over with a weird look on his face. Even as John opened his mouth, Alf came around the front and grabbed at his elbow, mouth coming close to John's ear.

"What's wrong?" Alf asked, his voice sounding loud and yet almost inaudible in the loud music of the club.

"Sherlock," John said, turning his head to get closer to Alf's ear. "Do you have a minute?"

"Does he know you're here?" Alf asked, apparently ignoring John's question.

"We had a fight."

Alf's head thudded onto John's shoulder and he could practically feel that huge sigh that went through him. "Stay here," Alf said firmly. "Jesus, John. You are trouble when you're pissed. I'm like your bloody Mecca, apparently."

"That's 'cause you're not as much of a wanker as everyone else," John shouted back as Alf pulled away. Alf must have heard it because he grinned and gave John an odd salute as he backed off towards the back again.

Feeling a little better (and he owed Alf a million times over for being so good about all of this tonight) John felt himself start to relax a little. Turning, he watched the dancers thoughtfully, half wondering if he'd have to start going on the pull again.

The idea, when he examined it closely, wasn't that appealing.

When he turned away, Victor Trevor was standing next to him.

Hudson had skulked off, despondent at being called useless. It was hardly Sherlock's fault that the man was proving himself to be exactly that.

Admittedly, he wasn't exactly being tactful. That he could admit. But John was at the back of his head, driving him mad and-

Perhaps getting Dahlia to answer the phone hadn't been a wise move. John had clearly been phoning to...well, not apologize because John Watson didn't do that well, but something akin to it perhaps. Leaving the bar, Sherlock studied the phone in his hands, trying to decide what to do next.

John needed to be seen to be under his protection, and yet it appeared John didn't want to give him any more chances.

Why was everything so...wrong? Why couldn't John just see and understand what was happening?

He answered his phone before he bothered to read the screen, half desperate to hear John's voice.

"John?"

"Alf," came the correction. "And, for the second time tonight, I have something of yours."

"He went to the club?" Sherlock asked, pausing mid-step.

"He's at the club," Alf corrected, sounding endlessly unamused. "Not as drunk as he was earlier but I'm on shift. I can't leave the club."

"Is Victor in?" Sherlock asked, turning to make his way to the nearest taxi rank.

"Yeah," Alf said, his nerves almost resounding down the phone. "He is."

"Haven't seen you in some time," Victor mused as he leaned against the bar, looking completely at ease, his voice just about heard over the music. In the light, John could see a slight bump on his nose and there was a perverse amount of satisfaction boiling within him.

"Just wanted to talk to Alf," John said.

"What was that?" Victor asked, pushing off the bar to lean in close.

"I..." All of John wanted to pull away but that would look weak and pathetic and he wasn't going to damn well do it. "Came to talk to Alf. He has a break soon."

Victor nodded. "Sherlock's given you a long leash, hasn't he?"

The implication made John clamp down his jaw, not really sure what to say that wouldn't allow Victor to goad him further.

"Or are you here to find me?" Victor asked. "Had a fight? Want to spite him?"

Yes but...Jesus, not with Victor. John shifted, still not sure what to say and suddenly...suddenly Sherlock's weird speech earlier seemed a lot more plausible.

"We should talk properly," Victor said, nodding towards the staff door at the side of the bar.

"I'm not that stupid," John said, staring at the bar and the door where Alf had disappeared.

"I think you're already that stupid," Victor hissed in his ear. There was an odd pinching sensation at John's side and he blinked, looking down-

There was a knife.

The world seemed to suddenly disconnect from him; the music faded slightly and the lights didn't quite seem to touch him.

Victor was holding a knife at his ribs and he probably knew exactly how to use it.

"You can't stab me in the middle of a club-"

"My club," Victor corrected with a smile. "My people. My place."

Oh.

Shaken by the sudden realisation of what Victor had meant last time, John threw one last look at the bar.

Was Alf really gonna risk his job and his life for John? Was he really gonna put Alf in that position?

Swallowing, John nodded and started to head towards the staff door, all too aware of how closely Victor fell into step with him. The situation seemed to make the drunk freedom fall away and all that was left was fear.

He wanted to ask questions but that was probably a stupid idea too. Past the door were some steep metal steps that John walked down, Victor still at his back. With every step down it was like John was becoming more and more trapped, the dim light in the staircase not helping matters

Downstairs, they made their way to the office and being back in there after what had happened last time, John started to brace himself.

"Take a seat," Victor said, not bothering to close the door behind them. He pulled out a chair for John, one that would mean he had his back to the door and John glanced at it, hesitating.

Victor sat behind the desk, as if this were some weird

meeting and gave John a pointed look. Now that he was far away, there was no way that John was going to sit and-

Even as he turned around, three men came through the door. All of them big, all of them looking like they could beat John into the ground with a swipe of bearlike hands.

Shit.

Turning slowly, John walked to the chair and sat, folding his arms as if that would protect him. The men that stood close seemed to copy his stance and the last one shut the door behind him.

Jesus Christ, what was Victor planning?

"I'm guessing that you must have rethought my job offer," Victor said, reclining into the chair with a casual ease that seemed impossible for John right now. "I mean, why else would you come here? To me? After what you did."

John licked his lips, trying to work out what to say. "I just came to see Alf," he said slowly. "I'm drunk. Wasn't thinking."

"So you came to distract my staff?" Victor asked, a smug smile crossing his lips. "You gonna cover him?"

No. John breathed in deeply, trying to control the hammering of his heart as it thudded wildly in his chest. He looked down at his hands, at the bones and veins and skin, half wondering if he'd ever see the sight again.

"And if you're gonna cover him," Victor said, "then you must have rethought my job offer."

He could say yes. But it wasn't what Victor wanted and chances were it would piss him off even more. Terrified, John squared his jaw and shook his head.

"No."

The triumphant smirk made John swallow, trying not to look at the men around him because why the hell would it help to see where the first blow came from when Victor gave a nod.

Thing was, it wasn't a blow. Instead, one of the men (a huge ginger haired man who looked like he could hold an entire tree with his arms) leaned forward and pressed on the back of John's chair, tipping him back onto two legs.

He hated it. He wasn't in control and that was pathetically clear now. It was impossible not to reach out for the chair arms and grip them tightly, trying to find some way to claw back control of his balance.

"My father has rules," Victor said, still sat behind the desk. "Strict rules, even for me. Can't kill you. But there are ways of convincing you to take my offer."

What? Baffled, John glanced between them all and tried to get his breathing under control as one of the men left and walked to the other side of the room and out of his eye line. Without any clues, John's mind raced as to what the hell Victor could possibly do to him.

It was enough to bring fearful tears to his eyes, even as he tried to blink them away.

Sherlock had done something, John tried to remind himself. Something that meant Victor had boundaries, that he had limits. He had to trust Sherlock-

God, the fucking irony. He'd been so convinced, so blind.

"How?" he heard his own shaking voice ask, and wasn't that embarrassing.

"Same way I used to control your boyfriend," Victor sneered as he stood, hands flat on the desk, and leaned over, a cruel flicker in his eyes catching the light.

What? What was that meant to mean? What the fuck was-

When the man reappeared, John bolted, trying to get out from the chair. The ginger guy let go of it, allowing the chair to crash back to the floor and dazing John briefly as he hit the floor. In the seconds that he struggled to crawl away from the chair and the shock of the sudden fall, there were hands grabbing his arms, pinning him down. Someone was on his legs as one arm was pulled out, spread out on the floor and *he was* so fucking vulnerable it made him almost want to beg.

They tied the tourniquet around his forearm, cutting off

the circulation. Not wanting to see, John tried to look away but hands gripped at his face, twisting his neck to look.

Victor had the needle now, was grinning as he started to prepare it. "You saw how Sherlock got on with this mix. You can compare notes now."

How Sherlock... "No," John said, thrashing as best he could. "No, don't you dare-"

"Don't I dare?" Victor hissed. "Don't I dare? How dare you? Coming here, after what Holmes has done to my family? After humiliating me?"

John tried to twist away and suddenly the hands left his head. The sudden disappearance made him hope that maybe, just maybe he could wriggle free and-

The sharp edge of a blade was pressed against his neck and he froze. The blade pressed further in and- Shit, they were making him turn his head, making him keep himself still.

"You said you can't kill me," John said, trying desperately to keep his voice steady.

"You turn into the blade then that's your choice," Victor said, leaning down.

It was impossible to keep still. He thrashed, trying to get his arm free and his shoulder buzzed painfully as it was wrenched by those holding him. Trying to wriggle and roll away just shoved the crook of his shoulder into the knife and warm stickiness flooded his shirt-

Sherlock's shirt.

The needle went in.

The world seemed to crack and shift, falling far away even as the pain became sharper, clearer in some way.

"You're gonna love this," Victor said, his voice bending and shifting far away as his lips brushed John's ear. "Nothing like it in the world."

John was hit with the strangest wave; everything was crashing and out of focus and too loud and bright and dim and blurred.

He couldn't breathe.

CHAPTER
TWENTY-TWO:

Cognitive Restructuring

THERE WERE A FEW STRANGE looks as Sherlock strode across the road, heading for the club. Gabe Fowler, the newest bouncer, was on the door and hesitated, looking around as if for help.

"You're giving me far too much credit," Sherlock hissed at him as he shouldered past and continued his quick pace down the steps and into the dimly lit stairway.

What the hell was John thinking? Why had he come here, to this place-

Because you didn't tell him, part of Sherlock whispered. You never explained properly. Why wouldn't he feel he couldn't come to Back Door?

Victor was walking up as Sherlock was going down. There were stains on his expensive shirt.

"You," Sherlock sneered, pinning him against the wall. "If you have done anything-"

"Seriously?" Victor asked, staring at him. "Here?"

"Where is he?"

Victor shot Sherlock a scolding look and nothing was going to be gained by allowing his emotions to rule. Steps sounded out and then stopped and Sherlock glanced down at the three men who were following Victor up.

He'd hardly be of use to John if he pushed his luck here. Pulling back, Sherlock released Victor and waited pointedly.

Infuriatingly, Victor seemed more concerned with his image as he adjusted his shirt collar and smoothed back his hair. Sherlock glanced down at the men but he barely had time to sweep his gaze over them before Victor spoke, dragging his attention back. "Now apologise."

"I do not have time-"

"You really don't," Victor agreed.

Panic flooded through him. "What did you-"

"Apologise."

It was tempting to simply shoulder past the four of them and find John but he would still need to leave and keep John safe and...

For a split second, Sherlock despised John for this.

"Sorry," he said, staring at the wall behind Victor's head.

"Downstairs, in the office," Victor said with a dismissive wave, hands stained with something dark. "You'll have plenty to bond over."

Sherlock turned, already racing down the rest of the stairs, shouldering past the burly henchmen Victor seemed to enjoy carting around. Until he saw John, it was pointless to consider what Victor meant by that. John had been in the club for twenty minutes, out of Alf's sight for fifteen. What could he have done that quickly?

His mind produced far too many answers as he headed down the second set of stairs. It didn't take long from there to get to the bottom, throw open the office door and-

There was blood on the carpet.

Sherlock froze suddenly, not wanting to see because... Victor couldn't have...that wasn't...

Alf was hunched over a pair of legs in jeans, John's shoes on the feet. As if he'd heard a noise, he turned, eyes bright with tears and a streak of blood across his face. The side of his face was swelling, he was sitting awkwardly and-

Sherlock didn't want to look. Couldn't-

"I called an ambulance," Alf said, swallowing back tears. "They're on their way. We-" he looked down at something Sherlock couldn't see. "Do I take the needle out?"

Needle?

Sherlock edged forward, trying to brace himself. Slowly, John's flung out arm came into sight, the discoloration on the wrist already present because they must have held him down-

To put a needle in his arm.

It was empty and Sherlock stared at it, unable to compute what he was seeing because the sight was wrong. John should never have a needle in his arm. Never.

Stumbling forward, Sherlock went to grab the needle and then blanched as the rest of John came into view. Pale face, sweat soaked and slack. The opposite side of his neck covered in red that spread like finger painting up over his face, into his hair and across the shirt that John had borrowed.

It was obscene. Turning, Sherlock vomited, gasping frantically for breath as his stomach heaved out everything as he reached out blindly for the desk.

"Is he-"

"Breathing," Alf said, his voice unstable. "I don't...Jesus there's so much blood," he whispered. "I don't know-"

Blood. John could bleed out.

No.

Stumbling forward, Sherlock crashed down next to Alf as he took off his jacket and pressed it into John's neck, trying to put pressure on the wound. That was what John's lecturer had said, back when Sherlock had been trying to impress John by turning up to his lectures. Pressure stops bleeding, stops death.

"Don't you dare," he said to John's hair, burying his face in the golden strands. It was sticky and smelt nothing like John's hair usually did. "Don't you fucking dare," he hissed. Pressing himself as close as he could to John, as if contact might help in some way, Sherlock looked up at Alf. "When did you call?" he asked, ignoring the way the world blurred and shifted as his eyes filled.

"Three minutes ago," Alf said, scrubbing a hand over his mouth.

Three minutes. Sherlock turned his face back into John's hair, just so he could feel the breaths that lifted John's chest and kept him alive.

Don't you dare.

The arrival of the ambulance and the journey to the hospital passed in a blur of green paramedics dancing in and out of his vision. The image of John, pale and bleeding on the carpet was all he could see; splashes of green and red and John's face and it all seemed to be a sickening blur of colour that he didn't want to deal with.

They didn't make him let go though. He could hold John's hand, stroking it with his thumb as if that somehow would will strength into the man he loved to get him to wake up.

And then they took him away.

Not family.

Not family?

Somehow, he ended up in a dull little waiting room with too harsh lighting that turned the blood stains on his and Alf's clothing to a strange, almost green brown colour and made him hang his head between his hands, bent over his knees almost in a crash position.

Drugs.

Victor had given John drugs. The one thing that Sherlock had always sworn would never, ever happen. The one thing that he could, no, would protect John from. John who wanted to be a doctor, who was good and kind and the thing he loved most.

He could die.

People died from speedball. John had never taken it, had no resistance to anything that had been shot into him. And his neck…there were arteries and veins in the neck that could mean he might bleed out or have extra complications and the two together-

"Here," Alf's voice said, deep and gravelled beyond what Sherlock had ever heard from him before. When he looked up, there was a plastic cup with water being held out to him.

He stared at Alf.

"Have you taken anything tonight?"

Yes. Reluctantly, he held out his hand and accepted the water, not realising how thirsty he had been until he took those sips. "Should you be here?"

Alf shrugged as he sat down. "Dead people in a club are bad for business," he said, staring at a poster. "I can excuse it."

Part of Sherlock wanted to scream at him but what was the point? They had both worked for the Trevor family, both knew how this worked. The plastic cup suddenly became the most interesting thing in the world as he tried to find something else to focus on.

"You," Andy's voice suddenly echoed out as he burst through the doors. Sherlock had barely looked up before hands were on him, sending what was left in the cup to crash to the floor. Hands tried to grab at his throat and he weakly tried to push them away, not even sure if he wanted to.

In the end, it was Mike and Alf who dragged Andy back, leaving Sherlock slumped on the chair and blinking up at the three, watching as Mike talked into Andy's ear. He wasn't entirely sure if it was because Mike had a quiet voice or whether it was because he wasn't able to focus, but it was as if there was a glass wall between him and the rest of the world, dulling everything to the point where it became blurred and insubstantial, something he couldn't possibly interact with.

Alf and Andy were talking in the corner, quiet clipped tones that he probably should have been able to follow. The chair shifted as Mike sat next to him and Sherlock sat himself back up properly, stunned by how much effort it seemed to take.

"I phoned Mary."

Mary. Right, yes. And they'd said family. Pained at the idea, Sherlock closed his eyes. "They'll try to call his mother," he said.

"Mary's John's next of kin contact," Mike said and Sherlock knew that, had known that. Why had they spoken? "She's talking to the doctor's now."

Sherlock nodded, his gaze darting back to Andy and Alf.

"It wasn't your fault," Mike said softly. "Andy knows that but...he's Andy. You weren't even there so how could it be your fault."

For that very reason, Sherlock thought as he closed his eyes.

It seemed to take an age to be allowed in to see John. The dark sky outside was staring to break with streaks of colour when the doctor came through and said something which made the others gently push Sherlock forwards to follow him down winding halls that were filled with medical staff and trolleys and equipment and then it was quiet and there was a machine that kept beeping.

John's heart was still beating.

"He's stable," the doctor was saying. "We can let you know more once Ms Morstan arrives but you can sit with him until then."

Nodding, Sherlock stepped closer, half-aware of the doctor sighing and leaving until he was alone with John. Helplessly, he plucked at John's sleeve, staring at the bandages that were thick at John's neck and shoulder.

"I'm sorry," he whispered, crouching by the bed suddenly, hands clutching at the bed sheets. "I'm so sorry."

He needed him, god did he need him. Lifting himself up again, he leaned over John and buried his lips in John's hair, breathing in the smell of him and then nearly sobbing in frustration when antiseptic, alcohol, blood and the smell of a damp carpet got in the way, burying John's natural scent.

He wanted to gather John in close, touch him until he could completely absorb him, keep him safe and whole. But there were too many drips and machines keeping an accurate measure of John's heart.

It could have been worse. If there had been more heroin than cocaine then John would be dead.

"Wake up," Sherlock begged John, brushing his lips against cold cheeks. "Please, wake up."

The machine beeped in reply.

By ten in the morning, Mary sat quietly in the corner. She hadn't said a word to him, though he could tell that the anger was simmering away under the surface. Her arms were folded and every time she caught his eye she stared for a few seconds and then looked away.

"I'm afraid until he wakes up we simply won't know," the useless doctor said. "The coma is most likely due to the sudden chemical imbalance caused by the drugs. The damage is difficult to predict. The neck wound isn't critical but added trauma complicates matters."

It was said in a way that that had Sherlock turning to him. "It was a forced administration," he hissed. "John is not an addict."

"We need to move him down to the ICU and take him for tests. He will have a catheter fitted, and we will have to monitor him closely. The longer he stays like this the more at risk he is from contracting pneumonia and atelectasis."

Not happening. Sherlock stroked John's hand carefully.

"Is there any way to limit it?" Mary asked, her eyes tracing the movement of his hands.

"Ensuring that he is as mobile as possible," the doctor said. "Should he be in this state for a long time we will start to discuss exercise options with you if you wish.

"You must also understand that coma patients are not

depicted accurately on television. He will move about; his breathing will speed up and slow down. He will not suddenly return to consciousness – it will be a steady process and he will be aware of very little the first few times he wakes up."

"Which will be when?" Sherlock asked, staring at John's sleeping face.

"I'll know more once we have run the tests."

Reluctantly, Sherlock sat back as the staff came in and pulled the railing up to keep John on the bed and started to do whatever it was they did with the machines.

"Go home," the doctor suggested. "This will take a few hours. You can come back this evening and sit with him."

Mary met his eyes again. The hard stare echoing the doctor's words but for completely different reasons. Sherlock could feel his strength in this waver.

"You should change," Mary said as the doctor left the room.

"I-"

"Don't," she snapped. "Let me have some time with my brother."

For the first time in his life, he didn't bother to argue.

It took some time but, by the late afternoon, he was starting to get double vision and his skin was crawling.

On the table in front of him was cocaine. The idea of so much as touching it made his- well his skin was crawling already. It made him shudder though, feel sick to his stomach.

The image of John forced to take this kept hammering its way through his mind. Tears blurred his already terrible vision and he put his head in his hands, staring down at the carpet.

A break. That was all he wanted, a few days or weeks without so he could help John-

It was an unequivocal fact that he couldn't help John in this state. The hospital staff would be far too aware of what a-

Sherlock closed his eyes.

-what a junkie looked like when they needed a hit.

The sentence made his mind stop. Slowly he lifted his head, hands sliding down his face to cup his mouth and nose.

It had hurt John and he couldn't stop.

It had hurt John and there was nothing he could do. Using or not using would leave him useless for John. Both risked having him being dragged from John's side.

If there was a switch he could just flip, one that would turn off the urge and the high, he would do it immediately, without hesitation or thought.

He wanted to be clean. Desperately wanted it suddenly. He wanted control; the control that had been slipping through his fingers for months now.

Sherlock looked down at the table, at the substance on it.

How terribly stupid, he thought, to risk everything for such a small, innocuous looking bag of powder.

He trailed a finger along the bag suddenly snorting with bitter laughter. How ironic – the one time he actually did need to take it, the one time he was forced to take it, was the one time that made him realise it was no fucking different to every other time.

He'd never been in control of this.

But the fact remained; he could not go through withdrawal until he was sure John would be all right. He would not risk being taken from his side.

But the idea of injecting it seemed heinous. Disrespectful in the most horrific way.

He snorted it in the end, eyes streaming as he did so.

The sky was starting to darken and, though all time had escaped him, he knew it was getting too long. Almost an entire day had passed since John had last been conscious, since they'd last talked and it was...well...it was far too long.

He wasn't sure he could bear another day like this.

"Wake up," Sherlock whispered against John's ear. "I need you. Please. Wake up."

John's breathing was ragged. It was easy to delude himself into thinking it was a sign he was about to open his eyes.

"For me," Sherlock pleaded, stroking his hair. "Look at me."

A shift, muscle spasm from inactivity. John remained silent, his features slack. It was wrong, desperately wrong for someone who was so open, so expressive. So multifaceted and fascinatingly interesting. The blank sleeping expression was hateful.

"It should be me." Sherlock trailed a finger down smooth skin. "I'm the one who does it night after night. I'm the one who deserves it. Not you. Never you." He pressed his face into the side of John's head. "You were never supposed to be touched by this." Sherlock pressed his lips together as his eyes threatened to spill. "I was meant to keep you safe."

Gasping in air, he shook, trying not to cry. "I wanted to keep you safe," he breathed helplessly. "You were mine. From the minute I saw you. My mystery, my challenge. My surprise. Everything I didn't realise I wanted."

He pressed a kiss to soft skin, tasting John finally and unwilling to move and give that up. "Wake up," he begged. "Wake up and I'll do anything. Anything."

"No offer to be clean then?"

Sherlock tightened his grip on John warily and then turned to face Mary.

"No," he said sitting back, eyeing up the extra coffee in her hand and took a deep breath. "That's unconditional now." Sherlock sat back, an iron grip on John's hand. "As soon as he wakes up, as soon as I know he's fine."

Mary simply raised a doubting eyebrow and how could someone put so many doubts into one facial movement?

Sucking in a breath he stared at John and then swallowed, as if to gather his strength. "I have just had to snort cocaine to keep myself aware enough to sit here by his hospital bed while he lies there in a state that the same drugs I use caused," he said, trying not to associate any emotions with his own words. "Do not talk to me about what I am capable of doing."

Mary stared at him, horrified, and nodded slowly as she sat down, staring at the floor. Slowly, she held out the extra coffee and he accepted it, not entirely sure it would be a good idea but not really having any other options if he wanted to function.

It wasn't the only thing that he'd need to keep taking. In his pocket, the cocaine felt like shackles.

CHAPTER TWENTY THREE:

Defensive Wounds

AFTER DAYS SPENT IN THE bright, white hospital and ducking out to snort cocaine in a bathroom, standing in a darkened alleyway seemed suddenly very...different.

He hadn't dared go back to his flat, not after the last visit had him opening the door to a wreck. The lamp and bedding overturned, slashes to the wall, to any fabric. It didn't take a genius to work out who had done it, especially as the people that had been in the flat had known exactly where his drugs had been stashed.

The places that Victor had once smugly suggested as being places that people rarely looked at.

It was a net closing in. He hadn't retaliated after John, he'd been barely able to function in the past week and there was only one way that the Trevor's interpreted his recent actions.

Weakness.

Tilting his head up to the sky, he took another drag of the cigarette as he waited. The smoke puffed up into the air, fading into the clouded, darkening sky above. The nicotine helped a little but every small noise that he heard, every time a gang of voices wandered by, Sherlock could feel himself stiffen slightly, waiting for the moment that-

Christ, he didn't even know. All he knew was that, for the first time since he'd lived in London, there was a pit in his stomach and it twisted unbearably inside of him.

He'd made his way through five cigarettes in a row by the time a familiar shadow walked over to him, glancing around in a way that made Sherlock's teeth grind in irritation.

"You have it?" he asked, pushing himself off the wall and tossing the still lit cigarette to the side. The ember flared for a moment and then started to flicker and die as it hit the ~~still~~ pavement, still damp from the last onslaught of rain.

Summer weather his arse.

"Here," Hudson said, handing over a small package. "Own stash." He folded his arms.

Part of him desperately wanted to snort the cocaine that second and part of him never wanted to touch it. His hands shook as he instead tucked it into the inside pocket of his jacket.

"They think they've won," Sherlock muttered.

Hudson hummed. "It won't go anywhere; what happened to your fella. The club's pleading ignorance, CCTV shows nothing. And this..." Hudson scrubbed a hand over his face. "You're no further along than you were the last time we spoke."

"The money?"

"The only thing that's gone to plan," Hudson huffed. "Which was what I was in charge of," he added in a tone that sounded far sulkier than a man of his age had a right to be.

"It will work. When John wakes up-"

Hudson let loose a low noise of frustration. "You are crashing," he muttered. "The kid weren't supposed to survive it and all he did was break Trevor Junior's nose. You blackmailed Jim. Do have any idea what-"

Sherlock flapped a hand at him, eager to make the noise stop. "I will handle it," he said, turning to make his way back to the hospital. "There'll be a pub or some toilets on the way-"

"I don't want to do this-"

Ridiculous. Almost laughing, Sherlock turned to stare at him. "And how are you getting out of it?" he asked shaking his head. "You can't go back and fix it, you can't turn me over to them because then they'll know exactly how much you've been fucking them over, including your earlier attempts to get me to turn against them."

Hudson's face was in shadow and he stayed silent for so long that Sherlock shook his head in disgust. "We're fucked," Sherlock suddenly laughed, the strangest feeling bubbling within him, as if he were about to melt. "Either way, we're fucked. And I am not going down without fighting back."

Slowly, ever so slowly, Hudson started to nod his head. "Then...if by some fucking miracle this works...I have an idea for that money."

May as well have a goal in mind, Sherlock supposed as he took a step towards Hudson in order to listen.

There was a strange heavy pressure on John's hand. A thumping ache resounded through his head and the idea of moving seemed like an impossible effort.

When he opened his eyes, it was just white. Bright white light that hurt his eyes and lanced through his skull with a painful intensity. John gasped, sucking in air as he closed his eyes again and winced.

"Shush," a gentle, familiar voice soothed. There was a strange press of wetness on his hand. "You'll be fine. I'll make sure of it."

Trusting the voice, John sunk back down into the darkness.

The next time he opened his eyes someone was moving his arms. An unfamiliar person was pushing at his leg and it was beyond uncomfortable. He tightened up in protest, whimpering slightly.

Then there was a touch to his hair, a soothing stroke and a gentle press of lips that made him hum in satisfaction.

"And how many need to be done?" Sherlock was asking.

None. No more. He could move his leg if he wanted to, he just chose not to. John shifted and looked up at Sherlock whose hand stroked a little firmer.

Half way through the woman's speech, Sherlock suddenly stiffened and looked down.

Sherlock had dark circles around his eyes. John's brain couldn't process any more than that. But he could see those ever-changing eyes widen slightly as Sherlock suddenly ducked down, his face level with John's.

His head hurt so much.

"He's alert," Sherlock declared, looking over John's head.

"I know it looks that way but-"

"Do you think I don't know when he's awake?" Sherlock snapped with frustration. "Go and get a doctor, now."

Then he looked back down. "Stay with me," he whispered. "Concentrate on my voice."

"Hurts," John gasped, trying to turn into the pillow.

"Your head?"

John wanted to nod but the idea of that much movement seemed torturous. "Yes," he answered as Sherlock looked up again and seemed suddenly fixated.

"John?" a new voice asked. "Can you hear me?"

"Yes." John swallowed. Too many voices, too bright.

A hand touched his chin, cupping it as the doctor leaned in close, pressing a thumb by John's eyes.

Too much.

John rolled back into darkness.

There was a steady noise. It kept going on and off, on and off like an alarm.

Someone should really turn it off.

Annoyed, he opened his eyes and stared at the heart monitor blankly. Then followed the wires down, down and onto his own chest.

It hurt to move his head, but he risked it, looking about. The hospital room was empty.

Hospital room? What the hell was he doing in a hospital room?

His neck ached fiercely and a tentative touch confirmed that there were bandages at the crook of his neck and across his shoulder. A vague memory of a knife and a carpet and laughter surfaced.

What the hell had happened?

In the foot-well at the end of the bed was a chart sticking out and John tried to lean forward then hissed as it pulled the wires that were stuck onto him and into him. His head spun and his stomach protested, so he just lay back, trying to keep as still as possible until the nausea faded away.

It was easier to do with his eyes closed.

Footsteps approached softly and John kept his eyes closed, determined to not throw up on whoever was approaching. It seemed to be strangely tempting fate if he threw up on a doctor's shoes.

A gentle finger stroked the back of his hand. "Relax," Sherlock said in possibly the softest voice John had ever heard him use.

"Why, what are you planning on doing?" John muttered suspiciously, still fighting down the nausea.

"John?" The gentle fingers became an iron fast grip on his wrist. "John?"

"Shush." Sherlock's voice sounded far too loud. John wanted to say something else but was suddenly terrified that if he opened his mouth he'd throw up.

Hands were stroking his face. "Open your eyes."

Normally, John would have told Sherlock where to go, but he sounded so desperate, so pleading and uncertain that John opened his reluctant eyes to look up.

Sherlock had moved around the bed to face him and was staring down at him with what looked like sheer wonder and relief. To John's stunned amazement, Sherlock's eyes were bright with tears.

"You okay?" John asked, reaching up with his good arm to touch Sherlock's cheek. Sherlock caught the hand and nodded into it, pressing a deep, long kiss to the skin on the back of his palm.

"Get Doctor Meadows," Sherlock ordered suddenly, looking at someone on the other side of John. He squeezed at John's hand for another second and then focused. "What's three plus four?"

"Seven." John squinted up at him. "Are you feeling all right?"

"Does your head still hurt?"

Still? "Yeah," John winced. "Feel sick," he confessed.

Sherlock nodded. "And your neck?"

"Aches," John said honestly. "What-"

"Ah, Mr. Watson?" John watched as Sherlock backed off fractionally. "I need you to tilt your head for me, careful of you neck please."

A man, Doctor Meadows John assumed from the clothes and Sherlock's earlier request, came into his line of sight and John obediently did as he was told and suffered through the doctor checking his pupils and responses.

"You know who this is I assume?" Doctor Meadows asked with a friendly smile.

"Yeah." John glanced at Sherlock who seemed to have pasted himself to a wall.

"Okay, I'm going to have to send you for a few tests, Mr Watson, but I'll give you two a few minutes. What's the last thing you remember?"

What was the last thing he remembered? It all seemed so vague and blank. Fuzzy, as if his memories had been coated in a thick layer of paint and he could sort of see vague outlines underneath, but nothing that made sense or formed a cohesive picture.

Sherlock turned to him, taking a deep breath. "What I'm about to tell you, I need you to stay calm."

That didn't help. John's hand clenched even tighter around Sherlock's shirt in fear and Sherlock gently brought a hand down to tug it loose and entwine John's fingers in his own.

"Victor dosed you," Sherlock said frankly.

Dosed? What did-

Oh god.

His heart started to hammer in panic as a dim memory of a red carpet and the smell of boots, sex and ash filled his mouth, arms holding him down like a vice-

"John," Sherlock said with such fierceness that John turned his head back to meet Sherlock's intense stare. "Look at me, just breathe."

"What was it?" John begged, voice wavering.

Sherlock licked his lips hesitantly, as if he needed the saliva. "Speedball," he said hoarsely.

Speedball. Heroin and cocaine.

Oh god almighty.

Sherlock leaned forward suddenly, dragging a hand through John's hair. "You are fine. I promise. You're fine."

He said it with such fierce sincerity that John just pressed his lips together and nodded, scared beyond anything he'd ever felt before as Sherlock pressed a kiss to his forehead and then gathered him in close.

"I don't..." he breathed into Sherlock's jumper. "We had a fight?" he asked, curious. He felt Sherlock nod and draw in a long breath. It was unnerving to forget something that had clearly been so vitally important, something that had ended him up in hospital.

"How bad-"

Sherlock shook his head, his breathing sounding ragged and uneven, as if he were trying not to cry and John curled his good arm up and around his boyfriend, trying to steady him.

"I'm fine," he whispered to Sherlock. "I'm...shush," he soothed, not at all sure what to do. "Everything's okay now."

But Sherlock shook his head and somewhere, deep down, John had a sinking feeling that even he knew he was lying.

CHAPTER TWENTY FOUR:

Endurance Tests

IN THE THREE DAYS SINCE he'd woken up, Sherlock had been there for one. One day of pestering and nagging and running the hospital staff ragged before John had ordered him to go home. Especially because he looked like he was close to crashing, and the last thing John wanted was to argue about the cocaine.

The last thing he ever wanted to do was to argue about the cocaine again.

It was strange. The memories seeped back through into his mind at odd moments, like remembering a name when you'd given up on trying. The sudden bursts of recollection were...difficult. Unpleasant at best and enough to make him want to scream at Sherlock at worst.

Confusing.

And Sherlock was devastated by what had happened. Other than his snipping at any doctor or nurse that he thought wasn't treating John like he was bloody God himself, he was a quiet lurking presence, looking like a scolded dog waiting for a beating.

And John couldn't quite bring himself to have an argument with Sherlock when he looked like that.

Mary seemed calmer with him than expected. She watched him with thoughtful, considering eyes. In fact, she watched them both that way, as if she knew more than both of them.

That wouldn't surprise him.

It was only when Mycroft came around the day before John was to leave that it made some semblance of sense.

It was a strange moment when he had walked through the door and into the private hospital room that John was starting to suspect Sherlock must have had a hand in because neither he nor Mary could afford this. Strange because the last person John had expected to visit him when Sherlock wasn't around was Mycroft.

The man stood at the side of his bed looking uncomfortable as he glanced at the chair Sherlock usually occupied. If John didn't know better he'd almost say that Mycroft was there against his will, but he'd seen Mycroft go toe to toe with Sherlock far too many times to believe Mycroft did anything against his will.

"You are to be released tomorrow," Mycroft started, picking up a card and eyeing it with some distaste.

"Yeah," John said as he watched him.

"You cannot go home." Mycroft put the card down with some finality. "Not at the moment."

"Because of Victor?"

"Mm," Mycroft hummed. "It seems unlikely that he will be convicted for this."

Outside, he could hear the general thrum of the hospital, and it seemed so typical and ordinary that he could barely believe what he was hearing. "Sherlock...he said something about the Trevor family being powerful."

"There are no witnesses," Mycroft said. "Your friend, Alfred Baird..." He seemed to hesitate. "It would be unwise for him. His statement to the police was extremely vague."

God, he hated that he'd put Alf in this position. Thudding his head back against the wall, John stared at the ceiling. He'd put everyone in a shit position.

"I guess Sherlock knows."

There was a long, unexpected silence and John lifted his

head curiously to stare at Mycroft. The man looked around and then reached for the chair. Easing himself into it, Mycroft seemed to debate where to start from.

"What's going on?" John asked, sitting forward, suddenly worried. The amount of things that could have happened... the only comfort was that Mycroft looked uncomfortable but not upset. Even Sherlock's fancy lawyer brother would be upset if his little brother had been hurt.

Right?

"Sherlock has decided, with his usual impeccable timing, that now is the moment to go through withdrawal."

Withdrawal. He couldn't help but feel sheer relief. Even though the timing sucked and god, the last time John had seen him had been yesterday and he'd seemed a little off then, it was still...

Sherlock was giving up cocaine.

"Yes," Mycroft said at whatever dumb expression was probably plastered on John's face. "However, him staying in London like this, it would not be wise. We have a family house in Sussex. I sent him down there last night."

Okay. Wow. The idea of Sherlock not being around for a while...

"How bad will it be?" John asked, looking at Mycroft closely.

"You've looked it up," Mycroft said simply. "Sherlock has been using drugs since he was seventeen years old. That many years of hard drug use? You know how bad it will be."

Shit. John hadn't...he'd wondered, but they'd never discussed that side of Sherlock's life. Plucking at his bed spread, John tried to imagine what the reality was going to be like.

"You will also need to leave London. Until this is sorted out or..." Mycroft settled back. "Your name is known by the sewage of London. Once that happens...your name and face will always be known in certain circles. We'll have to be careful with this and, with any skill, you may be able to return to university next year, living in a different area of course."

Oh.

It seemed like something from a dream and yeah, he knew why all of these suggestions were being made and that it would be like a red rag to a bull to return and keep living as he had been, but it felt completely like giving up. Or surrendering.

"Spare me," Mycroft said, standing. "You are going to have to set your pride aside. Perhaps you can reflect on the uselessness of your attempts to be helpful."

Sherlock was right: his brother really was a complete dick.

"Where is he?" John asked, tracking Mycroft with his gaze as the arsehole put the chair back.

"I told you," Mycroft huffed. "In Sussex. Do try to-"

"I want to help him," John said firmly.

A well-groomed eyebrow rose as if, for all Mycroft's intelligence, he hadn't guessed that John would want to help Sherlock through the withdrawal. "Why?"

"Seriously?" John asked. "You're asking me why I want to help the man I love get over a drug that is likely to ruin his life?"

Under other circumstances, it would have been funny to see how Mycroft looked like he wanted more information about this. As it was, Mycroft simply seemed to hesitate, turning the idea over and then nodded.

"I will have a car pick you up tomorrow," he said. "Ask a friend to pack your things."

There was no way he was asking Andy to do that. Fuck knew what he'd end up with.

The cottage was like something from a National Trust postcard. It was squat and made with flint. Vines and flowers seemed to be holding the whole thing up and there was even a slightly sunken garden with a tiny crumbling wall around the edge.

Inside, the cottage was actually rather sturdy and modern looking (which was lucky because Sherlock would probably lose his mind if he had to suffer without technology for a few months). The nurse earnestly lectured him. John half listened as he was told that she would be back in the morning and afternoon every day and that he should call her if he had any questions or needed any advice.

It seemed to take forever before he was allowed to go upstairs. He ignored the two spare rooms for the bedroom door that had been closed over. Peeking into the darkened room, John slid through the door and stared at Sherlock who was on the bed, back to the door and shaking.

He didn't say anything. Instead, he carefully took off his trainers and jacket then eased onto the bed, slightly grateful that the way Sherlock was laying meant that John didn't have to lean on his bad shoulder.

"You shouldn't be here," Sherlock muttered, curling away from him slightly.

"You're a dickhead," John told him frankly, scooting down as he pressed a kiss in-between Sherlock's shoulder blades. The shirt smelled fresh so Sherlock had probably recently changed it. Under him, he could feel Sherlock sigh.

"How are you feeling?" John asked after a while, sitting up a little so he could reach over and press the back of his hand to Sherlock's clammy forehead. His brown hair was plastered against his skin, his body already showing signs of a struggle despite the recent shower.

"Shit."

Yeah, that probably was fair. Shifting again, John swept his hands through Sherlock's hair. "Mycroft seems to disapprove. Is that just default?"

It didn't make Sherlock laugh. Instead, he simply clenched his fingers into the pillow.

"I didn't..." John sighed, uncomfortable and unsure. "I'm proud of you," he whispered close to Sherlock's ear. "How come you're doing it?"

That made Sherlock turn. He looked like he hadn't slept properly for a while, his face exhausted. His hand lifted to stroke John's face and then trail down to the bandage on his neck before tracing down further to John's arm.

"I...I couldn't stop," Sherlock whispered. "He...you were in hospital because someone had dosed you with speedball and I still had to go home to do it, just so I could stay by your side." There was a long, shuddering pause as he seemed to struggle with the idea. "It could have killed you and I still had to-"

John gathered Sherlock to him because the man looked like the mere idea was enough to make him burst into tears. Half of him expected to be shoved away, but then Sherlock's fingers clutched at John's t-shirt and he pressed into John's chest, still careful not to jostle John's bandages.

They lay there, quietly in the bedroom, holding each other.

At some point John must have fallen asleep. Hardly surprising given how long he'd spent in hospital and how long he'd spent just festering in a bed. Getting up, packing and sitting in a car had been trial enough (embarrassingly).

What he did know, was that when he woke it was to hearing Sherlock throwing up in the toilet.

It was bad that, at first, he was tempted to just roll back into sleep because god was he tired. But the second time he heard liquid hitting the bowl, John rolled out of bed and stumbled to the door that lead to the en-suite.

"Come in and I will kill you," Sherlock snapped as John started to open the door.

"Seriously?" John asked, leaning his head against the wall as he debated going in anyway. The sound of spitting made John roll his eyes. "Am I allowed to pass you water and a blanket?"

There was a long silence. "Yes," Sherlock replied eventually.

How fantastic. John turned and wandered down the hall and then down the stairs to fumble with the kitchen and swear at cupboards as he tried to find a glass or something that he could pour water into.

In the end, he picked up a china cup which he was going to pretend was not expensive. The offer of a blanket suddenly seemed stupid because he had no idea if there was one and like fuck was he gonna give Sherlock their duvet when he was throwing up.

When he got back into the room, Sherlock was sat outside the bathroom, knees drawn up and arms resting upon them as he watched John come in. "Did you get lost?"

"You could have got it," John pointed out as he handed over the cup. "Don't start," he warned when Sherlock quirked an eyebrow at the china. "Do you know where a sheet or a blanket is?"

"Just grab something from one of the other beds," Sherlock said dismissively as he drank the water. It seemed to quickly vanish and then there was that demanding look again.

"You trying to put me off?" John called as he walked out and into another bedroom that seemed to have a red theme going on. Dragging the bedding off, he pulled it back into the room and chucked it at Sherlock before reaching for the cup.

"Is it working?"

"Nope." John stepped into the bathroom to refill the water. "I'll get a bottle of water up here tomorrow."

"You should be a nurse instead of a doctor."

Were they really going to do this? John hung onto the sink for a moment and then turned back to bedroom. Slowly, he walked back out, half tempted to pour the water over Sherlock. "You done?"

Sherlock's hazel eyes glinted up at him, the pupils just catching the light from the hallway. His jaw clenched and he flinched away, as if he'd seen something he hadn't wanted to in John's gaze. But he took the water quietly, which John counted as a win.

"You don't need to be here for this," Sherlock said eventually, taking smaller sips this time.

It was hard to know what to say. Sitting down opposite him, back to the huge double bed that they'd been sharing, John mirrored Sherlock's pose, tapping his thumb against his forefinger. "I know that," he said quietly.

"I don't want you here for this," Sherlock corrected.

"Why?" John asked, half glad that his face was in shadow. Sherlock probably could pick up the signs anyway but, given the state of him, there was a small chance that John may actually get through the conversation without Sherlock deducing his every whim.

It didn't seem like that was a question that Sherlock wanted to answer.

"The withdrawal-"

"I can handle it," Sherlock snarled. "Mycroft has a nurse and a driver and a candlestick maker for whatever I need. Trainee army surgeons are not on the list."

"-is emotional," John continued as if the arsehole hadn't spoken. "It's psychologically demanding."

At that, Sherlock made a derisive noise.

"Have you looked it up?"

The silence was answer enough.

John didn't leave the room but Sherlock was prickly enough and suffering from enough insomnia that he did, as if his petulant protest would have John packing up and demanding a car out of the cottage at first light. Sherlock also seemed to think that not talking to John would help his cause in some way but the cottage had a full package Sky subscription so John just put the rugby on.

Really loudly.

Day seven started with Sherlock triumphantly announcing that they could go home.

"Home?" John asked, keeping his gaze on the game.

"I'm fine now," Sherlock said imperiously, moving to

block John's view. "We can return to London and I can actually ensure that Mycroft tries to prosecute the Trevor family successfully."

Ah, that. John studied him and sat up a little. "Have you talked to Mycroft about the conviction?"

"He can't," Sherlock dismissed with a wave of his hand. "But he doesn't know what I do and so I need to return."

"Why?"

There weren't many times that John could point to and say 'that was the moment I rendered Sherlock speechless' but this seemed to be one of them. Sherlock's mouth opened and then closed as he glanced around.

"Why?" Sherlock asked with disbelief, his voice raising. "Why? Why do I want to see Trevor behind bars? Oh John, I can't imagine why-"

"Given that you've refused to talk to me for the past few days," John said, twisting as far as he dared without putting too much pressure on his neck. Sherlock was irritatingly in the way of the TV.

"I..." Sherlock backed off a little and then stared out the window. The game was rubbish anyway, so John let his gaze switch to watch him instead. The summer light outside did wonderful things to Sherlock's eyes and actually gave him some colour rather than the sick, sallow look he'd had so far in the cottage.

"It is not something I wanted you to see," Sherlock said eventually, still gazing outside. He seemed to have fixated on something though, given that they were in the middle of nowhere, John could only imagine it was a sheep or a stray postman.

Wanted?

Not saying anything, John reached for his phone and typed in withdrawal symptoms for long term cocaine use.

"Has your insomnia gone?"

"I can cope with that," came the quiet reply.

Okay. "Run up the stairs."

That made Sherlock turn around, looking pissed off. "I am not running up. Why would I?" he asked, clearly perplexed.

"Check your energy levels," John as he scrolled through. In his periphery, he could see Sherlock stiffen when he saw the phone and guessed what John was doing. "You seem to think that you're over this-"

"I'm no longer sick. The aches and pains have gone as have the temperature fluctuations-"

"Great. We'll cancel the nurse's twice daily visit."

"I know my own body," Sherlock snapped. "Do not think that Wikipedia can challenge my own knowledge."

"Not on Wikipedia," John replied absently. "Why haven't you looked it up?"

"Fuck off," Sherlock hissed, striding out of the room.

Right. Well. John lifted the remote and used the rewind function. Upstairs, he could hear Sherlock moving something around and then later on there seemed to be strange banging and thudding noises coming from somewhere on the ground floor. There had been two rooms that had been locked when John had explored a few days ago so he assumed that Sherlock had probably grabbed the key from somewhere.

Sherlock ignored John making some food (thankfully the nurse came over with food already prepared because John was half sure his cooking would finish Sherlock off), ignored any calls and in the end, John went to bed, determined to let the arsehole sulk. There hadn't been any more noise about returning to London so either Sherlock had looked up his symptoms or Mycroft had squashed the notion far more thoroughly than John had. The room had all the drawers opened as if Sherlock had gotten half way through packing and then changed his mind. Refusing to tidy his mess, John crashed into bed and then swore when it made his shoulder yelp in pain.

Fucking thing. The wound was getting really boring now.

He couldn't see what was happening. There was someone in the room and he couldn't move. His shoulder hurt-

They were here. They were pinning him down, the knife at his throat and laughter because he was being weak and he couldn't wriggle free or escape.

He couldn't stop them and someone was grabbing at him.

There was a strange noise as he sat up in the bed and his throat ached as if he'd been screaming. The person by him-

It was Sherlock, backing off with his hands held up and god what if Victor was in the house? Panicked, John whirled to look at the door, trying to get his breathing under control.

"John?"

It had been a nightmare. Just a nightmare and Victor Trevor probably wasn't hiding in the house. It was an irrational, embarrassing fear that he was not letting leave his lips.

A hand stroked through his hair and John kept his eyes on the door, glancing between the shadows. His neck was aching fiercely and there was a sudden pause in the strokes.

"Have you torn the stitches?"

That would require looking away from the door. Sherlock sighed and moved away-

"No," John said, and then closed his eyes, mortified. If Sherlock left then he would be somewhere in the house where John couldn't see him and...

It was so stupid.

He was used to Sherlock just knowing things. It was strange to see him hesitate, a confused look on his face that was tinged with irritation and the growing realisation that he didn't know what to do.

"It's stupid," John whispered.

The bed dipped as Sherlock shuffled closer. John glanced back at the door and stared at the shadows.

"No-one's there," Sherlock murmured gently.

He knew that. He knew that but it didn't stop him from being terrified that there could be someone there. Someone that could make him helpless and hold him down and hurt him. Feed his veins with poison in the hopes that John would always be weak and powerless.

Sherlock was shifting again, sidling down and turning John a little so that he was facing the door. It was comforting to have Sherlock's weight and warmth at his back and John adjusted his head a little.

"The windows are locked," Sherlock said in his ear. "The trellis outside couldn't hold anyone so no-one can climb up. The front door is triple locked and the back door hasn't been opened since we got here. The gate squeaks and I'll hear it," Sherlock promised.

It was weird but comforting. Snuggling back into him, John nodded a little as he tried to calm down.

"Victor?" Sherlock asked eventually.

"Not now," John murmured pulling Sherlock's arm around him. "Please, not-"

A kiss was pressed to his ear and he could feel Sherlock sigh. Slowly, he felt himself being lulled into sleep, safe in the knowledge that Sherlock was with him.

He woke still in Sherlock's arms even though he could feel that the man was awake. It was rare that it happened, enough so that he turned further into Sherlock's body, pleased at the easy comfort.

"You stayed," John murmured.

"You had a nightmare," Sherlock responded. "You...how many of those have you had?"

"First one," John said, sitting up a little. Sherlock let him go but watched him steadily. Drawing up his knees, John reached to the bandage at his neck, pretty sure he hadn't pulled the stitches there.

"It's fine," Sherlock said, shifting on the pillow. "I checked once you fell asleep."

Huh, John couldn't decide whether that was sweet or potentially annoying. "You didn't sleep," he asked, scrubbing at his eyes.

"I..." Sherlock reached under the pillow and held out John's phone to him.

"What? Did you send messages to Japan or something?" John asked, reaching out to accept the phone.

"No. I looked at the websites on your search history."

Oh. That. "And?"

"Cognitive functions may not return properly for a while." Sherlock turned his attention to the ceiling, staring at it as if it was to blame for the situation.

"Full cognitive function," John argued. "There was someone...they said it was a bit like being in treacle or cotton wool. Things don't connect properly."

"Statistically, with my amount of usage, it could be two years before I can function at full capacity again."

Yeah. John shifted a little to look down at him. "You saw the rest as well?"

"Appetite is depleted or boosted. Insomnia, lethargy, paranoia, mood swings, obsessive behaviour and an overwhelming, continuous need to use again to get rid of it all," Sherlock snapped. He looked so taut that John was half sure he was about to strain something.

"So...the list...there are some symptoms-" He stopped when Sherlock closed his eyes and snorted. Lost, John watched him.

"Unless I'm missing something, there don't seem to have been that many," he said, confused.

Sherlock levelled a hard gaze at him and then sighed and got up out of the bed. He was still in his jeans and hoodie from the other day and he reached to toss a t-shirt at John.

Like hell was Sherlock over the temperature fluctuations.

He followed Sherlock down quietly, away from the lounge and towards the kitchen as Sherlock opened one of the locked rooms.

It was... There was no way to sugar coat it because, Jesus, it looked like a serial killer's room.

On the walls were pictures; grainy from the printer and stuck with blue tack or pins. Thick Berol pens had been used to draw lines and scrawl ideas onto what had once been a mint coloured wall. All the furniture had been pushed to one side and piled up high, a rug tossed over them to hide the stack. The floor was wooden and covered in pens, paper and post-it notes. The shipping folders that Sherlock had stolen all those months ago were open and John guessed that the useful contents were probably on the wall. After a moment of searching, he could spot passenger lists and pen lines that drew out to the people on-board, most of whom had their picture crossed out with an 'x'.

"Well," John said, staring at it all, "you're not obsessively neat?"

In a way that only they could, they paused talking about it while John made some tea and coffee and breakfast (half wondering about the wisdom of giving Sherlock coffee). Sherlock went upstairs to shower and it was only twenty minutes later that he appeared, hair still damp, but clean and fresh smelling and John felt that familiar kick of want.

He pushed it away. Neither of them had mentioned the sexual aspects to withdrawal and John wasn't touching that one with a barge pole.

Or any other kind of rod.

"So," John said as he took a seat on the floor, mouth full of toast and one hand balancing a tea precariously on his knee. "You didn't just get this since we've been here."

"No," Sherlock agreed as he took a sip of coffee,

apparently preferring to stand for this bit. "I...it used to be blackmail material."

Blackmail material. Right. Because this was John's life now. "Who were you blackmailing?"

"James Armitage."

When John shrugged at Sherlock's almost expectant look, Sherlock nodded and leaned against one of the chairs that he'd left out of his bizarre stack. "Jim Trevor," he corrected. "Victor's father."

Victor's father? Glancing between Sherlock and the wall, John shifted curiously. "So he has two names?"

Sherlock nodded, eyes dancing across the mess on the wall. Now dressed only in a thin t-shirt and some jeans, it was painfully obvious how much weight he had lost recently.

It seemed Sherlock had lost himself in the problem in front of him. Still not entirely sure what it was, John glanced back at it. Perhaps serial killer wall had been a bit quick, he admitted. Maybe...it was more like a police wall that you saw in the CSI shows.

"You were blackmailing him to keep me safe," John said, suddenly realising.

"Yes," Sherlock said, still not looking over. "It wasn't...it was a difficult few meetings." Only the slight twitch of his jaw seemed to give away just how difficult it had been. "I needed to have enough evidence to make him worry but," he trailed off with a frown, "until now I never considered that it could be used to..." He broke off again, worrying at his bottom lip.

"Used to?"

Now, Sherlock did look over at him, worry and hesitation clear in his expression. "The only way to ensure that Victor is convicted is to ensure his father is powerless."

Powerless. Right but-

Everything froze for a minute as John stared at Sherlock, unable to quite compute what he was hearing.

"That would mean bringing down an entire crime syndicate," John said, blinking at him stupidly.

"Which is why it's not proving to be easy," Sherlock grated out, staring back at the wall.

Holy mother of fuck!

"This is why your brother removed you from London," John said, thudding his head backwards. "You're in worse shit than I am now, aren't you? If his father knows you have this information and you were trying to keep me safe-"

Sherlock waved it away as if the issue was minute. As if the fact that he'd gambled his whole life for John not getting the shit beaten out of him was no big deal. "Look," he said, sounding as if he'd rather focus on his clever facts. "James Armitage was a murderer. He killed many and was ruthless, cold. An admirable strategist. He realised that to have a new start he'd have to find a way to get the entire government to stop looking for him."

John glanced at the picture Sherlock was pointing at. "That looks like Victor," he breathed, placing his tea to one side as he stood up to study the low-quality picture.

"Indeed. James had plastic surgery but..." Sherlock shrugged. "By the time Victor's likeness became apparent, James was well known as Jim Trevor and likely felt little need to cover anything up. Arrogance is always a costly weakness," he murmured, eyes narrowing on the picture.

Sherlock would know, John couldn't help but think, slightly bitter still. "So he'd committed identity fraud."

"Al Capone was caught for tax evasion," Sherlock said thoughtfully. "But..." He stepped back shaking his head, gaze still fixated. "There is nothing here that can avoid being dismissed as circumstantial evidence." Sherlock reached out for a passenger list. "There were some experimental ships in the late seventies, early eighties. A way of dealing with the overcrowded prisons. They took some prisoners out on a large ship and anchored in the ocean. Less chance of escape, less 'heart-warming' conditions. There were six commissioned before the Gloria Scott mutiny occurred."

Gloria Scott? Why did that ring a bell? Curious, John looked at Sherlock who smirked.

"The second time we met. Someone had tried to contact me. They never showed that night or were put off by you and me." Sherlock gestured with a pleased smirk. "It was only later that I wondered why he had been so adamant that we meet there, during the anniversary service for the families of the crew."

Was that what it had been? "I think Andy asked them all who'd died," John hissed, wincing at the idea.

There was a flash of a smile, rare as gold. "Do you know anything else about it?" Sherlock asked.

John shook his head. "But I know there was a mutiny. The crew were killed and they ended the whole prison ship idea." At Sherlock's almost impressed look, John glared at him. "I go to university. I do occasionally know stuff."

"Armitage seemed to be the mastermind behind it. One of the crew members was likely to be in on it too, though which one has never been confirmed. All that's known is that the ship was found, sinking from an explosion with all of the crew members dead and the prisoners unaccounted for. Given where they were, some ship must have picked them up. The scale of the operation was..." Sherlock shook his head. "Impressive. It seems unlikely that Armitage did it all himself."

"So he just came back?"

"He made some money in Australia," Sherlock explained with a scoff, "and I'm sure there's a certain irony there to a prisoner making his fortune in Australia." He shrugged it away. "He returned rich and with an associate: Beade. An American who knew the drug trade inside out. They built up their business and," Sherlock shook his head, "they knew things about criminals. Too much. They jumped the ladder of power ridiculously quickly."

"And these are the people you want to bring down?" John asked.

Sherlock eyed him up for a moment and then tapped on the passenger list. "This is his weakness," Sherlock said decisively. "He treated them like disposable goods. Like his minions, and these are not men who take well to it. The week we met for the third time, Beade had been killed." Sherlock traced the picture back to the passenger list. "His name was actually Evans. Roughly a month afterwards, Hudson got a letter," he said, tracing the name back again to the passenger list. "A threat. After what happened with you, he came to me. Offered me this whole scheme to blackmail Armitage."

Sherlock tapped a finger onto another prisoner. "Pembroke was in charge of blowing up the ship. But he objected, said he wouldn't kill people like that. Hudson said that the prisoners took care of the deed themselves and then tossed him off the boat."

Jesus Christ. John swallowed as he stared at the man in the picture, trying to imagine that.

"I have Hudson, I have the ship records, I have the records of Jim Trevor and of James Armitage-"

"How-"

"Stolen," Sherlock dismissed. "Every time Armitage tried to put pressure on me, I needed to have something else. But... he knows most of what I have," he confessed, hands turning clawed as he studied his work again. "I never intended to have evidence that would be damning in a court of law."

"Why not?"

"People won't sell snitches drugs."

Ah. Trying to side step that issue, John folded his arms. "Can't Mycroft do something with this?"

"No. Even I can see how I'd argue against all of this," Sherlock said as his hand finally smoothed out and relaxed. "I need more. And I can't think," he snapped suddenly, banging his hand against the wall.

Reaching out, John took Sherlock's hand and pulled it

back, all too aware that Sherlock was simply letting him. "If you can't-"

"Then I cannot go back to London," Sherlock said. "And, quite honestly, neither can you. Not to live or study there. Not for long periods of time. I know too much-"

"What they gonna do? Kill you?"

Sherlock looked away and shrugged as if he had no clue what they would do.

That was it then. They ran away or they fought back. Turning to the wall, John studied it again as he slid his hand into Sherlock's. Moments later he felt a squeeze and smiled at the sensation.

CHAPTER TWENTY FIVE:

One Step Backwards...

OBSESSION. COMPULSION. PARANOIA. IT WAS hard to say how many of those Sherlock was suffering from considering the situation they were in, but probably the strangest thing about watching Sherlock now was how long he could give something his full attention.

In the time John had known Sherlock, he had never seen him so focused. Nine times out of ten, Sherlock lost interest, became bored with what he was doing and simply wandered off for the next new project or object. In fact, the only thing that John knew to have successfully held Sherlock's attention for any length of time was himself.

"Take a break," John suggested as he found Sherlock in the den first thing in the morning for the third time in a row. "You might see something if you take a step back-"

"I cannot see anything because I cannot think," came the snapped reply, and it was going to be one of those days apparently. With some hesitation, John took a seat opposite Sherlock and tried to ready himself for the rant that was likely building.

"There is something," Sherlock almost snarled at the wall. "Something I am missing. Something..." he hissed, pursing his lips before he turned and paced, hands opening and closing while they shook. The signs were dangerously familiar, enough to make John hope to hell there was no way for Sherlock to score while they were in the cottage.

It was kind of freakish, he thought as he stared at the picture of James Armitage, back when he was Victor's age. Looked more like a clone than a son. That must have been a blast from the past for anyone who had worked with Trevor before the Gloria Scott. How many of them had experienced that dawning realisation?

There was something tugging at the back of his mind.

"Did someone react to Victor?" John asked.

"No...what?" Sherlock asked as he turned.

"I thought...didn't someone react in a weird way to him or...or a picture..." that sounded kinda right in his head.

For a long moment, Sherlock stared at him as a confused frown crossed his features. Doubt crept over his face as he glanced between the wall and John. "I..." he cleared his throat looking uncomfortable. "My knowledge may not be reliable," he said, and John winced, knowing exactly how much that confession had probably cost Sherlock.

"I think...I'm sure you were there." John waved the idea away. "I dunno. I just...maybe it was someone reacting to someone else?"

Sherlock nodded slowly, though he didn't seem convinced. The deep line in his forehead didn't fade away as he seemed to ponder on the idea. It made his movements slower as he traced the people on the wall, trying to find some connection as he thought.

It was torture watching him get that frustrated. To see Sherlock that worried that he was missing something obvious or that he couldn't rely on his mind. It was a relief when his phone buzzed and John could scroll through his messages to read Andy's latest rant about the whole situation.

Because he was dumb and a glutton for punishment apparently, John flicked across the Facebook page. It wasn't exactly the first time that he'd checked. Not because of the well-wishers or the people fishing for information (though

356

having that much attention on his page was kind of nice) but because he still hoped that maybe Harry might get in touch. Offer some...something.

When he glanced up, Sherlock was staring at him, a strange expression on his face. He opened his mouth as if to say something but then looked away. Probably for the best, John thought mutinously as he scrolled through, even though it was obvious Harry hadn't sent him a fucking thing.

It jarred something in his mind. Someone reacting strangely, him flicking through his page and photos and...

Doctor Harrison had recognised the picture of Victor on Facebook.

Slowly, John raised his eyes to Sherlock and then, without moving a muscle, stared at the wall.

Harrison had trained in the 80s. Harrison had experience in prisons and ships.

Prison ships?

The doctor on-board the Gloria Scott. Who had he been-

The moment was shattered by Sherlock thumping his hand flat against the wall and hanging his head, his breathing suddenly ragged. "I can't think," he whispered, almost sounding crushed by the idea.

And then he slid down the wall, crumpling as if he'd lost all structure.

Doctor Harrison. How much had he- John cut his thoughts off as he stood and then knelt by Sherlock, pulling him into a hug. The man's shoulders shook as he leaned into John, clearly trying to fight back the wave of emotion.

"Take a break," John whispered in his ear, even as his mind raced. "Have you slept at all?"

The lack of response was answer enough. "They'll come for us," Sherlock whispered. "They'll come-"

They wouldn't. Not this far out where the Trevor family couldn't show off what they'd done. If John knew that then Sherlock should.

Paranoia. Anxiety. Fear. Doubt.

Jesus. Pressing a deep kiss to Sherlock's hair, John tightened his grip. He should get him up to bed, should let him rest.

Or...

How often had he wanted to scream at Sherlock for not saying anything about the Trevor family? And if Sherlock was suffering from paranoia then...

He was going to regret this.

"Harrison recognised the picture of Victor on Facebook."

For a moment there was no reaction, almost as if the words hadn't sunk into Sherlock's mind. Then, slowly, Sherlock started to sit up and John let him. He stayed still as Sherlock rose up to kneeling position, eyes narrowed upon him.

"Harrison?"

"Doctor Harrison," John said, taking the plunge. "The guy on my course who trained on ships and in prisons."

Sherlock blinked. Once. Twice and then turned to look at his wall.

"Are you misremembering or-"

"I don't know," John said, still trying to remember if the two had been combined. "But I know that he recognised me. Then he warned me off of you." When Sherlock's face tilted curiously, John shrugged. "You were both in the picture."

Sherlock sat back, looking up at his wall like a child might eye a tricky climbing frame.

"How long had he been practising in 1981?"

"I dunno. I think that was when he started practising," John said, hesitant. "In the eighties-"

Sherlock held up a hand, eyes darting with some speed across the wall now.

"I mean, he might have met Armitage in prison-"

"Or on a ship," Sherlock said, still looking around. He leaned up suddenly and tugged down the crew list from the Gloria Scott, curling over it to scan the names.

Harrison wasn't on there. John was pretty sure he wasn't that stupid. Instead, he shifted, wrapping his arms around his knees as he watched Sherlock fly into action.

Then Sherlock tapped the page.

"Trainee," he said. "The original name is almost illegible," he said, switching between the neat typed sheet and the original, mottled copy from the print sheet that was under the document. "The typist lists him as L Ramzon."

John held out his hand and switched back to the original. There, clear as day, was Harrison's fancy shit writing and his weird H.

"Sam Harrison," John corrected as he stared at it, eyes lifting to Sherlock's. "You never said-"

"It said trainee," Sherlock defended. "It could have been a trainee acrobat for all I knew." He seemed to pause at that and then looked back at the wall.

"He might have treated Armitage," Sherlock breathed. "He'll recognise him. There must be something that Armitage didn't change, something that we can use as evidence. If he-"

"If," John warned, slowly standing up and brushing off his jeans. "That's a big if, Sherlock. And if he knew Armitage, saw him lead a mutiny." John kicked at nothing. "Gay Alf won't risk standing as witness at the moment. How likely is it-"

"Alf is too entrenched to take that risk when he knows nothing would come of it," Sherlock dismissed. "But a doctor? One who seems to have escaped Armitage's notice. A trainee? He must have simply assumed that Harrison died in the ship."

"How didn't he?" John asked, baffled. "I mean, the crew all died."

"We will ask him," Sherlock decided, turning with purpose as if he intended to just stroll out the front door and get the next train into London.

"No."

It was enough to stop Sherlock in his tracks. Apparently baffled, he stared at John and then around as if it wasn't quite comprehending. "We have a lead, a way forward-"

"You likely have people watching for you," John argued. "And-"

"And?" Sherlock questioned, his eyes narrowing dangerously.

"Run up the stairs," John challenged again. "No, run the length of the garden. I'll time you. Take your pulse-"

The door slammed as Sherlock kicked at it in fury. "I will not be babysat," he spat. "Not when we are so close to getting-"

"Getting one man to tell us something we already know," John protested. "You want to get him to go to the police?"

"No," Sherlock said quickly. "No, he can't...I need to work out..." He hummed and then scraped a hand through his hair as if that would jumble his ideas together in the right way. In the end, he dropped his head in defeat and spoke to the floor. "I don't know who to trust," he admitted, as if the information was being torn from him.

"You can trust me-"

Sherlock waved that away with such a dismissive snort that John nearly laughed. "I know that," he said. "I meant the police. Armitage is persuasive. He finds ways to make sure people owe him favours. I don't know..." Sherlock sighed. "We need to talk to Harrison."

"I'll do it," John said slowly.

"You will not-"

"Go to university to catch up with a lecturer?" John asked. "Why the hell wouldn't I? They don't care about me, they probably don't even know yet what you're gonna do. We have time and this? This looks natural. I'll go to Harrison, see what he knows-"

Sherlock was almost vibrating at the idea and so not in a good way.

"You know you're treating me like I'm so pathetic I can't even manage to do something I did regularly before the attack?"

That seemed to have mixed results. For a moment, his old

Sherlock was back, raising an amused eyebrow. "That was almost manipulative," he said with some approval. "Still no."

"Not asking for permission," John said as he moved to side step Sherlock. A hand shot out, not as quick as usual, and grabbed his triceps. They stared at each other and it was unfair that the red-rimmed bloodshot eyes almost made the Sherlock's hazel iris look more green than usual.

"You said you trust me," John reminded him. "I'm not gonna be stupid. I go in with Andy or Mike, ask Harrison some questions. I leave with Andy or Mike and I come straight back here. Unless you think I'd be followed-"

It took four blinks for Sherlock to eventually shake his head. "Unlikely," he said softly. "Far too much effort. Armitage has better things to do than that."

"Right," John said. "So let me go."

Sherlock's eyes rose, as if he were looking at something over John's head. It was obvious the moment he relented, shoulders slumping in defeat as he leaned close into John. For a moment, it was as if Sherlock were going to attempt osmosis and fuse them together in some way.

"No heroics-"

"Like what?" John asked, almost amused. "I love that you think I could do anything remotely heroic."

That almost got a smile.

Almost.

"You know you're gonna owe me for this," Andy said as they walked into the lecture building the following day. "When I become a famous journalist, I'm so using you two to sneak into places and be my distraction."

"As opposed to the times you used us to sneak after girls and distract their friends?" Mike asked.

As awful as it was to say, it was almost a relief to be away from Sherlock, just for a few hours. Any longer and John suspected that he might get a bit...you know...clingy. Funny, everyone raved about the countryside and the beauty there but walking in London during a work day when it was busy and alive was a thousand times more interesting.

The idea that it could be taken away from him, taken away from Sherlock, who seemed to haunt all the streets he walked down.

Well, it just wasn't gonna happen.

Inside the building the air conditioning was on so high that it almost felt chilly again. There were students milling around as the lecture had finished a few minutes ago and, typically, Doctor Harrison was still at the front dealing with questions.

How was John meant to start this conversation again?

Mike led them to some seats halfway down and they sat, talking about Andy's latest girlfriend who was apparently a little bit too loud at night. Andy seemed to think it was hilarious.

It was only five minutes later when the crowd began to thin that John managed to catch Harrison's eye.

There was a blink of surprised recognition and then, just as everyone else had, Harrison's gaze dropped to John's neck. Probably knew that John should have taken the bandage off a few days ago and, like the worst doctor in training ever, was ignoring advice because that was something he couldn't quite deal with seeing in the mirror yet.

Harrison seemed to get rid of his dedicated followers quickly after that. One or two of the first-year students glanced at John thoughtfully but didn't seem to know anything about what had happened, which at least meant it wasn't gossip flying around the campus.

"John," Harrison said as he climbed up the stairs to take a seat in the row in front of him. "How're you feeling?"

"Better," John said honestly. "Almost healed up now."

"I saw the email," Harrison said quickly. "You should focus on healing for now, John. Don't try to catch up or get ahead for next year."

Harrison thought he was there for work? Andy looked

away and John was sure the git was sniggering. "Yeah, that's not why I'm here." John took a deep breath and got out his phone, the picture of Victor and Sherlock stored on it now. "You know him, don't you?" he said, tapping at Victor's face.

Mike winced, shooting him a baffled look as if disagreeing with John's method, but fuck it, John wasn't as smooth or as subtle as Sherlock and he sure as hell wasn't going to try and be.

There was little reaction on Harrison's face. He simply looked at the picture and then at John, then at John's neck. As if piecing together the dots, Harrison sat back and sighed, the noise long, heavy and exhausted.

"Yes," he said quietly. "I did tell you to stay clear."

Right. Yeah. John sucked in a long, steeling breath. "His father is Jim Trevor. He runs a drug..." John hesitated, actually not sure what the proper word for it was. "Company?" he tried, his voice rising in a question. "My boyfriend tried to blackmail him to keep me safe because I got in a fight with Victor here."

Harrison blinked at that information, his mouth opening once or twice, as if to correct John but thinking better of it.

"But you know his father as James Armitage, right? A man who's been dead for almost thirty years."

That, Harrison reacted to. He sat back with a long exhale and looked away, back down at the last slide of his PowerPoint.

"He hurt John," Andy said suddenly. "Injected him with speedball."

Why the hell was that gonna be relevant? Shooting daggers at Andy, John shook his head in disbelief.

"Oh, you can wade in like a kid knocking over toys but I can't?" Andy demanded, sitting back and folding his arms, apparently in a huff. "Seriously, I mean-"

"Come on," Mike said, standing up. "We'll be right outside, John. Okay? Text us when you're done."

John nodded, grateful, because clearly Andy was going to be worse than useless. Shifting a little to let his still muttering friend get by, John waited until they'd left to turn his attention back to Harrison.

"Never thought I'd have anyone ask me about him," Harrison confessed.

"You said you'd trained in a prison and on ships-"

Harrison nodded. "There were years where I'd make sure I didn't mention either," he said slowly, still looking a little shaken. "The things I saw..."

"The mutiny."

Harrison nodded. "Prendergast ...I was training under a doctor called Matthew Garrot. Horrible man. He treated me like a skivvy and the men like they were dogs. He dismissed a problem that Prendergast had and I didn't. Got a right rollicking for it too. Showing off or something stupid."

"Prendergast saved you," John murmured.

"And died for it. Told me to hide, pretended he couldn't find me. Told me where to hide in the ship in case some of the fuses went off..." Harrison's eyes were shadowed, distant. "He shouldn't have been there," Harrison said softly. "He was in there for forgery. That was all it was. He forged a few documents to get more money to put his kids through school."

John swallowed and shifted. "Did you know? That Armitage was back?"

Harrison shook his head. "Not until...I wondered if maybe his son was traveling but...he's here? In London? Selling drugs?"

"Killing," John corrected. "And others sell his drugs for him. His son..." John gestured to his neck. "In a night club. One of my best friends, he can't come forward because it's where he works and no-one else will have a statement that matches his-"

Harrison rocked back again, hands covering his mouth. "He's that influential?"

"There he is," John admitted, not sure if this was the smartest thing to do. "Look, I know that it will be hard but-"

"Hard?" Harrison demanded suddenly, his voice back to the usual strong boom that John was used to in a lecture. "Hard? Believe me, this is the easiest decision I'll ever make. He slaughtered those people, killed a man who did nothing but show compassion. This-" he said, waving a hand in John's direction. "Armitage was a killer then and worse now. I have no problem with coming forward."

"Can you offer anything substantial though?" John asked.

It took a moment to sink in and Harrison's eyebrows drew together. "Playing police officer now, John?"

"My boyfriend is. Sort of at the moment. He's...it's hard to explain," John said, squirming at the idea he was being looked at like a kid playing dress up. "I just...his brother's a lawyer and Sherlock was...uh..." fuck it, "blackmailing Armitage to keep me safe. So he has some information just not quite enough-"

"Blackmailing..." Harrison shook his head. "More fool him," he said quietly. "I have pictures-"

"So do we," John said. "But Sherlock reckons he's had plastic surgery."

Any other time it would have been funny to see how Harrison repeated Sherlock's name with a slightly bemused expression. "I have the medical notes."

John stared at him. "How-"

"People are reluctant to question trauma victims and the eighties weren't as anal as we are now. Doctor Garrot was an abysmal human being but a brilliant doctor when he put his mind to it. His philosophy was to always try a new experience in order to get ahead, one that I have taken on." Harrison smiled faintly. "And so I kept his notes. Our notes."

John barely breathed. "And?" he asked, trying not to lean forward in eagerness.

"And James Armitage has been in far too many fights in his younger days to hide all his scars and old fractures," Harrison said. "Certainly, not on an x-ray. But that won't get him for the drugs-"

"It'll get him for identity fraud and for the murders he committed while using his previous name," John said, sitting up. "It'll get him for what we need."

CHAPTER TWENTY SIX:

The Game Is Up

I T WAS TAKING TOO LONG.

For the first twenty minutes it had been a relief to have John completely out of the house. The endless worried looks and hovering were annoying enough without John glancing at the NHS website every five seconds.

There had once been a time in his life when he'd revelled in being alone. Now, it was too quiet, there was no audience or dry remark to come from the corner of the room.

What if Trevor was looking for John? What if there was a lucky coincidence? What if Alf decided he needed to get back in the Trevor's good books and John had sent off some stupid friendly message? What if-

What if, what if, what if? That was all he could think now. The paranoid possibilities haunted him and stopped him from seeing the correct clues, the relevant facts and finding something tangible, something real.

It was hateful.

It was even more hateful that it was John who had put everything together. That wasn't John's role in their relationship. He was meant to be, well...not the stupid one, but not the perceptive one either. John was practical and had common sense and was the people person. If he kept on going like this then he wouldn't need Sherlock and maybe he'd realise this while he was visiting Harrison and then never come back. Just a polite message to end their liaison.

Paranoia.

Clutching at his head, Sherlock bent over and tried to get his rambling thoughts under control, all too aware of how useless he'd suddenly become.

There was something else. There had been something nagging at him and he was certain that John had never mentioned Harrison's reaction to the picture. It was too obvious a moment for Sherlock not to have noted so that surely couldn't be the thing that had been bugging him.

There was something else and all his mind could do was whirl around in confused circles, like a pet chasing its own tail, because the cocaine had stolen his ability to think in a straight line, to see proper connections. Almost as if it had lit up his brain to the extent that, without the drug, his mind was now plunged into a dark maze that twisted every thought into a muddle. There was nothing to focus on and no reason to pretend that he could now that John had gone-

Gone, not coming back, in danger, running away-

He punched the wall.

It took a moment for the realisation and the pain to filter through. For a moment, Sherlock simply stared stupidly at his fist in the wall, behind the plasterboard that gripped at his wrist. Slowly, he started to pull it out and winced at the pain that was both dull and sharp. Blood welled up out of the graze on his knuckles and his fist ached as he pulled back and tried to stretch his fingers back out.

It was entirely possible that he'd broken something. Rocking back onto his heels, Sherlock inspected his hand, trying to remember a few of the lectures he'd sat through with John.

John. He wanted him here. Needed him to come back.

What if he didn't come back?

The circular thoughts were driving him mad. They never went anywhere, simply returned to the first fear as if it were a new revelation. The blood tricked from cuts and scrapes on his knuckles and Sherlock could just imagine the unimpressed look on his partner's face.

But then who was John to talk? The wound on his shoulder was deep and Sherlock was haunted by the image of John bleeding onto the office carpet at Back Door. So pale and fragile, and the memory of that terrible moment when Sherlock had thought that he was too late.

It made him sick to imagine it again. Raising his hands, he cupped his mouth and took a few steadying breaths; the iron smell of his blood giving him something to focus on and helping rather than hindering which was probably nowhere near normal.

John could come back soon.

There was blood on Sherlock's jumper; both on the sleeve and on the chest. He should probably find some way to make the hole less noticeable because John might see it and realise just how mad Sherlock was getting and leave-

Annoyed at his own thought process, Sherlock stood up on shaky feet, stumbling his way to the downstairs bathroom and smacking his palm on the light switch. He almost fell into the sink, his hands bracing himself at the last moment as he stared at his reflection.

His hair was on end from the amount of times he had ran his hand through it and was streaked with blood from his fingers. His face was still sallow and getting thinner every time he looked. Dark bags hung around his eyes, draining the colour from his iris and turning the whites into a dull, almost yellow grey. The blood from his hand smeared across his lips, cheek and chin where he'd rested his hands.

He was a mess.

Disliking the physical reminder, Sherlock slowly reached for the taps and started to run the water, washing his hands carefully, almost meticulously. Part of him sneered at the idea, and yet he kept on washing.

When his hands finally felt clean he inspected the wounds. His hand probably wasn't broken but there would be some swelling, and the knuckles were deeply grazed. Dimly, he blinked at them, trying to work out how you were meant to bandage up a hand.

He should be able to work this out. Mothers with moronic children managed to work it out. Lifting his gaze to himself again, he glared at the mirror and then at his lip.

It almost looked as if he'd been punched.

The memory of John being hit months before crashed into him. He'd had a bruised lip the first time they'd woken up together. He could have been hit again. Victor raising his hand again, bringing down that fucking ring onto-

Sherlock blinked at his reflection and reached out, tracing the reflection of his bloody lip in the mirror.

Oh.

John was probably going to kill him. A lot. Though it would be debatable as to whether John's biggest issue with what Sherlock was doing was going to a place that he could get cocaine in his sleep or going to see Victor.

Neutral ground was easy enough to find in London. Especially if you went into central London and the tourist areas. Victor enjoyed going there every so often to impress girls, to show off and play the normal rich boy when he felt like blowing off steam.

Such as a few weeks after nearly killing someone.

The bouncer (an irritant by the name of Jaz, if Sherlock remembered correctly) stared at him as if trying to remember him and then his eyes widened in horror as Sherlock strode over. He shook his head as if to warn Sherlock away but that was easily dismissed with a smirk as Sherlock stepped over the red rope sectioning off part of the roof top bar in Kensington.

Victor glanced over from where he had his arm wrapped around a girl's shoulder and froze momentarily. The panic was washed away almost in the same second, as if he'd realised he couldn't possibly look weak at this moment.

Sherlock sat himself opposite him with ease and reached for one of the spare glasses on the table, pouring himself a glass.

"Can we help you?" the girl asked, her chin raising in a way that made him desperately hope that she managed to somehow get involved with the bastard sitting in front of him.

"I was wondering," Sherlock said as he took a sip and settled himself back into the sofa, his spare arm stretching out to lay across the back of it. "Where I could find James Armitage's son? Any ideas?"

Victor stared at him for a long moment and then squeezed the woman. "Why don't you get a round of cocktails for your friends back out there. Or champagne."

There was a momentary war on her face as she tried to decide between the gossip and the moment to show off. With a dramatic huff, she nodded and momentarily clambered over Victor's lap, her skirt lifting to reveal a generous amount of shapely thigh. "You will be making this up to me," she purred before kissing him.

Sherlock waited, amused. Behind the bar, Alec was working and that would always mean an easy score if he wanted it. Instead he shifted, trying to ignore the urge to take it, just this once, just to deal with Victor.

When the woman finally slid away, Sherlock took another sip, waiting for Victor to continue the conversation.

"How is John?" Victor asked after a moment or two. "Learned his lesson yet?"

"I think so," Sherlock said, keeping his tone light and musing. It seemed to annoy Victor who drummed his fingers on the arm of the sofa he was on, his brain clearly ticking away as to how he should handle this.

They weren't in one of his bars now. And while the manager might like Victor's money, Alec's cocaine operation wasn't one that was known about by the owner. A whiff of the threat of closure and the managers would kick Victor out as fast as possible.

Unsurprisingly, it didn't take Victor long to drop the cool and calm act. Within two minutes he had sat forward, as if to attempt intimidation, and was glaring at Sherlock.

"You should be here, begging me," Victor announced, his voice tight with what could either be rage or panic. "You try to blackmail my family? Us? We-"

"I'm not going to blackmail you," Sherlock dismissed with a wave of his free hand. For whatever reason, Victor seemed to believe that and couldn't quite hide the slump of relief. It almost made Sherlock wonder just how much Victor had been screamed at by his father.

He hoped it had been a terrifying and painful conversation.

"Yeah," Victor said, sitting back. "Yeah, 'cause no-one would ever sell to you again."

Idiot. His father wanted Sherlock's head but the threat still crawled under his skin because Victor was probably right, and that scared Sherlock more than it should. And it was starting to be even scarier that he had allowed himself to be controlled by that.

"But you're not working for me," Victor said, as if he'd suddenly regained the power in their conversation by the mention of cocaine. "And you're gonna have to do a few favours before I'll sell to you again."

"You won't sell to me again," Sherlock assured him, taking another sip, just to imbibe something.

"I might be persuaded. If you ask real nice."

"I'm not blackmailing you," Sherlock said, keeping his tone level. "I'm having you arrested."

Victor's reaction was to throw his head back and laugh, as if Sherlock were the funniest man on the planet. And that, that was something Sherlock could enjoy because in three minutes, all of it would tumble down.

"Why?" Victor said as his laughter faded away, but the triumphant grin remained. "As I explained to the officer, I was so worried to see that John had got into a scuffle with some unsavoury member of my club. If we see them again we'll be sure to alert the police. And given that us three had some... history...well..." he pulled a sad, pathetic face, "I'm afraid that John has such a grudge because I slept with you and you like to blame me for it. I just...I know it was wrong but-"

"You won't be arrested for that," Sherlock said, interrupting the histrionic story. And that fact would always grate on him, Sherlock suspected. Even if this worked (which of course it would) it still wouldn't quite be the justice that John deserved.

There was a flicker in Victor's eye; a moment of fear as he realised that Sherlock wasn't scared or begging or playing into his power game. "Then for what?" he asked, his voice wavering in a way that Sherlock imagined he wasn't happy with.

"Mm," Sherlock hummed at that. "Not sure yet. Drugs, fraud. Obstruction of justice, although thinking about it perhaps it would be best to not have you arrested. See if you sink or swim on your own."

The eye twitched again as Trevor tried to catch up. "On my own?" he echoed faintly.

"Without your father," Sherlock explained. "Did you know that a crew member on board the Gloria Scott survived?"

"No-one survived," Trevor said.

"Prendergast hid him," Sherlock explained. "And you know, that crew member? He doesn't like your father one bit. I wonder how hard it is to forge old documents. Let them leak out to your networks. Maybe we could add some details..." He pretended to muse on the idea. "Depression, anxiety, maybe even some continual anal tearing from being repeatedly made into the prison bitch. How long would you last if-"

Victor stood up and Sherlock continued to regard him while still running his mouth.

"-your contacts knew that. Especially as some are rather homophobic and you tell them all that you shove it in rather than bite the pillow. I could attest to how false that claim is." Sherlock smiled. "In fact, I could make up any story, couldn't I? While your father deals with this trial? How many enemies has he made? How many more could I entice? There was that dealing with Beade and the way your family has been skimming off the top of all deals-"

"That's a fucking lie," Victor snarled.

Sherlock shrugged as he finished off the glass and stood up. Adjusting his jacket, he smirked at Victor. "So?"

The hit came as predicted. A vicious backhand that Victor usually dealt out when feeling particularly threatened, as if he needed that type of hit to believe himself to be back in power.

Sherlock laughed.

"Please," he said, standing back up as the manager started to come over. "There's nearly two million missing from your latest deal."

Panic lit up Victor's face and the hit came again.

And again.

And-

This time the manager was there dragging Victor back and calling for the bar staff to help.

Sherlock smirked at Victor. "Or maybe," he said, standing back up. "Maybe I will have you arrested for assault after all."

Five steps.

Inside the police station, Sherlock sat back, watching the desk.

Five easy steps.

One.

Check that Hudson had kept to his part of the deal and had indeed taken the money. Less important but still something that could panic the Trevor family.

"We have some witnesses," the officer was saying doubtfully as she looked at Victor Trevor's name on the charge sheet. "But," she looked at Sherlock, "I guess you know how unlikely it is to stick."

Two.

Get taken to the same station that John was in. The one they'd been to a few months before, back when Sherlock had been charged for possession. The one where John would go to because he knew the officer who didn't have much of a brain but had some heart.

"I know," Sherlock said, staring at the wall. "But charge him anyway."

There was a long sigh and then a nod, as if she couldn't make up her mind to warn him off or commend him for what he was doing.

"And there's someone giving a statement. John Watson and Sam Harrison. They're likely being represented by my brother."

Three.

There was only one reason that John hadn't been back early and that was because he was trying to solve the crime. And that was good, that was excellent and wonderful but there was a risk that it was all one man's word against another's.

So he needed to see John. Needed to see the officer and he needed Mycroft (God help him).

But more than all of that, he needed Victor in a jail cell and out-manoeuvred.

"By the way," he said as Officer Clayborne stood up. "Would you mind taking his ring? I'd like to have a detailed record that his ring created this," he said, waving at his lip. "While it still has blood on it."

She nodded at that.

"And you might want to check it for other blood sources," Sherlock added, staring at the ceiling. "Maybe someone who was recently assaulted in Back Door."

At that she paused and turned to stare at him properly. "And is there anything else I should look for?" she asked, something like realisation crossing her face.

"Maybe check it against old records," Sherlock said musingly. "Perhaps an inventory list of prisoners, possessions on board the Gloria Scott." Sherlock hummed and nodded.

Four.

Unsurprisingly she didn't seem to understand that. "I-"

"My brother should know," Sherlock said, wriggling to get himself comfortable. "And I mean, let's say, for the sake of argument, that Victor Trevor was wearing the family ring of one of Britain's most notable criminals then it might be worth testing his DNA to see if they're related? Especially if he is the spitting image of the man."

"It's not a crime to be someone's son."

"No," Sherlock agreed. "But it is awfully suspicious when you're born two years after that man died in a noted accident? Surely enough to check for identity fraud? And maybe enough to check if his DNA matched old evidence from the Armitage case?"

She stared at him and then nodded and turned, as if in a daze.

Five.

"And find my partner," Sherlock called after the woman. "He's about three hours late home."

CHAPTER TWENTY
SEVEN:

Epilogue

"WHY ARE YOU ALWAYS LATE?" Sherlock complained. John rolled his eyes and shoved his hands into his pockets against the fierce January weather. "I was at a lecture," he murmured as he leaned in close to press a kiss to Sherlock's lips. "And you texted me to get here about an hour ago. This is the most fucking stupid tube station to-"

"Shut up," Sherlock muttered against John's mouth. "This way," he added, reaching out to take John's hand and pull him into a quick stride up the steps.

"Where are we going?" John asked as he followed the mad man along the road. Follow was maybe an overstatement, more like was dragged along by the nutter, and John wasn't entirely sure that Sherlock wasn't doing it just to piss off the few people that did a double take at the pair of them holding hands.

"I told you. To find another place to live."

Ah, that. With the others finishing their three-year courses and Mike wanting to live with his girlfriend, they were kinda, a little bit, maybe going to be homeless.

"No," John said as he planted his feet firmly against the pavement, pulling back against the hand that was dragging him. It was apparently surprising enough that Sherlock staggered a little and glared back at him.

"No?"

"We're in central London," John said, circling a finger.

"Do you want a medal for working that out?" Sherlock asked.

Fucker. "No," John said, trying to keep his voice even. "But, this is expensive. Even factoring in that you aren't paying for drugs anymore-"

Sherlock rolled his eyes and folded his arms, throwing him a withering look. "This is in our budget."

They had a budget? Dammit, when had Sherlock thought about budgets? When had he become the mature one?

"Do I wanna know what our budget is?"

When Sherlock cleared his throat, John could feel himself brace for impact. "Free," Sherlock said as he turned on his heel and continued to stride up the road.

There was a moment when John simply stood on the pavement, gaping at his boyfriend's retreating back.

That little...

John trotted to keep up with him, even as Sherlock made a left, turning them onto the main road and then stopped.

"What do you mean free?"

"Well, the rent's free," Sherlock explained, and then nodded at the building they were standing in front of. It was one of those huge, three floored affairs with a basement below. There were steps to get to the front door and a gap below for the basement flat to have a window, and the gap was protected by black iron rails.

There was no way they could afford this in their wildest dreams, let alone have it for free because no-one was that insane. Suspiciously, he watched Sherlock. "Why is it free?"

He could have sworn Sherlock's face fell slightly as he glanced at the building again, then scowled at John. "I...there was a small plan."

"A small plan?"

"In regards to Victor. I wanted him to pay for his attack on you."

Yeah. And?

The questions must have been clear from his face because Sherlock sighed and tapped his fingers against the rails. "I knew that... I know it's unlikely that he'll be convicted but..." he traced the top of the railings without looking at it. "But, compensation seemed fair."

"If this was his house-"

"No," Sherlock snapped. "I wouldn't do that; I'm not that insensitive."

Well...

They were spending way too much time together because Sherlock's face twitched with amusement and he stepped close to John, turning him to the building.

"I helped Hudson steal two million off the top of their operation."

That took a few seconds to process. "Would that be the two million pounds that their associates claimed had been stolen from them? That thing that made them testify?"

"Maybe," Sherlock's voice rumbled in his ear. "We split it. They don't need the whole house."

Ah. That started to sink in and holy fucking shit, that wanker. "You bought a house?"

There was a long hum. "We part bought a house with another couple."

We.

"You bought a house?" John exploded, unable to quite get his head around the idea. A house. In London? He'd accepted that he'd have to rent for the next gazillion years.

One of Sherlock's rare, delighted smiles crossed his face and he nodded. "Want to see it?"

John stared at him and then back at the house and let lose a sudden shocked laugh. "Sure," he muttered, allowing Sherlock to take him up to the door, and fucking hell he had some keys on him, and undo the locks.

Inside, the hallway was dark, not much light coming

through. The house was narrow, John realised suddenly, and the stairs even thinner.

"The Hudson's will be down here," Sherlock explained, seeming to get a little more excited now that they were inside. "There's a conservatory and something which approaches a back garden so..." he rolled his eyes. "There was a lot of chatter about growing things," he said with a dismissive attitude.

John giggled as he stared at the closed door and then at the stairs. "And up there?"

The answering smile made John feel like he was a kid on Christmas day. Together, they walked up the stairs, one behind the other because the stairs were seriously narrow.

Upstairs, the hallway was still thin but the rooms were far more open plan than he had imagined. There was what looked like a small study facing the street and behind was a rectangular room containing both an empty large space and a kitchen to one side. Almost like a stubby T shape.

In the longer rectangular room, John wandered to the window and stared out into the surprisingly long garden behind. He could feel Sherlock come up behind him and then he reached for the window, lifting it up. When Sherlock wriggled down and out, John peered out after him and saw a really narrow, metal, balcony.

"You're so not smoking out here," John scolded.

"Don't be such a doctor," Sherlock said. "Of all my faults that's hardly in the top five," he said, and then seemed to ponder it and leaned onto the railing. "Top ten even."

"Mm," John said. "And I could just lock you out here when I want to kill you."

Sherlock ducked his head back through and kissed John carefully on the lips. "I may spend some time out here then."

Probably. John stepped back and allowed Sherlock to come back into the room. "And upstairs?"

Sherlock nodded him up at the second flight of stairs. Creeping up again, fascinated by their house (fuck, their house!), he couldn't quite stop his grin as he got up to the top level.

It was all empty still. A large room that felt wonderfully roomy. The bathroom was on the other side of the stairs and it was small but functional.

"Is this really ours?" John asked as he turned to Sherlock.

"Yes," Sherlock said. "And...Andy can bring over what I boxed up if...if you're happy. It won't be everything but-"

John grinned and kissed his boyfriend with a resounding smacking noise. "Yes," he said. "I've fucking moved you enough times," he added when Sherlock raised a surprised eyebrow.

It never failed to amaze Sherlock that Andy could be surprisingly organized when he wished to be. Or perhaps it was the new woman in his life that he was seeing. The one that Andy seemed to be managing to keep happy for the past few months.

It had taken the better part of the afternoon to get the bed and bedside table in, taken from Sherlock's room in his mother's house. She'd promised a few other bits and pieces and Sherlock had a strong suspicion that she was about to use this as an excuse to renovate his entire childhood home.

As evening drew in, Sherlock found himself standing in the doorway, watching John thoughtfully as he placed Andy's article about the court case on the bedside table next to him. He didn't move when John got started on the bedding, instead choosing to continue his study of the man in front of him. The ropey knot of scars on his neck peeked out from the collar of his t-shirt but they were fading slowly. In a few years, the scars wouldn't be obvious to anyone who wasn't looking for them.

The Trevor family would rot in prison, Sherlock thought as he tried to calm the fury that raced through him. Already there were reports as to how terribly Victor was faring with the other prisoners.

He would always despise the fact that John's crime wasn't the one that Mycroft had used to prosecute that bastard. Hated how long it had taken for them to get settled, for John to start to trust him fully again.

They were getting there though.

"Is this..." John had finished with the bedding, apparently, and was instead rifling through the boxes they'd brought up into the bedroom. "Is this a violin case?"

Ah. That. "Yes," Sherlock said, pushing himself off the doorframe. "I used to play as a child. And then, some well-meaning relative got me this the first time I was caught."

"Caught?" John asked and then nodded. "Ah. How old were you?"

"Nineteen," Sherlock said, reaching out for the case and stroking a hand over it, half tempted to give the foolish notion a try now. "It was...it might have been an attempt to distract me. I imagine he was trying to be helpful."

"Can you actually play?" John asked doubtfully.

Sherlock lifted the case from the bed and rested it against the wall. "We shall find out," he said, and then hesitated before he turned around.

"Are you...you feeling all right? Not feeling suddenly sick at all this expectation?" John asked, teasing, but with a hint of something else in his voice. "I mean, we have a house together now, which is still fucking insane. You might need a month or two to-"

"Shut up," Sherlock breathed, turning to him. "I just...you and I...this is...it's a new start."

John's eyebrows rose. "I guess it is," he said, sitting down on the bed, his brow wrinkling a little with confusion.

Taking the risk, Sherlock walked over and slowly, infinitely slowly, he bent his lips to John's. The faintest chaste brush of lips that made his skin vibrate and nerves tingle. John's breath hitched hopefully and Sherlock brushed forward again and again.

Then harder, as if a dam had broken suddenly. John

stretched up to meet his touches and they battled with their tongues over and over until Sherlock was almost dizzy with it.

"I love you," Sherlock whispered in-between kisses.

John clutched at him harder. There was something about it that made Sherlock want to pull John to him and gather him up.

"I want to live with you, be with you," he added, dragging his lips from John's and tracing his jaw line with kisses as his hands dropped to pull at John's t-shirt. Dragging it over John's head, he allowed the few seconds pause in which his lips weren't attached to John in some way and then dived back as if starving.

Under his fingers, John was just as warm as he remembered; smooth skin and lines of muscle, tissue and bone that Sherlock traced with his fingers as John plucked at the buttons of Sherlock's shirt. Seconds later, his shirt fell to the floor with a quiet thump and John's hands were tracing over his chest.

Sliding a hand through John's hair, Sherlock kissed his lips again, harder, firmer than before and John groaned into his mouth, eager and blessedly responsive. His free hand slid down John's back until he hit the jean's waistband and dipped his hand underneath. John pressed against him encouragingly and Sherlock slipped his hand out and around to the front, popping the button and sliding down the zip.

Sherlock pushed at the material with both hands, sliding it down enough that, when he bent, one arm around John's waist while the other braced on the mattress. They tilted, then lay flat so he could pull at the jeans and boxers with ease, encouraging them the rest of the way down.

Part of him wanted to duck down John's body, to explore and ensure nothing had changed, that his memory of John was perfect, but he couldn't bring himself to leave John's lips or throat or cheeks or collarbone. Needed to be stretched out over him instead of leaving John bare and open. Instead his hands roamed freely, spider-webbing over skin.

One of John's hands had vanished and, in the silence of the room, Sherlock could hear the crash of the drawer against their breathing and part of him grinned at the thought that John had unpacked the important supplies first. Without looking, he swept a hand along John's arm and plucked the lube from him, coating his fingers and then pressing in, swallowing John's moans.

For the first time since he'd done this the aim wasn't the end.

It felt like an age to work John open, to the point where his fingers were nearly cramping from the effort. Every gasp and whimper was breathed in, every cry devoured. And just as he could hear the word start to form on John's lips Sherlock pulled back a little, pressing a kiss to the corner of his mouth and looking down to strip off his trousers.

John sucked in a breath and when Sherlock looked back up at him he was wide eyed, biting his lip, and the smallest smile was starting to form. Out of habit Sherlock started to reach for the drawer again, and then paused, suddenly unsure.

Seeing it, John reached up and dragged a hand through Sherlock's hair. "It's fine," he said, shifting a little. "Whichever."

Sherlock closed his hand over the condoms and John's expression didn't shift or change. Ducking his head to kiss John again, Sherlock shifted them carefully as he put the condom on. Reluctantly, he sat back and lifted John's legs over his shoulders, before leaning over to watch his face.

John's eyes darted between Sherlock's eyes and down to his cock as if unsure which he should look at. Lining himself up, Sherlock pressed a kiss to John's forehead and pushed gently.

John panted against the skin of his throat, hands suddenly gripped at Sherlock's upper arms. Tense and tight, he gasped raggedly into Sherlock.

It seemed too obvious to tell him to relax, to breathe. Sherlock just pressed small kisses to his face, encouraging with slow movements until John's grip on his arms lessened and he started to calm his breathing. Sherlock eased in carefully, noting the sweat that was starting to bead John's forehead and the breaths that were changing in tone. The tension drained away and John gasped with ease beneath him

Taking it as encouragement, Sherlock pressed in firmer, kissing John's lips and smiling as John started to meet him, thrust for thrust. John grinned and arched back, letting Sherlock sweep his mouth over John's wonderful throat, to feel the cries before they left him. Picking up the pace a little, he looked up to check John's reaction and stared at the bright eyes and happy smile.

"Love you," John whispered.

Sherlock buried his head into the crook of John's neck and nodded, reaching for John's hand, silently grateful to whatever was out there that he had waited until it was just them.

This was something he wouldn't have changed for anything.

Half dressed, Sherlock studied the bow, having tuned the violin carefully. John lay curled up around him, looking tired but sated and would every so often draw patterns onto Sherlock's thigh.

Raising the instrument to his chin in a move half remembered, Sherlock pulled the bow across the strings, listening to the notes and feeling the last pulling, dragging weight of tension halt as if the bow had sliced through his skin, a blade and barrier to the gnawing need that crept in the back of his mind.

A few of the easier classical pieces drifted through his head and he played slowly, noting the transitions he had difficulty with and the necessity of practice to improve the dexterity of his fingers and arm movements. John remained silent.

Waiting.

Dropping the violin from his chin, Sherlock put the bow in the hand that was holding the violin and reached down to stroke through John's hair, his mind trying to focus on what he wanted.

"Just play," John said quietly.

It seemed as good advice as any. Lifting the bow and violin again, Sherlock played, losing himself in the music, the feeling of actually being able to concentrate on something again, something that wiped through his mind and sharpened it again instead of being swallowed by the feeling of dust. It was if he were a great mass that was just breaking apart and falling everywhere without pattern. This was like collecting it all back up again and padding it together, honing his mind.

He paced forward, looking through the window as he played. Below him, people walked up and down the street and he could see a van parked up on the pavement; Mr and Mrs Hudson below already starting to argue as some familiar con artists unloaded a mattress.

"Who are they?" John asked, leaning against the window frame and peering down as well.

"Associates," Sherlock suggested, pausing the music.

John hummed and folded his arms. "They look a lot like the associates that helped us steal dinner once. And I've seen the older man before..."

It seemed wise to say little on the matter but Sherlock flashed him an amused smile. It was a relief to see the same reflected in John's face.

John glanced up at the sky and then back at him. "Come one and all, the door of 221 is open to all the crooks of London."

"I'll have to have something to keep me busy while you train for the army." Sherlock said, lifting the violin under his chin again and trying to keep back the smile as Mrs Hudson picked up some of her precious potted plants. "And it's 221b, they're having 221a."

"221b Baker Street," John sighed. "This will be interesting."

CONNECT WITH THE AUTHOR

For more information about the author, please visit:

LTBradystories.co.uk

Or contact on twitter @LT_Bradystories

Always dable chech.
And then triple chech.
And then get Jo to
read it!

Proof

72184142R00233

Made in the USA
Columbia, SC
13 June 2017